RESCUED
BY DR RAFE

&

SAVED BY
THE SINGLE DAD

BY
ANNIE CLAYDON

Stranded in His Arms

Falling in love in the face of danger!

As the water level rises in a Somerset village ambulance partners Mimi Sawyer and Jack Halliday race towards a pregnant woman fast approaching her due date. But when a river bursts its banks this fearless team is separated, and Mimi and Jack find themselves facing the strongest challenge yet to the walls around their hearts…!

Don't miss this exciting new duet by

Annie Claydon

Mimi and Rafe's story
Rescued by Dr Rafe

and

Jack and Cass's story
Saved by the Single Dad

Available now!

RESCUED
BY DR RAFE

BY
ANNIE CLAYDON

Published in Great Britain 2016
By Mills & Boon, an imprint of HarperCollins*Publishers*
1 London Bridge Street, London, SE1 9GF

© 2016 Annie Claydon

ISBN: 978-0-263-91510-5

Our policy is to use papers that are natural, renewable and recyclable
products and made from wood grown in sustainable forests.
The logging and manufacturing processes conform to the legal
environmental regulations of the country of origin.

Printed and bound in Spain
by CPI, Barcelona

Dear Reader,

I've often thought that to read—and write—romance you have to be a believer in redemption. Is it *really* possible to leave the past behind and make a new future? Mimi and Rafe have a tough task on their hands, because they've hurt each other before and have spent the last five years rebuilding their lives. The last thing either of them wants to do is go back and revisit that pain. So working together for even a few days, in a flood-ravaged area, is a particular challenge for them.

But sometimes tough times will give us the chance of a new beginning. Looking back on my own life, I can see the many good times have given me joy and hope, but it's the difficult times which have shaped me the most and given me the opportunity to change. And, of course, to appreciate those good times all the more!

Thank you for reading Rafe and Mimi's story. I always enjoy hearing from readers, and you can contact me via my website at annieclaydon.com.

Annie x

For my sweet sister

Cursed with a poor sense of direction and a propensity to read, **Annie Claydon** spent much of her childhood lost in books. A degree in English Literature followed by a career in computing didn't lead directly to her perfect job—writing romance for Mills & Boon—but she has no regrets in taking the scenic route. She lives in London: a city where getting lost can be a joy.

CHAPTER ONE

THE RAIN BEAT down hard on the windscreen, the wipers only clearing it for a moment before water blocked visibility again. Jack was sitting next to her, watching the road ahead carefully.

'Think we'll make it?'

Mimi was gripping the steering wheel tight, gauging the way the heavy vehicle was responding in the wet conditions. 'Yep. As long as the road doesn't disappear out from under us, we'll make it.'

The comment wasn't as unlikely as it would have sounded when they'd last come this way, two weeks ago. It had been raining then, a fine mist that barely covered the road ahead of them. But since then, the rain hadn't stopped. It had been a dismal summer and August had brought storms. Roads had been washed away in some areas of rural Somerset, and ambulance crews had been battling to get through to their patients.

'Just think. In two weeks' time you'll be away from all of this.' Jack leaned back in his seat. 'Miss Miriam Sawyer. Paramedic.'

Despite herself, Mimi grinned. She'd worked hard, and the sound of her own name, spoken with the coveted qualification attached still made her smile every time Jack repeated it. 'I'm not sure I would have made it without you.'

''Course you would. Although I like to think that my expertise and advice were helpful…'

'And the incessant nagging, of course. But we don't mention that.'

'No, we don't. Or my back seat driving.'

'Especially not that.' Two weeks seemed like a long time right now and Mimi's promotion from ambulance driver to paramedic a long way away. Just getting to this call was about as far ahead as she was able to think, right now.

'And I'll be trying to get used to a new partner. Missing your unerring instinct for finding every bump in the road…'

'Oh, put a sock in it.' Mimi felt her shoulders relax. Jack always knew when the tension was getting too much, and always seemed to be able to wind things down a bit. 'Anyway, you're assuming that they'll be able to find someone who'll put up with you.'

'Harsh, Mimi. Very harsh.' Jack chuckled, leaning forward to see ahead of them, down the hill towards the river. 'Looks as if the bridge is still there.'

'Yeah, but I don't think we should risk it. That bridge will only just take an ambulance at the best of times. I don't want to get stuck in the mud on the other side.' In the brief moments that the windscreen was clear enough to see any distance, it was apparent that the surface water, rolling down the hill on the far side of the river, had reduced the road to a slippery quagmire.

Jack nodded. 'Looks as if we walk the rest of the way, then.'

'We could try the A389.' They'd been directed around this way because of reports that the main road into the village was closed. But maybe that was just a precaution and the ambulance would still be able to traverse it.

'Nah, I checked and it's under three feet of water. We'd never get through.' Jack had been using his phone for updates while Mimi concentrated on the driving. 'Right now, I think we need to just get ourselves there.'

'And then?' If the chances of getting the ambulance across the bridge and up to the village at the top of the hill on the other side were slim, the thought of arriving on foot didn't appeal very much either. Bringing a pregnant woman back down that treacherous path was something that didn't bear thinking about.

'We can assess the situation. I've put a call in for a doctor to attend…'

'Yeah. Right.' She and Jack had delivered babies before together and, if needs must, they'd do it again. 'I hope they're not going to send some junior doctor who thinks he's the one who's going to save the world and that we should just stand back and make the tea.'

'As a paramedic you'll be making these kinds of decisions soon. What will you do?' Jack smiled.

'Oh, I think I'll put in a call for a doctor to attend.' Mimi grinned back at him, bringing the ambulance to a halt. She decided to stay put and not pull off the road on to the muddy verge. That was one sure way to get stuck, and a car could make it past in the other lane. Anything bigger wouldn't be getting any further anyway.

'Time to get your hair wet again.'

Mimi grimaced, tucking her blonde plait into the back of her shirt. Her hair had been wet so many times in the last week that she was beginning to wish that short hair suited her as well as it did Jack.

They pulled their wet weather gear on in the cabin and Mimi reached for the radio. The only response to her call signal was a burst of static. 'Looks as if there's a problem again…'

'Yeah?' Jack looked at the rain slamming into the windscreen. 'Have you got a signal on your mobile?'

'Probably not…' Even in good conditions, mobile reception was patchy around here. 'I might have to walk back up the road a bit. You go on; I'll be right behind you.'

The ambulance rocked slightly as Jack pulled his heavy bag out of the back, slamming the rear doors closed. Mimi saw him trudge past, rain bouncing from his waterproofs, as she pulled out her phone and dialled.

Nearly… A staccato ringtone sounded on the line, but it was breaking up and then it cut out completely. Climbing out of the ambulance, she toiled back along the road, rain stinging her face. Some way ahead of her she could see an SUV travelling down the hill towards her, going as fast as the pouring rain would allow.

'Careful, mate…' She muttered the words to the unknown driver. 'Any faster and you'll be in the ditch.'

Forty feet gave her another bar on her phone, and another twenty feet one more. That should be enough. The SUV was closer now, and the driver was flashing his headlights.

'Okay, I see you.' Mimi stepped off the road, stumbling over the uneven, sticky ground.

Then she heard it. A distant rumbling sound that might have been thunder, but there had been no accompanying flash of lightning. Mimi turned in the direction of the noise, looking upstream, and then she saw its source.

'Jack…!'

She shouted into the storm, at the figure on the other side of the bridge, screaming Jack's name again when he didn't react. It was impossible to tell whether he'd heard her this time, or the thunderous sound of water rushing downstream towards him, but he turned around.

Jack took one look at the water and dropped the heavy bag he was carrying. He seemed about to try and run, but the steep slope ahead of him was slippery with mud and water.

Mimi stared in horror, unable to do anything, and knowing that Jack had only seconds to make a decision. Run for it, or find something to hang on to. There was a large spreading tree at the side of the road and she willed him towards it. As the water crashed down, she saw him run for the shelter of the tree, clinging on to one of the four split trunks which rose up from the earth.

'Jack... Hang on...' She sobbed the words even though she knew he couldn't hear them. Maybe he knew she'd be saying it, just as surely as she'd known which decision he'd make.

The noise of the water was almost deafening and, in an apocalyptic touch to the scene, the storm chose this moment to shoot a bolt of lightning through the sky, followed by a deep growl of thunder. The rush of water crashed past, taking a few chunks of the bridge with it, and Mimi kept her gaze fixed on the spot where she'd last seen Jack.

'Hang on, hang on, hang on...' It was as if she could repeat it enough times to somehow make his grip firmer. The water was subsiding now as it followed the course of the river, and she could see him, tangled in the framework of twisted tree trunks.

Maybe he was holding on or maybe unconscious; she couldn't see from here. Mimi started to run for the bridge, hoping that it hadn't been weakened too much by the impact of the water.

A voice sounded behind her but the words were whipped away in the storm. And then someone grabbed her from behind, lifting her off her feet.

'Mimi...!'

'Let go of me.' She struggled and, when he didn't let her go, she kicked against him. The feel of him was familiar, but Mimi didn't even stop to wonder how. Another sickening roar was coming from upstream.

'Jack!' She screamed his name as the second wave of water came crashing down into the valley. This one was bigger and swept the bridge away almost in one piece as the water boiled and rushed downstream.

'You can't reach him, Mimi. You'll only kill yourself.'

That voice… Maybe her mind was playing tricks on her and it wasn't him at all. But Rafe's voice was unmistakable. A trace of public school, softened by years of not caring to mark himself out as any different from the next man, and currently spiced with an urgent growl. 'Let go of me! My ambulance…'

Water spilled towards them, this time reaching the parked ambulance, pushing it sideways across the road. For a moment, Mimi thought it was going to be okay, that the vehicle would come back to rest on the tarmac, but then it slipped onto the mud by the side of the road, tipping and coming to rest against a tree, as the water retreated again.

If Jack was injured, how was she going to get him back to the hospital now? In fact, how was she going to get to him at all? The bridge was gone and the river had burst its banks and become a lethal, fast-running torrent.

'Someone's coming for him—look.' The arms around her loosened and Mimi struggled free. She'd deal with the sick feeling in her stomach, prompted by the feel of his unrelenting body, later. She had more important things to think about right now.

She watched as five…no, six figures appeared from the trees on the other side of the river, scrambling and sliding in the mud. Two stopped to retrieve the medical bag, which had been deposited in a clump of brambles, and four made for the twisted tree trunks, where Mimi could see Jack's bright high-vis jacket.

For what seemed like an age, he lay motionless, tangled

in the branches like a broken doll. One of the figures squatted down next to him as if talking to him.

Please, please, please... Yes! Through the curtain of rain, she saw him move and then Jack was helped to his feet. She strained to see as the rescue party clustered around him, and then saw him turn towards her.

'Looks as if he's still in one piece...' Rafe's voice again, behind her.

She could see that. 'Jack, are you okay? I'll meet you up at the village...' she called across.

'There's no way through, Mimi.'

'Only my friends call me Mimi.' In the sudden shock of seeing him again, all she could think about was that she wished Rafe wouldn't call her Mimi. Everyone else did, but she'd never wanted to hear him say her name ever again. If he wanted to call her something, he could call her Miriam. Or actually Ms Sawyer would be just fine.

'All right then. Miriam...' He shot her a look that told her he knew full well that she was being petty. 'We both have the same information from the control centre. Unless you're considering sprouting wings and flying...' He gestured towards the raging stream, frustration written clearly in every abrupt movement.

Mimi didn't reply. The most satisfying course of action right now was to hold Rafe responsible for both the state of the roads and the fact that her ambulance was sitting at a precarious angle in a ditch, even if that wasn't fair. Rafe had gone out of his way to teach her that life wasn't always fair.

Jack was waving and she waved back, tears springing to her eyes. Then that familiar gesture, the one she'd seen hundreds of times before. *I'll call you.* She looked around for her phone, and Rafe picked it up from where she'd dropped it, handing it to her. Mimi took it without looking at him. She checked that the phone was still working and then signalled back a thumbs-up to Jack. *Okay.* Then she watched him turn, as the men with him helped him back up the hill, towards the village.

Now that Jack was out of sight, she couldn't put the moment off any longer. Mimi turned to face Rafe.

He was still the same. Dark hair, wet and slicked back with one wet spike caressing his brow. Deep blue eyes, so striking that it was difficult not to stare. He still stole her breath away, and right now that felt like robbery of the cruellest kind.

If anything he seemed a little taller, but she knew that was impossible. He was staring down at her, no hint of emotion on his face, and she wondered what he saw.

'We'll wait for Jack to call, and then I'll take you back to the hospital.' Finally Rafe spoke.

'You're not taking me anywhere. My vehicle and my partner are here.'

'Your vehicle doesn't look as if it's going anywhere, and you can't get to your partner.'

Rub it in, why don't you? Rafe had clearly not forgotten how to hurt her. His strong, silent approach, unafraid to face the facts and able to make hard decisions, had been one of the things that had made Mimi notice him in the first place. But this time it wasn't up to him to make the decisions.

'It's not your call, Rafe.' If he thought that a failed relationship gave him any right to tell her what to do then he was wrong. He'd given that up five years ago, when he'd walked out on her.

'Okay. So what *are* you planning on doing?'

'I'll wait until Jack phones. Then I'll decide.' That was final, and there was nothing that Rafe could do about it.

Rafe had steeled himself against the possibility that he might bump into Mimi when he'd volunteered to help in the area. When he hadn't, he'd had to steel himself against the possibility that he might not.

Something about the way she moved had told him that it was her as he'd driven towards the figure in the rain, but he'd dismissed the idea, deciding that the woman was just another of those ghosts which had appeared before him and then turned out to be someone else. But as soon as he'd seen her start to run, he'd known. The kind of passionate loyalty that had sent her towards the wall of water instead of away from it might be foolish but it was Mimi all over and he still admired it.

Not that she'd shown very much passion when he'd left. Perhaps cool indifference was all he'd deserved after the way he'd behaved, but it had still hurt. This bristling anger, the naked hostility would have been almost refreshing if it wasn't so badly timed.

'Come and sit in the car.' He gestured back to where his SUV was parked and she glared at him. He shrugged. 'Or you could just suit yourself...'

She marched towards the car and, in a series of hurried movements, she managed to get her waterproof jacket off without getting too wet. When she was inside, she took off her overtrousers and heavy boots, hanging her coat on the clip behind her and dumping her boots in the footwell.

'I hope you don't mind my getting your car wet.'

She was sitting in the front seat frowning at him, legs drawn up in front of her, her feet in a pair of thick woolly socks. One of the things that hadn't changed about Mimi was that she was wiggling her toes. She always did that when she was unsure of her next move.

'Nope. Any time.' Rafe hung his own coat in the back of the car, and it started to drip.

'We're staying here. Until I say so, right?'

'Yes. That's right.' Mimi and Jack had always been close

and always looked out for each other, but that had never inspired this sharp ache of jealousy before and it took Rafe by surprise. It had been five years. Even if it felt like just a few days since he'd last wrapped himself in her warm scent before drifting off to sleep. If she and Jack were together now, it was hardly a surprise.

She relaxed slightly into the seat. 'Might take a while. If you get tired of waiting…'

'You think I don't care about Jack?' They'd all been friends once. Whatever had happened since, Rafe still reserved the right to be concerned for him.

Her honey-brown eyes considered the question for a moment. 'No. I don't think that.'

She leaned forward, propping her phone on the dashboard, and Rafe wondered whether he should turn on the car radio to mask the silence. She looked just the same. Dark blonde hair, captured in a plait that was currently tucked into the back of her shirt. How many times had he watched her weaving it into that plait in the morning before she went to work?

'What are you doing here, Rafe?' The question had obviously been circulating in her head for a while and she didn't meet his gaze when she asked it.

'This area's the worst hit by the weather conditions. All the hospitals in the county are sparing staff where they can.'

'And you drew the short straw?'

'I volunteered.' Suddenly it seemed important that she know that. 'I'm on leave for two weeks…'

'This is your holiday?' She raised her eyebrows.

'Yeah. Beats the South of France any time.'

She gave a little nod. 'Thanks.'

The thank you was more likely to be on behalf of her hospital to his, but Rafe preferred to take it personally and think that Mimi was actually glad to see him, despite the evidence to the contrary. All the same, she seemed to be relaxing a little now.

'You and Jack are still a team, then?'

'Not for much longer. I passed my exams and I'm a qualified paramedic now.' She almost smiled. Almost but not quite.

'You're staying here to take up your promotion?'

'No, I'm moving.'

'Jack'll miss you.'

'I won't be going that far…' She broke off suddenly, staring at him. Maybe he'd been a little too obviously fishing for information. 'Who I'm going out with is none of your business, Rafe.'

'No, I know. But, out of interest, are you…and Jack?'

'Like I said, none of your business. What about you?'

'Nah. Jack's not my type.'

'I didn't mean…' The outrage drained out of her and she started to laugh. 'He'd be very glad to hear you say that.'

She fell suddenly silent, her brow creased in a frown, as if making her laugh had now become a hanging offence. Rafe settled back in his seat, watching the rain drum on the windscreen and wondering whether it was worth cracking a few more jokes, just to see how cross he could make her.

CHAPTER TWO

IT WAS A great deal easier to dislike Rafe when he wasn't around. Mimi stared gloomily at her phone, her finger tapping impatiently on the small screen.

The expected beep made her jump. A long text from an unrecognised number said that Jack was okay and in the Church Hall. He'd keep her updated as and when he knew more about the situation. And wasn't that Rafe he'd seen with her on the other side of the water?

When Mimi texted back that it was, she received a smiley face. Clearly Jack hadn't thought about the ramifications of the situation. She might have a lift home, but she would really rather have walked than it turn out to be Rafe.

She relayed the factual part of the message as dispassionately as she could, trying not to look at Rafe. The thought that she might need him wasn't particularly pleasant, but she was going to have to face facts. She'd get this over with as quickly and painlessly as possible.

Her phone beeped again. Another long text. Mimi read it carefully.

'What does he say?'

'The stuff in his medical bag's ruined. The water got to it.' Mimi had been hoping against hope that at least some of the medical equipment that Jack had been carrying would have survived the drenching. 'He's staying with the patient until he finds a way to get her out, and there are some people coming down to try and get a second bag across. We're to get it packed and ready, and wait for them to call.'

'Tell him okay.'

'Yeah.' She'd just done that. Mimi surveyed the torrent of rushing water in front of them and hoped that the people who were coming to meet them had some idea how they were going to get the bag across the river, because she didn't have a clue.

Rafe turned in his seat. 'I've got pretty much everything he might need.' He surveyed the boxes and bags in the back of the SUV. 'What's the patient's condition?'

Trust Rafe to come prepared. He always came prepared, never thinking that someone else might have the situation under control.

'She's pregnant.'

Irritation tugged at his mouth. 'I know *that*.'

'Well, that's all. She's not in labour yet, but we were going to transport her to the hospital anyway, due to the weather conditions. No complications that I know of, but best…' She was about to say that they'd best send whatever they could to deal with any eventuality, but Rafe had already got out of the car and was walking around to the tailgate. Opening it, he selected a sturdy holdall and began to stack it with boxes.

Mimi puffed out a breath and pulled her boots back on. She had no doubt that Rafe would do the right thing, or that she would, but it seemed that they were both going to do the right thing in the most unpleasant way possible.

The storm had done its worst and seemed to be easing off a little now. They didn't have to wait long before four figures appeared on the other side of the river, carrying what looked like climbing gear.

Her phone rang and she answered it.

'Hi, is that Mimi?' A woman's voice on the other end of the line, shouting over the roar of the water. 'I'm Cass... Fire and Rescue...'

At last, some good news. It was always good to have a firefighter around, even in the pouring rain.

'Hi Cass, Mimi here. How's Jack?'

'He's fine. We've taken him up to the village to dry off and we're going to try to get a line over to you now.'

'What's your plan?'

'Along the river to the east the land rises on this side. I'm thinking we may be able to throw a rope to you and winch the bag across.'

'Right you are; we'll meet you there. We have two bags.'

'That's great. Thanks.' The line cut and Mimi shouldered one of the bags. Knowing that Rafe would follow with the other, she slid carefully down the slope at the side of the road and walked into the trees.

Under the canopy of the leaves, the ground was wet but undisturbed and the clingy mud by the side of the road less in evidence. Rafe's long strides quickly caught up with her.

'There's some high ground on the other side of the river, about a quarter of a mile in this direction. They seem to think they can get a rope across.'

He nodded. Apparently he'd run out of things to say, or perhaps he'd decided that keeping the peace was the better option right now. In the silence, broken only by their footsteps and the drip of rain from the trees, Mimi resolved to do the same.

She thought she'd left this all behind. Taken charge, caught whatever life could throw at her and thrown it back. But right now she felt just as alone as she had five years ago, when Rafe had left, and still weighed down by the memories from her past.

Seventeen years old and clinging to her twin brother,

Charlie, on the night they'd heard their parents had died in a car crash. Promising that they'd always be there for each other...

That promise had been kept. And, as the pain of their loss had diminished, Mimi had known that Mum and Dad would be proud of the way that she and Charlie had stuck together.

Twenty-one years old. She'd thought that she'd been in love with Graham, and then he'd slapped her down with that list. A comprehensive catalogue of Mimi's faults and failings, which he had used to justify having slept with someone else behind her back.

She'd let him go, but somehow the list had been harder to shake. Stamped on her brain, a reminder that she was irretrievably flawed and a warning against ever trusting a man again.

But Rafe had made her believe that one last try might be possible. He had been the handsome doctor in attendance when Charlie was brought into A and E, so terribly injured, after falling from a window. It was thanks to his skill and quick action that Charlie still had some mobility left in his legs, and could pull himself up from his wheelchair and walk a few steps.

Twenty-three. When Rafe's mother had been diagnosed with cancer she'd tried so hard to support him, the way he'd supported her and Charlie, but he'd shut her out over and over again. Every day she'd felt him slip away a little more, and when he'd finally left it had been just a confirmation of everything that the list had taught her. She just wasn't good enough. And it hurt so much more to be not good enough for someone you really loved.

Mimi had picked up the pieces and set her goals. Helping Charlie regain his independence. Getting her paramedic qualification. Wiping Rafe out of her life, and never giving any man the chance to break her heart again. And she'd achieved them.

So how come she was wet through, trudging through a wood with Rafe? Feeling all the insecurities that she thought she'd put behind her. Wondering what he was thinking, and whether he might be comparing her with someone else and finding her lacking.

The straps of the bag were cutting into her shoulder and she shifted it a little. She would deal with it. She felt bad, but that had never stopped her before. It would pass. Rafe would be history again, very soon.

As they approached the place that Cass had indicated the canopy of trees thinned slightly, giving way to long grass, which had been flattened and muddied when the river broke its banks. On the other side she could see Cass's party, climbing a rocky outcrop that rose twenty feet above the level of the fast-flowing water.

'If they're going to get a line across, this is the place to do it.' Rafe had come to a halt, looking around.

'Yep.' Mimi looked up at the iron-grey sky. 'At least it's stopped raining.'

He nodded. Finally it seemed they'd found something that they could agree on.

Cass and the men on the other side were securing the end of a long rope around the trunk of a tree. She was as tall as the men with her, and seemed to be directing them. As she worked her hood fell back off her head, showing a shock of red hair, bright against the browns and dirty greens of the landscape.

Mimi's phone rang.

'We're ready.' Cass didn't bother with any preliminaries. 'I'm going to try and throw a line to you. Be ready to grab it.'

'Okay. Standing by…' Mimi looked up at Rafe. 'There's a rope coming over.'

He nodded, and Mimi saw Cass swing the rope and throw it. The coil at her feet played out, but the rope was too light to travel far and dropped into the middle of the river, immediately carried downstream by the current. The men behind her hauled it back and she tried again. It travelled further this time, dropping into the river just yards from their reach and Mimi heard Rafe puff out a breath almost at the same time as she did.

'They need to find something heavy to weight the rope…' His voice was loaded with frustration.

Mimi bit back the temptation to tell him that he was stating the obvious, and that it seemed that Cass was already doing something about it. She had to get a grip. Rafe was acting perfectly reasonably and she should at least try to be civil with him. But she was still reeling from the double shock of nearly losing Jack and then of seeing Rafe again.

She watched as Cass selected something from one of the backpacks they'd brought with them and tied it carefully on to the end of a thinner, lighter length of twine. When Cass threw again, the line came whizzing across, followed by a shout of triumph as it cleared the river, the weight dragging along the ground as the twine sank into the water and was pulled downstream.

Mimi ran for it but Rafe was faster and he was already there, catching the weight just in time. Mimi took hold of the twine and together they dragged it clear of the water, pulling it back and winding it securely around the trunk of a tree.

Her phone rang again and there were more instructions from Cass, which Mimi relayed on to Rafe. A rope was hauled across and secured, along with clips and a pulley.

'I wonder where she got all this stuff from.' Mimi could see that the nylon ropes were strong and of high quality.

'It looks like mountaineering equipment. This is a carabiner...' Rafe was securing the rope around the tree with a no-nonsense-looking clip. 'Watch your fingers.'

'Well, give me a chance...' Mimi whipped her hand away as Rafe tested the strength of the anchor and the rope snapped tight around the tree trunk.

He waved to the party on the other bank and the bag began to move. Slowly at first, and then speeding through the air, over the water. A small pause while it was unclipped on the other side, and then the pulley came spinning back towards them.

Mimi looked at the water, boiling over jagged rocks twenty yards downstream. She was afraid, but she wasn't going to let that stop her. She cupped her hands around her mouth, shouting across the river. 'You have a harness?'

Cass didn't seem to hear her, and Rafe shook his head.

'Leave it.' He clipped the second bag on to the pulley. As it began to move, he tugged at the ropes that anchored their end of the line around the tree trunk, assessing their strength.

Mimi knew exactly what he was thinking. Rafe was going to insist on being the one to make that perilous journey, with or without a harness. It had always been this way with him.

He'd been just the same when they'd lived together. Strong, dependable, always the first to get to grips with a problem and always the first to solve it. His quiet resourcefulness was one of the things that had drawn her to him but, after a while, standing back and watching Rafe deal with everything had begun to lose its charm.

And yet she'd done it. She couldn't bear the thought of losing Rafe and she'd tried so hard to be the woman he wanted, someone he'd think was good enough to spend his life with.

Fat lot of use that had been. His family had obviously been hoping he'd find someone from the same background as him—big house, private education, an appreciation of the finer things in life and the money to buy them. They had probably heaved a joint sigh of relief when Rafe had left her.

She wasn't about to let Rafe walk all over her again. 'I'll go first. I'm lighter than you are.' She spoke casually, even though she knew that the words would be like a red rag to a bull.

'You will not.'

'Just watch me, Rafe.' She threw the retort at him, watching as the group across the river retrieved the second bag. As they did so, a crack sounded across the water. One of the ropes came whipping towards them and she felt herself falling sideways as Rafe tackled her to the ground. The rope described an arc in the air above their heads and flopped down next to them.

'Ow! Did you have to do that?' Mimi rolled away from him, straight into a patch of mud. She'd been trying so hard to show him that he didn't need to protect her any more. Rafe sweeping her off her feet, however dispassionately he'd done it, was the last thing she needed.

'Nope. Could have just let it take your head off.' He had the audacity to grin at her.

'I'm beginning to wish you had.' She brushed herself down, resisting the temptation to thank him. Instead she turned to the group on the other side of the river, who were standing motionless, staring across at them.

Mimi took her phone out of her pocket, dialling Cass's number.

'Sorry about that. You okay?' Cass's voice sounded down the line.

'Yes, fine.' Rafe was behind her, muttering something about tying her to a tree to keep her out of trouble, and she ignored him. 'I'm going to try to get to you. I might be able to get through on the other road into the village…'

'I doubt anyone's going to get through safely tonight.' There was a pause. 'Jack said that he's getting in contact with the HEMS team. When the rain gives over a bit they might be able to make it. If there's anything he needs, you'll be the first to know.'

That was sensible. And, coming from Cass, it didn't sound like a put-down. 'Okay, thanks. Give him my love…'

'Will do. When this is over, there's a bottle of red with our name on it, if you fancy a night out.'

'I'll be there.' She waved across to the group on the other side of the river and ended the call. Thankfully, Rafe had decided not to make good on his threats and was already unclipping the remaining rope from around the tree, watching as it was hauled back across the water.

'We're going.' It was an obvious statement, but it made Mimi feel good to be the one to say it. Turning away from him, she started to walk back towards the road as the rain started falling again.

They made the journey in silence. Perhaps Rafe was figuring out what he was going to save her from next. When they reached the stricken ambulance, he walked over to it.

'I don't think I'm going to be able to tow you out…' He was peering underneath the vehicle. 'In any case, it looks as if there's a fair bit of damage, here.'

'I'm going to call for a tow truck.' *Thanks, Rafe, but you're no longer needed. You can go now.* Treacherous regret tugged at Mimi's heart at the thought.

'Don't forget the CD safe.' There was a barb in his tone. No, she hadn't forgotten the controlled drugs that the ambulance carried, and she did know that she had to remove them.

'I'll let you get on.' She turned, making for the back doors of the ambulance, and felt his grip on her arm.

'Let me go, Rafe.' She pulled against him, but he didn't relent.

'What are you expecting me to do? Leave you here with no shelter and no transport?' He gave an incredulous shake of his head. 'Think again.'

'Let. Go.' Every time he touched her, it was the same. The memories were almost like solid, living things, tearing at her heart and reminding her that once upon a time, in a land far, far away, she'd craved Rafe's touch.

He uncurled his fingers from her wrist. Not too fast, not too slow. Rafe had always been a master of the art of good timing.

'Stay if you must. I'm calling for the tow truck.' She forced herself to look away from him, scrolling through the list of numbers on her phone for the vehicle recovery company.

If he had to put a name to that look, Rafe supposed that hostile arousal might just about cover it. He had no doubt that the hostility was there, but the arousal was probably just wishful thinking on his part.

He supposed he didn't deserve anything else, but she didn't have to ram it down his throat. It was obvious that she could cope without him, but he wasn't entirely surplus to requirements. If she thought that leaving her hadn't hurt him as well, then she could think again.

Rafe kicked disgruntledly at the tyre of the disabled ambulance. Mimi had taken hold of her life with both hands, gained a qualification and got a new job. His life was back on track, too. When he'd left, he'd made the right decision and now was no time to start re-examining it.

The ambulance was tipped at a slight angle in the mud, but it was wedged firmly against a tree and seemed stable enough. Rafe gave the vehicle a good shove and it stayed put, so gingerly he opened the back doors and climbed inside, looking around to assess the damage.

'They're sending a truck out. The tow company's pretty busy, but they're giving me priority, so they should be here inside an hour.' She was standing in the rain, outside the ambulance, looking at him thoughtfully.

'Good. Not long to wait, then.' This couldn't be easy for her. Medicine was all about teamwork, and he knew that the nature of the ambulance crews' work tended to forge the tightest of teams. She must be feeling very alone right now.

She looked up at him and he thought he saw a flicker of confused warmth in her face. 'How much of the ambulance equipment can you take in your car?'

'Pretty much everything that's portable.' Rafe surveyed the inside of the wrecked vehicle. 'Apart from the stretcher.'

'I was reckoning on leaving that.' Mimi was standing stock-still, her arms folded. As if she knew what she had to do but just couldn't bring herself to start. Rafe picked up one of the bags, stowed away under the seat, and climbed out of the stricken vehicle, making his way to his car.

Rafe's sudden appearance seemed to have peeled away everything she had built up in the last five years, like a bad skin graft sloughing off a wound, leaving it red raw. And now she was leaving Jack behind and stripping her ambulance of everything that could be moved. She could almost reach out and touch the feeling of loss.

She *had* to get a grip. Mimi repeated the words in her head, in the hope that they might sink in.

As usual, it was practically impossible to see what Rafe was thinking, but as they worked quietly together the atmosphere between them seemed to relax. He watched as she checked through the contents of the Controlled Drugs safe, countersigning the inventory, and then set to work helping stow as much as they could from the ambulance into his car.

Typically, the rain seemed to slacken off just as they were finishing, and the tow truck chose that moment to arrive as well. Tired and shivering, Mimi clambered into Rafe's car and hung her dripping jacket in the back.

'Here.' He rummaged for a moment on the back seat, unzipped a bag and produced a sweater. 'Put this on.'

He ducked back out of the car, closing the door, and Mimi picked up the sweater. She didn't particularly want to follow his orders, nor did she want to wear his clothes, but refusing might give him the idea it meant something to her. And when she pulled it over her head it was warm and all-enveloping.

The key was in the ignition and she started the engine, putting the heaters on full and directing the ventilation up on to the windows. As they began to clear she could see Rafe, talking to the vehicle recovery men as the winch slowly pulled her ambulance out of the mud and on to the back of the truck.

He jogged back to the car and got in. 'I'm ready whenever you are.'

'Yes. Let's go.' She blurted out the instruction, knowing that he wouldn't go anywhere unless she allowed it, and realising that somehow that didn't put her in charge.

'Hospital?'

'Yes, thanks. We need to get the controlled drugs back there.'

He nodded, leaning forward to start the engine. Even

in these conditions it wouldn't take long before they were back at the hospital and then she could thank him and wave him goodbye.

CHAPTER THREE

RAFE WAITED WHILE Mimi argued with the ambulance control supervisor. They'd both turned around at the same time, to look at him for a moment, and then Mimi had turned away again, her eyes dead, as if he mattered rather less to her than the chair he was sitting on. The supervisor beckoned her into his office and she followed him, protest leaking from every movement she made.

He'd loved her fire. That unquenchable, unstoppable thirst for life that made the best out of everything had enchanted Rafe. It had challenged all the assumptions that his family had taught him. *Boys don't cry. A man should take care of the women in his life. He must handle his problems alone, not needing to talk about them.*

And Rafe had come so close to quenching that fire. When his mother had been diagnosed with cancer, and his family had descended into a state of restrained crisis, Mimi had wanted to help, had fought him to let her in. But Rafe couldn't. He'd already perfected the art of hiding whatever pain life threw at him and he didn't know how to do anything else.

He didn't blame her for giving up on him, but it had hurt all the more because Mimi never gave up on anything. Lying with her in their bed, unable to either sleep or to share his anguish, had taught Rafe the nature of true loneliness.

Leaving had been his way of keeping her safe from the silence that had descended on their home.

That was all history now. He'd thought it could never change but, as the door of the supervisor's office opened and he saw Mimi walk towards him, he began to wonder. He'd measured his failure in their relationship by the lack of emotion she'd shown when he left, but now anger was stamped all over her face and he had little doubt that most of it was directed at him.

'Everything okay?'

She shook her head. 'There are no spare vehicles and no one for me to partner with. They're sending me home…'

'Unless?' Rafe had seen enough of the situation here to be able to guess what Mimi's options were.

Her face was set in an expression of almost believable remorse. 'I apologise for what I said. I should have thanked you for getting me out of the way of that rope when it broke.'

Mimi was still thinking about *that*? Then Rafe realised that this was the precursor to something else.

'You're welcome. I apologise for what I said too. I had no real intention of tying you to a tree.' However appealing the thought had been at the time.

'No. It didn't really occur to me that you did. I think we were both letting off a bit of steam.' She screwed her face into a frown. 'My controller… He says that if you need any help I could always tag along with you.'

Deep down inside a primitive sense of triumph pulled at him. However much she disliked the idea, Mimi needed him. Rafe tried to think dispassionately. Two would be more effective than one, and he'd be able take more calls. Unless, of course, they spent the rest of the evening bickering over old grudges.

'Do you think that's going to work?'

Mimi took a deep breath, as if she was suppressing the urge to solve the problem by killing him and taking his car keys. 'I'll make it work, Rafe. I can't sit this out; I'll go crazy at home.'

There wasn't even a decision to make. Turning down any assistance, let alone that of a trained paramedic, would be reckless at a time like this. 'Happy to have you along. I'd appreciate the help.'

That was that, then. There was a lot of unresolved anger between them, but if they could put that aside this could work.

They stood for a moment staring at each other and then Mimi broke the silence.

'Look, this is difficult, but we could make it a lot easier.'

'Yeah, I guess we could. I'd like that…' Rafe remembered not to call her *Mimi* this time. That was just the kind of thing that might shatter this unstable truce.

'We'll make a new start, shall we?'

Pretend that none of it had ever happened? That he hadn't loved her and then left her, and that resentment wasn't colouring everything they did now. It was a tough prospect, but if that was what it took… It was, in fact, an opportunity. If there *was* unfinished business between them, then maybe now was the time to finish it for good.

'Yes. Okay, I'd like that. New start.'

Mimi felt better now that she'd had a chance to wash her face and comb her hair. She folded Rafe's sweater, making a conscious effort not to bury her face into its softness, trying to catch one last trace of his scent. This was hard.

She stuffed the sweater into a bag, dragged her jacket on and marched out into the rain. He was sitting in the car, waiting for her. Her colleague. The one she'd slept with once upon a time, but that had been a mistake and it was all finished now.

'Ready?' She settled herself into the front seat of the car.

He nodded, turning the radio down until it was just a gentle beat, swallowed up by the drumming of the rain on the windscreen. 'Yep. First one's near Shillingford. We'll have to go through Eardwell.'

Her home village. 'Yes, that's the best way.'

'You want to call in on Charlie?'

'He's… I spoke to him a few minutes ago. He says everything's okay.' Mimi wished that Charlie would accept her help a little more readily, but she knew better than to fuss.

'How's he doing?'

'A lot better. He plays in a wheelchair basketball team now.'

'Sounds as if he's a great deal more independent.'

'Yeah. As time went by we all learned how to make that happen.' The cottage that she and Rafe had rented, just across the road from Charlie's place, had been a factor in that. Close enough to help, without crowding her brother. When Rafe had said he was moving, to take up a new job and be closer to his mother, he'd known full well that Mimi couldn't abandon Charlie and follow him.

'I don't suppose he's got a spare flask he can lend us. If he could fill it up with coffee it would be even better.'

She couldn't help but smile. Rafe and Charlie had always got on well, and it seemed that Rafe still cared about her brother enough to find an excuse to pop in and see whether he was all right. 'You want a sandwich as well?'

'Sounds good. Call him and tell him we're coming.' Rafe swung the car out of the hospital car park and on to the road.

* * *

Rafe drove the familiar route, which he'd used to call the road home. He hadn't reckoned on it being quite so hard. When he stopped outside their cottage, it looked just the same as it always had, the white render gleaming pale in the pouring rain like a ghost from his past.

'You're still here?' He tried to make the question sound as casual as possible, as if there hadn't been a time when he had dreamed about walking back to that door every night.

There was a slight pause, as if she was weighing up whether it was all right to answer. 'Yes. I bought the place.'

'Mrs Bates died?' The elderly woman who had owned the cottage had gone into a nursing home and her family had rented the property out.

'Yes. Four years ago. The family didn't want the cottage and decided to sell, so I put in an offer.'

'Smart move...' Rafe bit his tongue. He wasn't in a position to give Mimi advice on what to do with her life any more. All the same, he'd thought more than once that if the roomy cottage they'd rented ever came on to the market they should put in an offer for it.

She nodded as if she didn't want to discuss it any more, and rather unnecessarily pointed to the driveway of Charlie's one-storey house, right across the road. It had only been five years, not a century. And Rafe hadn't forgotten.

He got as close to the front door as he could and switched the engine off, leaning back in his seat in an unequivocal signal that he'd wait. Turning up here with Mimi wasn't the most tactful of things to do.

'Come and say hello to Charlie.' She shot him a pretty fair counterfeit of a welcoming smile.

'I thought... Wouldn't you prefer me to stay here?'

'I told him you were here when I spoke to him. He's not going to eat you, Rafe.'

Maybe he would and maybe he wouldn't. But Rafe had often wondered how Charlie was doing and he wanted to see him. Mimi had already got out of the car and was running up the ramp which led to the front door, her jacket over her head. It opened as she approached and Rafe saw Charlie inside.

Rafe swung out of his seat, following Mimi to the front door. Charlie looked great. Strong and smiling as he pulled Mimi down for a kiss. 'You just couldn't resist, could you...'

'What?' Mimi broke free, giving a look which was far too innocent to be believed, and Charlie grinned at her.

'Couldn't resist checking up on me.'

'All I want is coffee. Then we'll go. If you want you can go lie on the floor and I'll step over you on the way out.' Mimi turned her back on her brother and walked towards the kitchen area at the far end of the open-plan space.

'You can finish making the sandwiches...' Charlie called after her and then turned his attention to Rafe, his face suddenly impassive. 'You're back then.'

'I'm here to help out, that's all.' Mimi seemed to be busy in the kitchen and Charlie was showing no inclination towards following her. Rafe sat down. If Charlie wanted to give him the third degree, he could do it face to face.

'I hear that Jack's marooned, and the ambulance was towed?' Charlie seemed to be fishing for information, and Rafe guessed that Mimi hadn't told him the whole story.

'Yeah, that's right. The river broke its banks near Holme and the bridge has been washed away. Jack got pretty wet, but we hear he's okay. Mimi had walked back up the hill to make a phone call.'

'Yeah. That's what I heard too. Did she try to get across the river?'

'She… Perhaps you should ask her.'

Charlie leaned forward. 'I'm asking *you*, Rafe.'

'I thought she might. I didn't give her the choice.' Rafe decided that telling Charlie he'd had to lift Mimi off her feet before she ran headlong towards a wall of water wasn't a particularly good idea. And if she hadn't mentioned anything about her plans for getting across the river he'd keep quiet about them as well.

'Yeah. I reckoned that's what happened.' Charlie seemed to relax a bit. 'Thanks.'

'My pleasure. Although I'm not sure it was Mi… Miriam's.' Mimi's full name sounded strange and very cold on his lips, but Rafe had made up his mind to play it safe and use it, since she seemed to object so much to his using her nickname.

'Miriam…?' Charlie's face broke into a grin. 'She *is* giving you a hard time, isn't she?'

'Do you blame her?' Somehow Rafe couldn't quite leave it at that. 'There were reasons, Charlie. For my leaving…'

'I dare say there were. That's between you and Mimi. She told me to mind my own business enough times.'

A quiver of unexpected warmth jabbed at Rafe's heart. Mimi could have said whatever she liked about him, and it was only to be expected that she'd bad-mouthed him to Charlie. He hadn't realised until this moment how much he'd wanted her not to.

'Do me a favour, though…' Charlie interrupted his reverie.

'Of course.' Rafe had absolutely no intention of trying to rekindle anything between him and Mimi, and sex for old times' sake definitely wasn't on his agenda. He could reassure Charlie on that score, at least.

'I know Mimi's job has risks attached to it, and I also

know she doesn't tell me about half the scrapes she gets
herself into…'

'They're not scrapes, Charlie, and she doesn't get herself into them. She's a trained professional.' Rafe surprised
himself by springing to Mimi's defence.

'Yeah, I know.' Charlie ran his hand through his hair.
'Look after her, will you? You know Mimi. She thinks she's
superwoman sometimes.'

'You have my word on that.' Rafe held out his hand, wondering if Charlie would take it. He did so without hesitation.
He was so like Mimi, in both looks and mannerism, and it
felt doubly warming that Charlie seemed ready to forgive.

'It's good to see you.' Charlie's irrepressible grin broke
through his reserve. 'I've missed our little talks.'

Rafe chuckled. Their *little talks* usually lasted until closing time in the local pub, when Mimi was working a late
shift. 'Me too. We should do it again some time.'

'Yeah. That would be good.'

Things were going okay. Not good, but okay. They were
adults and there was no reason in the world why she and
Rafe couldn't play nicely until the situation eased. There
was just one thing that needed clearing up.

'I heard what you said to Charlie.'

'Yeah?' He didn't turn his gaze from the road ahead but
Mimi supposed she shouldn't expect that. She wouldn't
have done if she'd been driving either.

'It's quite unnecessary.'

'Which bit of it in particular?'

'About looking after me. There's no need.'

Rafe's shoulders moved in a tight shrug. 'You want me
to go back on my word?'

'Far be it from me to get in the way of any male bonding that you've been engaging in, but I'd rather you didn't

involve me in it.' Mimi shut her mouth tight. That sounded sharper than it should, but when she'd heard Rafe and Charlie's quiet words she'd felt a little more hurt than she should too.

'I didn't say it to impress Charlie. It's what I intend to do.' The side of his jaw hardened in an obstinate line. She knew that look, and it had frustrated her when she'd been living with him. She didn't need to put up with it any more.

'I've been looking after myself for the last five years, Rafe, and I've met all the challenges that life can throw at me. I'm sorry if that tears a hole in your masculinity, but that's the way things are. I don't need you to look after me, and I'd appreciate it if you didn't go around pretending that I did.'

She felt a little breathless. Almost free, as if that was something that she'd been waiting for a long time to say. Mimi dismissed the idea. There was nothing…nothing that she'd been waiting to say to Rafe.

The car suddenly pulled off the road, jerking to a halt. 'You think this is all about my ego?'

'Well, it's not about mine…' The atmosphere was zinging with hurt antagonism.

'Not about you?' He turned around to face her and she saw her own anger reflected in his face. 'We all need each other at the moment. If you can't deal with that then that's all about you.'

'Stop trying to twist things around, Rafe…'

'I am *not* twisting anything. And I didn't promise Charlie that I'd look after you because you're a woman, *or* because we used to sleep together.'

Mimi caught her breath. He'd said the words they'd both been trying not to say. The words that could lead to all kinds of trouble…*we used to sleep together*. After all the efforts she'd been making not to think about it.

'That's all ancient history.'

His lip curled in disbelief, and suddenly he was very close. That scent of his, a little soap, a little sweat. She'd always loved the way that Rafe smelled, and it was just as intoxicating as it had always been.

'We need to get one thing straight. It's fine with me if you just want to come along for the ride. I happen to think that would be a shame, because I was hoping that I could rely on you.'

'What for?' The words almost stuck in her throat. Suddenly she couldn't think of one thing that Rafe would want to rely on her for.

'You know these roads better than I do. You know the best way to get to where we need to go. And you have a lot of experience of working with people outside the hospital, which I don't have. I could really do with your help.'

'I… I want to help.' Although they'd worked at the same hospital for over a year, Mimi had never worked with Rafe. She knew he was a fine doctor and had often wished she could have that opportunity.

'Right then. So we're a team?'

'Yes… That would be good.'

'In that case, I get to look out for you. The same way that I hope you'll look out for me.'

Mimi swallowed hard. 'You want *me* to look out for *you*?'

'Why not?' His sudden grin burned into her soul like a red-hot brand. 'It's expensive to train new doctors. You'd be doing the economy a favour.'

Right now, the economy was the last thing on her mind. She tried to drag her attention away from the curve of his lips.

'Okay then—partners. I'll look after you and you can look after me.'

He held out his hand and she took it, almost in a dream. One of those bright, happy dreams that had so often been shattered when she woke and found that Rafe wasn't sleeping next to her.

'Partners it is, then.'

Suddenly the dream cracked. Mimi had promised herself not to risk falling for another man and fantasising about Rafe, of all people, was plain crazy.

She let go of his hand, settling back into her seat. Five years ago she'd been foolish enough to believe that she meant something to him, and now… He'd be gone soon and he wouldn't look back.

Perhaps that was the advantage of having a heart that had once been broken. It was stronger now, and well defended. Rafe couldn't just walk back into her life and steal it.

The shining look on her face, the way her lips were parted slightly, had obliterated everything else. Mimi might be as tough as they came, but when she made love she was the softest, sweetest thing.

Don't do this. Don't even think about it.

He'd made one promise to Charlie, and another to himself. He wasn't going to break either of them. Rafe switched on the engine, jamming the car into first gear with more force than was strictly necessary, and started to drive.

CHAPTER FOUR

THEIR FIRST CALL was to a man with cuts and bruises, from where a dry-stone wall had collapsed onto him. In better circumstances he might well have just turned up in A and E, but he'd called first and been passed on to the Disaster Control Team, who had told him to stay put and wait for someone to get to him.

With Rafe there, it was possible to treat him in situ. Not the best use of his skills, but it saved time and resources where they were needed the most. The kitchen table was turned into a temporary treatment area, and Eric's arm lay supported on a wad of dressing as Rafe carefully injected the local anaesthetic on either side of the wound.

'You're the doctor's assistant?' Eric's wife came to sit next to Mimi at the other end of the long table.

'No.' She flipped her gaze towards Rafe to check that he wasn't grinning and saw that his concentration was wholly on what he was doing. 'I'm a paramedic. Only my ambulance got washed away in the river.'

'Up by Holme? I heard about that on the local radio news; they're completely cut off now. No one hurt, I hope.'

'No. Just got a bit wet.'

A baby started to cry in the other room and the woman hurried out, returning with her child in her arms. 'We're sorry to bring you out all this way. Eric was going to go into A and E, but I was worried about him driving and I called first. They said they'd send a doctor to us.' Her tone was apologetic.

'That's all right. We're trying to get as many people as possible treated at home because A and E is pretty stretched at the moment. It's a lot better this way, all round.'

'Not for you. It looks as if it's going to be a filthy night again.' The woman turned the edges of her mouth down in sympathy, and Mimi smiled.

'I'll be in bed, drinking cocoa and reading a book soon enough.' Mimi thought she saw a movement from Rafe out of the corner of her eye, but when she turned he was already looking away again.

'Whatever you earn you deserve more...' Eric broke in, and his wife nodded.

'I tell my boss that all the time.' Mimi grinned, picking up a soft toy from the table and waggling it in front of the baby. There wasn't much else for her to do. 'What do you say to my making a cup of tea?'

'Tea?' Rafe seemed to hear the magic word. 'That would be nice, thanks.'

Mimi swallowed the temptation to tell him that the tea was intended for their patient. Picking the kettle up and finding it empty, she went to fill it up at the sink.

Rafe stood at the end of the path, surveying the small cottage for any signs of life, and Mimi knocked on the door again. No answer.

'I don't suppose we've got the wrong address...?'

'Nope. This is the right one.' Mimi bent down to shout through the letterbox. 'Toby. Open the door.'

Obviously she'd been here before. Or maybe she knew the elderly man who lived here. They'd been summoned by a concerned neighbour, who had noticed that he was limping and had seen an infected sore on his leg.

'Do you think he might not be able to get to the door?' Rafe suggested, wondering if they were going to have to break in.

'Shouldn't think so. He's probably hiding out in the kitchen.' Mimi walked to the side of the cottage, squeezing through the narrow space between the wall and a waterlogged hedge, and Rafe followed, avoiding the branches that sprung back behind her.

She clambered over a low wall, walking past a small kitchen garden to the back door. He stopped and waited, reckoning that Mimi probably knew what she was doing. She pressed her face against the glass, rattling the handle.

'Toby, open up.'

There was a short pause, and Mimi banged on the door again. Then it opened, to reveal an elderly man.

'You might have said it was you…'

'Can we come in, Toby?'

'You'd better. You'll catch your death out there.'

Mimi entered and Rafe hung back from the door as Toby eyed him suspiciously.

'This is Dr Chapman.'

'Where's the other lad?'

'Jack's up at the top of the hill, in Holme. He's a bit tied up at the moment.'

Toby nodded sagely and beckoned Rafe inside. A black and white collie was sleeping by the fire and raised its head to inspect the visitors, then rested it back onto its front paws. The little kitchen was old-fashioned, yet clean and neat as a new pin.

'What can I do for you?' Toby sat down at the kitchen table, its polished surface dark and pitted from years of use.

'Mrs March called us. She says you've got something wrong with your leg.' Mimi's tone was firm, but she was smiling.

'It's nothing.' The old man's chin jutted in a show of defiance. His face was like the surface of the table, dark from years spent in the open air, with deep lines at the side of his eyes.

'No, probably not. But the thing is, now I'm here I have to have a look at it. Those are the rules.'

'And him?' Toby gestured in Rafe's direction.

Mimi looked around, a trace of the smile that she'd bestowed on Toby still lingering on her face. After the uneasy truce between them, which seemed to have started to crumble as soon as it was made, it was like a ray of sunshine. 'Yeah, he's got to look at it as well.'

Toby sniffed. 'One of you not good enough, then.'

Mimi directed a bright grin at Toby and the old man's face softened. 'Come on, Toby. Give me a break, eh?'

Toby shrugged and Mimi knelt down in front of him, pulling a pair of gloves from her pocket and carefully rolling Toby's trouser leg up. Halfway up his calf, a large sore blazed red against the pallor of his skin.

'Have you been wading in flood water?' Mimi voiced the first question which occurred to Rafe. Flood water frequently carried a high concentration of bacteria, and in the circumstances it was the most likely candidate for turning a small injury into an angry, obviously infected wound like this.

'Mebbe...' Toby shrugged non-committally.

'I'll take that as a yes. You've been with your grandson up at the farm, have you?'

'The lad needed some help to get all the animals inside. The pasture's waterlogged.'

'And when was this?'

'Day before yesterday.'

'Okay. This looks as if it hurts.' Mimi gave Toby no chance to reply, clearly suspecting that he wasn't about to admit it if it did. 'I'd like the doctor to take a look at it, and he'll tell us what needs to be done.'

Toby raised one eyebrow, pursed his lips and regarded Rafe steadily. The effect was something like the assessing stare of his first tutor, back when he was a student. Rafe took his coat off, hanging it on the back of one of the kitchen chairs, and bent to examine the leg.

'Yes, there's some infection there.' Rafe stated the obvious and tried not to notice that Mimi was rolling her eyes. 'I'll get some antibiotics and we'll dress the wound…'

'That's okay. I'll get them.' Mimi was on her feet already. 'I'll pop in to see Mrs March on the way, and I need to make a phone call.'

'Okay, thanks.' Rafe supposed that the visit next door and the phone call were going to be about making sure that Toby was looked in on every day. The wound would heal, but not if he didn't take care of it. She caught up her coat and breezed through to the front door, leaving Rafe and Toby staring at each other.

'Nice girl. Reminds me of my Joan.' Toby broke the silence.

'This is her?' Rafe craned over to look at the photograph on the sideboard, and Toby nodded. 'She's beautiful.'

'That she was. Right up until the day she died.' Toby's eyes lingered for a moment on the image. 'Had a temper, like your girl.'

'She's not my girl. We're just working together.'

Toby gave a short barked laugh. 'My Joan and me, we used to argue like cat and dog, but we never let the sun go down on a quarrel. Five kids to show for it, and twelve grandkids.'

'Sounds like good advice.' Rafe wondered what Toby would think of letting things simmer for five years.

'It is. You and your girl…'

'She's not my girl, Toby.'

'Aye. Well, take your eyes off her when she's not looking, and look her in the face when she is, and then I might believe you.'

There was no answer to that. Not one that Rafe could think of anyway, and that allowed Toby to warm to his theme.

'Sun's almost down. Puts you on borrowed time.'

Rafe had been congratulating himself that, whatever their private differences, neither he nor Mimi had allowed them to bleed into their work and they'd remained entirely professional in front of their patients. But it appeared that he'd been mistaken.

'It's…complicated.' Rafe decided that denials weren't going to work this time. Toby might be elderly, but that was no reason to treat him as if he was stupid.

'No, it's not. You find a girl you like and, if she likes you, you lead her up the hill to the church.' Toby folded his arms in a gesture of finality.

The front door slammed, saving Rafe from the difficult task of working out how to answer that. Mimi's footsteps sounded in the hall and Toby twisted around in his seat as she appeared in the kitchen doorway.

'Right. I've spoken to Mrs March and she's given me your daughter's number.' She waved a piece of paper at Toby and put the dressings down on the table, avoiding Rafe's gaze when he went to thank her. He wondered if she watched him when he wasn't looking, and wished he'd thought to ask Toby.

'Are you going to call her, or would you like me to do it?' Mimi gave Toby her most persuasive smile.

'Since you've come all this way, best you do something.' Toby's retort was accompanied by a slight gleam in his eye.

'Yeah, right. Because you wouldn't want me to be bored while the doctor sees to your leg.' Mimi grinned at him good-humouredly and pulled out her phone, turning her back on Rafe as she dialled the number.

He had been about to ask Mimi to assist him, but apparently he was going to have to juggle scissors, tape and a dressing pad on his own. That wasn't what worried Rafe. What worried him was the feeling that he and Mimi weren't so much working together as working in close proximity to each other.

He disinfected the wound and dressed it, then broke open the blister pack, taking the first of the antibiotic tablets out. 'Take this one now. Then three times a day for the next week. It should start to feel better in a couple of days, but if it gets any worse call us again.'

'Wasn't me as called you the first time.' Now that Toby was reassured about his leg, a mischievous sense of humour had begun to surface. Mimi remonstrated with him and, after another short battle of wills, it was time to pack up and go.

'You know him?' Rafe asked as he settled back behind the wheel of the car.

'Yeah. He broke his hip about three years ago, up at his grandson's farm, and Jack and I attended. I went to see how he was doing in hospital, and he had all the nurses wound around his little finger. When he got better, he turned up at the ambulance station with two bags of home-grown strawberries, one each for me and Jack.'

'Nice.'

'They were. They had a real flavour to them, not like the ones you get in the supermarket.' Even though they were alone in the car, Mimi's smile wasn't for him. It was for

Toby and the strawberries, and maybe for Jack. She must be missing Jack.

Rafe reminded himself that he shouldn't need her smile in order to work effectively. Despite all their good intentions, he and Mimi just weren't functioning as a team and they needed to address that. Quickly, if Toby was to be believed, because the sun was going down. He leaned back in his seat, trying to think of some way to broach the subject casually.

'So, marks out of ten. What would you give us?' Rafe accompanied the words with a smile, hoping that it would soften them. 'I reckon ten out of ten for individual performances, and a lot less for teamwork.'

She coloured suddenly. 'What do you mean?'

'Well, how many marks out of ten do you give *me* for teamwork?'

Mimi shrugged. 'Can't we leave the psych assessments until later?'

Something in her tone made Rafe press the point. 'I'd say one. Two if I was being generous. How many marks do you give yourself?'

She turned her gaze on him, luminous in the gathering dusk. Her eyes, wide and dark, seemed almost to be pleading with him.

'I... I probably don't deserve any more than one. But I can do better.' Her words were almost a whisper.

She looked so deflated, so hurt, that he instinctively reached out for her, stopping only a moment away from touching her hand. The problem was almost entirely of his making and he'd blundered in, trying to fix it. And somehow all he'd managed to do was to wound Mimi.

'It's me that needs to do better, not you.' Mimi looked as if she was on the edge of tears and the impulse to comfort her was almost irresistible.

None of his old coping strategies were going to work. Rafe knew that he needed to try something new.

'We need to talk.'

She was doing it again, judging herself, doing herself down, before Rafe got the chance. And now he wanted to talk? Somewhere in the universe, something very big must have jolted out of alignment because Rafe didn't talk.

Even though she'd cursed him a million times in her head for not sharing how he felt, now that he'd offered she didn't want to hear it. The thought that Rafe's list might be far more damning than anything which Graham might have concocted terrified her.

'You want *me*…?' She couldn't even say it.

'I'll give it a go if you will.' His voice was suddenly tender. 'We're both so busy doing our own thing that… Well, neither of us has put a foot wrong with a patient yet, but that might be only a matter of time. I want to do better, and I'd like you to help me.'

There wasn't enough air in here. Her heart was labouring and her head was spinning.

But he was right. They had too much baggage, and it could so easily blind them to something important.

'We…can't do it now.' She needed some time to think.

'No. Later?'

She looked at her watch. 'It's eight o'clock…' It would take them at least another two hours to get through the calls they already had. She would rather have the option of going with him to a pub or a coffee bar, but they'd barely make it before closing time. 'Are you staying in town tonight?'

'I've got one of the on-call rooms at the hospital.'

That wasn't going to work either. The last thing that Mimi wanted was to be overheard by anyone there. She needed to be clear about what she was offering, though.

'Before you go back there, you can come to my place. Just…
half an hour.'

'Thanks. I'd really appreciate that.'

CHAPTER FIVE

THE MOOD HAD lightened between them. It was eleven o'clock before they had worked through the list of calls they had to make, but they'd done it. There had even been a couple of bad jokes, which they'd both laughed far too loudly over in an attempt to prove that they were at ease with the situation. Rafe knew that, in reality, about the only thing that they shared any more was the certain knowledge that what lay ahead of them wasn't going to be easy.

He was about to swing into the parking space to one side of the cottage, and then realised that this was no longer his home.

'Where can I park?'

'Use the hardstanding. My car's at the hospital.'

He should have thought of that and offered to take her there, so she could drive it back here, but it was too late now. He manoeuvred the heavy vehicle into the tight space and switched off the engine.

'Is this okay? If you're tired...'

'It's okay.' She seemed to have screwed her courage up for this, and he knew Mimi didn't back down. She got out of the car, and made a dash for the porch, unlocking the front door and not looking behind her as she disappeared inside. Rafe followed her, trying not to drip too much water on to the hall floor.

When they'd rented this place together, the decor had been gloomy and tired and Rafe had asked if he could apply a few licks of paint. The landlord had agreed willingly, and he and Mimi had chosen a cream colour for the walls, with an oatmeal-coloured carpet to match. She'd hung a few pictures and suddenly the place had become clean and welcoming.

Now, it was like a different place altogether. She'd ripped up the carpet and laid a wooden floor instead, and the walls were painted a faded plum colour, which suited the age of the cottage perfectly. An old dresser, which looked as if it had been lovingly restored and polished, stood in place of the flat-pack hall table.

She took off her coat and motioned for him to come through. Rafe followed her into the kitchen. Here, the new cabinets he'd put in were gone too, the wooden doors replaced with shiny white ones. No better, no worse. Just completely different.

'Hang your coat here. It'll dry off a bit.' She pulled a chair that he didn't recognise away from a table he didn't recognise, and put it close to the old wood-burning stove, which was about the only thing that still remained from when he'd lived here. Rafe imagined that it had gained a reprieve only by dint of being too large and too heavy for Mimi to disconnect and drag out of the house.

He sat down, watching as she took cups from the cupboard and boiled the kettle. Rafe had taken nothing with him when he'd moved out, just his clothes and personal belongings, reckoning that the least he owed Mimi was to leave the home that they'd built together behind for her. She hadn't wanted it, though. Even the cups and the tea towels were different.

'You've made a good job of the place.' His first instinct was still to hide his feelings and pretend that nothing had happened, but he was trying to do things differently. If he couldn't quite bring himself to tell her how much it hurt to see how ruthlessly she'd expunged any sign that he'd ever been here, he could at least acknowledge that there was a change.

'Thanks.' She looked around the kitchen thoughtfully, seeming to decide that saying nothing was her best option.

'So you've been studying, renovating the cottage and looking out for Charlie.' Rafe imagined that every penny she earned and every moment of her time must have gone into those three things. 'Anything else? You must have had at least five minutes' spare time since I saw you last.'

Her face broke into a sudden smile. 'It was six minutes. And I wasted them quite shamelessly, eating chocolate in front of the TV.'

A faint echo of the life they'd had together here smacked Rafe squarely on the jaw. The evenings when she'd raided her not-so-secret chocolate stash and curled up on the sofa with him, feeding him the odd square as they talked. 'I'm glad to hear it.'

She threw the tea bags into the cups and made the tea, giving each one a perfunctory stir before carrying them over to the table. She seemed to be about to sit down and then had second thoughts, clearly unwilling to go to the lengths of sharing a table with him just yet.

He should give a bit more. Something about his own life, perhaps. 'I'm working at the new emergency care unit at Hartsholme Hospital.'

Surprise registered on her face. 'I heard about that. I gather there's some groundbreaking work going on there; I didn't realise you were involved.'

'I was looking for a challenge, a chance to push the boundaries a bit, and I found it. I've been there four years and it's all been good.'

She nodded. 'I was wondering… Your mother…?'

'She's well. In full remission.'

Suddenly, Mimi's smile held nothing in reserve. 'I'm so glad to hear that.'

'Thank you. She and my father moved up to Scotland a few years ago, but I talk to her regularly. I'll tell her you were asking…'

She pressed her lips together, shaking her head. 'She probably doesn't even remember me. I'm just pleased to know she's okay.'

Rafe remembered what Toby had said and looked her straight in the eye. His chest tightened suddenly, as if his body was instinctively trying to strangle the words that he was determined to say. 'What is it? What are you not saying?'

She took one controlled breath, as if she was trying to steady herself. 'The job you had, before Hartsholme. It fell through?'

'No. I was covering for someone on maternity leave. It lasted longer than I thought.'

'And your parents? They suddenly decided to up sticks and move?'

He could see the way this was going, but he couldn't stop it now. 'No. They'd planned to go when my father retired. The cancer delayed it a bit, but…'

She turned her back on him, planting her hands on the counter top, her head bowed. Something that sounded like a sob escaped her lips. 'Rafe… How could you…?'

This was a far cry to the indifference she'd shown when he'd left. Then, she'd accepted his reasons without question, but now she knew that they were excuses, given because he didn't know how to tell her the truth. The thought that maybe this was truly how she felt made him shiver with guilt.

When she faced him again her face was twisted into a mask of anger. Somehow that was worse than the tears he'd expected, because he knew now that her fury disguised an awful, unknown hurt.

'Get out.'

There was only one thing he could do. Only one thing to say.

'No.'

Mimi stared at him. Now was a fine time to suddenly decide he wanted to stay around. 'I said…'

'Yeah. I heard. Not until you listen to what I have to say.' His jaw was set in an immovable line.

'I don't want to hear it, Rafe.' She felt breathless, almost giddy with rage. 'I was never good enough for you, but you know what? I'm over it. This is *my* house, and *my* life. If you want to pick holes in it, then you can go and do it on your own time.'

'What…?' Shock registered on his face. 'What on earth do you mean, not good enough?'

'Don't pretend you don't know.' She'd vowed she wasn't going to do this, but it was all too much. The feelings were flooding out with as much force as the water that had separated her from Jack. 'I'm not a doctor, or a lawyer like your sister. My mum and dad didn't live in a big house, and I didn't go to private school.'

'You think I care…'

'Well, clearly you do. You didn't even let me try to help when your mother became ill; you just got in the car and went over there on your own.'

'But you had enough on your plate. Charlie…'

'Don't make my brother into an excuse, Rafe. You just shut me out. After all you did to help me cope when Charlie was injured…' She felt tears well in her eyes. 'How do you think it made me feel when you turned your back on me when I tried to help you?'

He didn't answer. Probably didn't *have* an answer, because he wouldn't have thought of that. In the silence she felt her heart begin to slow, and the burden of things left unsaid shifted slightly. Maybe she should have told him this before.

'It wasn't like that.' He was looking at her steadily but his hands were trembling. The thought that she'd finally goaded him into some kind of reaction was a bitter triumph because it was all too late now.

'Don't…' Suddenly her legs felt as if they were going to turn to jelly, and she leaned back against the counter top. 'You can rewrite history all you like, Rafe. Don't ask me to countersign the last page.'

'Fine. Now you listen to me.' He was on his feet now, pacing restlessly.

'No… I don't want to.' Now that the rush of anger was subsiding, the feeling of loss was tearing at her. Along with a horrible feeling that Rafe could talk her round if he really wanted to, because he'd always been able to.

He came to a halt opposite her. When she looked away, she felt his fingers brush her arm. 'Look at me.'

She didn't move.

'All right then. Just listen. I wanted to accept your help but I just didn't know how. I was brought up to cope, not talk. Never to talk, because that was a sign of weakness in a man.'

'All you had to do was ask, Rafe…' She looked up at him and the pain in his face silenced her.

'It's not that simple. My own father, the one who taught me how to behave, was failing my mother when she needed him most. He couldn't deal with not being able to make everything right for my mother, and he just shut down. I was doing the exact same thing. I was keeping everything bottled up inside, and I was failing you.'

'Why didn't you tell me?'

'It wouldn't have made any difference. And telling you…' He shook his head. 'Like I said. I was brought up to believe that talking about things was a sign of weakness.'

'And leaving fixed everything, did it?' In a strange way she supposed it had. When Rafe was around she'd filled the silences with her own fears and they'd thrived on that fertile ground. When he'd left she'd filled the void in her heart with ceaseless activity. She'd stopped measuring herself by what the men in her life thought of her and found ways to feel proud of herself.

'I think it did. Look at what you've achieved.'

'And… You? Your mother…?'

'I had to learn how to deal with things better and how to give my mother the support she needs. It wasn't easy, but I did it. My father…' He turned away from her, flexing the tension out of his shoulders. 'He learned to text.'

'And…texting helps?'

'Yeah. When something's up he texts either me or my sister. Both of us if it's bad. We call Mum and she gets it off her chest, then she goes and tells Dad what she wants him to do.' He shrugged. 'Seems to work for them.'

'They're happy with that?' Somewhere, at the back of her mind, Mimi could hear an insistent voice. If Rafe's father could change, then why not him?

'Happy as clams.' He gave a wry laugh. 'Very understated clams. My dad's not all that different; we just found a way to work around it.'

He walked over to the stove, picking his coat up. 'I should go.'

'Wait.' She'd told him to go. She'd wanted him to go. But

the haunted look in his eyes had changed her mind. 'You haven't finished your tea.'

'Thanks.' He put his coat back over the chair and sat down. 'There's one more thing…'

'No. Please, Rafe, no more…' She'd had enough for one night. More than enough. She couldn't process it all yet.

'Okay.' He picked up his tea and sipped it. It was probably cold by now, but that seemed not to matter to him. Just being in the same room, without tearing chunks out of each other, felt calming.

'What did you…?' She pressed her lips together. She'd told him 'no more'.

'What?' He turned his blue eyes on her and suddenly the question seemed important.

'What were you thinking? Coming here tonight? Coming here at all, for that matter; you must have known we might bump into each other.'

'I knew how stretched the emergency services are here, and I really did just want to help. I reckoned on dealing with bumping into you if and when it happened. And tonight…' He shrugged. 'Perhaps it's only fair that if you're going to hate me, it's for what I did, not what I didn't do.'

Mimi was about to tell him that she *did* hate him, but something stopped her. Maybe she didn't after all. She turned away from him, pondering the question, and in the silence his phone started to buzz insistently.

She heard his quiet sigh of frustration. Then he picked the phone up from the table in front of him.

'Yeah… No, it's okay, I wasn't sleeping… Yeah, I'll go. Text me the details… Thanks.'

'What's up?'

'The house down by the lock. The fire brigade are in attendance and they've called for medical help.'

'I'll come with you.'

His gaze met hers and Mimi found the solid ground she'd been looking for. The place where they could work together, knowing that there was never going to be anything else between them.

'Okay. Thanks; it'll be good to have you along.'

He was trying to keep his attention on the road ahead, dark and glistening with rain. But Rafe could still see her. She'd been wearing a white cable-knit sweater and jeans. Trainers and blue spotted socks, with a blue ribbon twisted into her plait. A plaster wound around her middle finger from where she'd cut herself the day before. Every detail was burned into his memory.

He'd made her sit down at the kitchen table, and he'd told her that he was moving out…

'You're right. It's the best thing.' She'd agreed with him almost before he had been able to get the words out of his mouth.

'I'll just take my own things…' Something inside him had been screaming that this wasn't right, but she'd seemed so firm, so sure.

'Take whatever you want.' She'd shrugged as if none of it meant anything to her and then stood up, in a clear indication that the conversation was now at a close. *'I've got to pop over to see Charlie.'*

How could he have believed her? He should have known that her lack of emotion was just a front. But he'd struggled so agonisingly with this decision that the thought that Mimi didn't care whether he stayed or left was almost welcome. It assuaged the guilt.

When he'd packed his things, put his bags in the car and driven away, he'd thought he was being strong, protecting her. But now he knew the truth. He'd messed up, and he'd hurt her.

The thought that she still hadn't told him everything, that she'd given no reason for this crazy assertion that she wasn't good enough for him, wouldn't go away. But he'd already pushed her too far tonight.

'Wait... Is this right?'

Yes. It was right. They might have done it in the worst way possible, but it had unquestionably been the right thing to do.

Suddenly Rafe realised that she'd actually spoken the words and that she was referring to the fork in the road a couple of hundred yards behind them, not a decision made five years ago. Occupied with his thoughts, he'd instinctively taken the same road he'd taken then, which led on to the motorway.

'Ah... Yeah, of course. Lost my bearings for a moment.'

'Visibility's terrible. I nearly missed it.'

It was so easy to fall back into the pattern—Rafe driving, Mimi at his side, tactfully applying a corrective nudge from time to time. It made him feel strong to have her there, which was worrying in any number of ways.

He turned the car in the deserted road, driving back the way he'd come. It was still raining, and they still had a job to do. And Rafe was becoming increasingly certain that he couldn't leave until he found out what it was that Mimi had refused to tell him.

As he manoeuvred around a car parked right on the corner, he heard Mimi catch her breath.

'Oh, no!'

Water was pouring over the lock gates, spreading out in a huge pool on the other side. The lock house, converted now to make a holiday home for someone, was surrounded by three feet of water. A fire engine stood on solid ground, further up the hill.

'There's someone in there?' She was peering through the rain-drenched windscreen.

'Apparently. Must have been trapped and called for help.' Rafe drew up beside the fire engine and got out of the car. He identified himself to the senior firefighter and they shook hands.

'We can't get over there with ladders; they won't reach. We'll have to go by dinghy. We have information that someone's injured in there, but we don't know how badly.'

'Okay. We'll come with you.' He'd rather go alone, but leaving Mimi behind wasn't an option at the moment.

'Only one of you. Those guys are going and, with two of my men, that leaves only one place in the dinghy.' The firefighter jerked his thumb towards two men standing up close to the fire truck to get what shelter they could from the rain.

'Who are they?'

'Plain clothes police. The place is being burgled.'

'What?' Rafe hadn't been aware that Mimi was standing next to him until she spoke.

'Yeah. The alarms went off and the security company alerted the police. When they got here they found that the place was cut off and called us.'

'You think they're still there?' Mimi frowned, clearly taking stock of the situation.

'We know they are. The alarm system in the house is state-of-the-art—heat and pressure sensors, webcams, the lot. The ones downstairs are out, but upstairs they're still working. It looks as if there are two lads and one of them has suffered some sort of injury.'

'And the police are keeping a low profile not to spook them.' Rafe remembered the car, parked on the corner.

'Yeah. If they think that it's just the fire and ambulance services, then hopefully there'll be less chance of trouble.

I'm sending over two of my men with the police officers, so that'll be enough to contain them if things get nasty.' The fire officer looked around at the activity going on behind him. 'We'll have the dinghy ready in ten minutes. Then we'll get you over there.'

'Thanks. We might wait in the car.'

'Yeah.' The firefighter looked up at the falling rain. 'Don't blame you.'

They walked back to the car in silence. Mimi got in, sitting quietly in the passenger seat.

'All right. I'll go.' Rafe decided to make his position clear, right from the start.

Mimi turned to him, no trace of the anger that he'd seen in her face more times than he could count today. 'This is my job, Rafe.'

He didn't care. Mimi was *not* going into a dark house which was in the process of being burgled. He didn't care if it was just kids, or that there was going to be backup. She wasn't going.

'Look, Mimi…' He heard the exasperation in his own tone and took a breath. 'In a situation like this, I'm handier with my fists than you are.'

'You're thinking of hitting the patient?' She was annoyingly calm.

'Don't be smart.'

She pressed her lips together, as if she was trying not to rise to the bait. 'Teamwork, right? You're a gifted doctor, Rafe, but I'm a first responder. I've been trained to work with the fire services and the police and I know exactly what to expect of them and what they're going to expect of me.'

Rafe grabbed the last and only argument he had. 'And, professionally speaking, a paramedic usually defers to a doctor in any medical situation.'

'Okay.' She sat back in her seat, folding her arms. 'Make the decision, then. From a professional standpoint.'

She'd pulled the last plank out from under him. Rafe had made some tough decisions in his life, but that didn't make this one any easier.

'All right. You should go. You're the one best qualified to do the job.'

'Thanks.' Her face suddenly softened. 'Don't worry.'

She went to get out of the car and Rafe caught her arm. 'If you don't take care out there, so help me I'm reporting you...'

She grinned at him, irrepressible as ever. If this was all he could have, the camaraderie of working together in a potentially volatile situation, then he'd take it.

'You need to have a word with Jack. He usually threatens to string me up and flay me to within an inch of my life.'

'What you and Jack do on your own time is your own business.'

Mimi chuckled. 'I'd like to see him try.'

'Just go, before I change my mind. And be careful.'

'Yeah. I will.'

Rafe let go of her arm and she got out of the car, walking over to where the dinghy was being pushed out into the water. One of the firefighters helped her in and she sat down. Someone must have cracked a joke because Rafe saw a couple of the men laugh, and Mimi joined in.

He got out of the car and went to stand next to the senior fire officer, who was watching as the boat steered a path across the water. It drew up alongside a small balcony on the upper floor of the house, and two figures climbed up onto it. The crack of breaking glass sounded above the rush of the water and then the figures disappeared inside.

CHAPTER SIX

MIMI WATCHED FROM the boat as the two police officers gained entry into the house and were followed in by one of the firefighters. Glancing across the expanse of water, she could see Rafe, standing by the fire truck. Suddenly, she was glad that he was there.

The firefighter appeared and beckoned her inside. She knew that the place would have been searched and that it was now deemed secure. A hand reached down and she grasped it, struggling to find a foothold on the balcony, before an undignified shove from the firefighter in the boat behind her boosted her upwards.

'Through there. If we give the order to evacuate the house, you don't wait. We'll be getting everyone out.'

'Understood.' Mimi waited for her bag to be passed up and hurried through to the bedroom on the other side of the house.

The room was in darkness, apart from the light from torches and a lantern. A youth of about twenty lay on the double bed, groaning in pain. One of the policemen was with him and the other was guarding a younger boy, who sat on the floor in the corner of the room.

'He's got no weapons on him and I can't see any signs of blood either, apart from his fingers.' The policeman had obviously made some kind of preliminary check.

'Thanks.' Mimi climbed on to the bed. Looting was considered the lowest of the low, but this was a patient and he wasn't much more than a boy at that.

'Hi, I'm Mimi. I'm with the ambulance service.'

No answer. The lad's eyes were resolutely closed, although he seemed to be conscious.

'What's his name?' She turned quickly towards the boy in the corner, who had his face in his hands and seemed to be crying.

'His name.' The policeman standing over him bent towards the boy. 'Come on. You need to help your mate.'

'Terence Arthur Wolfe.' It seemed that now the boy had decided to talk, he was going to tell all. 'We call him Wolfie.'

'Okay. Wolfie...?'

'Not now, baby. I'm not in the mood.'

She heard the firefighter who had come with her chuckle quietly and shot him a grin. 'Just as well. Neither am I.'

She tapped the side of Wolfie's face with her finger and he opened his eyes. 'Ambulance service, Wolfie. I'm here to help you.'

She started the basic checks, calling over her shoulder to the boy in the corner. 'What happened to him?'

'It wasn't my idea...' The boy started to sob.

'What happened, lad?' Another prompt from the policeman.

'He... He went downstairs, said there was stuff down there. I didn't go. All the furniture was floating about. He got hit by a wardrobe and it squashed him against the wall...'

'Did his head go under the water?' Mimi felt Wolfie's hair and it was dry.

'No.'

'Was he unconscious at any time?'

'I pulled him out and got him up here.'

'Has he been unconscious?' Mimi tried the question again.

'I don't think so.'

It looked as if Wolfie might have a cracked rib and two of his fingers were broken. But his breathing was okay, and if there was any bleeding it was internal. She turned to the firefighter. 'We'll need a carry cot. You have one on board?'

'Yep, we've got one.'

'Great.' She felt in her pocket for her phone and dialled Rafe's number. 'The boat can go back and fetch it?'

Rafe was holding his phone in his hand, and answered on the first ring. As he did so, he saw the boat, pushing away from the house and moving back towards them.

'Mimi?'

'I've got a young male, crushed by a floating wardrobe, of all things. We'll need to evacuate him by stretcher. I'll call an ambulance.'

'Okay, got it. I'm coming across with the boat. Anything you need?'

'No, I'm good. Thanks.'

By the time the boat arrived back, a carry cot had been taken from the fire truck and they were ready to go. The dinghy was manoeuvred carefully across the dark water, bumping against the wall of the house, and Rafe waited for the go-ahead before he climbed up on to the balcony.

On his way through to the bedroom, a policeman led a young boy past him, ready to ferry him back to dry land and take him into custody. It seemed, from what Mimi had said, the other hadn't been so lucky.

She'd enlisted the help of one of the firefighters to hold a breathing mask to the boy's face and was kneeling on the bed next to him. A new-found respect for her bloomed in his heart. In this vital fifteen minutes she'd worked alone and by torchlight, improvising and taking the help she needed from whoever was there at the time. His responsibilities were different, heading a team of doctors and nurses in the hospital.

He'd been so close to making the wrong decision. Rafe had told himself that it was concern for Mimi's safety, but maybe he just hadn't respected her enough. He'd allowed himself to fall back into his old way of thinking—he was the man and he had to protect her. He did, but he had to protect her as an equal.

'Quite a few minor cuts and bruises, and pain in his upper left abdomen and shoulder. BP and heart rate are on the lower end of normal.'

'You're thinking a ruptured spleen?' Everything that Mimi had said pointed to that, but Rafe supposed she hadn't given her diagnosis out of deference to him.

'Yeah. I don't smell any alcohol on his breath, and his mate says he's not taken any drugs.' She twisted her mouth grimly. 'Not that he would have wanted to admit it, but the policeman made it very clear to him that he'd be in a lot more trouble than he is already if he didn't tell us. *Oof...*'

The air rushed from Mimi's lungs as her patient grabbed at her jacket, pulling her down on to the bed next to him.

'Gimme something, baby.'

Rafe and the firefighter both moved at the same time to release her from his grip, but Mimi had this under control too.

'Let go, Wolfie.' Her tone was suddenly commanding. 'I can't give you anything for the pain if you don't let me go.'

Wolfie let go and started to moan loudly, his hand moving to the left side of his chest, as Mimi moved clear of him.

'All right?' The firefighter moved his free hand to restrain Wolfie, and clamped the oxygen mask firmly back over his face.

Mimi grinned. 'Yes, thanks. He's surprisingly strong.'

'Okay, let's have a look.' Rafe got on to the bed and Mimi grabbed hold of Wolfie's flailing arm. A careful examination prompted howls of protest from Wolfie, the assertion that his pain levels were twelve out of ten, and a not so polite request for anaesthesia.

'I think you're right.' Rafe turned to Mimi. 'We'll keep him warm, continue the oxygen and monitor his BP and heart rate.'

She nodded as if that was an instruction.

'Agreed?'

'Oh.' She shot Rafe a surprised look but regained her composure immediately. 'Yes, agreed.'

'You're carrying morphine sulphate?'

'Yes and Naloxone.' Although it didn't appear that Wolfie had been taking narcotic drugs, the Naloxone would reverse the effects of the morphine if necessary.

'Okay…'

She left Rafe to keep an eye on Wolfie and turned to fetch the morphine from her medical bag. When she offered him the syringe, Rafe shook his head.

'Your patient, Mimi.' He murmured the words. Now that she was a qualified paramedic, she was allowed to give a patient morphine.

Her grin felt like a reward, when he'd only given her what was her due. Rafe held Wolfie still, while she slid closer to him. 'Wolfie… Wolfie, listen to me. I'm going to give you something for your pain. Just lie still; you're getting what you want.'

Rafe felt the tension in Wolfie's body relax, and he started muttering. Mimi carefully swabbed his forearm, and when she slid the needle in Wolfie hardly noticed. She disposed of the syringe and then sat back on the bed, her hand on the side of Wolfie's face, soothing him while the drug took effect.

Rafe stood back, ready to step in if he was needed, but Mimi was handling everything correctly and efficiently. She managed to insert a cannula in Wolfie's arm which, given the bad lighting and the fact that Wolfie seemed to be trying to proposition her while she did it, was nothing short of miraculous. She was monitoring him carefully and the lad responded to the sound of her voice, lying quietly.

The firefighter who had been helping Mimi had gone to get an update on evacuating Wolfie from the house, and Rafe saw him appear in the doorway. 'How long before we can get him out of here?'

'Five minutes, maybe ten. We'll winch him down on to the dinghy and walk it over.'

Rafe had no clear idea of what that might involve, but Mimi seemed to and she nodded. 'We'll strap him into the carry cot as tight as we can. He seems a lot calmer now.'

'Hope he stays that way.' The firefighter winked at Mimi. 'Baby…'

She laughed. 'Wanna try calling me that when I don't have my hands full?'

'Nope.' He walked away, chuckling.

When everything was ready, Wolfie was carried through to the balcony and lowered down on to the dinghy. Men were standing, waist deep in water, on four sides of the craft, ready to guide it back to the waiting ambulance.

Mimi seemed about to climb over the balcony, to accompany the dinghy but Rafe lay his hand on her arm.

'My turn, this time.'

For a moment he thought she might argue with him, even though it was obvious that his height and strength made him the one for this particular job. Instead she nodded. 'Better take this.'

She pressed the EpiPen, containing the Naloxone, into his hand. It was highly unlikely that he'd need it now, but it was a kind of acceptance, that he was right.

'Thanks.' Rafe climbed over the balcony, wading through the freezing water towards the lights on the other side.

They'd handed Wolfie over to the ambulance crew, and Rafe had called the hospital to make sure that they were aware of the possibility that the incoming patient had a ruptured spleen. Then he'd made for the car, found a pair of sweatpants in his overnight bag and stripped off his soaked jeans in the cramped confines of the front seat.

The sky was beginning to show the first signs of an approaching dawn as Rafe drew up outside Mimi's cottage. Now that she had nothing to do, fatigue had taken over and she was already yawning. As soon as he got back to the hospital and into a hot shower, Rafe reckoned he'd be yawning too.

'What day is it?'

He had to think about the answer. 'Thursday.'

'Yeah. That's right, Thursday. I'm off duty for three days, now.'

'Right. Get some sleep.'

'I'll text Jack first…' She felt in her pocket for her phone and then seemed to give up, unequal to the task of finding it.

'If he's got any sense he'll be sleeping. Probably in a warm bed in the church hall.' A warm bed sounded like heaven at the moment but, however cold and tired Rafe was, he couldn't resist stretching these few moments out just a little.

'Suppose so.' Mimi stifled another yawn. 'What are you doing now?'

'I should get back to the hospital. Get a few hours' shut-eye and then back on the road.'

She thought for a moment. 'Why don't you stay here? You won't get any sleep in the doctor's on-call room today, and anyway you need to wash and dry your clothes. And you won't have to drive back out here to pick me up later on.'

'Pick you up? Where am I taking you?'

'I don't have a vehicle or a partner, remember?' A little quiver of her lip betrayed her uncertainty. 'If you still want me around, that is.'

He wanted her. 'Think you can put up with me?'

A tired grin. 'I'll try.' She opened the car door and started to climb wearily out. 'So are you coming…?'

Rafe reached for his overnight bag and pulled it out. Locking the car, he followed her up the front path and into the house.

Mimi fussed about a bit, leading the way into the spare room and switching on a lamp by the bed, which gave so little light that it served only to stop him from bumping into the furniture. She gathered a few items of washing that were drying by the window and then collapsed the drying rack.

'Leave your clothes in the basket in the bathroom and I'll put them in the washing machine tomorrow morning.'

Rafe nodded.

'I'll get you a towel…' She walked out of the room, re-appearing a few moments later with a clean towel and putting it on the bed. 'Bathroom's all yours.'

'Thanks.'

'Have you…' She frowned as if she'd forgotten what she was about to say. 'Is there anything you need?'

'Go to bed.' He could have slept on a washing line at the moment, and Mimi looked as if she was half-asleep already.

'Yeah.' She swayed a little as she turned, and Rafe wondered whether he should follow her to make sure she got to her bedroom without falling asleep on the way. Then she left him, closing the door behind her.

Rafe waited until he heard the door of the main bedroom close and then walked the few steps across the hallway to the bathroom. He showered off the bits of river mud, revelling in the hot water, and then made his way back to the spare room.

He had neither the energy nor the inclination to worry about what he was doing here, or how awkward things might be when they woke. Rafe loosened the towel from around his waist and crawled into bed.

He woke slowly, knowing that he wasn't anywhere familiar but unable for the moment to work out exactly where he was. In fact he probably wasn't awake at all because he could smell the citrus scent of Mimi's favourite soap. Rafe considered the possibility of lucid dreaming and whether he could control what happened next. Then he opened his eyes.

Not bad for a first try. Mimi wasn't draped over the end of the bed, wearing black lace. On the other hand, the smell of cooking was wafting up from the kitchen. Bacon sandwiches would be his second choice of things he most wanted to wake up to at the moment.

He tried again and failed. He must be awake. Rafe stumbled out of bed and drew the curtains, looking up at the sky. It was iron-grey and threatening, but at least it wasn't raining.

Turning, he caught his breath. If none of the rest of Mimi's house held any memories, this room was full of them. The walls were a plain cream colour, and the pale

blue patterned curtains and bedding were unfamiliar, but
the bed was the sturdy pine one that he and Mimi had
shared. And against the far wall was an old mahogany
wash stand.

The memory hit him like a punch to the chest and
Rafe wondered for a moment whether his heart had really
stopped or it just felt that it had. They'd found the washstand in an auction, sitting unwanted in the corner and
covered with grime. But Mimi had seen some virtue in it
and so Rafe had put in a bid and secured it for her. When
they'd got it home, she'd gone to work on it, carefully pol-
ishing up the wood to reveal an age-old patina, removing
the brass handles and making them shine. It had sat in the
corner of their bedroom, transformed from a piece of junk
to something precious.

He supposed that Mimi's ruthless purge of the cottage
had been tempered by practicality. Here in the spare room,
she didn't have to look at the furniture all that often, and so
the few things that reminded her of him which she hadn't
wanted to throw away had been consigned to this room,
where she could shut the door on them.

The bed, rumpled on one side only, filled him with an
unexpected sadness. He'd told himself that he was over
Mimi. That had been a mistake, but he could rectify it.
Last night had given him hope that perhaps they both might
find some closure.

He wondered briefly whether he should pull some
clothes from his overnight bag to make the three strides
across the hallway to the bathroom door, but the towel was
large and thick and it was easier to just wrap it around his
waist. From the mouth-watering smells coming from the
kitchen, Mimi was downstairs cooking, anyway.

He opened the bedroom door at almost exactly the same
time as hers opened. Rafe caught a glimpse of her star-

tled face, her green ambulance uniform, and then the door closed with a loud slam.

'Sorry. You first…' Her voice came from behind the door.

Rafe called back a thank you, wondering how she could be in two places at once. This was nothing she hadn't seen before, more times than either of them could count. So why had her sudden startled look sent an electric pulse travelling across his bare shoulders? And why had she slammed the door with such agitated force?

He padded across the hallway, shut himself in the bathroom and locked the door, switching on the shower. Clearly he had some more thinking to do before he could work out what either he or Mimi really felt.

CHAPTER SEVEN

MIMI HAD WAITED until she heard the shower running and then gone downstairs to see how Charlie was doing with the breakfast and put away the shopping he'd brought for her. When she heard Rafe's footsteps again, and the door of the spare room close, she ventured up to the bathroom to empty the washing basket.

'Doing his washing, now?' Charlie raised an eyebrow.

'Oh, be quiet.' The thought had already occurred to Mimi and she was trying to ignore it. 'He's meant to be staying at the hospital and he can't get these washed there. And we don't have time to visit the laundrette...'

She pressed her lips closed. Charlie was grinning, holding his hands up in a gesture of surrender, and she was protesting far too much. Mimi dumped the pile of clothes on to the floor, almost glad that the nasty-smelling mud on the legs of Rafe's jeans was enough to overwhelm his scent.

Automatically, she felt in the pockets. A little loose change in one, and in the other... Held securely in his pocket by a clip, Mimi knew what it was before she even drew it out.

'What's that?' Charlie's question made her realise that she was staring at the watch, running her thumb slowly across the face of it.

'He must have taken his watch off last night, so it didn't

get caught in anything.' It was an expensive watch, but that wasn't what made it special. It wasn't obvious at first sight but, when you looked more closely, an old silver sixpence was set in the centre of the dial, behind the hands.

The strap was different, and he'd obviously had the glass replaced because the scratches that she remembered were gone. But the sixpence was what mattered. Rafe had said that his grandfather had carried it in his pocket for years, and then had the watch made for his only grandson when he went to medical school, saying he'd had all the luck he could stand and he was passing it on now.

Something tugged at her heart. She'd seen Rafe take this watch off the nightstand every morning and put it on. Having grown up in a world where he was surrounded by things of material value, this was the only one he seemed to care all that much about. He must have been so tired last night that he'd forgotten that it was in his pocket.

'Still got his lucky watch, then.' Charlie chuckled. 'Good thing *that* didn't go into the washing machine.'

'Yeah.' Mimi put the watch down on the table. Even there, it seemed to be radiating some signal, activating memories that she'd rather not think about at the moment.

She stuffed the clothes into the washing machine and was fiddling with the dial when Rafe appeared at the kitchen door. Thankfully he was dressed now.

She could hardly look at him. His thick, dark blue shirt was open at the neck and tucked into jeans that fitted better than they had any right to. Mimi thought she recognised the brown leather belt, or one quite like it. Suddenly this was almost worse than seeing him half-naked. The shirt couldn't conceal his broad shoulders, and the jeans only accentuated his slim hips. And her treacherous memory was busy filling in the gaps, reminding her that she knew every inch of his body and that it had always been beautiful.

'Have you seen…?' He was clearly looking for something.

'On the table.'

'Ah… Thanks.'

Mimi turned her back on him, studying the instructions on the packet of washing powder as if this was the first time she'd ever washed clothes. She'd armed herself against all the obvious things, his smile, his scent, but she'd forgotten all about the watch and it had sneaked in under her defences. She'd deal with it, though. Just as long as she didn't have to see him put it on…

Charlie came to her rescue. 'Hey Rafe. Good night's sleep?'

'Yes, thanks. Much better than if I'd stayed at the hospital.' He seemed to want to explain his presence here.

'I imagine so. Sit down; breakfast's almost ready.'

The scrape of a chair and then a sudden laughing exclamation from Rafe. 'Really?'

Mimi turned and saw that Charlie had pulled himself out of the wheelchair and was sitting on a high stool next to the cooker.

'Yeah, really. Took a bit of work.'

'I'll bet. Nice one.'

Rafe was grinning from ear to ear. The same grin that Mimi had worn for days when she'd seen Charlie wave away his physiotherapist's help, leaning heavily on the parallel bars for support as he took his first laborious steps. Now, standing and even walking a little was something he did many times a day.

Suddenly it seemed all wrong that Rafe had missed out on that. She could have at least sent him a text to let him know how well Charlie was doing. She could have, but she hadn't.

'Have you heard from Jack?' Rafe was leaning back in his chair, still smiling.

'Oh… Yes. He texted me. Holme's completely cut off at the moment, so he'll be staying there for the next twenty four hours at least.'

'Everything's okay with him, though?' Charlie interjected.

'He said so.' Jack hadn't gone into details about exactly what he was up to, and Mimi had been happy to take his lead. 'Apparently ambulance control told him the same as me—that they don't have a spare vehicle and he should take his days off. They'll sort something out for when we go back on shift.'

'And, in the meantime, you and Rafe are doing your thing.'

Shut up, Charlie. Mimi gave him a withering look and he ignored it and began to dole out the contents of the pans on to three plates. Like so many other weekends when the three of them had eaten together, only then it had been either Mimi or Rafe doing most of the cooking.

Now, Rafe was sitting back, watching. He knew as well as Mimi did that you only helped Charlie when asked.

'Come and get it, then.' Charlie had finished serving the food and Mimi went to collect the plates and transfer them to the table.

'This looks good.' It was a full English breakfast and Charlie had crammed as much as he could on to each plate. 'I'm starving.'

'Me too.' She heard Rafe behind her but didn't dare look round at him. His hand shot out of nowhere and suddenly he was shaking Charlie's hand. 'Really good to see you on your feet, mate.'

'Thanks.' Charlie shifted on the stool and Mimi got out from in between them, carrying two of the plates over to the table. When she looked around, she almost dropped them. Charlie was on his feet and Rafe had him in a man hug. It wasn't so out of the ordinary for Charlie—he did that kind of thing all the time—but Rafe… All the same, there was no trace of stiffness or reluctance on his part.

'I'm sorry I wasn't there to see it.' The admission startled her even more. The old Rafe would have just sucked up his regret and walked away, never mentioning it.

Mimi put the plates down on the table. She was going to have to find a way of not watching Rafe's every move, hoping to find evidence that he'd changed. She was going to have to find a way of not caring, and do it quickly before he left again.

As expected, they didn't have to wait long before they had a call from the control centre. With eight hours sleep and a good meal inside her, Mimi felt a great deal better about that. Being able to see where they were going was no bad thing either. As they moved closer to the flood area, large puddles had become lakes and the fields were now deep in water.

The car slowed and came to a halt. In front of them, a dip in the road was knee-deep in water for the next couple of hundred yards.

'Can we manage that?'

Rafe was surveying the path ahead of them. 'I'd rather not try if there's an alternative.'

Mimi nodded. The surface of the water was almost serene but that could be deceptive. The road underneath could be strewn with sharp rocks and potholes, any one of which had the potential to put them off the road.

'That looks a better bet.'

Rafe turned the car abruptly on to a track that wound upwards and Mimi saw a handwritten notice pinned to a tree: *Diversion and Manor Hotel*.

'Yep.' She clasped her hands tightly in her lap. The

Manor Hotel's main driveway was three miles further along this road. If they could get up to the hotel from here and then drop back down again they'd avoid the flooded section of road.

She wondered if Rafe remembered. Because, as the old stately house loomed on the horizon, she was having difficulty forgetting.

Date night. Although it had been more than five years ago now, it was suddenly fresh and clear in Mimi's memory, a treasure that had remained untouched and unchanged. Preserved in every detail, right down to the note she'd found on the kitchen table when she'd come home from work.

Going out tonight. Dress up.

By the time Rafe had arrived home she'd been almost ready. He'd showered and changed into a suit, and complimented her on her dress. Then he'd kissed her, refused to tell her where they were going, and led her to the car.

They'd driven here. It had been a summer's night and they'd dined on the patio, with flickering torches lending a sense of drama to a good meal. As dusk had begun to fall he'd dropped a room key into her hand...

'A four-poster!' The solid, dark wood structure had been big enough to close the curtains, shut the world out for a night and have Rafe entirely to herself. 'I've never slept in a four-poster before.'

'You want to sleep?' Rafe's wicked, seductive smile had made it very clear that sleep wasn't on his agenda.

'Got a better idea?' she'd teased him.

'Much better...' He'd taken off his jacket and loosened his tie. Picking up a wooden chair from the corner of the room, he'd placed it carefully and sat down. Mimi had known just what he wanted. If she stood in front of him he would be able to see her back, reflected in the big mirror over the dressing table, which would give him a three-sixty-degree view when she unzipped her dress.

Undressing slowly, she'd revelled in his gaze, his murmurs of approval pricking at her senses like fingers running over her skin. Finally she'd shaken her hair free across her shoulders and advanced towards him, perching on his knee.

'What next? Since you seem to have a plan.' Whatever it was, she had really wanted to hear it.

'Call it a fantasy.' He'd nuzzled against her neck, running his hands across her body. 'You up for that?'

'Fantasy night…? Yes, I'm up for it.'

He'd had to help her unbutton his shirt because her hands had been shaking with anticipation. When he was naked, his clothes flung in an untidy heap on the floor, he'd broken away from her kisses, moved the chair a few inches and sat down again, his legs stretched out in front of him.

'Come here, honey…'

He'd settled her on to his lap, astride his legs. She had been completely exposed to him, her back reflected in the mirror.

'You like what you see?'

'You know I do, Mimi. More than I can say.' Rafe had spread his hands possessively across her back. 'I want to see everything. Touch every part of you.'

She'd clung to him as his gentle hands did just that and she'd been blind to anything other than Rafe. When he'd lifted her, she'd reached to guide him inside, sighing with him as he'd lowered her back down.

'You like what you feel?' He'd whispered the words, his breath caressing her neck.

'I love what I feel.'

The heat had started to build. Locked in each other's gaze, breathing together, hearts beating together more and more urgently. His hands had found her hips, suddenly clamping firm, moving her in the urgent rhythm that her body craved.

'Rafe… I can't wait…'

'Then don't.'

He'd seemed intent on making her come as fast and as hard as he could, and she'd known that if he kept this up he would get exactly what he wanted.

'Just let go, honey…'

The fantasy vanished abruptly as Rafe jammed his foot on the brake and the car jolted to a halt. Four other cars were all trying to negotiate the forecourt of the hotel and the man standing outside, trying to direct the traffic, wasn't helping very much. Rafe wound down the window, exchanging good-natured hand signals, and the car that had shot out in front of them backed up.

She could still almost taste his kisses. The last time they'd been here together, she'd been thinking about them for days, but then she'd been basking in a rosy glow of satisfaction and now the memories just left her hanging.

'Sorry…' Rafe was looking at her, and Mimi realised she'd let out a gasp when the car had stopped and she'd been thrown forward against her seat belt.

'Okay. His fault; he was lucky you managed to miss him.' She tried to swallow down the languorous warmth that she heard in her voice.

'Getting a bit crowded around here…' He waved another car past and pulled on to the main driveway, which led back on to the road.

'Yeah.' Too many memories. Mimi wondered if Rafe could feel them, hovering in the air. It was impossible to tell; his face was impassive, his gaze trained on the route ahead.

He had been a wonderful lover. Tender, thoughtful, with

enough raw passion that they'd lost themselves in each other. But now they'd both found their way again. It was just a pity they'd only been able to do that when they were apart.

The car turned back on to the main road, clear of the water that had blocked their path. 'What's the next call again?' It was better to keep her mind on the job. Better to stop re-examining old wounds and concentrate on moving forward.

'It's a Mrs Potter. The controllers couldn't get much sense out of her; all she would say was that her son might be unwell.'

'Might be?'

'We'll see.'

It turned out that Mrs Potter was panicking because she couldn't get in touch with her son on the phone. Rafe had swallowed the frustration that Mimi knew he must feel and spent a few minutes checking the number that she was calling. The addition of a zero at the beginning worked wonders and her son answered immediately, clearly in the best of health. They left her in the sitting room, talking animatedly on the phone, and let themselves out.

CHAPTER EIGHT

THREE MORE CALLS and Rafe had successfully managed to scrub the Manor Hotel from his mind. He was about to congratulate himself on that, and then realised that remembering to congratulate yourself on forgetting something was a contradiction in terms.

He could do with stretching his legs, and there were no more calls for them to respond to. 'Time to take a break?'

Mimi nodded. 'The park's only five minutes away.'

That was exactly what he had in mind. The nature park's picnic area was likely to be deserted and the trestle tables would be too wet to use, but there was a nice view. Maybe Mimi needed to stretch her legs too.

'Stop!'

Rafe heard Mimi rap out the word at the same time as he saw two small creatures ahead of them, standing in the middle of the road, and braked sharply. As he skidded to a halt, the pair didn't move.

'What the blazes…?' The tiny animals clearly weren't wild or they'd be long gone by now instead of regarding them solemnly. Wet and bedraggled, they seemed to be all eyes and shivering limbs and very little else.

'It's Tommy and Tallulah.'

'Who?'

'Tommy and Tallulah. They must have escaped from the

petting zoo.' She reached for the passenger door, opening it slowly so as not to spook the animals.

'Where's the petting zoo?' Rafe didn't recollect a petting zoo in the area and he supposed it must be a new addition.

'Not far. Jack and I took Ellie there and she had a whale of a time.' Mimi started to walk slowly towards the animals and Rafe got out of the car.

'Ellie…?' Clearly a lot had been happening in the last five years and he needed to catch up.

'Oh, sorry. I didn't tell you, did I. Ellie is Jack's little girl. She'll be five at Christmas. She loves the petting zoo.'

Rafe tried to get his head around an arithmetical problem that seemed simple but obviously wasn't. 'Did I miss something? Jack wasn't even married…'

'No, he wasn't… Isn't… It's complicated. He didn't know about Ellie…' Mimi's attention was on the tiny creatures ahead of them. 'Come on, sweetie… Tallulah…' She advanced towards the closer of the pair, which regarded her steadily.

'What exactly are they?' They looked like tiny bundles of wet fur with little hooves and big eyes. Given the rather more pressing possibility that Mimi might be about to get bitten, Rafe decided to leave the question of Jack's love life until later.

'Miniature goats. Get with it, Rafe…'

'Okay. You take the white one and I'll get the one with the brown splodges.' Rafe eyed up his goat warily, wondering how fast a miniature goat could run.

Clearly Mimi was a better goat whisperer than he was. She walked right up to hers and bent down, picking it up carefully in her arms. 'There you go, Tallulah. What are you doing here, sweetie…?'

Tommy took one look at Rafe and turned, trotting along

the road away from them. Rafe followed, and Tommy picked up the pace a little.

'Get him, Rafe.' Mimi chose that moment to shout an encouragement and Tommy took fright, trotting into the long grass at the side of the road.

How fast could a miniature goat run, anyway? Rafe walked up to the animal and made a lunge for it and it darted to one side, cantering towards a clump of trees. It was certainly agile enough.

He heard Mimi let out a cry of dismay behind him and ignored her. If he was going to be outwitted by a goat, he'd actually prefer that it didn't have to happen with an audience. 'All right, then, mate. It's just you and me...'

Apparently this was some kind of game. Tommy stood stock-still, waiting for Rafe to approach and then dashed for cover. Rafe might be a lot bigger, but Tommy had four legs and was quick on them. A final desperate lunge and Rafe tripped on a tree root, crashing down on to the wet leaves.

'All right. You win.' Rafe rolled over on to his back and Tommy approached. They regarded each other steadily and Rafe reached out towards him. Tommy nuzzled at his hand and then tried to climb up on to his chest.

Carefully, Rafe wrapped his arms around him. Tommy trained his innocent eyes on to him, and Rafe unzipped his jacket, allowing the small, shivering animal to nestle against his chest.

Gingerly he got to his feet. Tommy seemed quite happy where he was now and was trying to eat his sweater. Rafe climbed the bank, back up to the road, and saw Mimi, sitting in the front seat of the car, her head bent over Tallulah, who was lying in her lap, wrapped in Mimi's ambulance service jacket.

'Poor little thing; look...' Mimi was wearing a pair of

surgical gloves and had *his* surgical scissors in her hand. She looked up at him and frowned. 'You've got wet leaves all over you.'

'Yes, I know. Spare me the details. What are you doing?'

'She's got a piece of plastic wrapped around her leg. Look, it's bleeding.' Two pairs of wide brown eyes were trained on him and Rafe frowned. This was an unfair advantage.

'You're not a vet, Mimi.'

'I know that. We're Good Samaritans.' She snipped the tight plastic away from Tallulah's leg, exposing a red raw wound. 'There. That's better, isn't it, sweetie.' She bent down, allowing Tallulah to lick her cheek.

There was no point in telling her that it wasn't a good idea to allow random animals to lick your face, or to mention that the scissors would have to be sterilised now. He had another pair somewhere. 'All right, so where is this petting zoo, then?'

'Half a mile along that track.' Mimi pointed to a new road that branched off ahead of them, leading into the trees.

'Right. We'll get them back there as quickly as we can.' Rafe wasn't about to admit that the large eyes and little shivering bodies of the goats had made him wonder whether taking them back to his house was an option. He got into the car, depositing Tommy at Mimi's feet, where he nuzzled against her legs.

'Drive slowly. We don't want them flying around…'

No. Flying goats were the last thing he wanted. 'If we get a call…' If they got a call, he wasn't entirely sure what he was going to do. People before animals always, but Rafe was not sure that he could bring himself to dump Tommy and Tallulah.

'We won't.' Mimi hugged Tallulah close on her lap. 'It won't take us long.'

* * *

He drove slowly into a large paved area, surrounded by low buildings. A woman appeared from one of them, jogging out towards the car. When she saw Tallulah in Mimi's lap she smiled broadly.

'Thank you so much...you've brought her back.' She opened the car door and Tommy jumped out, nuzzling at her legs. 'And Tommy, too.'

Rafe couldn't help grinning at the little creatures' obvious joy at being back home. He'd meant to just drive away and leave them, but instead he got out of the car, opening the passenger door so that Mimi could carry Tallulah.

'Do you have to go yet?' The woman looked at the ambulance markings on Mimi's jacket, and Mimi looked up at him imploringly.

'Not for a minute. We're on a meal break.'

'Well, come inside and eat. I'll make some tea.' The woman smiled up at him. 'I'm so grateful you brought them back. The rain washed away some of the fences last night, and some of the animals escaped. We've tracked down all the others, but we couldn't find Tommy and Tallulah.'

'They didn't get too far.' Mimi followed the woman inside the building. 'But Tallulah has a wound on her leg, where she got caught in an old plastic bag.'

The woman gave a tut of disapproval. 'I wish that people would think before they leave those things lying around in the countryside. You wouldn't believe the number of animals that are injured by them one way or another.'

She led the way through to a room that was kitted out with examination benches, not so different from a hospital surgery, only generally speaking the hospital didn't have cages for its patients. A young man appeared, white coat and all, and set about examining the wound on Tallulah's leg.

Mimi showed no signs of wanting to leave just yet and

Rafe picked up her jacket, brushing the inside down. There were a few wet patches but they would dry in the car. Something nuzzled at his legs and a plaintive bleat reached his ears.

Tommy had been towelled dry and looked even more appealing now. Big eyes and a fluffy brown and white coat. Rafe bent down to pet him.

'Oh, look. He likes you.' The woman set two cups of tea down on the counter and Mimi took one, thanking her.

'I think he likes my sweater, actually.' Tommy was busy trying to nibble at his sleeve.

'Yeah. Goats. They'll eat anything.' The woman bent down, nudging Tommy away from Rafe's arm, and he started to lick his hand.

'It's not much of a hole. You could darn that.' Mimi was sipping her tea, looking at him speculatively.

'Darn it?' He raised an eyebrow. The Mimi he knew couldn't sew on a button and, unless she'd fundamentally changed in the last five years, darning was way out of her skill set.

'I said *you* could darn it.' For a moment the old warmth flashed between them and Rafe found himself snagged in a tingling sensation, which reached all the way to his heart.

'It's an old sweater.' He stood up to collect his tea and Tommy followed him over to the counter.

'Be careful. He'll be wanting to go home with you.' Mimi chuckled and he saw the smile that up till now she'd kept for her patients and for Tallulah. This time it was unmistakably his, and Rafe found himself luxuriating in it.

'He's a great little guy.' Rafe took a swig of his tea and bent down to stroke Tommy's head.

The vet looked up from his patient, smiling. 'Well, she's okay. Just a bit of a scrape and the skin's broken where she tried to untangle herself. All she did was manage to pull the plastic even tighter. It was acting as a tourniquet, so it's a good thing you got it off when you did.'

Mimi nodded. 'I'm glad she's all right. I bet you've had a lot of animals brought in here after the flooding.'

'Quite a few. Not so much domestic pets—people are keeping them inside mostly—but a lot of wild animals have been washed out of their homes by the floods. We've had birds, foxes, voles, you name it. Even a couple of grass snakes.'

'Really?'

'Yeah.' The vet pointed to a large, leaf-lined aquarium in a quiet corner of the room. At first glance there was nothing in it, but then Rafe saw something green coiled around one of the tree branches, which was propped against the glass. 'Take a look if you like. But don't get too close; they're very shy and you'll spook them.'

Rafe smiled as she approached the container warily, stopping a couple of feet away from it. 'I can see them…' Her voice was hushed with wonder. He wanted to walk over and fold her in his arms so they could watch the shy creatures together.

His phone rang. Mimi turned and the moment was gone.

Resisting the temptation to pull his phone from his pocket and stamp on it, he looked at the caller display. He shrugged and took the call, listening carefully to the instructions that the ambulance controller was reading out at the other end.

'Got to go?'

'Yep.' Rafe checked the text that had just arrived, confirming the name and address of their next call. 'Got to go.'

Men holding small fluffy animals with big eyes. *Rafe*, with his strong arms and gentle way, and a small fluffy animal with big eyes. It was a little too much to bear.

Maybe it was emptiness in her stomach causing that pang. More likely, it was the thought of Rafe's tenderness, and her own instinctive reaction. There was only one thing that could have struck any closer to her heart.

'Where are we headed?' Mimi tried to switch back into professional mode.

'One of the farms, out by the A375. Three-month-old baby.'

If Mimi had been alone, she would have screamed and buried her head in her hands. What was this? Did fate have some sort of grudge against her? If the sight of Tommy in Rafe's arms had pushed all her buttons, then a baby was going to be even worse.

'A baby?' She tried to keep her tone level. Maybe Rafe would decide that it wasn't medically necessary to pick the child up.

'Yep. Probably just colic, but we'll make sure.'

'Yes. Good to make sure.' He was going to pick it up, she just knew it. Maybe a baby throwing up all over him wouldn't be so mind-bendingly difficult to watch. Mimi wasn't at all sure that would be the case.

CHAPTER NINE

THE TRACK WHICH led to the farmhouse was submerged and the house itself surrounded by almost a foot of muddy water. Rafe parked on the road and got out of the car.

'Looks as if we're getting our feet wet.' Mimi surveyed the muddy, rippling water in front of them. Her wellingtons were in her car, which was still parked back at the hospital.

Rafe opened the back of the SUV and leaned in, pushing bags and boxes to one side and pulling out a pair of heavy-duty wellington boots. At least he'd be keeping dry. Perhaps she could roll her trouser legs up far enough to avoid the water.

'Want a lift?' Rafe was grinning broadly.

No. The idea of being carried around like a rag doll didn't much appeal to her. The idea of being carried around by Rafe… Mimi swallowed hard.

'Come on.' He'd obviously had second thoughts about teasing her, and was now trying to keep his face straight. Somehow that was worse. 'We've got more to do today, remember? There's no time to go home and change.'

And if she got wet, that was only going to get in the way of the job. It was a first principle. Stay safe, stay dry, because your ability to help others was compromised otherwise.

'All right. Thanks.' She kept her eyes fixed on the

ground, feeling her muscles tense in stiff, silent protest. He tried to pick her up, but had to set her back down again.

'Hey. Loosen up, will you. You're going to need to bend your legs.'

'Yeah. Sorry.'

'One medical professional assisting another to the scene…' He muttered the words under his breath and Mimi wondered if he believed that any more than she did.

She laced her fingers together behind his neck and he picked her up. It was actually more like taking her in his arms, holding her close. Mimi hung on tight, squeezing her eyes shut and burying her face in his shoulder.

'That's better.' He started to walk, the sloshing sound of water accompanying his slow strides.

Mimi clung to him, trying to think of anything else. The shopping list for Charlie. The forms she had to fill in for her new job. That was just making things worse. Every time she went to the supermarket now, the stronger image was going to take hold and she was going to have to deal with remembering this moment.

He was walking carefully, testing each step, but a sudden eddy of water made him pause, instinctively holding her tighter. Mimi felt herself move against him, her cheek brushing his neck.

No, no, no… She felt her face redden in anguish. She hadn't done that, had she?

She had. Without thinking, and entirely by instinct, her lips had formed the shape of a kiss when she'd jolted against him. When he'd started walking again the kiss had been planted on his neck.

He hadn't felt it. He couldn't have. One quiet murmur of approbation told her that he had.

By the time they got to the farmhouse her cheeks were flaming. He leaned over the row of sandbags, protecting the small flower garden in front of the house, and let her down on the other side.

Maybe his hand was just travelling in that direction, in a movement of uncharacteristic awkwardness. But his fingers brushed against her cheek and Mimi looked up into his face.

The cocky grin she'd expected wasn't there. Instead, a look of silent pain and uncertainty. Had she been so caught up in her own feelings of rejection that she'd missed his unspoken feelings?

'Rafe, I'm… I'm sorry.'

'What for?' He glanced round at the farmhouse behind her. They had a job to do and right now the people inside were probably watching them.

'Whatever it is, it's all right.' He straightened up. 'You're standing in a puddle.'

'Oh. Thanks.' Mimi stepped to one side quickly.

'Got your phone?'

'Uh?' She felt automatically in the pocket of her trousers. 'Yes.'

'I'll go back to the car and get the bag. Have a quick look at the patient and call me if there's anything else I need to bring over.'

'Okay. Will do.' Mimi turned and saw that a woman was opening the front door of the farmhouse, smiling at her. She smiled in return, walking towards her without looking back at Rafe.

Mimi had wanted to keep going, but when she'd received a call from the ambulance controller saying they were no longer needed tonight Rafe had stopped her from arguing.

'She said they were managing, right? We need to pace ourselves; we both have another week's work ahead of us. Isn't there something you need to do?' Rafe couldn't think of a single thing that he wanted to do more than spend time with Mimi. Certainly not a meal, eaten alone, and a bed at the hospital. But he supposed that she might have a greater range of options.

'Not really…' She turned away from him and got into the car. As she did so her phone rang.

'Charlie?' Something seemed to be going on because she frowned. 'Yeah, okay; that's fine. I'll do it. Text me the address, will you?'

She turned to Rafe. 'I don't suppose you could give me a lift to the hospital, could you? I need to pick up my car.'

'Yes, of course. What's up?' Rafe had been planning on going back to the hospital. Last night had been an exception.

'Couple of friends of Charlie's. Their house is in an area that's prone to flooding and he told them to come and stay with him if they needed to.'

'And they need to?'

'Yes. He's getting a room ready for them, and he wanted to know if I could go over there and pick them up. My car's got a much bigger boot than his.'

'They'll be bringing as much as they can with them, I imagine.'

'Yes.' She was squeezing her fingers together in what seemed like an agony of indecision. Rafe wondered whether she was also wiggling her toes.

'My SUV can fit a fair amount in. We could fetch your car, dump the medical gear back at yours and go together.'

'Would you? I…didn't want to ask… But if the house is flooded…'

Rafe started the engine. 'That's what we'll do then.'

Mimi could barely see his SUV in front of her on the road, it was raining so hard. It had taken almost an hour to get here, but she'd called Janet and Matthew to let them know that they were on their way. When Rafe pulled up outside the house, the door opened and Matthew ran out and knocked on the window of her car.

'Better bring your wellies, Mimi.'

'I've got them.' She slid over into the passenger seat and felt in the footwell for them, pulling them on over her socks. Mimi hadn't been about to lay herself open for a repetition of the carrying incident.

Rafe was already jogging towards the front door. Matthew led them through to the kitchen, where Janet was drying cups and plates and stacking them in a high cupboard.

It was evident that they hadn't got here too soon. Water was leaking in under the back door, sloshing around on the kitchen floor. Janet was shaking.

'Mimi, thank you so much for coming.' Janet put the tea cloth down and turned to Rafe. 'And...?'

'Rafe. It's a pleasure.'

'Thanks, both of you.' Matthew held out his hand and Rafe shook it. 'We've loaded our car up, but anything else you can bring along would be much appreciated.'

Rafe smiled—the smile he kept for emergencies, which showed both his readiness to take on any challenge and his utter certainty that things were going to work out fine in the end. 'I'll help you carry your things out to the cars.'

Janet seemed to be sizing Rafe up. 'Matthew...the cabinet...'

'It's too heavy, Jan; we tried it already...'

'But...' Janet lapsed into silence, picking the tea cloth up and folding it carefully. She was in shock, resorting to small tasks that were not going to make any difference so she didn't have to face the one big task ahead of her.

Mimi nudged Rafe. 'They've got a really nice china cabinet in the sitting room. Maybe you and Matthew could manage to get it upstairs?'

'Good idea.' Rafe strode out into the hallway, and Matthew followed.

'We really appreciate your help, Mimi.' Janet was looking around the kitchen abstractedly, as if to make sure that it was tidy before she received visitors.

'It's a pleasure.' Mimi took Janet's arm. 'Are these boxes to go?' She pointed to the cardboard boxes on the kitchen table.

'Yes. Our tea service. It was a wedding present.' Janet's eyes filled with tears.

'Right then. We'll stow that carefully, in the front seat of my car.'

'Yes.' Janet didn't move. 'Thanks.'

She seemed to be paralysed, dreading what was coming next. Mimi picked up a waterproof jacket that was lying on the table next to Janet's handbag. 'This yours?'

'Yes. I got it in the sale.'

'Yeah? It's a lovely colour. Where did you get it?' Mimi gave Janet the jacket and she automatically put it on.

'The place down by the cinema in town. The one that does camping gear…'

'I'll have to pop in and see if they have anything that suits me. Yours is really nice.' Mimi picked up a box and put it in Janet's arms. 'Let's get started.'

Once Janet had something to do, she worked with a will. The necessities had already been packed into Matthew and Janet's car, and now some of their most precious items could be brought along too, instead of leaving them upstairs and hoping for the best. After a bit of bumping and banging about on the stairs, Matthew and Rafe got the cabinet from the sitting room safely out of the water's reach and Matthew appeared with a pretty wooden box in his arms.

Janet beamed with joy. 'My sewing box! Is there room for it?'

'Of course. We've still got my car to load up.' Rafe strode down the path after Matthew to open the passenger door of the SUV so that the precious box could be placed carefully on the front seat.

Then it was time to leave. Janet picked up her handbag from the kitchen, took one last look around and then they walked outside into the pouring rain. Matthew locked the front door, as if in some way that would keep the water out.

Matthew put his arm around his wife's shoulders. 'We'll be back before long, you'll see.'

'Yeah.' Janet smiled up at her husband.

'No looking back now, Jan. Come with me.'

Janet nodded and the couple walked to their car together. When Mimi looked up at Rafe he was watching them go.

'It's such a shame.' Suddenly the sadness of it all struck her. 'They're losing almost everything...'

'You think so?' He couldn't seem to tear his gaze from the couple, walking so close, as if they were in their own little bubble. 'Seems to me that they're taking everything that really matters with them.'

Rafe led the small procession of cars back to Charlie's house, parking outside, while Mimi backed her car into the sideway, ready to unload it. Charlie had obviously been looking out for them and the garage doors swung open, light flooding out.

'I thought we could stack everything in the garage and sort it all out tomorrow.'

'Thank you, Charlie.' Janet had a hug for him.

'My pleasure. Dinner's nearly ready. Jan, come and help me, eh?' He caught hold of Janet's hand.

'I'll be there in a minute. I want to bring my sewing box into the house...'

Rafe gave her his car keys and she skittered off through the rain to the SUV.

'Mimi, Rafe, you're joining us.' Charlie spun his wheelchair round as if the matter was already settled, making for the door that led from the back of the garage into the house.

'I should really get going.' Matthew had followed Janet and they were alone suddenly in the open doorway of the garage.

'Do you have to? You could have a meal with us and stay with me.' When Mimi looked up at him, Rafe realised that he didn't *have* to do anything. But even though a meal in the hospital canteen and a disturbed night's sleep in one of the doctors' on-call rooms didn't appeal to him very much, it was infinitely preferable to the mess he might get himself into if he stayed.

'It's not a good idea, Mimi.' It really wasn't. Last night he'd gone to sleep not realising that he was in the same bed they'd made love in, but tonight it was doubtful whether he could ignore that.

'I hurt you, didn't I?'

'It wasn't your fault, Mimi.'

She tossed her head, her fair hair slipping from the collar of her jacket and streaming over her shoulders. He wanted to touch it so badly, to clear the damp strands from her face. He wanted to touch *her*.

'But still…'

Then he realised. He'd hidden his pain from her but she needed it, just the same as he needed hers. Just as he had wanted some small expression of regret that it was all over, so did she.

'Mimi…' He took a step closer, and they were almost touching. 'Leaving you tore my heart out. And yes, it hurt a lot and for a long time. But, looking back now, it was for the best.'

'You think so?' There was an edge to her voice, a hint of anger. The final refuge of the broken-hearted.

'Don't you?'

Her cheeks flushed. 'I've no idea, Rafe. Not a clue.'

She turned away from him before he had a chance to answer. Walking to her car, she hauled out the heaviest box, staggering a little under its weight, until Matthew rushed to help her.

'I'm hurting now...' Rafe walked to his car, murmuring the words under his breath, even now not able to say them out loud.

He unloaded the car, working steadily so that he didn't have any chance to stop and think, let alone stop and talk. When he was done, he exchanged handshakes and hugs with Janet and Matthew and bade goodbye to Charlie, waving away all of his protests that he'd cooked far too much for four and that only five would do.

Then Mimi. She was hanging back, fidgeting in one corner of the garage.

'What time shall I pick you up tomorrow?'

'Eight would be fine. If you get any sleep.' She seemed determined to leave him in no doubt that he was being petty and that thought was unexpectedly warming.

'Eight it is. Make coffee.' He turned, walking away from her to the SUV.

'You'll need it. They tell me those mattresses in the on-call rooms are like boards.' She flung the words after him and Rafe hid a smile. It seemed that cold acceptance wasn't Mimi's style any more.

CHAPTER TEN

MIMI WAS ALMOST surprised when she saw Rafe's SUV draw up outside the cottage at eight sharp. She'd slept last night, but it was only a long day and a very full stomach that had facilitated that. This morning she'd woken early in a fever of uncertainty as to whether Rafe wouldn't decide that she was surplus to requirements and that he'd be much better off working alone today.

She'd drawn the curtains back carefully, leaving a small chink next to the wall so that she could watch for him without standing at the window. Aware that pulling them straight might produce a telltale curtain-twitch, she left them as they were and ran into the kitchen. It wouldn't do to let him know that she was anything less than one hundred per cent confident that he would come. Unless he didn't, in which case she'd decided to text him and tell him that she hadn't expected him anyway.

It seemed an age before the doorbell rang. She almost took up her position at the window again, wondering if he'd changed his mind and driven off. But he was there, on the doorstep. Unshaven and looking slightly the worse for wear, but a night at the hospital would do that to you.

'I'm just making breakfast. Care to join me?' She made the request seem as off-the-cuff as she could manage.

'Yeah. Thanks.'

He followed her into the kitchen, taking off his coat and putting his phone on the table. Mimi set two places, taking juice from the fridge and setting the coffee machine to brew. The croissants were warming in the oven, and she piled them on to a plate and set it on the table.

'Charlie bought them for me. He got me some shopping yesterday.' There was enough for two here, and Mimi didn't want to give the impression that she'd gone out of her way. In fact, she'd already been out this morning, catching the local bakery when it opened at seven.

Rafe nodded. 'They smell good. I couldn't face the canteen this morning; I was going to pick something up when we got on the road.'

'You can't work without a good breakfast.' Mimi wondered whether that sounded as if she was mollycoddling him. Whenever she wasn't working, she'd always sent him off in the morning with a good breakfast and a kiss.

'Neither can you.' He motioned her to sit. 'I'll get the coffee.'

Mimi sat down, watching as he walked over to the coffee machine. He had a kind of grace, an economy of movement that served to emphasise the gestures he did make. Unshaven suited him. Jeans and a sweater suited him. Everything suited Rafe.

'Aren't you going to ask me how I slept?' He was leaning against the countertop, his arms folded, his lips twitching in a half-smile.

'Do I need to?'

'Not really. Just thought you might like to make the point.'

'All right.' She couldn't help shooting him her most innocent look. 'Sleep well?'

'Nope. I've got an ache in my shoulders you wouldn't believe.'

Time was that she'd offer to massage them for him. But

then time was that he wouldn't have even mentioned it, considering that any aches and pains were his to deal with. It was an odd form of sharing, but nonetheless a break in his stubborn self-sufficiency.

'I dare say it'll ease once you get moving.'

He turned back to the coffee, grinning. 'Dare say it will.'

It was a busy day again. A good day. As long as they both kept up the pace, working as hard as they could, not leaving room for anything else, they were able to slip into the kind of relationship they'd never enjoyed when they were sleeping together.

Although Rafe was the doctor on the team, he was standing back, letting her take the lead with their patients whenever possible. Mimi could feel her confidence growing, and she was beginning to live for his quiet nods of approval.

By four o'clock she was aching from long hours spent in the car and her head was buzzing with both exhilaration and fatigue. Rafe stopped by a coffee shop, overlooking a pretty village green. 'Time for coffee?'

'Definitely. I'll get it.'

By the time Mimi had queued, passed the time of day with a couple of people and returned to the car, he was gone. She could see him over the road, sitting on a bench under a tree which was usually three feet away from the banks of the river which snaked through the green space but was now on the water's edge.

'You've got something to explain to me?' When she sat down next to him and handed him his coffee, Mimi saw that he had a pad of paper balanced on his lap.

'Nope. We're on a break.' He gave her one of his most gorgeous smiles. The one that said the world could wait for a moment. This was Rafe's safety valve. Some people talked things out of their system, a couple of her colleagues had their own blogs, but Rafe seemed to have developed the capacity to just change gear, leave it all behind for a while and divert all of his attention to something else.

'So what *are* you doing?'

'I'm making a boat.' He tore a leaf from the pad and started folding.

Mimi put the coffee down on the bench between them. When talking about things just sent you round in circles, sometimes Rafe's solution was the better one. It was usually a great deal more fun.

'Give me a sheet, then.'

Rafe's boat turned out to be a complex, double-hulled affair which took more than one sheet of paper and sported a sail. Mimi stuck to a basic coracle shape, but she could make three in the time it took for Rafe to make his one.

They walked to the water's edge. Like a pair of kids with nothing else to do but mess around with paper boats. Mimi carefully placed her boats and, as the surface of the pond rippled in the breeze, two of them floated towards his.

'Watch out, Rafe, my pirates will be boarding you any minute…' She grinned up at him.

'No, they won't.' He picked up a stick, nudging his boat away from hers, and it began to drift slowly toward the centre of the pond. 'And anyway…'

He produced a wrap of paper from his pocket. 'What's that?'

'Duck food. My secret weapon.' He gave her a Machiavellian grin. 'Found it in the glove compartment.'

He'd been feeding the ducks without her. Of course he had. She couldn't have expected Rafe to go five years without taking time out to feed the ducks.

He tipped a measure into his hand, and then hers. Then threw some of the food into the water. 'Here they come…'

A large green and blue duck was making for the food,

diving for it as it sank beneath the surface. Another well-aimed throw hit one of Mimi's coracles and the duck tipped it upside down in its eagerness to get at the food.

'Hey! Two can play at that game.' She aimed for Rafe's boat and it wobbled slightly on the water as the grains hit it. 'Come on…' She urged a smaller brown speckled duck on, which was paddling across the water towards it.

'No, no, no…' Rafe clapped one hand to his forehead as his boat lurched and relaxed as it righted itself. 'Yesss…'

They were both laughing. Rafe managed to lure another duck towards her second boat and it nudged its beak inside before lifting it out of the water entirely. The little brown duck was making his boat wobble dangerously, but somehow it survived the onslaught.

Mimi still had one boat left, caught amongst the roots of a tree. Picking up a fallen branch, she clambered across to nudge it out on to the water. Leaning out to free the boat, she felt herself begin to tip.

'Rafe…!' A knee-jerk reaction—screaming for him before she knew quite what she was doing. And, by the same instinct, he was there, pulling her back from the water's edge.

He didn't let go. Mimi dropped the stick, turning in his arms.

'Nearly…' He was holding her tight. In a sudden, controlled movement, he threatened to spin her backwards into the water, and then pulled her back again. Mimi clung to him.

'You wouldn't…'

'Is that a dare?'

She knew better than to dare Rafe, particularly when he was in this mood. He might not actually push her in, but he'd find some way of dangling her so close to the water that she'd be hanging on to him, begging him not to.

'No.' She tightened her grip on his jacket.

'Because a dare would be…' Something melted in his eyes. The reserve that had been keeping them both safe.

'Dangerous…' She whispered the word.

'Yeah. Very.' He didn't let go of her. And Mimi couldn't let go of him.

Getting wet was the least of her worries. Rafe had her in his arms and the look in his eyes… Suddenly nothing was impossible. A vision of their naked limbs, twisted languidly together, flashed into her imagination, making her heart pound.

He was so close. His lips a whisper away. If he kissed her… If he *didn't* kiss her, she was going to kiss him.

'Please… Let me go.' If he didn't move away now, she wasn't sure that she could. And kissing him would only open up old wounds, not heal them.

Wordlessly he moved back, holding on to her hand as she stepped away from the precipice. Steadying her when she almost tripped over a tree root.

'Ready to go back to work?' His gaze was thoughtful. Tender.

'Yes.'

He glanced over her shoulder and Mimi followed his gaze. There was no trace of the remaining boats, both of them having been scuppered by the ducks.

'What do you reckon?' He was searching in his pocket for something. 'A gaggle of ducks?'

She grinned. 'No, I think that's geese.' Rafe had changed gear again, turning away from the things that threatened to hurt them. But this time he seemed intent on bringing her with him, lightening her load.

Mimi picked up the empty coffee cups as Rafe tapped a search into his phone. 'A sabotage of ducks?'

He chuckled. 'Yeah. Actually, it's not as good as that. It's a paddling or a waddling. Depending on whether they're in or out of the water, presumably.'

Mimi strolled to the car with him as he laughed over the list of collective nouns he'd found on the Internet. A murder of crows. A parliament of owls.

It was time to go back to work.

This was going to be the last call of the day. If it hadn't been for the fact that each call meant that someone was in trouble then Mimi would have been sorry.

'They should be on the road, here somewhere.' She leaned forward, straining to see through the rain and the darkness. A light shone briefly and disappeared. Then describing an arc, up ahead of them.

'I see them.' Rafe slowed to a crawl in the teeming rain as the car headlights illuminated a figure standing in the middle of the road, signalling with a distress lantern. Another figure was sitting, hunched over, in the shelter of a tree by the side of the road, and a few yards further up a car was nose-down in the ditch.

The white rear number plates reflected in the glare of the headlights and Mimi saw that it was a European registration, with a D under a circle of stars to denote the country. 'What's that? German?'

'Yep. Hope they speak English.' Rafe stopped the car and got out, jogging towards the figure in the road, and Mimi followed.

It was a woman. She spoke a hurried sentence that Mimi didn't understand, and Rafe frowned in incomprehension.

'Wir werden ein Krankenwagen.'

The woman gave her an uncomprehending look and Mimi tried again, hoping that the woman might get her drift. If she didn't, then Mimi was going to have to call the translation service.

'Ich brauche einen Arzt.' She smiled, jerking her thumb towards Rafe, and the woman raised her eyebrows. 'Um… *Sprechen Sie Englisch?'*

'Ja… Yes, I speak English. *Danke.'* She caught Rafe's sleeve, pulling him towards the figure by the side of the road. 'My husband is hurt. Please can you help us?'

The woman's English was slightly accented, but seemed fluent enough. It was common to find that people under stress spoke first in their own language, and that calming them down would improve their English no end.

Mimi found the woman's hand and took it. 'The doctor is here and he will help your husband. Do you understand?'

'Yes… Yes, I understand.' The woman watched as Rafe hurried over to the man by the side of the road.

'I need you to help us.'

'Yes. What can I do?' The woman looked frightened and stressed but she was keeping it under control.

'My name's Mimi. Yours?'

'Annaliese.'

'Okay, Annaliese. I want you to help translate for us. Can you do that?' If her husband was hurt, then it was important they hear everything he had to say.

'Yes, I can do it.'

'Good. Thank you.' Mimi led Annaliese over to where Rafe was kneeling in the mud next to the man. 'What is your husband's name?'

'Leo,' Rafe answered. He'd already got that far and it seemed that he'd also checked the man for any life-threatening injuries as well. 'He's been moving around but I'll put a neck brace on him anyway, and then I think it's best we get him over to the car.'

Annaliese translated quickly for her husband but he was already trying to get to his feet.

'All right...' Rafe laid a hand on his shoulder. 'Stay still for one minute. Let us help you.'

Mimi jogged back to the car to fetch the neck brace and, when Rafe had fastened it securely, they got him on to his feet. With one at each side to support him, they walked him slowly over to the SUV, sitting him in the back seat. He was wet through and shaking.

'It's ten minutes to the hospital.' Mimi looked at Rafe. She knew that he was weighing up all the factors. It was impossible to treat him effectively here, and the quickest way to get him warm was to go straight to A and E.

'Yeah. He seems alert and I can't find any signs of major injury.' Rafe considered the question for a brief moment. 'We'll take him now?'

'Yes, I agree. Would you like me to drive?'

'The steering's pretty heavy...' Rafe hesitated and then smiled, handing over his car keys. 'Why don't you drive? I'll sit in the back seat and keep an eye on him.'

Good call. If she could handle an ambulance, she could handle Rafe's SUV. 'Don't worry. I'll be gentle with your car.'

'You'd better be.'

The A and E department of the hospital was always busy, but tonight it was *busy*. The doctor in charge recognised Rafe, though, and after an exchanged greeting waved them through to an empty cubicle. It seemed that they were going to be keeping their patient for a little while longer.

Mimi sat Annaliese down in a chair in the corner and helped Rafe get Leo out of his soaking clothes. There was only a gown to dress him in, but Mimi found a couple of blankets and tucked them around him on the bed.

Rafe's quick nod told her that he could continue with

the examination on his own and she turned her attention to Annaliese, who was crying quietly now.

'Let's get your coat off. You must be cold.'

Annaliese nodded gratefully, allowing Mimi to help her off with her coat and overtrousers. She was moving stiffly, her arms shaking.

'Are you hurt?' Mimi had already asked the question out on the road and Annaliese had said she was fine, but she didn't look all that good now.

'No. I am okay.' Annaliese was holding her arm.

'May I see your arm?' Annaliese nodded and rolled her sleeve up to expose a livid red friction burn. 'That's from the airbag?'

'Yes. I think so.' Now that they had reached the safety of the hospital, Annaliese seemed about to break down. Mimi had seen that many times before. People's courage brought them through to the point where they knew that they and their loved ones were safe and then took a back seat, allowing them to cry.

'The doctor's examining Leo now.' She leaned towards Annaliese confidingly. 'He's the best.'

'I heard that...' Rafe murmured the words without taking his attention from what he was doing.

'So did I. Thank you.' Annaliese smiled and seemed to relax a little.

Mimi took off her own jacket and dropped it on the floor in the corner. She'd known that the tension between her and Rafe was unsettling for their patients and now it seemed that the warmth was making itself felt too.

She set about cleaning Annaliese's wound. 'When I first spoke to you, in German...'

'Ah. Yes.' A sense of fun suddenly showed in Annaliese's face.

'What did I say? You looked a bit puzzled.'

'You told me that you were turning into an ambulance.' Annaliese smiled. 'But I understood. You made a mistake that is common with English speakers.'

'What did I say afterwards?'

'You said that you needed a doctor.'

Mimi pulled an embarrassed face and heard Rafe chuckle quietly. 'At least you were somewhere in the ball-park.'

'*Ja*... Yes, it is good to try.' Annaliese turned to her husband, speaking quickly to him in German, and he nodded, managing a smile.

'I don't suppose you could write the correct wording down for me, could you? I meet a lot of different people in the course of my job and it might come in handy in the future.'

'Yes, of course. I have paper...' Annaliese reached for her handbag eagerly, and Mimi stopped her.

'We'll get your arm sorted out first. Then you can give me some lessons.'

Annaliese was wrapped in a blanket, sitting by the side of her husband's bed, sipping a hot drink. Mimi had ascertained that her clothes were wet only around the shoulders and fetched a spare T-shirt from her own locker, along with a blanket and a drink. Annaliese received the comb that Mimi handed her with a smile. It was the little things that did the most to reassure people sometimes. Taking the time to comb your hair was a step back into normality.

Rafe had concentrated on Leo. Now that he was warm and dry, and his distress levels were reduced, it became clear that his English was good enough for them to communicate directly, without needing a translator. His injuries were relatively minor but needed treatment and care—a broken wrist, shock and slight concussion, along with rapidly forming bruises on his face and chest.

Rafe beckoned to Mimi and she followed him out of the cubicle. 'I'm going to see if I can find a bed for him. I wouldn't normally admit him, but he needs care and rest. I assume they have nowhere to go?'

'No. Annaliese said that they left their hotel in Exeter to drive to one here, not realising that it was flooded. Apparently the hotel didn't think to phone people and let them know, just expected everyone not to come.'

'Great. Masterpiece of forward thinking.'

'Yeah. They were looking for other accommodation when their car went off the road.'

'So what are we going to do with her?' Rafe knew that the correct procedure was to alert hospital services and they would find somewhere for Annaliese but, from the snatches of conversation he'd heard between the two women, maybe Mimi had other ideas.

'I've called Charlie. With Jan and Matthew there, he can only offer her the sofa bed, but I reckon it's better than a mattress on the floor in a community centre somewhere. She'll never get a hotel tonight, and Charlie will be around tomorrow to get her to the hospital.'

'She's okay with that?'

'Yeah. Fine. Charlie's got room for Leo as well, if you want to release him.'

'I'd prefer he stays here, if they have a bed for him.'

She nodded, reaching into her pocket and pulling out a bunch of keys. Slipping a familiar one off the ring, she handed it to him. 'Here. I'll go on ahead with Annaliese and you can follow when you're finished.'

'Are you sure?' Rafe had resolved not to go back to

Mimi's cottage again but, now that he had the key in his hand, temptation made him waver.

She hesitated, her cheeks flushing red. 'I'd like to talk to you.'

He couldn't say no now. Rafe nodded, pocketing the key.

CHAPTER ELEVEN

CHARLIE HAD BEEN ready with hot soup for Annaliese. Janet had fussed over her, going out of her way to make her welcome, and Mimi had left the four of them in the sitting room around a roaring fire, getting to know each other. She half wished that she could have stayed.

But her own quiet cottage was waiting for her. Rafe would be home soon. The thought twisted in her stomach. It wasn't his home any more. She'd erased almost every trace of him from the place, working in a fury of hurt and anger.

Maybe all the feverish effort had just been her own attempt to prove that she *was* good enough. And maybe she hadn't needed to after all. She opened the kitchen cupboard and, taking the bottle of emergency brandy out from the back of the top shelf, poured herself a measure.

Slipping off her heavy boots, she settled herself down on the sofa and swirled the amber liquid in the glass. No answers there, but it felt warm and relaxing. They couldn't change what they'd done, now. But perhaps there was some way that they could come to terms with it and get on with their lives. She reached for the TV remote and then threw it back on to the cushions beside her. She had too much going on inside her head to be able tolerate anything other than silence at the moment.

Her back ached and her limbs were heavy. Stretching out on the sofa, she sipped the brandy slowly...

'Hey...'

'Geroff...' She could feel someone's hand on her shoulder, gently shaking her. Mimi swatted it away and rolled over. The sound of breaking glass, and Rafe's sudden exclamation of surprise, brought her back to wakefulness.

'Careful...'

'Yeah, sorry. Didn't see the glass.' He was kneeling down next to her.

'That's okay. Have you cut yourself?' The glass must have fallen on to the floor when she fell asleep.

'Don't think so.' Rafe was collecting the larger pieces, picking them up gingerly between his finger and thumb.

'Well, you will do...' She huffed at him and sat up. 'Don't do that; I'll get a dustpan and brush.'

She stumbled into the kitchen, blinking when she switched the light on. On an afterthought, she collected up the brandy bottle and a couple more glasses from the cupboard on her way out.

'Have you taken to drink?' he teased.

'No, of course not.' That smile would drive her to drink if she wasn't careful. Or something far more dangerous.

'Watch out...' He frowned, and Mimi realised that she was about to tread on a piece of glass in just her socks. 'Sit down, I'll do it.'

He knelt down, collecting up the glass and brushing the shards out of the carpet, then disappeared for a moment to empty the dustpan into the bin. Mimi picked up the bottle of brandy, pouring a large measure into each glass. Tomorrow was the last of her days off, and so tonight might be the last opportunity she had of talking to Rafe. She had to make it count.

* * *

'I've been thinking about what you said.' She came right out with it as soon as he walked back into the sitting room, as if waiting might chip away at her resolve. That was typically Mimi and it had always made him smile.

'Okay.' He sat down beside her. 'What have you been thinking?'

'I think that I owe you an apology.'

She'd tried to apologise about something that afternoon, after he'd carried her across to the farmhouse, and Rafe had brushed it off. He was as mystified now as he'd been then.

'You have nothing to apologise for.'

She shook her head, brushing his objections away. 'You pushed me away, Rafe. That was your fault. But I was too afraid to ask why. I never tried to stop you from going.'

Rafe shook his head dumbly.

'And that must have looked a lot like a rejection to you.'

Emotion blocked his throat. The way it always had, and probably always would. Rafe took a sip of the brandy. 'Yeah. It did. But it doesn't matter… What I really want to know is why?'

She looked at him blankly. 'Why what?'

'Whatever gave you the idea that you weren't good enough?' She began to frown and Rafe stuck to his guns. 'I really need you to tell me.'

She took a mouthful of brandy. 'Okay. If you must know. The guy I went out with before you… After that friend of Charlie's…'

'The one you never used to talk about?'

'Yeah. Graham. He cheated on me. When I found out and confronted him, he said that he couldn't help it. He had a whole list of things I did wrong…'

'What? What things?' Maybe he shouldn't ask. But he couldn't believe that any of them were justified.

She turned to him, mortification sparking in her beautiful eyes. 'He said that I was boring. And that he couldn't help doing what he did because this other woman was dynamite in bed. Is that what you want to hear?'

Rafe stared at her. 'He said... Are you serious?'

She rolled her eyes. 'No, I joke about that kind of thing all of the time. Of *course* I'm serious.'

'It's rubbish. He's an idiot.' Rafe reached for her and she pushed him away.

'Don't. Just...don't.'

He couldn't believe that she could have taken something that was so obviously a cruel jibe to heart. Mimi was the most exciting woman he'd ever known, both in and out of bed, and this guy had to be certifiably insane. But she'd listened to him, and it had worked into her system like poison.

'Didn't *I* make you feel good enough?' Rafe knew the answer to that as soon as he'd asked the question. When she didn't answer, it confirmed everything. He'd never confided in her, and then he'd left, without giving any proper reason. He'd done nothing to repair the damage that had already been done.

She shook her head. 'It's... It doesn't matter.'

It *did* matter. Nothing he could say was going to make her believe how completely wrong all this was. Only one thing would do. Rafe leaned forward and kissed her.

She gave a little squeak of surprise and then she kissed him back. It was a proper kiss, not the brushing of lips against skin which hardly knew how to respond because it was all so brief.

They were both breathless, holding the kiss for so long that Rafe felt almost giddy. He pulled her close in a sharp, strong motion and she gasped. Then she climbed on top of him, sitting on his lap, her legs folded on either side of his thighs.

This time he would tell her how irresistibly beautiful she was, how much she meant to him in every way. He'd make her understand...

She nuzzled against his neck and he felt her lips move against his ear. 'What's your number, Rafe?'

'You have it, don't you? Why...you want to call me?' Maybe this was some kind of complicated telephone sex game that Mimi had dreamed up. He couldn't help wishing it might be.

'No, idiot. How many girlfriends? Proper ones.' She nipped at his ear with her teeth and his whole body jerked with desire.

He knew just what she was asking. She didn't care about the ones who came before they'd lived together. Since then... He wanted to know who she'd been with since then too.

'Six. That's my number. And there's been no one since you...' Rafe decided that full disclosure was his only option. Her body was too close to his for anything else. 'No one serious, that is. I've asked women to dinner or the theatre but that's all. The odd barbecue...'

She silenced him with a kiss. One that told him, without any doubt at all, that barbecues didn't count and six was the right answer.

'Three,' she whispered into his ear and he felt uncertainty tear at him. Two before him; he knew that. Maybe someone had helped her move the furniture and repaint the walls. 'Including you.'

An instinctive warmth spread through his whole body. No one since him. Rafe swallowed hard.

'And this tells us something?'

'I just wanted to know. Didn't you?'

'Yeah.'

She grabbed his wrists, forcing them back on to the

cushions behind him. Then she kissed him again, somehow managing to tease and take both at the same time.

The anger, the new self-confidence which had been the source of so many arguments in the last few days, had translated into the physical. He'd always tried to be a considerate lover, and he knew that he could take them both into a state of dizzy satisfaction. But she didn't want that this time. *She* was going to take them there.

A sharp jolt of arousal spun through his veins. He stretched his legs out in front of him, longing for her to play out the fantasy.

She stilled suddenly, her lips a hair's breadth from his. 'Say my name. The way you used to.'

He knew just what she wanted. Rather than call her Miriam all the time, he'd simply stopped calling her anything. 'Mimi. Beautiful Mimi.' He felt his lips brush hers as he said the words.

'I want to know...' She was dropping kisses on his cheek, working her way across to his ear. 'I want to know how far I can take you.'

'Then find out, honey.' He wouldn't beg just yet. Not while he still had the choice. He had a feeling that Mimi might be depriving him of that quite soon.

'Be careful what you wish for.' One hand loosed its grip from his wrist and slid down to the buckle of his jeans. Rafe closed his eyes, feeling the scintillating fumble of her fingers.

'I know just what I'm wishing for.' Whether or not he was going to be able to stand it was another question.

She had the button on the waistband of his jeans open now and he couldn't wait. He just wanted to be inside her, to feel her taking him. Maybe she'd do it here. She could do it wherever she wanted and, when she'd had her way, he was going to take her upstairs and have his. She'd be coming underneath him, breaking apart so softly, so sweetly...

She seemed to know how much he wanted her. Her fingers trailed up his chest, finding their way to his face. 'You like this?'

'What do you think?'

'I think you do.' She kissed him again. He could taste the brandy on her mouth…

Brandy.

He didn't want to think about this right now, but the question cut through all of the sensations that were radiating from her touch. How much had she had? He couldn't remember, but he knew that she'd poured herself a large measure and that she'd been drinking while they were talking. Maybe it didn't matter…

It mattered. They'd had drunk sex before. Tired sex, no-time-for-it sex, practically every kind of sex in the book. But that was when they were living together.

And yet simply turning away from her now was unthinkable. Hadn't she just admitted to being the victim of one of the cruellest taunts possible, and hadn't he just told her that it wasn't true. If he remembered rightly, he'd kissed her to prove his point.

Okay. He could do this. He was quivering with molten desire, and Mimi was moving against him, but he could do it.

'Mimi. Wait… Wait…' He put as much gravitas into the words as he could muster.

'Rafe…?' Suddenly she was still, a look of uncertainty on her face. The realisation that this wasn't going to happen now, that he couldn't let it happen, almost broke him.

He cupped her face in his hand. 'How much have you had to drink, honey?'

Rafe felt her cheek burn hot under his fingers. Clearly she wasn't going to tell him, which wasn't a very good sign.

'Is this your idea of being…chivalrous?' She made the word sound as if chivalry was a deadly sin. Rafe dismissed the notion that if she could pronounce *chivalrous* she couldn't be that drunk.

'Would you get into a car right now?'

She shook her head. 'Probably not. But you never used to breathalyse me before taking me to bed. What's so different now?' Her body started moving against his. That sensual rhythm of hers that Rafe couldn't resist.

'The difference is that we've not been together for five years. If we really want to do this, then we need to make that decision with clear heads and in the cold light of day.'

'We won't, though, will we?' She was still again.

Loss seared through him. They both knew that this couldn't work. The only way he would ever get to touch her again was in a moment of madness like this one.

In that case he'd never get to touch her again. Rafe was *not* going to be the guy who took advantage of her when he knew that she'd had a few drinks. 'No. We probably won't.'

She nodded and climbed off him, getting to her feet and marching out of the door. 'You know, at this moment I could really slap you, Rafe.' She threw the words over her shoulder.

'You'd be doing me a favour…' He leaned back, covering his face with his hands. If she knocked his head off it would at least take his mind off his aching groin.

He heard her stomp upstairs, and then back down again. 'Don't even think about driving tonight; you've been drinking too. You can sleep on the sofa; it's a lot more comfortable than at the hospital.' Her voice was matter-of-fact, brooking no argument. 'And lock the door.'

He looked at her between his fingers. 'We don't need…' Maybe they did. He hadn't got around to thinking about what he'd just missed out on yet.

She dropped the duvet that was in her arms on to the floor. 'Lock the door. And, in case you're thinking about changing your mind, I'm locking mine too.' She turned, slamming the door closed behind her so hard that the key rattled.

He got to his feet, twisting the key in the lock, wondering if he should swallow it or throw it out of the window just to be on the safe side. Even when she was angry and he didn't much feel like it, Mimi still made him smile. He threw himself down on to the sofa, tipping half the brandy left in his glass away into Mimi's empty one and settled down to brood over the rest.

Mimi heard the click of the key turning in the lock. Almost overbalancing as she tiptoed back across the hallway, she sank silently to the floor outside the door, pressing her cheek against it. She wasn't used to drinking more than the odd glass of wine with a meal, and when she closed her eyes she felt dizzy. Perhaps she *was* a bit tipsy...

You started it, Rafe. She mouthed the words into the cool darkness. Maybe he had, but she hadn't exactly beaten him off. She'd been so turned on, and he'd been... She knew that he'd loved it too.

And in the morning a headache would have been the least of her worries. Mimi brushed her fingers lightly over the wood panelling of the door.

'Thank you.' She knew he wouldn't hear the whispered words. Slowly she got to her feet, her socks muffling the sound of her footsteps across the wooden floor in the hall. Then she climbed the stairs and fell fully clothed on to her bed.

CHAPTER TWELVE

Rafe opened his eyes and closed them again. Sunlight was spilling into the living room, and he felt as if he'd lost the use of his arms. When he tried to move, he realised that he was rolled tightly in the duvet.

Disentangling himself, he sat up. He was going to have to face Mimi. Somehow that seemed just as difficult as if he'd slept with her. But at least he could make sure he wasn't going to have to do it naked.

He picked his jeans up from the floor and stretched his cramped limbs. Unlocked the door, and then walked towards the sounds of activity coming from the kitchen.

She looked up from the coffee machine. 'You're up early.'

Rafe looked at his watch, frowning at the sixpence, which had clearly been falling down on the job lately. Seven o'clock. If he'd realised, he probably would have stayed put on the sofa for another half hour.

'Coffee?'

'Yeah. Thanks.' He eyed her suspiciously. She looked as bright as a daisy. Maybe he'd overestimated how much she'd had to drink last night. 'Do you have a headache?'

'No. I haven't got a headache.' She reached into the cupboard for a second mug, putting it on to the counter top with a clatter, as if to prove her point.

'Good.' Rafe sat down at the kitchen table and waited. This probably wasn't the time to tell her that it didn't matter if she was angry with him. Anger, any kind of emotion, in fact, was better than the way they'd parted the last time. And he was suddenly under no illusions. This *was* another parting.

She walked across to the table, setting a mug of coffee in front of him and sitting down. 'Last night…'

'It doesn't matter.' The words sprang to his lips by instinct and then he shook his head. 'Actually, it does.'

She took a deep breath. 'You were right, last night, and I'm sorry. I was crazy to even contemplate…'

'I contemplated it too. And it would have been a mistake, for both of us.'

He wanted to tell her that he *had* loved her, and that maybe he still did, but that was no use because she deserved a lot more than Rafe knew how to give. She deserved someone who could share his feelings openly, who could heal her wounds and make her see herself as Rafe saw her. Beautiful, funny, talented… That was the kind of list that she deserved.

Her gaze met his, and he realised that he wasn't going to say any of those things. He didn't trust himself, not after he'd so nearly made the wrong decision last night. It was better to just leave it.

She rubbed her forehead with her fingers. 'Then we're done?'

'Are you okay about that?' There was nothing else left to say.

She ignored the question, getting to her feet in a sudden burst of energy. 'Why don't you go and take a shower? I'll make some breakfast.'

It was an undisguised invitation to leave her alone for a while. Rafe needed that time too. As he stood in the shower,

wondering whether being able to cry about it would make
things any better, it occurred to him that this was the final
confirmation that they'd made the right choice. Mimi was
downstairs in the kitchen, probably crying into her coffee.
And yet going to her was unthinkable, just as he knew that
she wouldn't come to him. When neither of them could
even do that, the best they could hope for was a civilised
parting and a little closure.

Last night's rain had brought another round of injuries
with it. Cuts, sprains, a dislocated finger, and a broken
arm where a man had fallen out of a tree, trying to rescue
a cat. At lunchtime they took advantage of a sudden lull in
the stream of calls and parked up by the side of the road
where groups of men were digging ditches, using the earth
from them to make a barricade to contain the river on this
side and protect the village which lay half a mile away.

Mimi watched as Rafe strode over to the men to speak
to them. She didn't join him. It was better to let go a little
now, before she had to do it for good this evening, and she
was grateful for this opportunity to just relax back into her
seat and close her eyes.

Last night had been a turning point. They'd come so
close and then drawn back, acknowledging that sleeping
together would be a huge mistake. She'd known it, but saying it made it real. She had to say goodbye to the fantasy
that they might somehow pick up where they'd left off five
years ago, and deal with the reality. She repeated the man-
tra that she'd developed over the morning. She and Rafe
were no good for each other. He would break her heart just
as surely now as he had then.

Someone knocked on the car window and she opened
her eyes. One of the men who had been digging was stand-

ing there, his clothes spattered with mud and rain, his face creased in a smile. Mimi rolled the window down.

'Come and eat your lunch with me, miss.' He jerked his head towards a tarpaulin, strung beneath the branches of a tree.

It looked nice. A little patch of grass that hadn't been rained on steadily for the last two weeks. There were a couple of old deckchairs and a large metal barrel for a makeshift table.

'Thanks.' Mimi reached for the bag with the sandwiches and flask and opened the car door. In a gesture of old-world courtesy, the man held out his hand for her to take as she got out.

His bright blue eyes twinkled as he saw the size of her lunch bag. The cutting of sandwiches this morning had been more of a therapeutic effort than anything, and she had no idea how she and Rafe were going to eat them all.

'You need to sit down and eat a good lunch. Keeps you going.' The man was probably sixty if he was a day, but all the same he tucked her hand in the crook of his arm, in case she needed to lean on him on the way over to the tarpaulin.

It was a small act of kindness, magnified by the emptiness in her heart. 'You've got yourselves all set up here.'

'We've been digging along this stretch for days, all the men of the village in shifts. There's another gang down the road.'

'And no flooding so far?'

'Touch wood.' The man tapped his forehead.

'What about the other side?' The fields on the other side of the river were already deep in water.

'Can't do anything about the farm; Chris knows that. We've done what we can to help him. My wife's up at the farmhouse at the moment, helping lay sandbags.' The man took off his cap and scratched his balding head. 'The water's got to go somewhere.'

'She's not overdoing it, I hope.'

The man chuckled. 'If you happen to be passing, you might just stop and tell her that; she doesn't listen to me. Now, you just sit down here.'

He brushed the dingy canvas of the most stable-looking deckchair and motioned her into it. Then he produced an impossibly clean white handkerchief from inside his jacket and spread it on top of the barrel.

'Thank you. This is nice.' The view over the river would look almost idyllic if she hadn't known that the bright reflections in the distance were the result of flooded villages and fields.

'Pleasure. Always a pleasure to see one of your people.' He nodded towards Mimi's bright ambulance service jacket. 'You're doing a fine job.'

'Thank you.' Tears were beginning to mist Mimi's eyes. She could just about handle the brittle good humour between herself and Rafe, the thought that after today she probably wouldn't see him again, but right now kindness was the only thing that could threaten to break her.

Rafe was still with the other men, clearly discussing earthworks, five heads turning one way and another in synchronisation as the men surveyed the digging. Mimi put her Thermos down on the handkerchief, hearing a dull clang as she did so.

'What's in the barrel?'

'That's from the brewery, miss.' The man tapped the side of his nose in a gesture of friendly conspiracy. 'Came floating down the river. We called them, but they've got enough to worry about at the moment.'

'The Old Brewery's flooded?' That didn't come as much of a surprise; it was right by the river.

'Three days ago. They're clearing out the mess now but I say it's too soon. There was more rain last night and the river's too high just now.'

'I'll bet you've seen a few floods...' This area was on a flood plain and the rivers broke their banks regularly every few years.

'This is the worst. Never seen nothing like this.' The man surveyed the expanse of water before them. 'Want a sip of beer with your lunch?'

'You're drinking it?' Mimi looked at the barrel more closely and saw a large shiny patch of metal where it had been cleaned and a tap inserted. 'It's been in the water.'

'You're telling a Somerset man how to drink his beer?'

'Well, no...' That would be sacrilege. And, anyway, Mimi knew that she'd be wasting her breath.

'Just be careful, though; that water's filthy. If I find you've made yourself ill I'll rat on you to the doctors and they'll be giving you every precautionary test that the hospital can throw at you.' If she had no jurisdiction in the question of beer-drinking, she could at least exert some authority on the matter of infection control.

The man chuckled. 'We gave the barrel a good wash before we tapped it. Made sure of that.'

Maybe she should get Rafe to enquire more closely on the matter. Or confiscate the barrel, or get the men to pour the beer away in the river. She glanced towards him. He was standing with his hands in his pockets, deep in conversation, obviously now a temporary member of the gang. He'd probably just clap the men on the back, congratulate them on their ingenuity and accept a pint from the barrel.

Mimi puffed out a breath and reached for her pack of sandwiches. For the next ten minutes she was off duty.

Rafe had strolled across and helped himself to a sandwich from the pile. 'These look good.'

She nodded. The coldness between them was already beginning to set in. When they were working and there was a shared objective, it was a little easier to ignore. 'Did you know they're drinking from there?' She pointed to the barrel.

'Really?' He inspected the tap. 'Looks as if they've cleaned it up...'

'All the same. I wouldn't take the chance on it...'

'Yeah, you're right. Leave it with me. I'll have a word.' He walked back over to the group of men, taking a large bite from his sandwich.

Ten minutes of welcome relaxation and then Rafe was back, jogging towards her, hastily putting his phone back into his jacket. 'Time to go.'

'What's up?' Mimi was on her feet instantly, grabbing her flask and the rest of the sandwiches and stuffing them into the bag. There was an urgency in Rafe's movements which meant only one thing.

'You know where the Old Brewery is?'

'Yeah, just follow the barrels floating down the river.' She threw the bag into the car and scrambled in. 'It's a couple of miles that way...'

Rafe started the SUV up with a jolt, spraying mud from the back wheels, and then they were on the road again, the group of men returning her hurried wave goodbye.

This call was going to need an ambulance in attendance, but they were nearby and every minute might count. A man working at the brewery had got careless and touched a live cable running from a generator.

'The ambulance controller told us not to move him. But the water's rising again...' The man who greeted them was obviously in authority here and he guided them quickly towards the redbrick building. The yard was awash with water and duckboards were laid across it.

'Where is he?' Mimi seemed concentrated on only one goal, striding towards the building. Rafe followed, carrying the holdall which contained the emergency resus gear.

He moved past her to lead the way, reckoning that since they were barely talking to each other she could hardly object. They went up a flight of steps, leaving the sludge-covered ground floor to find that the rooms upstairs were clean and dry, their white-painted walls seeming to defy the mess downstairs.

They were shown through to a large open area which smelled strongly of malt. A man was lying on the floor, a folded coat under his head. The small group of his fellow workers parted as they saw Rafe and Mimi.

Mimi was on her knees next to him. She looked down at the man and smiled. 'Hi there. Stay still now; the doctor's here.'

Rafe heaved a sigh of relief. He was obviously breathing and conscious. He dumped the bag and knelt down on the other side of the man. As he examined him, he heard Mimi questioning the men who were standing around, getting the information that he needed to know. The man hadn't been unconscious; he'd been thrown clear of the cable. His name was Grant.

'I'm going to clip something on to your finger now...' Rafe turned to fetch the pulse monitor and found that Mimi was already holding it.

'Thanks.' Rafe checked the small display and nodded in satisfaction. The man had some nasty burns on his arm and had cracked his head on the concrete floor when he fell, but he was breathing and his pulse was fast but steady.

The sound of running footsteps behind them, and a man's voice. 'Mr Harding... The water's rising fast...'

Everyone's head turned towards the man who had ushered Rafe and Mimi inside. 'How much time have we got?'

'Fifteen, twenty minutes. The water's building up at the back and it'll be coming in through the windows soon…'

Mr Harding turned to Rafe. 'We need to evacuate the building as soon as we can. The ground floor's about to be flooded again.'

Rafe turned to Mimi and she nodded in answer to his unasked question. 'Okay, we'll move him now.' He looked around for something that might be pressed into service as a makeshift stretcher.

'We've got a carry cot.' Mr Harding gestured towards a large canvas bag which lay on the floor.

'Really?' Mimi's eyebrows shot up and Mr Harding smiled grimly.

'Health and Safety. We don't take any chances.'

'Nice one.' Mimi was already unzipping the bag and taking out the tubular framework. The cot wasn't as sturdy as the ambulance issue ones, but it would do.

'I want everyone out of here. Pete and Stan, supervise that, will you?' Mr Harding gave the crisp order and no one moved. Clearly no one was going anywhere until they saw their workmate safely down the stairs and out of the building.

Mimi snapped the carry cot framework open, testing its stability before she laid it next to Grant. 'You, and you…' She pointed to Mr Harding and another man. 'I'll need you to help us hold the cot steady and lift him on to it.'

She put everyone exactly where she wanted them, issuing directions to everyone. Grant was lifted carefully on to the carry cot and she tucked the pulse monitor alongside him.

'I need a coat…' Everyone immediately started to take their coats off and Mimi smiled. 'Thanks, guys, just one.

That'll do.' She took a light waterproof jacket and tied it over Grant, securing the sleeves together under the cot to augment the flimsy-looking straps.

'Ready?' Rafe had been keeping an eye on Grant, trying not to notice that Mimi was both unstoppable and magnificent when she swung into action.

'Yep. I want three volunteers to help with the stairs…' Mr Harding signalled to two burly men, who stepped forward with him. 'Right, now. This is what I want you to do.'

Under Mimi's direction, Rafe and the two volunteers manoeuvred Grant safely down the stairs. Dirty brown water was already sloshing around on the concrete at ground-floor level, and two ambulance men met them at the bottom of the stairs.

'We need to get a move on. Looks as if we don't have as much time as we thought…' Mr Harding was looking anxiously towards the back of the building, which faced the river.

'Okay.' Rafe allowed one of the ambulance men to take over his place at the carry cot and turned back up the stairs. 'You go on ahead; I'll fetch the medical bag.'

He took the stairs two at a time, glancing behind him when he got to the top to see Mimi, standing alone in the middle of the loading bay. 'What are you doing, Rafe? We need to get out…'

'I'll only be a minute. You go.'

'Forget the bag; we can collect it later…' She turned as an ominous groaning came from the back of the building, accompanied by the crash of metal hitting metal.

'Mimi. Go…' He shouted the words but she still hesitated, as if she was waiting for him. 'Now!'

She glanced at the stairs, then the entrance to the loading bay, obviously gauging which she should make a run for. Then she started to sprint towards the sunlight pouring through the entrance.

She didn't make it.

A loud crack sounded and a metal door at the far end of the loading bay flew off the wall, a great plume of water behind it. It travelled six feet and then crashed down, catching Mimi on the side of her head. Rafe heard her scream above the roar of the incoming flood, and then he lost sight of her.

'Mimi...' Her name tore from his throat in a ragged cry as he raced down the stairs. Pausing for one moment to try and locate her, he ripped off his jacket and plunged into the water.

Buffeted by the powerful force of the flood, he waded through waist-high water to the spot where he'd last seen her. Groping for her, almost blinded by mud, he plunged down into the water again and again. Choking and retching as dirty water found its way into his throat, he ducked under the torrent again. If he couldn't find her, then he too would be lost.

His hand touched something soft. He reached for it and found her arm, and tugged her towards him. Now that the water was reaching the same level as it had been at the back it was calmer and he managed to haul her lifeless body up into his arms. As he did so, a long shape disentangled itself from her leg and Rafe saw it borne away from them in the rush of water.

As he pulled her over his shoulder, it registered at the back of his mind. The dark brown body of the snake, with black zigzag markings. It looked like an adder, but he couldn't stop to find out. His first priority was to get Mimi out of here, and get her breathing.

He heard her choke, one feeble sign of life, and pushed doggedly forward towards the light coming in through the open shutters of the loading bay. Willing hands were there at the door, guiding him up to dry ground. Carefully, he laid her down on her side, on the bed of coats that had hurriedly been prepared for her.

'Mimi…' Rafe cleared her mouth and dirty water dribbled from her lips. Then she choked again, expelling the rest of the water from her lungs.

'That's right, honey. Breathe for me.' She had to breathe. If she didn't he would suffocate too.

She took one huge gasp of air and then her eyes snapped open suddenly, wide and frightened.

'All right. It's all right, Mimi, I've got you.'

Her hand moved unsteadily to the side of her face, where blood was trickling from a nasty gash. Rafe caught it in his.

'I see it. Just lie still for me, honey; you're going to be all right.'

She started to whimper, hanging on to his hand. Mr Harding was kneeling down on the other side of her, watching anxiously, and Rafe spoke quickly to him. 'I think I saw an adder in the water. Tell everyone to be careful…'

Mr Harding nodded. The word was passed around the group of men behind them as Rafe wiped the blood from her face, hoping that none of it was the result of a bite.

Nothing. Just the cut, running along her jawline. Mimi was moaning fitfully and Mr Harding caught hold of her hand, talking to her and keeping her still. Rafe turned his attention to the leg of her trousers, which was ripped and soaked with blood.

There was a four-inch cut on her ankle, and blood was pumping from it. Above it, three double puncture marks, just below her knee. The snake, washed out of its home and terrified, had bitten her repeatedly, probably releasing its full supply of venom. Rafe pushed back the instinctive dread which clutched at his heart. No one had died from an adder bite in years.

'Mimi...?' A man's voice behind him. Rafe glanced round and saw one of the ambulance crew who had come for Grant.

'I need gloves, a dressing pad and a splint for her leg. We go in two minutes.' Rafe rapped out the words and the man nodded, turning.

'Rafe... Feel...sick.'

'I know. I want you to stay still, honey. Can you do that for me?' He wrapped his hand around hers.

'Yes. Stay still.' Somehow she managed a lopsided smile. 'Hold on to me...'

'I'm here.' Her breathing was becoming increasingly laboured and she had started to wheeze. Her eyes fluttered closed and Rafe shouted for adrenaline.

CHAPTER THIRTEEN

THEY RAN ON sirens and flashing lights, Grant on one side of the ambulance, Mimi on the other. She had gone into anaphylactic shock, but prompt treatment with adrenaline had stabilised her. Rafe had splinted her leg to keep it still and now all he could do was watch and wait until they could get her to the hospital.

A team was waiting for them in A and E. Rafe followed the gurney in a daze, pushing past the nurse who caught his arm.

'I'm sorry…' He felt the nurse's grip on his arm, tighter now and more insistent, and he stopped, keeping his eyes on the retreating back of the doctor who was walking beside Mimi. 'But I have to go to her…'

'You have to step back now.' The nurse looked up at him, oozing no-nonsense sympathy. 'We need to get you clean and dry and then examine you.'

'I'm all right.'

'Maybe. But you're in the way here.' Rafe didn't move and the nurse leaned closer. 'Mimi's one of ours. We'll look after her.'

Rafe had called Charlie and they'd waited together in one of the family rooms. Finally the doctor who had been treating Mimi appeared, her face impassive.

Rafe had hung back, knowing he had little right to stand with Charlie and hear what the doctor had to say, but Charlie had beckoned him over. They listened together and Rafe numbly shook her hand, thanking her.

'Now tell me what all that means.' Charlie spun his wheelchair around, motioning Rafe to a chair opposite him.

'It means…' Rafe could hardly bear to think about it, but he knew that Charlie needed to know and he had to be strong for him. 'She's come through the worst of it. Mimi's very ill at the moment, but she's strong and fighting back. There's no reason why she can't make a full recovery.'

Charlie nodded. 'What is she facing now?'

'She went into anaphylactic shock when she was bitten. That means they probably won't use any antivenom unless they absolutely have to, in case her body reacts by going into shock again. At the moment she's fighting back, but they'll need to keep a close eye on her. She's also inhaled a lot of dirty water, and that's irritated the lining of her lungs. That'll mend, but she's been admitted to the ICU and sedated. Rest and care are the best things for her right now.'

'What else…?'

'Everything else is relatively minor. She has some cuts, a lot of bruises and a fractured ankle. I missed it when I first examined her…' Rafe was still kicking himself for that.

Charlie rolled his eyes. 'Yeah, you missed it because you were busy saving her life.'

'I just did…' *What any doctor would do?* He hadn't. He'd felt close to many patients, battled for them with every ounce of his strength. But he'd always been able to maintain enough distance to keep himself sane. Never felt that his own fate was inextricably linked with the person whose life lay in his hands and that if they died he would too.

'How long will it take? Before she's up and around again.'

Rafe really didn't want to look that far ahead. He'd seen

all the things that could go wrong in the course of his work, and he didn't want to think about any of them. But Charlie needed as much information and reassurance as Rafe could give.

'From what her doctor says, she'll be in the ICU for two, probably three days, if everything goes well. The inflammation on her lungs should resolve by itself in a few days…'

'And the snake bite?'

'It depends, Charlie. We need to wait and see. They won't transfer her down to the general ward until she's through the worst of it. But, after that, an adult can experience swelling and pain for up to nine months.'

'Nine months! But what about her new job?'

'I'll contact them and let them know what's happened. I can ask them to keep the post open for her but… To be honest with you, I think they'll be needing to fill the post before she's well enough to go back to work.'

Charlie shook his head, puffing out a breath. 'She so wanted that job.'

'Look, Charlie. At the moment, the best thing we can do is to take each day at a time. Looking ahead is just going to be overwhelming. She was treated promptly, she's being well cared for and her condition is stable. That counts for a lot.'

'Yeah, I understand.' Charlie reached forward, gripping Rafe's hand tightly. 'Thanks. When will they let us see her?'

'Soon. I'll go with you, and ask.' Rafe still knew enough people here and his word might carry some weight. At the very least, he could stay and explain what was happening to Charlie.

'Thanks. I appreciate that.'

It was the least that Rafe could do. If he hadn't gone back for the medical bag. If they hadn't been arguing about it… Overwhelming guilt gripped at his chest, leaving him breathless with remorse, and he tried to shake it off. That was for later. Right now he had to give Charlie as much support as he could.

'We'll go up there now and see what's happening, and then we'll go to the canteen for something to eat.'

'I can't eat, Rafe...'

'We'll do it anyway. The next couple of weeks are going to be hard, and you need to pace yourself.'

Charlie nodded. 'Just don't bring me chocolate.'

'You remember that?' Suddenly the years fell away and he was walking up to the ICU, a sandwich and a bar of chocolate in his pocket for the pretty ambulance driver who spent every waking hour sitting by her brother's bedside.

'I remember thinking it was just as well that someone was feeding her up. I had this idea that I'd sneak out when the nurses weren't looking, get to a phone and order up a pizza for her.'

Rafe nodded. 'Happens a lot. I've seen people who are seriously injured, and who think they just need a minute before they can get up and walk away.'

'I guess we all think we're indestructible.' Charlie's eyes were suddenly full of tears. 'Mimi always has...'

'She's going to come back to us, Charlie.' Rafe felt himself choke, and in a sudden terror wondered whether this was a response to the fact that Mimi too was choking. Maybe intubated. Frightened and unable to speak. He hoped that someone was holding her hand.

He *had* to stay calm.

'When you see her, I want you to remember this. She's going to look pretty bad. But I want you to remember that they're looking after her well, and that she's going to mend.'

Charlie took a deep breath. 'Thanks, mate. Got it.'

Visiting hours were over, but the ICU doctor had allowed them in for ten minutes. Mimi's body seemed very small in the bed, overwhelmed by the paraphernalia around her that was monitoring her and keeping her stable. Rafe breathed a sigh of relief when he saw that she was breathing on her own.

'Why is she in this room?' Charlie's brow creased.

'It's nothing to worry about. They'll put patients where they can best manage them; a separate room doesn't mean that she's any better or worse than anyone else.'

'Okay.' Charlie looked at the cannula in her arm. 'Is she in pain?'

'The drugs they're giving her will be enough to keep her comfortable.' Rafe looked at the label on the bag suspended above her head. He had every confidence in the people here, but he still couldn't help checking.

'Her toes…' Charlie was staring at the lightweight cast that encased her right foot. The other leg was hidden under a canopy, and Rafe dreaded to think what that looked like. Probably swollen, blistered and almost black by now.

'Her toes are just the way we want them to be.' He couldn't resist brushing them with his fingers, just to check that the cast wasn't too tight. The small, intimate act almost brought him to tears.

Looking at her face was an almost unbearable effort, but he made himself do it until the shock began to numb. One eye was bruised and closing fast, and a row of stitches ran along her jawline.

'I… I want her to wake up.' Charlie reached for Mimi's hand, taking it in his.

'I know. She's better asleep right now, mate. Just hold her hand and tell her you're here.'

'Will she hear me?'

'Maybe. Hopefully not, but tell her anyway.'

It was such an effort to stand back, watching Charlie

touch her and hold her hand. Hearing him say the words that Rafe wanted to say to Mimi. But he had no right to say them.

They'd eaten and then left the hospital. Charlie had given Rafe a lift back to the brewery to collect his car, and Rafe had followed him home. The lights of the bungalow were ablaze, and clearly Charlie's house guests weren't going to bed until he returned. Rafe nodded in satisfaction and accelerated on down the road, not looking at Mimi's house when he passed it. There was no way he was going to be anywhere other than the hospital tonight.

He dumped his overnight bag in the small cubicle that adjoined the duty doctors' rest room and lay down on the bed, fully clothed, trying to tell himself that he wasn't going to do what he was about to do. Then he gave up all pretence of sleep and went upstairs to the ICU.

He'd expected a gentle invitation to go and get some rest from the ICU staff. But the doctor on duty knew Rafe and beckoned him inside.

'She's very restless. I don't want to give her any more medication if I can help it.'

'What's she on now...?' Rafe held out his hand for the notes, knowing that he was pushing his luck.

'Just go and talk to her, see if you can calm her down.'

'Yeah. Of course...' Rafe followed the doctor to Mimi's room and walked inside.

In the muted light, he could see her hand twitching. Grasping for something. Maybe she was still back at the brewery, fighting to find something to hold on to, in the rush of water. The feeling that his heart was going to break, right there and then, hit Rafe.

'She's been like this for a while. She tried to pull the cannula out...'

Not good news. Rafe looked at Mimi's arm and saw that a bandage had been put over a new cannula insertion, to try and prevent her from getting to that one. 'Can I sit with her?'

'That would be good.'

Rafe pulled up a chair and sat down. Whoever Mimi was reaching for probably wasn't him, but that didn't matter. She was reaching for someone, and he could be anyone she wanted him to be if she'd just calm down and go to sleep.

He took her hand and felt her fingers curl around his. It was probably just an automatic reaction, but she seemed to relax a little.

'You're safe, Mimi. Nothing's going to hurt you.'

She lay still. He stood up, leaning over to brush a few strands of hair from her forehead. 'Go to sleep now. You're safe.'

Although her eyes were closed, he could see movement behind the lids as if she was dreaming. She was still fighting it, though. She moved in the bed and seemed to stiffen, as if in pain.

'Honey, please try not to move. You need to rest.'

Suddenly her eyes snapped open. They seemed unfocused and Rafe had no idea whether she could see him or not. But he repeated his reassurances, hoping that he was getting through to her.

She blinked twice. Then her lids drooped and she lay quiet. Rafe sat down beside the bed, holding her hand, feeling the tears course down his cheeks. This was the only place he needed to be tonight. Every night, until Mimi woke up again.

Three nights. Three nights when he'd been able to sit with her while she slept. Charlie had been there every day. Jack had come in, looking gaunt and tired, and been allowed to spend half an hour with her. But that was the daytime. At night Mimi was still his.

Rafe knew that he shouldn't be doing this. He was pushing his luck, asking more favours than he should, but he didn't care. He drove home for a couple of hours' sleep first thing every morning, and then back in the afternoon to speak to Charlie. If the ICU staff were willing to allow him to stay on and sit with her during the night, Rafe wasn't going to question it.

Mimi was improving. She'd been breathing for herself, her lungs recovering from the assault of the water. Each night she seemed to sleep more peacefully. On the third morning, as he tried to slip unnoticed out of the ICU, her doctor caught up with him. Eddie and Rafe were old colleagues and he had always made time to speak to Rafe when he visited.

'We're going to discontinue the sedative and if she's still stable we'll transfer her on to one of the general wards.'

The small spot of light at the end of the tunnel suddenly turned into brilliance. 'Thanks...' Rafe tried to catch his breath. 'Thank you.'

'I'll get someone to call you. When she wakes up? Or are you going to get some shut-eye?'

In a world where Mimi was awake, Rafe doubted whether he could get any sleep. 'Thanks, but... Let her brother spend some time with her first. I'll wait.'

Eddie raised his eyebrows quizzically, but didn't ask. 'Okay. Just to let you know.'

'Thanks.' Rafe took the doctor's hand and shook it, gripping tight. 'You know when people tell you they don't know how to thank you?'

Eddie chuckled. 'Yeah, I know that one.'

'Well, trust me. They don't. I'm indebted to you...'

'Watch out. I might just collect.' Eddie turned and

walked away, leaving Rafe to wander down to the canteen for breakfast in a daze of happiness.

'Thought I'd find you here…' Rafe was holding the paper in front of him, pretending to read it so that he didn't have to look at anything else. But Charlie's voice made him look up.

'You're early. Can I get you anything?'

'How can you eat at a time like this?' Charlie peered at Rafe's plate, where his untouched breakfast was beginning to congeal. 'Correction. How can you buy food and not eat it at a time like this?'

'Force of habit. Never let a meal break pass you by. They called you?'

'Yep. Said they were waking her up. The doctor said she might not be fully conscious until lunchtime.'

'Probably not. Everyone takes their own time.'

'I remember when I woke up in the ICU…' He saw Charlie's hand fist around the wheel of his chair.

'I know that was a very rough time for you, but you were badly injured, Charlie. It'll be a lot easier for Mimi. Remember that.'

Charlie took a breath. 'I will. Thanks.'

'She'll be drowsy, and she might well be uncomfortable. But this is a real step forward.' Charlie had been looking to him for advice and Rafe had been careful to keep his expectations realistic, but at the same time stay positive. He knew that Charlie's worst fears were grounded in his own experience.

'When should we go up, then?'

'I reckon an hour or so. They'll let you in early if they're waking her.'

Charlie narrowed his eyes. 'What's with the *you*? You're not coming?'

'She's…' Rafe shrugged. 'It's you she wants to see, mate.'

'Right. You two were arguing, weren't you?'

'Yeah.' Every time Rafe thought about it, it was as if a knife had been slid into his heart.

'More than you were when you first turned up?' Charlie grinned.

'A lot less than that, actually. In fact we were in complete agreement...' In the last three days the dogged determination that she was going to get better had overwhelmed everything else. But now... The sadness that Rafe had felt on their last morning together, when they'd both known it was over but hadn't been able to say the words, washed back over him.

She was waking up. And he had to go.

'You and Mimi broke up again, didn't you?' Charlie's voice was heavy with resignation.

'Well...we were never together, so it follows that we couldn't have...'

'Oh, for crying out loud. So you were never together, which is none of my business anyway, but you still managed to break up. Only you and Mimi could do that.'

'It's complicated.'

'Yeah, I don't doubt that for a minute.' Charlie was squeezing the bridge of his nose between his thumb and finger. 'But I'd really appreciate it if you'd wait with me. I need some company...'

Charlie seemed suddenly on edge. As close to panic as Rafe had seen him since the difficult days when he'd had to come to terms with the fact that he wouldn't walk again. This was the one thing that Rafe had feared, and the only thing that could persuade him to stay.

'I'll stay for as long as you want. She'll be okay, you'll see.'

'Yeah.' Charlie took a deep breath. 'I know. Thanks.'

'Let's have some coffee. There's plenty of time, and I

could do with a cup.' Rafe's limbs were aching with fatigue, but the thought of a few more precious moments with Mimi made sleeping out of the question. Just as long as he left before she woke.

CHAPTER FOURTEEN

THEY SAT AT Mimi's bedside as she slept. Charlie had moved from his wheelchair to the perching stool which he had brought from home, the extra height allowing him to lean over and see Mimi's face, but after half an hour Rafe persuaded him to sit back down again and save his strength for when she was awake.

They talked, one on each side of the bed. Speaking quietly about the weather, how it had stopped raining. The wheelchair basketball league, the best beer gardens. Anything and everything, so that she might hear their voices.

'So some of us were thinking we'd have the basketball club crest tattooed on our arms. Only we don't actually have a club crest, so we'd have to get one first. And no one can agree on what to have…'

'Don't do that.'

Charlie suddenly fell silent. Mimi's voice had been quiet but clear, and when Rafe glanced at her she seemed to be sleeping still. Charlie rapidly hoisted himself to his feet, twisting urgently towards the perching stool, but he slipped and ended up on the floor.

Now was no time to stand back and let Charlie deal with it. Rafe rounded the bed, keeping his gaze on Mimi's face, and offered his hand. Charlie gripped hold of him, swinging himself up and finding the stool.

'Mimi. No tattoos, I promise. Just wake up… Please…'
Charlie leaned over her, his knuckles white on the bed's
safety rails.

She lay unresponsive. This was agony.

'She might be like this for a while, Charlie. It's quite…'
Rafe stopped short as Mimi's eyelids fluttered. They'd done
this before and she'd drifted back to sleep. But this time…

She opened her eyes.

Tears spilled suddenly from Charlie's eyes and he lifted
Mimi's hand to his lips. Mimi blinked a couple of times
and licked her lips.

'Dry… Rafe…'

Rafe had told himself that he would leave as soon as
Mimi showed any signs of waking, and let Charlie have this
moment, but when he heard her say his name he couldn't
help it. He leaned over the bed, careful not to obscure her
view of her brother.

'Mimi…? Welcome back, honey. You want some water?'

'Yes… Tell Charlie…'

'You can tell him yourself. He's right here.' Rafe turned,
brushing away his own tears as he reached for the beaker
of water.

'No tattoos. I promise…' Charlie was babbling almost
incoherently on the other side of the bed, and Mimi batted
her hand as if to shut him up. Rafe dipped a swab into the
water, holding it against the side of her mouth.

'Good… More…'

Rafe handed the water to Charlie. 'Careful. Don't let
her drink just yet. A drop of water on the swab, just to
moisten her lips.'

'Yes. Thanks, mate.' Rafe watched as Charlie carefully
brushed the swab against Mimi's lips.

'My legs… Can't move…' She moaned, shifting restlessly in the bed, and Rafe stroked the side of her face

to quiet her, the way he'd done so many times in the last three nights.

'You have a fractured ankle and it's in plaster. But it'll mend.'

'Snake...'

Rafe exchanged a glance with Charlie. He hadn't realised that Mimi had known about the snake. An image of her, underwater and alone, struggling for air and feeling the snake coil around her leg and bite her...

'I know. That's all been dealt with. You're in the hospital and you're safe, Mimi. No snakes here.' He wondered whether he should make the point by checking under the bed, but Mimi's eyes were closed now and she wouldn't see him. The thought that she'd faced terrors in her sleep made him want to wade into her dreams and protect her from whatever her unconscious mind could throw at her.

She seemed to calm, drifting somewhere between awake and asleep. Then she moaned again, her eyelids fluttering.

'Got to go to work...'

Charlie looked helplessly at Rafe. 'What's the matter with her?' He mouthed the words silently.

'She's okay, just a bit confused. You were just the same when you woke up.' Rafe smiled reassuringly.

'Was I?' Charlie shook his head. 'I don't remember that...'

'What's the time? Got to go...' Mimi's eyes were still closed but she was trying to raise her head from the pillow.

'It's your day off. No work today. Just rest.' Rafe took hold of her reaching hand and she quietened again.

'Good. Tired...'

Charlie leaned over the bed, his shaking fingers brushing her cheek the way Rafe's had earlier. He seemed to be getting the idea of what he needed to do now. 'You can go back to sleep for a while, Mimi. Just rest. We'll be here when you wake up again.'

She heaved a sigh and then lay still again, drifting away from them, back to sleep. They watched her for almost an hour as she slept peacefully. Rafe knew she'd be waking again soon, and that this time she'd be more lucid. And he knew what he had to do.

Slipping his watch off his wrist, he looked at it one last time and smiled. Then he held it out to Charlie. 'Give her this.'

Charlie stared at him. 'You're going, aren't you?'

'I'll be downstairs.'

'But… Don't you want…?'

More than anything. He wanted to see Mimi wake up, hold her hand and talk to her. 'I think…it's time for me to take a back seat, Charlie. Mimi and I made our decision, and it's best if I don't hang around now.'

Charlie seemed to be turning it over in his mind. Then he took the watch, his thumb grazing the glass over the lucky sixpence. 'I'll make sure this gets back to you…'

'No, I…' Giving something that Mimi knew was precious to him was the only way that Rafe knew of showing that he did care. That he hadn't just walked away, the way he'd done the last time.

'She should keep it; it'll bring her luck.' Rafe forced a grin. 'And she'll be able to check the time when she wakes up and thinks she needs to go to work.'

'Okay. I'll give it to her. You'll be in the canteen?'

'Yeah. Come down and let me know how she's doing? I'll wait.'

'Sure. I'll be down later.'

Charlie had found him in the canteen and Rafe had listened, greedily absorbing every detail of how Mimi had woken again and what she'd said. Rafe had extracted a promise from him, to call if there was anything he could do, and walked to Charlie's car with him, dangling his own car keys in a vain attempt to convince himself that he too was going to get into his car and drive away.

He'd told himself that he would just go up and check with the doctor on her progress. That she'd be sleeping now, and that if he looked in on her one last time she'd never know.

The doctor had told him that they'd tried to take the watch from her, but that Mimi had protested so fiercely that he had relented. The watch had been carefully folded inside an elastic bandage, and she had been allowed to keep it on her wrist. Drawn in, he sat beside her bed, watching her sleep.

'Rafe…?' He'd been staring at her wrist, wondering if the watch was too heavy for her to wear it like that, and he hadn't seen her eyelids open. But in the half-light he could see her gaze now, fixed on him.

'Everything's okay, Mimi. Go back to sleep.'

Her lips twitched into a smile. 'Again? That's all you ever say to me…'

She'd heard him. Those long nights when he'd wondered if she knew he was there. Rafe blinked back the tears.

'I'm thirsty…'

'Okay.' He operated the controls to raise the head of the bed. Then he poured some water into a glass, letting her take some water through a straw. 'Better?'

'Thanks. That's good.' Her fingers found the elastic bandage around her wrist, plucking at it. 'I'll take good care of this.'

He'd wondered whether she would try to give it back to him. The fact that she didn't, that she wanted to keep it, made his heart swell with happiness.

'It's supposed to be taking care of you. When it comes to good luck, you can't beat a sixpence.'

'No. You can't.' Her eyelids fluttered and Rafe thought they were closing, but then she shifted in the bed, turning her head to look at him. 'You should go home. Get some sleep.'

'I will. In a minute.' When she was asleep. It hurt to even think about getting up and walking away and although there were many things he wished he could share with Mimi, the pain of parting wasn't one of them.

'Thank you for staying, Rafe. I would have been…so lonely…'

He brushed the tear from her cheek, forcing a smile. 'I was at a loose end…'

'Yeah. Me too.' She became suddenly agitated. 'You should go now. I want you to go home…'

This was the one thing that Rafe had hoped to avoid. He took her hand, soothing her. 'It's okay, I know. We made a decision and I'm honouring that.'

'Thank you.' She yawned, clapping her hand over her mouth. 'Didn't mean to do that…'

Rafe chuckled despite himself. 'I know you didn't. One thing before you go back to sleep. I want you to call me if you need me. Any time. Will you promise?'

'I can't…' She furrowed her brow, as if she was trying to remember why. 'My phone…'

Rafe turned, sliding open the drawer which held her personal bits and pieces. Her phone was inside, but smashed so badly that it was practically broken in half.

'Your phone's broken. So you'll have to get Charlie to call if you need me. Will you do that?'

She nodded. 'Promise.'

'Good. Go to sleep now, Mimi.'

'Yes. I'm…tired.'

She yawned again, and then seemed to settle. Rafe waited. He'd seen enough people pretending to be asleep or unconscious in A and E to know the difference, and Mimi wasn't making a very good job of it. Soon enough, though, the tension seemed to leave her body and she was really asleep.

Time to go. Rafe tried to come up with some parting words that he might whisper, something to sum up how he felt, but he couldn't. Leaning over, his lips formed the shape of a kiss, which didn't even touch her forehead for fear of waking her. Then, swiftly, he turned away.

Mimi heard the door close. Despite her jumbled thoughts and the almost irresistible desire to sleep, she knew that Rafe had left now.

He'd looked so tired. Despite that, she knew he would have stayed if she'd asked him, watching over her. But it was time now, and she'd wanted him to get some rest.

Her fingers felt for the watch on her wrist. Still there. The most precious thing he owned...

A great tide of fatigue overwhelmed her. She'd feel better in the morning. The lucky sixpence would see to that.

The watch had stayed on her wrist for the last eight days. It had gone with her from the ICU down to a general ward, and now it was going home with her. Mimi was dressed and sitting by her bed, waiting for Charlie to come and fetch her.

'All set?' He was all smiles when he appeared at the door of the ward.

'Definitely.' She'd been looking at Rafe's watch every five minutes. In addition to the clear message that it carried, it was also useful for telling the time.

'Let's get out of here, then.' Charlie picked up her bag

and laid it across his knees. 'Matthew's outside with the car, and Jan's just rustling up a wheelchair for you.'

Mimi winced with embarrassment. 'Sorry. It's all such a business…' Jan and Matthew's house was still drying out and they had given up Charlie's spare bedroom for Mimi. They'd be sleeping at her cottage now, and coming back to Charlie's during the day.

'Oh, be quiet. It's a well-oiled machine, Mimi, so just sit back and watch the cogs go round.'

'I'm beginning to regret giving you such a hard time when you got out of hospital. I can't wait to be able to get around by myself.' Mimi screwed her face up and Charlie laughed.

'You were right.' He leaned forward, doing the mad scientist impression which had always made her laugh when they were kids. 'Now, my pretty, I get my revenge.'

The cool breeze on her face was wonderful. It was as if the world had been waiting for her for the past two weeks and had spruced itself up for her return. The sun shone and the late summer sky was cloudless.

Mimi was installed on the sofa in Charlie's sitting room and Jan bustled off into the kitchen, reappearing with a bouquet in one hand and a parcel in the other. 'These came for you this morning.'

Pink and white roses, with purple freesias for scent. Rafe. He knew she loved freesias.

'I'll get a vase and some water so you can arrange them.' Jan put the flowers down on Mimi's lap and handed her a small white envelope.

She opened it with trembling fingers.

With love from everyone…

No. That wasn't right. Mimi realised her mistake with a stab of regret.

'Who are they from?' Jan was watching her.

'Oh… Everyone I used to work with.' A salt tear reached the stitches on her face and she snatched a tissue from the box on the table and dabbed it gingerly. 'That's so nice of them.'

'They're lovely.' Jan put the package down on the other end of the sofa and turned towards the kitchen.

Mimi reached for the parcel, trying to work up a bit of enthusiasm for it. Everyone had been so nice over the last couple of weeks, visiting her and sending cards. She'd known that Rafe wouldn't come. It would have only drawn out the sadness of knowing they were inevitably going to part.

But every step she'd made, coming out of the ICU, coming home, had been bittersweet because it was another step towards regaining a life that didn't include Rafe. Mimi shook her head and grabbed the package, taking her frustration out on the tape that secured it.

She almost gave up and left it for Charlie to undo when he came back with the tea. Everything seemed like an effort at the moment. But someone had taken the trouble to wrap it up and send it for her, and the least she could do was to show some interest.

Inside was a pretty patterned box bearing the name of an exclusive skincare company. When she lifted the lid, the fresh scent was gorgeous after the dry, utilitarian smell of the hospital.

Someone had been very thoughtful. Mimi knew she looked a mess; her hair was flat and her nails needed filing and that was just the tip of the iceberg. One leg was in a cast and the other was still swollen, blistered and discoloured from the snake bites. When she'd first been allowed to go to the bathroom at the hospital, the large mirror above the basin had revealed what she'd only glimpsed in the pocket mirror the nurse had given her. Livid bruises on her face, a line of stitches and her own eyes staring back at her in shock and dismay.

She picked up a bar of soap, closed her eyes and smelled it. Her skin itched from antiseptic soap and wipes and this was just what she'd been craving. There were bottles of lotions and shampoo. Mimi picked up a tube of hand cream, squeezing a small dab on to her finger and rubbing it on to the back of her hand, still bruised from where a cannula had been inserted. It was luxurious and smelled just gorgeous.

'Who's that from?' Charlie appeared with a plate of cakes.

'I don't know.' Mimi looked around for a card but couldn't see one. 'But look, Charlie. So thoughtful…'

'Hmm.' Charlie leaned over to inspect her gift. 'Suppose you'll be wanting to stink my bathroom out with this lot.'

'Oh, stop. You should be so lucky. And if you lay one finger on any of these, you're dead.'

'Hardly likely.' Charlie rummaged around amongst the torn packaging. 'Must be a card somewhere… What's that?' He pointed at a slim package, slipped into the side of the box.

'Don't know.' Mimi tore the tissue paper and caught her breath.

'Very smart.' Charlie peered at the phone in her hand. 'Top of the range. Who's it from, though?'

Suddenly she knew. Mimi pressed the power button on the phone and the screen lit up immediately. There was an unread text.

'How do I…?' She jabbed her finger on the screen and the text appeared.

If there's anything you need, call. Hope you enjoy washing off the smell of the hospital. Love Rafe.

Dumbly, she clasped the phone in both hands, holding it to her heart.

'When did this come, Charlie?'

'Came by courier this morning.'

'It's from Rafe. How did he know I was coming out of hospital today?'

'I've been…' Charlie shrugged. 'I've been keeping him up to date, and asking a few questions about things. You know…texts. Couple of calls.'

From the guilty look on Charlie's face, it had been more than a couple of calls.

Suddenly it was all too much. Mimi felt tears welling in her eyes and she started to cry.

'Hey…sis…' Charlie seemed to manoeuvre almost sideways to get next to the sofa, and slid across to hug her. 'I'm sorry… He said I should call…'

'It's okay. I'm glad you did.' Mimi snuffled into his sweater. 'Is he… Is he all right?'

'He's fine. He was just worried about you and I thought…'

'You thought right. Thank you.' Mimi dabbed at her face with a tissue, wishing that she could at least cry without something hurting. 'Will you call him? Tell him I'm happy to be home, and that I said thank you.'

'Of course.' Charlie hesitated. 'Don't you want to tell him? If he sent you this, then doesn't that mean he wants *you* to call?'

It was tempting, but… 'No. We broke up, and that was the right thing for us both.'

'Yeah. That's what he says. But you know he'll come, don't you? If you want him to.'

'I know. I don't want him to. We don't work that well together, me and Rafe. Never really have done.'

Charlie hugged her tight, rocking her gently in his arms,

the way he had the night their parents had died. 'You…
loved him, didn't you?'

'Of course I did. Love isn't everything, though. You've
got to be able to live with someone.'

'Well, come and live with me. I'll buy your chocolate.'

'You might have to until I get another job.'

Charlie squeezed her hand. 'Don't worry about that, sis.
One thing at a time, eh?'

'Yes. One thing at a time.'

She heard the doorbell ring, and Jan's quick footsteps.
Then she appeared in the doorway holding another bunch
of flowers.

'They're nice.' Charlie turned to look. 'Who are they
from?'

'From…' Jan looked at the card which was taped on to
the wrappings. 'Joe Harding and everyone at the Old Brewery. Aren't they just lovely?'

'They're beautiful.' Mimi poked Charlie in the ribs. 'Is
there anyone you *haven't* told about my coming out of hospital today?'

'Must be someone.' Charlie grinned, sliding back into
his wheelchair. 'Right, we'll have tea and then you can get
down to some flower arranging. Then a nap…'

'A nap? What? Am I ninety?'

'*Then* you can have a shower.' Charlie nodded towards
the box that Rafe had sent and he grinned. 'Then we'll hang
out a bit, have some dinner, and tomorrow you can start on
the getting well thing. Okay?'

'Okay. Thanks.' Charlie made it sound so easy. They
both knew it wasn't, but it paled into insignificance alongside the journey she was going to have to take before she
stopped missing Rafe.

It had to be done, though. All of it. Starting tomorrow.

CHAPTER FIFTEEN

MIMI HAD BOUGHT a new dress. She had been exhausted by the shopping trip with Jan, but had refused point-blank to go home until she'd found what she was looking for. A pretty, dusky pink summer dress that she'd got in the sales because everyone was looking forward to the winter fashions now, but which had the advantage of covering her knees.

Tights would have gone some way towards making her leg look a little better, but she still couldn't bear to have anything touch the swollen, discoloured skin around the snake bites. The supportive brace on her other foot didn't do much for the outfit either, but at least it allowed her to walk and she opted for a pink canvas sneaker on the other foot.

She'd applied a deep conditioner to her hair, drying it carefully, and was pleased with the shine it gave. There was nothing she could do to make the scar on her face go away, but a little foundation made it less obvious.

'Bit more cleavage, maybe…' Charlie gave her outfit a cool, assessing eye.

'The neck doesn't go like that. Anyway, what happened to being a woman of mystery?' Mimi pulled at the lace-edged top of the dress.

'There's something you need to learn about men, Mimi. Cleavage is always better than mystery.'

'You think I don't know anything about men?'

Mystery was going to have to do. She had too many imperfections now to consider anything else, and Rafe was going to have to take her as she was. Mimi pulled on her coat and got to her feet.

It had been ten weeks since her accident and, now that the cast was off, it was a lot easier to get around. She couldn't walk very far and still needed elbow crutches to support her, but every day she managed a little more.

Charlie held up his hands in an expression of surrender. 'Not getting involved, Mimi. I'm just giving you a lift.'

'Good. Thanks. Let's get going.'

Rafe's road was a nice road. Nice houses. If he'd had to spend all this time away from her, Mimi was glad that he'd found somewhere pleasant to live. Charlie drove slowly, pulling up outside the house on the brow of the hill.

'Oh…!'

'Told you.' Charlie looked at the path, sloping upwards with a couple of steps along the length of it, and three more leading to the front door. 'Not all that accessible.'

'Well, what do you do then?'

'I go round the back.' Charlie pointed to the concrete slope where Rafe's car was parked. There was a passageway in between the house and the garage, just wide enough to take a wheelchair.

It was bad enough turning up at his front door; the back door was out of the question. And if she could get this far, then a few steps weren't going to stand in her way. Even if they did look virtually insurmountable from here.

'Why don't you just call him? That would be much easier.'

As if the rest of this was a walk in the park. 'I'll manage. I'll take it slowly.'

Charlie shrugged. 'Okay. I'll wait.'

'It's okay. Thanks for the lift.' Mimi grabbed her handbag, looping it across her body, and got out of the car, pulling herself upright.

'Call me when you want me to come and get you...'

Charlie waited anyway, while she laboriously made her way up the steep path. The last three steps looked pretty much impossible, but she could reach the bell from the bottom if she stretched up. Turning around, she flapped her hand at Charlie in a signal that he was going now, and the car moved off.

This was it. Charlie had mentioned more than once that there were easier ways of getting to see Rafe, but she'd been determined. It was going to be just her and Rafe. Away from the echoes of their past which haunted her own cottage, and certainly not anywhere else. What she wanted to say needed to be said in private.

She reached for the bell and rang it. No answer. Rafe's car was there and, anyway, Charlie had called to make sure he was in, on the pretext that he might drop round at some point in the morning.

Perhaps he'd gone out for a few minutes, knowing that Charlie would let himself in at the back. Maybe he'd forgotten. Or maybe there was some kind of emergency at the hospital and he'd been called in. But then he would have taken his car.

Mimi tried again, this time keeping her thumb on the bell for long enough to make sure that Rafe was out. Then she carefully made a one-hundred-and-eighty-degree turn and sat down on the front steps.

There was just one cloud in the sky, but it was a big one and it was coming this way. The breeze was fresh and she drew her coat around her, wishing she'd brought her umbrella. It didn't matter now. However long she had to wait, she wasn't going to call Charlie and get him to come back for her.

She waited and then saw him, turning the corner at the end of the road, the Sunday paper tucked under his arm in a thick wad. There were a few moments to appreciate his long stride, the way his dark woollen sweater mimicked the shape of his shoulders. She could just see that he hadn't bothered to shave this morning. She'd always thought that a couple of days' worth of stubble suited Rafe.

She wondered if she should stand up or remain sitting, and decided to stay where she was. The long stretch of front path seemed horribly steep from this angle and she was afraid of falling.

So very afraid of falling. But she was here now, setting herself up for whatever Rafe could dish out. Cold distance, uncertainty, outright rejection. Or the terror of hearing him say *yes*. She'd deal with it when it came. She clasped her hands together tightly, wondering if she'd know when he saw her. Maybe he'd pretend not to for a few strides, to give him time to work out how he was going to let her down easily.

He saw her. The precise moment was clear and unequivocal because he dropped his paper and started to run. When he reached the front path he slowed and suddenly stopped, his gaze on her.

'Mimi. What…?'

'You…you said that if there was anything…' She gulped the words out.

He took the path in long strides, stopping in front of her. 'Come in.'

She swallowed hard, trying to remember the words that she'd rehearsed so many times. Suddenly her courage deserted her. 'I… I can't.'

He sat down next to her on the step, one arm planted on

the paving stone behind her, his face a mask of concern. He was being careful not to touch her.

'Okay. We'll stay here, then.'

She wanted this moment to last. Even the tearing uncertainty was something she wanted to hang on to because she was here with him.

'Mimi...?' He craned around to look into her face. 'What is it? Why won't you come inside?'

'Because...' Suddenly it all came tumbling out. 'Because there's something I want you to do for me. I believe in you and I want you to believe in me...'

He opened his mouth to speak and she waved him into silence.

'I believe that we can make it work between us, if we just trust enough to help each other change. I'm daring you to try.'

'You...' He gasped out the word, turmoil showing in his face. 'You're daring me?'

'Yes.' She was twisting her fingers so tightly together that they hurt.

'Then I dare you back, Mimi.' He was closer now, his mouth an inch from hers, his gaze all-encompassing. 'I dare you to come inside.'

'You might be sorry...'

'I won't be. I'll make sure you aren't either.'

'Then I accept.' She held out her hand to shake on the deal, and he pulled her trembling fingers to his lips.

Pulling his keys out of his pocket, he put them into her hand. Then he lifted her in his arms and turned towards the door. In a dream—no, this was far too good to be a dream—Mimi opened the door.

'Last chance, Mimi.' He was smiling down at her. 'If you come inside then you stay until we've seen this one through.'

'I know.'

He stepped over the threshold and the warmth of the house tingled against her cheek. Rafe kicked the door closed and let her down, his arms around her waist, supporting her against his body. She dropped her handbag and slid her coat off her shoulders, letting it fall to the floor.

'Aren't we going to go and sit down?' He wasn't moving, just staring at her.

'I have to do something far more important first.' He held her close, kissing her. Tender at first and then the connection between them snapped into place, something hot and wild flooding through them both.

She'd lived for this. Dreamed of it, every moment that they were apart.

Rafe was showing no sign of wanting to move and she kissed him again. Yesterday was gone and tomorrow wasn't here yet. And today was turning out to be just perfect.

'Maybe we should...talk?'

'Not yet.' He smiled down at her. 'There might be a few constructive arguments along the way...'

'I imagine so. I'm almost hoping there will be.'

'In which case I want to remind us both how sweet it'll be when we make up.'

That sounded like an excellent plan. 'And this is the best you can do?' She knew for sure that it wasn't.

He kissed her again and her legs started to tremble. He felt it and supported her the few steps to the stairs, sitting down before he pulled her on to his lap. 'Better?'

'Much.' She could feel his body against hers. Wound tight, like a coiled spring. 'Rafe, I've missed you so much.'

'Me too...' He grinned. 'I'm not dreaming, am I?'

'If you are, then we're both dreaming together.' Maybe this would shatter the dream. She had to trust him enough to believe it wouldn't.

She swung her feet up, looking at her mismatched footwear. Suddenly her swollen, discoloured leg seemed so much worse than it had looked this morning when she'd got out of bed and her fingers itched to pull her dress down and cover as much of it as she could. But being in his arms gave her courage.

'I feel a mess, and I'm afraid that's all you'll see. I want you to be honest with me…'

'Mimi…' His fingers brushed her cheek, almost finding the healing scar on her face and instinctively she flinched. When his gaze found hers again, tears were glistening in his eyes.

'Mimi, please don't ever feel that you're not the most beautiful woman in my world. Please don't ever think that I'm judging you.'

'You don't care, do you? About my leg…the scars…' Finally she could manage to say it.

His chest heaved as he sucked in a deep breath. 'I care about them, but only because they hurt you. I love you.'

'And love is blind?'

'Never.' His finger was under her chin, tipping her face up towards his. 'I see every part of you. And I love every part of you. Please don't be afraid, sweetheart, because there's nothing for you to be afraid of.'

'And I…'

He laid his finger over her lips. 'There's more I want to tell you. Your turn in a minute.'

She couldn't help smiling. Rafe was clearly taking this decision to change seriously and it looked as if she was going to have difficulty in shutting him up. 'Okay.'

'I stayed away because it was what we'd agreed, and I thought it was best to let you recover properly without having me around. I wanted to let you make this decision, but I hoped every day that you would.'

'Yes…' It made Mimi feel so good to hear him say these things.

'I want to love you and take care of you, but I want to let you take care of me too.'

'Yes.'

'When you were arguing with me, that night on the sofa when you climbed on top of me…' She felt him shudder.

'That was a mistake. I know.'

He chuckled. 'It was challenging. And, in or out of bed, that's the thing that excites me about you most. I want you to love me, but I *need* you to challenge me, and I need you to make me hear it.' He dropped a kiss on to her cheek.

'Because I'm always right?' She giggled.

'No. Because neither of us is always right. But together we've got a fighting chance.'

'You've been thinking about this, haven't you?'

'All the time. Every day, honey.'

He kissed her again. Rafe had always known all the right things to do to make her body crave him and to make her heart thump with longing for him. An emotion that she couldn't name shivered through her. Desire, happiness. The feeling that she was coming home… No. The knowledge that she *was* home.

This was all she needed. Everything else could take its time.

'Maybe we should take things slowly.' She waited for his agreement.

It didn't come. 'What? Don't you agree, Rafe?'

'What things?'

She dug him in the ribs. 'You know what things. Sex. Leave the gymnastics until later.'

He shrugged. 'Yeah, I can do without the gymnastics. If you honestly want to know, then the sex is going to be a bit harder.' He kissed her cheek. 'I'm not going to pretend that I don't want you. Mimi, I'm done with that. But I'll wait until you're ready, however long that takes.'

He was making this very hard. Mimi wanted him too, but the thought that she might disappoint him held her back. 'I just think... Well, I get tired easily. And my legs are still weak. I can't do all the things we used to.'

'Would it be all right if I just kissed you?'

She looked up into the warmth of his eyes, wondering how she could have lived this long without having him close. 'Yes. It would be more than all right.'

'Hold hands. I'd like to do that.'

She took his hand in hers, kissing his fingers. 'How's that?'

'Wonderful. You want to try something new?'

She grinned. 'What sort of new?'

He kissed her cheek again, working his way round to her ear, and Mimi shivered. 'I'll kiss you and touch you. I'll make you burn for me, the way I do for you, only I'll take it slow. Very slow. Very gentle.'

She could almost feel him doing it. Her fingers clutched convulsively at his sweater. 'Yes. Only you don't need to be all that gentle. I'm not going to break.'

He kissed her, his hands tender and his mouth hot, almost savage. 'Oh, yes, you are, honey. You *are* going to break...'

Rafe had carried her upstairs in a move that seemed romantic rather than a response to need. Mimi sat down on the bed, looking around. Cream walls, cream curtains, cream linen. It was...

It was neat and tidy, but the room could do with some loving care. It felt like a place where you just crashed out to sleep.

'This is…nice.' The bed was large and the mattress comfortable. It was a bit like a high-class hotel room.

He chuckled. 'Needs a woman's touch.'

'Ah. Well, maybe I'll…' Mimi suddenly forgot all about soft furnishings as Rafe pulled his sweater and shirt over his head together in one fluid movement.

'Maybe you'll what?' He knelt down in front of her, gently taking off her shoe and sock.

'I'll touch it later. First I'll touch you.' She ran her fingers lightly over his chest, feeling the muscles quiver and tense. 'I tried so hard to hold you in my imagination, but I couldn't. I was too angry, and you're too beautiful.'

'No more of that now, sweetheart.' He kissed her, smoothing her hair back from her face. 'I want to look at you.'

Suddenly she wanted that too. With all the frailties, the scars, the red blotches on her leg. Even though he was flawless, smooth skin rippling over muscle and bone. 'Help me…with my dress.'

CHAPTER SIXTEEN

HE UNDRESSED HER SLOWLY. Lavished attention on her, trailing his fingers across every inch of her body. When Rafe took his jeans off, she gave him a little gleeful look and he knelt in front of her, holding her close.

'I don't think I ever said this before...' He kissed her lips lightly. 'You make me feel so loved. So wanted.'

'You are loved. You are wanted.' It felt good to say it, and even better to have him hear it.

'I thought...' He seemed to give up any pretence of thought for a moment, in favour of the sweet sensations that his caress, and her answering touch, engendered.

'What did you think?'

'I thought that taking it slow was going to mean a bit of self-restraint. But I want this so much, Mimi. I won't be cheated out of a single moment of it.'

They kissed for a long time. Talking, caressing, both knowing where this was leading and in no hurry to get there. When he finally lifted her on to the bed, Mimi didn't care that he could see all her imperfections, all the injuries that she examined every morning in the mirror. In his eyes, she was beautiful.

'Comfortable?' He put an extra pillow behind her back.

'I'm fine.' She caught hold of his hand, pulling him close, feeling the heat of his skin. 'Where were we?'

The list of things they liked about each other, with a caress and a kiss for each one. He nuzzled against her shoulder, his lips brushing her ear.

'Breasts…' He paused. Hesitation wasn't Rafe's style and he was just letting the thought sink in while his fingers traced across her ribcage. Stopping, just as she began to tremble with anticipation.

'You are such a bad man…'

'Yeah?' His grin confirmed it. 'Is that something you like, or just an observation?'

'Something I like…' She caught her breath as he ran his tongue across her nipple, lavishing slow attention on it.

They moved past the point of mere arousal to a place where every touch sent sensation spinning through their bodies. Every breath, every word, tangling in a web of pleasure which captured them both.

When the time came, there was no need for Rafe to ask if she was ready. He reached for the condom and handed it to her. Mimi ran one finger down his length, making him groan. Then she rolled the condom down carefully, in an exercise of sensuality triumphing over practicality.

He couldn't believe that this was really happening, but it was much too good to be a dream. Mimi was in his arms, making love with him. More than that, they were at one in a way they'd never been before. Carefully, he propped her leg on to a pillow, then levered his body over hers.

She was staring into his eyes and when he pushed inside her, she murmured his name. Rafe held still for a while, feeling the tremble of his limbs match that of hers. She reached up, her fingers tracing over his face and lips, and he allowed a little of his weight to press down on to her, pouring all his furious need into one kiss.

They were both too greedy for these moments for him to do anything that would snatch them away. He made love to her slowly, luxuriating in her gaze. Every sensation, every emotion shared.

'My beautiful Mimi.' He knew that she was close to breaking point and he wanted her to hear it, and believe it, one more time. When she smiled back at him, he knew that she'd finally learned to accept that compliment completely and that she would accept everything else he had to give.

One hand found his, guiding it to the top of her swollen leg, asking for what she needed silently but without apology. He wrapped his fingers around her thigh, holding her leg steady on the pillow so his movements didn't jolt it.

She felt his other hand curl around her shoulder, steadying her against his thrusts, so she could feel each one more keenly. Mimi raked her nails across his back, feeling him shudder with the sudden sensation, and his rhythm changed. Pushing her further and higher until she came so hard that the earth seemed to tilt.

He held her tight as aftershocks spun through her body. Keeping her safe, telling her all the things she so needed to hear. How he loved her. That she was beautiful and he was never going to let her go. It was then that Mimi realised that the world hadn't tipped upside down. It had simply righted itself.

Rafe could have just watched her for hours. But then he felt her leg arch around his back, and her fingers touching the place where their bodies were joined.

'Now you...' She didn't really need to tell him; he was already helpless in her hands. She knew he couldn't resist when she did that...

Rafe held on, through each exquisite sensation, until finally it was almost a relief when his shaking limbs began to relax. Knowing they were probably about to turn to jelly, taking his brain along with them, he rolled over to one side of her, pulling her close to feel the beat of her heart against his.

'Wow…' He felt her snuggle in tight as she voiced the only word that was currently available from his own vocabulary.

He kissed the top of her head, feeling his whole body plunge into satiated warmth. 'Mmm. Wow.'

He fetched a sturdy stool with slip-proof feet, for Mimi to perch on while they showered together. Rafe planted his hands firmly on the tiles behind her shoulders so she could hold on to his arms to steady herself while she soaped him.

'All done.' She ran her fingers through his wet hair, slicking it back from his face.

'You were all done a while ago.' The last ten minutes had been an exercise in sheer pleasure, just for the sake of it.

It was so good to hear her laugh again. So good to feel her limbs tangling with his.

'The last time…' She wrapped her arms around his neck. 'The last time we were in the water together, you carried me out. You saved me, Rafe.'

'I couldn't have made it out of there without you, honey.'

'Can we do it again? Save each other.'

'I'm relying on you, Mimi. I've been lost and I need you to save me.' Warm water tumbled on to his back as he kissed her. It was the sweetest sensation because he knew that he was safe in Mimi's arms.

One hand trailed across his chest and Rafe braced his limbs securely against the side of the shower. He was strong enough to support her, and keep her safe too. Her fingers tantalised, moving lower, and the words she whispered in his ear told him exactly what to expect next. Rafe closed his eyes…

* * *

She was tired now. He let her rest for a while, watching her as she slept. More than once, during those silent nights at the hospital, he'd wondered if maybe they shared the same dreams. Now he knew.

When she woke she was hungry and he pulled on his clothes and went downstairs to make tea and toast. When he returned, she was wrapped in his dressing gown, smoothing the creases in her dress.

'Can you stay tonight? I can run you home to get whatever you need, and we'll pick up some shopping. I'll do a Sunday roast, with all the trimmings.' Living on his own, he'd got into the habit of making do with pizza on Sundays and it would be good to cook again.

'Sounds wonderful.' She took the elbow crutch that he'd retrieved from the front step and stood up.

'You want my arm?'

'No, that's okay. Let me manage it on my own.'

He waited while she walked carefully down the stairs, and then fetched the tea from the kitchen. She settled comfortably on to the sofa, leaning against him, and he put his arm around her shoulder.

His heart beat fast and suddenly he couldn't keep the words to himself. 'I want to be with you, Mimi. All the time.'

She flushed red. 'Are you asking me to move in with you?'

'Yeah. Or we can stay at your cottage, if you prefer.'

'Your work's here. And I can't have you doing all that driving...' She broke off, smiling. 'The truth is that I'd rather be here with you, if that's okay. We're going to do things differently from when we were at the cottage.'

'Yeah. I think so too. So you'll come here? Warm my bed at night?'

'Yes, my love, I will.'

Happiness burst into yet another neglected corner of his heart. He took her hand, pulling it to his lips. 'I'm going to make you glad you said that.'

'And I'm going to make you glad you asked.' She grinned impishly. 'Maybe…'

Rafe leaned back against the sofa cushions, chuckling. 'All right. What have I let myself in for now?'

'Well, there are a few little bits and pieces I could bring with me. Only if you wanted me to. My breadmaker, perhaps.'

'Bring as much as you like.' Rafe looked round at the sitting room. Plain walls. Good quality furniture. But it had always felt a little cold and empty. He'd known for a while now that there was one vital thing missing. 'I said that this place needed a woman's touch. What I actually meant was that it needs *your* touch.'

'Really?'

'Absolutely. There's a bit of a space, up in the bedroom. I think it needs something…'

'A washstand?'

Rafe laughed. 'Perfect.'

'I've got some other things up in the loft. Things we bought together. You could go up there and have a look around if you wanted.'

'You didn't throw it all away?'

'No. I couldn't bear to. I just didn't want to look at it.' She shifted in his arms and settled again comfortably. 'Maybe this is how we do it. Keep the things we want, but make a new start.'

'I'd like that.'

They were silent for a moment. Dreaming the same dreams.

'What are you thinking, Rafe?'

Rafe bent to kiss her. 'I was just thinking about coming home every day to find you in my bed. Naked. Or maybe something lacy...'

'You will not.' She poked her tongue out at him. 'That's only every other day. Alternate days, you're the one who gets naked. In the kitchen.'

He chuckled. 'Right. Okay, I see how this is going to go...'

'And there are rules.' She pulled herself up on to his lap and he curled his arms around her.

'Yeah. I was really hoping for rules.'

She'd never felt so loved before. Never felt that she was so exactly in the right place.

'Rule Number One...' Mimi kissed the tip of his finger. 'We talk about it. Whatever it is, however hard it is.'

'Agreed. That's a good one. Number Two...' He laughed as she kissed his next finger. 'You remember that I love you. And if I ever do anything to make you feel you're not good enough, you make me crawl on my hands and knees to ask for forgiveness.'

'I think you're pretty safe on that score. But yes, I can do that.'

'Good. Number Three...'

'Hey, don't I get to make the next one?'

'Do you have one?'

She thought for a moment. 'No. Not at the moment. Okay, you take Three and I'll have Number Four.'

'Fair enough. Number Three is that we don't let the sun go down on an argument.'

'Yes, that's a good one. That can be Number Three.' She kissed the top of his third finger. 'Where did you get that one from?'

'Remember the old guy we went to see?' He frowned

in thought for a moment. 'Infected cut on his leg. What was his name?'

'Toby? His name's not really Toby, but his surname is Jugg, so everyone in the village calls him Toby.'

Rafe chuckled. 'Okay, well, the wise Mr Jugg suggested it to me.'

'When did he do that?'

'When you were off fetching the dressings and conspiring with his next-door neighbour. He gave me some relationship advice.'

'I wasn't gone *that* long, was I?'

'It was a pretty one-sided conversation and he came directly to the point. Toby seemed to think that the fact I was looking at you when you weren't looking, and looking away when you were, was a sign that I was madly in love with you. He was quite right, of course, and naturally I denied it all.'

'It's a good rule. Did he happen to mention anything else that might come in handy?'

A faint gleam appeared in Rafe's eyes. 'That was man-to-man advice. Don't interfere.'

'Okay. Rule Number Four is that I'm going get it out of you.' She kissed the sensitive skin on his neck.

'Yeah, I imagine you will. Soon, probably.'

Step by step, she was moving back into the world. Rafe had talked to the HR department where he worked, and it had been arranged that Mimi should go in four half-days a week to mentor trainee ambulance technicians. It was unpaid, but it was a start. And, to her surprise, she found that she loved teaching just as much as she loved being on the road. It was one more new possibility in a world that felt full of promise.

Although the snake bites were still painful and she was

unable to put her full weight on that leg, her other leg was strong enough to make walking easier. And although the scar on her face was still there, it was no longer the only thing that Mimi saw when she looked in the mirror.

When the invitation to the grand reopening of the Old Brewery came, Rafe had voiced his concerns that it might awaken traumatic memories for her. But when Mimi had told him that with him by her side she could take that risk, he'd simply hugged her and promised his support. With his trust, she felt she could do almost anything.

The afternoon was bright and clear. The colours of the autumn leaves were especially vibrant this year, deep reds and oranges lining the road, and, as they turned into the car park of the Old Brewery, Joe Harding came to meet them.

'So glad you could come.' He offered Mimi his arm, helping her out of the car. 'This way.'

He led them through to the visitor centre, which had been cleared and hung with bunting for the party. A barbecue had been set up in the beer garden behind the building and there were several different kinds of beer on tap.

Grant made a point of bringing his wife and children over and introducing them, and then Joe Harding made a speech, which was received with general approval, in particular because it was short and to the point. A little girl dressed as a fairy appeared from somewhere and everyone clapped as she presented Mimi with a posy of flowers. Rafe seemed so happy that he was almost shining. And then Charlie turned up.

'Who's that?' She turned to Rafe, tugging urgently at his sleeve.

'Um...one of the nurses from the ICU, I think.'

'Really? You mean I was lying unconscious and Charlie was busy chatting up the ICU nurses?'

Rafe nodded, grinning. 'Looks like it.'

'Good for him. She's pretty, isn't she?'

'Not as pretty as you...' He leaned down to whisper the words and then grunted in protest as Mimi jabbed him in the ribs.

'It's not a competition, you know. Aren't you glad that Charlie's found someone nice?'

'Of course. Think he'll introduce us any time soon?'

'He'd better...' Charlie seemed to finally realise that Mimi was staring at him and she gave him a wave. 'Go and ask them if they're free for lunch tomorrow.'

'Ask them yourself. They're coming over.' Rafe turned his smile on to the petite brunette who was with Charlie.

It had been a lovely afternoon. Fireworks were promised for the evening, and Mimi and Rafe had escaped the heat of the visitor centre for a while.

'Ah! It's better out here.' She had left her elbow crutches behind, in favour of leaning on his arm. 'Fewer people around.' She turned and kissed him.

'What's that for?'

'To thank you for today. And to remind you that I might want to thank you a bit more comprehensively when we get home.'

Rafe chuckled. 'You know what, I'm sending you back to work full-time. Four half-days a week isn't enough to keep your mind occupied.'

'You love it. Anyway, if you want me to stop thinking about sex, then you'd better stop with the *How many ways can we do this without my leg swelling?* thing.'

'That's Continuous Professional Development. Not every doctor has his very own adder bite patient to experiment on, you know.'

'So that's what you call it, is it? What happens when I get better?'

'I experiment a bit more. Long-term effects.'

They walked a few steps in the darkness and Rafe found a bench. It was obviously designed for visitors to watch the comings and goings at the working brewery because it looked out over the river and across to the floodlit loading bay.

'Do you want to go down there?' His voice was very tender. 'Joe Harding lent me the key.'

'You know...' Mimi thought for a moment, wondering if she really did or she really didn't, and decided that she did. 'Yes. Yes, I would.'

He fetched her coat, wrapping it around her, and carried her across the rough ground between the visitor centre and the loading bay. It wasn't strictly necessary, she probably would have managed it on her own, but she needed him close.

'I'd like to go inside.' She could feel herself trembling, but she wanted to do this. She'd shared everything else with Rafe over the last weeks, and both of them had known that she'd share this sooner or later.

He bent down, unlocking the padlock and pulling the shutter up from the door beside the main bay. Reaching inside, he found the light switch.

'Sure about this?'

'Yeah.'

He wound his arm around her waist, helping her inside. Everything was clean and orderly, and the smell of the brewing beer was stronger here now than it had been the last time. She looked around. The stairs where Rafe had been standing. The metal door which had flown off the wall. The shuttered entrance that she'd made a dash for before the door had hit her and the water had swept her off her feet.

She'd dreamed of this place, waking up in the night to

find him holding her, comforting her. And, now she was here, it had somehow lost its power. Something bad had happened here, but that was all in the past.

He helped her across to a bench, which stood against the wall, and she sat down on his lap. When she looked up into his face, she saw tears in his eyes.

'Hey... We made it, Rafe.'

'Yeah. We did. Are you okay?'

Funnily enough, yes. Mimi hadn't expected to be, but then she imagined that Rafe hadn't expected not to be.

'Yes. You're not, though, are you?'

He smiled. 'Just being here... I thought I'd lost you. When you were under the water and I was searching for you...'

She kissed his cheek. 'And you found me. That's what matters, Rafe.'

'Yeah. I know.'

She hadn't expected that this would be the time or the place, but it was. Mimi reached into her handbag.

'I have something for you.'

He brushed his hand across his face. 'Yeah? What?'

'Your watch. I know you said you wanted me to keep it...'

She pulled the jeweller's box out of her bag and gave it to him. Rafe shot her a questioning look and opened it.

'Mimi...' His face broke into a wide grin. 'That's... It's great.'

'You don't mind?'

'Mind? It's wonderful.' There were two watches in the box—Rafe's along with a smaller one for her, each with half the lucky sixpence mounted behind the hands.

'Put it on...' She could hardly sit still, hardly wait to see it on his wrist.

'Yours first.' He slid the bracelet of the smaller watch

over her hand, fixing the clip to secure it tight. Then he took off the watch he'd been wearing for the last couple of months and let her put his grandfather's watch back on to his wrist.

'I had to have the dial redone.' She traced her finger over the glass. After some debate, she'd opted for a dark blue semi-circle, studded with stars, to replace the other half of the sixpence. 'It's a reminder of the nights you sat with me. How much that meant to me.'

'It's perfect, honey. I love it, thank you.' He stared at the watch for long moments and Mimi hugged herself with glee. She hadn't dared hope that he'd like it as much as he obviously did.

'I've got something for you too.' He reached into the inside pocket of his jacket. 'I was going to save it for later, but you're right. This is the place.'

He was hiding something in his hand and, when curiosity got the better of her and she leaned over to see what it was, he smiled.

'Are you ready?'

'I might be, if I knew…' Mimi caught her breath. Suddenly she *did* know.

She gazed up into his eyes and he nodded, as if the question was already asked and answered.

'Will you marry me, Mimi?'

'Yes, Rafe. I will.' She didn't need to think about it. Something had clicked into place as soon as he'd spoken the words, a final, all-engulfing happiness which knew no half measures and allowed no hesitation.

'You sound pretty sure of it.'

'I am. I love you, Rafe, and I want to marry you.'

'Then the sooner I can get this on to your finger…' He opened his hand, showing her a box with a ring inside. A pretty, twisting trail of sapphires with a large diamond in the middle. Suddenly it all became real, and tears sprang into her eyes.

'How long...?'

'I chose it last week, but the jeweller had to resize it. I picked it up when I went to town this morning, reckoning I'd give it to you tonight... Do you like it?'

'It's gorgeous, Rafe. Beautiful... Too much...'

He shot her a reproving look. 'Nothing's too much for you, Mimi. I just want to see you wearing it.'

'I... I really want to wear it too.' She held out her hand.

He kissed her finger and then slid the ring on to it. Mimi stared at it. 'Am I dreaming?'

'If you are, then so am I. For the rest of my life.'

You find a girl you like and...you lead her up the hill to the church...

Toby Jugg's advice. In a moment, Rafe would tell her that this was Rule Number Four, the one he'd set for himself that day when Mimi had appeared on his doorstep. But, for now, he was complete in a way that he'd never thought possible. He'd carry her out of here one more time and give her a moment to show Charlie her ring. And then he'd take her home.

EPILOGUE

IT WAS THE first wedding of the New Year. Charlie had decided to wait at the church, to accompany Mimi down the aisle and give her away, and she snuggled into the horse-drawn carriage with Jack and his daughter, Ellie.

'Are you warm enough, sweetie?' Mimi's wedding dress had a matching brocade coat, with white fur at the collar and cuffs, and Ellie had a similar coat over her dress.

'Yes.' The little girl was trying very hard to be grown up, and to act like a princess, after her father had told her that this was really a fairytale carriage.

'That's good.' Mimi twitched a rug over Ellie's lap, covering her satin slippers. 'Look at the people, coming to watch. You can wave if you like.'

A small knot of people had tumbled out of the village Post Office and were waving to the carriage as it went by. Ellie scrambled up onto her knees on the seat, waving back, almost dropping her posy of flowers out of the window, before Jack retrieved it and stowed it carefully under the seat.

She felt for the heavy pearls around her neck, making sure that they were still there. Rafe's mother had given them to her, saying that her own mother had worn them on her wedding day. Rafe had stopped Mimi from protesting that she couldn't possibly take such a precious gift, and his mother had beamed with pleasure when she saw that they complemented her dress perfectly.

'Are you all right?' Jack must have asked the question at least twenty times, but it still seemed to require an answer.

'I'm fine. Just thinking about…everything. A lot's happened in the last few months, for both of us.'

'Yes.' Jack looked out of the window. 'Might be more to come. You and Rafe can think about me battling through three feet of snow, while you're off on your honeymoon.'

'I'll do no such thing. I'll be…' Mimi laughed as Jack's hands moved for Ellie's ears.

'Okay. We all know what you'll be doing.'

'What will she be doing?' Ellie climbed onto her father's knee, and Jack rolled his eyes.

'Exercises, sweetheart. Mimi has to exercise her leg for a while longer, so that she can walk properly.'

It had been a long, hard journey to get here. The snake bites had weakened Mimi's leg to such an extent that at one point it was doubtful whether she'd be able to make it up the aisle unaided. Rafe had been quite prepared to carry her, saying that he didn't care how she got there, just as long as she did, but Mimi had been determined not to compromise either the date of her wedding, or the manner in which she arrived.

As they pulled up at the church it started snowing again. Large umbrellas shielded her as Jack helped her down from the carriage, and then he stepped back so she could join Charlie in the vestibule of the country church.

There was a moment's pause while Ellie was coaxed to stand a few feet in front of her, ready to scatter petals. Charlie suddenly caught her hand.

'Can you do it on your own?'

'Yes. I can do it.' She wasn't going to stumble, now. She

knew exactly where she was going, and falling flat on her face was no longer an option.

Charlie nodded. 'Off you go, then.'

'But Charlie…? You're supposed to be walking me down the aisle?'

'Yeah. Since when did we care what we were supposed to do? *I* want to see you do this by yourself.' Charlie pressed her hand to his lips in a gesture of old-fashioned charm. 'Go to him, Mimi. I'll be right behind you.'

'I love you, Charlie.'

'Love you too. Just get on with it, will you.'

Mimi turned to face the congregation. Everyone's face was tipped round, towards her. All their friends and family. There would be time for all of them later, but right now all she could see was Rafe.

He looked so handsome in his dark suit and brocade waistcoat, the subtle pattern of which matched the theme of her dress. The organist struck up the Wedding March, and the sudden wall of sound made Ellie jump and run back towards Mimi, instead of walking up the aisle, scattering petals as she was supposed to.

Charlie caught Ellie, lifting her up onto his lap, and she decided that now was a good time to start throwing petals. Rafe was chuckling, holding out his hand towards her. Mimi couldn't wait any longer. Leaving Charlie to follow with Ellie, she almost ran up the aisle towards him.

* * * * *

Look out for the next great story in the
STRANDED IN HIS ARMS *duet*

SAVED BY THE SINGLE DAD

*And if you enjoyed this story, check out these
other great reads from Annie Claydon*

*DISCOVERING DR RILEY
THE DOCTOR SHE'D NEVER FORGET
DARING TO DATE HER EX
SNOWBOUND WITH THE SURGEON*

All available now!

SAVED
BY THE SINGLE DAD

BY
ANNIE CLAYDON

MILLS
BOON®

Published in Great Britain 2016
By Mills & Boon, an imprint of HarperCollins*Publishers*
1 London Bridge Street, London, SE1 9GF

© 2016 Annie Claydon

ISBN: 978-0-263-91510-5

Printed and bound in Spain
by CPI, Barcelona

Dear Reader,

When I started to write *Saved by the Single Dad* I knew that my heroine was going to be a bit special—so she needed a special name. And when I settled on one it meant a phone call to one of my friends—did she mind if I appropriated her name for my heroine? The real Cassandra rather liked the idea that the fictional Cassandra would be six feet tall, flame-haired and able to lift the hero off his feet, and so my heroine was born. She's very different from my friend, but in my eyes they have one thing in common. They're both true heroines.

Of course a heroine like this needs a special hero. Many men would be challenged by Cass's do-anything attitude but Jack loves it—which is precisely what I like about him.

Thank you for reading Jack and Cass's story. I always enjoy hearing from readers, and you can contact me via my website at annieclaydon.com.

Annie x

For the real Cassandra

Books by Annie Claydon

Mills & Boon Medical Romance

The Doctor Meets Her Match
The Rebel and Miss Jones
Re-awakening His Shy Nurse
Once Upon a Christmas Night...
200 Harley Street: The Enigmatic Surgeon
A Doctor to Heal Her Heart
Snowbound with the Surgeon
Daring to Date Her Ex
The Doctor She'd Never Forget
Discovering Dr Riley

Visit the Author Profile page at
millsandboon.co.uk for more titles.

**Praise for
Annie Claydon**

'A compelling, emotional and highly poignant read
that I couldn't bear to put down. Rich in pathos,
humour and dramatic intensity, it's a spellbinding
tale about healing old wounds, having the courage to
listen to your heart and the power of love that kept me
enthralled from beginning to end.'

—*Goodreads* on
Once Upon a Christmas Night...

CHAPTER ONE

JACK PUT HIS head down, trying to shield his face from the stinging rain. Behind him, his ambulance was parked on the road, unable to make it across the narrow bridge that was now the only way into the small village of Holme. Ahead of him, a heavily pregnant woman who should be transported to hospital before the late summer floods in this area of Somerset got any worse.

He and Mimi had been in worse situations before. They'd crewed an ambulance together for the last seven years, Mimi in the driver's seat and Jack taking the lead in treating their patients. They were a good team.

But, however good they were, they couldn't stop it from raining. The main road to the hilltop village was under three feet of water and this back road led across a narrow bridge that was slick with mud. Rather than risk the ambulance getting stuck halfway across, they'd decided to make the rest of the journey on foot.

There were still plenty of options. The patient wasn't in labour yet, and maybe a four-by-four could bring her down the hill to the waiting ambulance. Maybe the storm would clear and the HEMS team could airlift her out. Maybe the support doctor Jack had requested would arrive soon, and maybe not. If all else failed, he and Mimi had delivered babies together before now.

His feet slid on a patch of mud and he gripped the heavy medical bag slung over his shoulder, lurching wildly for a moment before he regained his balance. 'Careful...' He muttered the word as an instruction to himself. Slipping and breaking his leg wasn't one of the options he had been considering.

'One, two, three...' In a grim version of the stepping game he played with Ellie, his four-year-old daughter, he traversed the bridge, trying to ignore the grumbling roar of thunder in the hills. He'd wait for Mimi on the far bank of the river. She'd walked back up the road a little to get reception on her phone and check in with the Disaster Control Team, but they shouldn't lose sight of each other.

He thought he heard someone scream his name but it was probably just the screech of the wind. Then, as the roar got louder, he realised that it wasn't thunder.

Jack turned. A wall of water, tumbling down from the hills, was travelling along the path of the riverbed straight towards him.

His first instinct was to trust the power and speed of his body and run, but in a moment of sudden clarity he knew he wouldn't make it up the steep muddy path in front of him in time. A sturdy-looking tree stood just yards away, its four twisting trunks offering some hope of protection, and Jack dropped his bag and ran towards it.

He barely had a chance to lock his hands around one of the trunks and suck in one desperate breath before the water slammed against his back, expelling all of the precious oxygen from his lungs in one gasp as it flattened him against the bark. A great roar deafened him and he kept his eyes tight shut against the water and grit hitting his face. *Hang on.* The one and only thing he could do was hang on.

Then it stopped. Not daring to let go of the tree trunk,

Jack opened his eyes, trying to blink away the sting of the dirty water. Another sickening roar was coming from upstream.

The next wave was bigger, tearing at his body. He tried to hold on but his fingers slipped apart and he was thrown against the other three trunks, one of them catching the side of his head with a dizzying blow. There was no point in trying to hold his breath and a harsh bellow escaped his lips as his arms flailed desperately, finding something to hold on to and clinging tight.

Then, suddenly, it stopped again. Too dazed to move, Jack lay twisted in the shelter of the branches, his limbs trembling with shock and effort. He was so cold…

Mimi… He tried to call for her, hoping against all hope that she hadn't been on the bridge when the water had hit, but all he could do was cough and retch, dirty water streaming out of his nose and mouth.

He gasped in a lungful of air. 'Mimi…'

'Stay down. Just for a moment.'

A woman's voice, husky and sweet. Someone was wiping his face, clearing his eyes and mouth.

'Mimi… My partner.'

'She's okay. I can see her on the other side of the river.' That voice again. He reached out towards it and felt a warm hand grip his.

He opened his eyes, blinking against the light, and saw her face. Pale skin, with strands of short red hair escaping from the hood of her jacket. Strong cheekbones, a sweet mouth and the most extraordinary pale blue eyes. It was the kind of face you'd expect to find on some warrior goddess…

He shook his head. He must be in shock. Jack knew better than most the kind of nonsense that people babbled in situations like this. Unless she had a golden sword tucked away under her dark blue waterproof jacket, she was just an ordinary mortal, her face rendered ethereal because it was the first thing he'd seen when he opened his eyes.

'Are you sure? Mimi's okay?'

The woman glanced up only briefly, her gaze returning to him. 'She's wearing an ambulance service jacket. Blonde hair, I think…'

'Yes, that's her.' Jack tried to move and found that his limbs had some strength in them now.

'Are you hurt?'

'No…' No one part of him hurt any more than the rest and Jack decided that was a good sign. 'Thanks…um…'

'I'm Cass… Cassandra Clarke.'

'Jack Halliday.'

She gave a small nod in acknowledgement. 'We'd better not hang around here for too long. Can you stand?'

'Yeah.'

'Okay, take it slowly.' She reached over, disentangling his foot from a branch, and then scrambled around next to him, squeezing her body in between him and one of the tree trunks. With almost no effort on his part at all, he found himself sitting up as she levered her weight against his, her arms supporting him. Then she helped him carefully to his feet.

He turned, looking back over the bridge to find Mimi. Only the bridge wasn't there any more. A couple of chunks of masonry were all that was left of it, rolling downstream under the pressure of the boiling water. He could see Mimi standing on the other side, staring fixedly at him, and beside her stood a man who he thought he recognised. Behind them, the lights still on and the driver's door open, was a black SUV.

'All right?' Now that he was on his feet, he could see that Cass was tall, just a couple of inches shorter than him.

'Yeah. Thanks.' Jack felt for his phone and found that he had nothing in his pocket apart from a couple of stones and a handful of sludge. 'I need to get to a phone…'

'Okay. The village is only ten minutes away; we'll get you up there first.' She spoke with a quiet, irresistible authority.

Jack waved to Mimi, feeling a sharp ache in his shoulder as he raised his arm. She waved back, both hands reaching out towards him as if she was trying to retrieve him. Moving his hand in a circular motion as a sign that he'd call her, he saw the man bend to pick something up. Mimi snatched her phone from him and looked at it for a moment and then turned her attention back on to Jack, sending him a thumbs-up sign.

'Did you mean to park the ambulance like that?' There was a note of dry humour in Cass's husky tones.

Jack looked over the water and saw that the ambulance had been washed off the road and was leaning at a precarious angle against a tree. He muttered a curse under his breath.

'I'll take that as a no.'

Jack chuckled, despite the pain in his ribs. 'What are you?'

She flushed red as if this was the one question she didn't know how to answer. In someone so capable, the delicate shade of pink on her cheeks stirred his shaking limbs into sudden warmth.

'What do you mean?'

'None of this fazes you very much, does it? And you've been trained in how to lift…' Jack recognised the techniques she'd used as very similar to his own. A little more leverage and a little less strength, maybe. And, although Cass didn't give any orders, the men around her seemed to recognise her as their leader.

'I'm a firefighter. I work at the fire station in town, but I'm off duty at the moment. On duty as a concerned family member, though—my sister Lynette's the patient you're coming to see.'

'Then we'd better get going.' Jack looked around for his bag and saw that one of the men was holding it, and that water was dripping out of it. He really was on his own here—no Mimi and no medical bag. He turned, accepting a supportive arm from one of the men, and began to walk slowly up the steep path with the group.

This wasn't what Cass had planned. She'd hoped to be able to get Lynette safely to hospital well in advance but, stubborn as ever, her sister had pointed out that it was another two weeks before her due date and flatly refused to go.

The hospital was now out of reach, but a paramedic was the next best thing. And the floods had finally given her a break and quite literally washed Jack up, on to her doorstep.

Despite the layers of clothing, she'd still felt the strength of his body when she'd helped him up. Hard muscle, still pumped and quivering with the effort of holding on. It had taken nerve to stay put and hang on instead of trying to run from the water, but that decision had probably saved his life.

He was tall as well, a couple of inches taller than her own six feet. And despite, or maybe because of, all that raw power he had the gentlest eyes. The kind of deep brown that a girl could just fall into.

Enough. He might be easy on the eye, but that was nothing to do with her primary objective. Jack was walking ahead of her and Cass lengthened her stride to catch up with him.

'Lynette's actually been having mild contractions. She's not due for another two weeks, but it seems as if the baby might come sooner.' It was better to think of him as an asset, someone who could help her accomplish the task ahead. Bravery had got him here in one piece and those tender eyes might yet come in useful, for comforting Lynette.

'Her first child?'

'Yes.' And one that Cass would protect at all costs.

'Hopefully it'll decide not to get its feet wet just yet. The weather's too bad for the HEMS team to be able to operate safely tonight, but we may be able to airlift her out in the morning.'

'Thanks. You'll contact them?'

'Yeah. Can I borrow your phone? I need to get hold of Mimi as well.'

'Of course, but we'll get you inside first. Who's the guy with her?'

'If it's who I think it is, that's her ex.' A brief grin. Brief but very nice. 'Mimi's not going to like *him* turning up out of the blue.'

'Complicated?'

'Isn't it always?'

He had a point. In any given situation, the complications always seemed to far outweigh the things that went right. Which meant that someone as gorgeous as Jack was probably dizzyingly complicated.

'She'll be okay, though? Your partner.'

'Oh, yeah. No problems with Rafe; he won't leave her stranded. He might have to tie her to a tree to stop her from killing him, but she'll be okay.' Despite the fact that Jack was visibly shivering, the warmth in his eyes was palpable.

Maybe Cass should have done that with *her* ex, Paul. Tied him to a tree and killed him when she'd had the chance. But he was a father now, and probably a half decent one at that. He had a new wife, and a child who depended on him.

'I don't suppose there's any way we can get some more

medical supplies over here?' Jack's voice broke her reverie. 'Rafe's a doctor and, knowing him, he'll have come prepared for anything. I could do with a few things, just in case.'

Cass nodded. 'Leave it with me; I'll work something out. You need to get cleaned up and into some dry clothes before you do anything else.'

'Yeah.' The tremble of his limbs was making it through into Jack's voice now. 'I could do with a hot shower.'

'That's exactly where we're headed. Church hall.'

'That's where we're staying tonight?' He looked towards the spire, which reached up into the sky ahead of them like a beacon at the top of the hill.

'Afraid so. The water's already pretty deep all around the village. In this storm, and with the flash floods, there's no safe place to cross.'

She could count on the water keeping him here for the next twenty-four hours at least, perhaps more if she was lucky. He might not want to stay, but there was no choice.

'I'm not thinking of trying to get across. Not while I have a patient to tend to.'

'Thank you. I really appreciate that.' Cass felt suddenly ashamed of herself. This guy wasn't an asset, a cog in a piece of machinery. He was a living, breathing man and his dedication to his job wasn't taken out of a rule book.

She reminded herself, yet again, that this kind of thinking would only get her into trouble. Paul had left her because she'd been unable to get pregnant. Then told her that the problem was all hers, proving his point by becoming a father seven months later. In the agony of knowing that she might never have the baby she so wanted, the indignity of the timing was almost an afterthought.

That was all behind her. The tearing disappointment each month. The wedding, which Paul had postponed time and time again and had ended up cancelled. Lynette's baby was the one she had to concentrate on now, and she was going to fight tooth and nail to get everything that her sister needed.

Jack was taking one thing at a time. He fixed his eyes on the church steeple, telling himself that this was the goal for the time being and that he just had to cajole his aching limbs into getting there.

Slowly it rose on the horizon, towering dizzily above his head as they got closer. The church had evidently been here for many hundreds of years but, when Cass led him around the perimeter of the grey, weatherworn stones, the building behind it was relatively new. She walked through a pair of swing doors into a large lobby filled with racks of coats. At the far end, shadows passed to and fro behind a pair of obscure glass doors, which obviously led to the main hall.

'The showers are through here.' Cass indicated a door at the side of the lobby.

'Wait.' There was one thing he needed to do, and then he'd leave the rest to Cass and hope that the water was hot. 'Give me your phone.'

She hesitated. 'The medical bags can wait. You need to get warm.'

'Won't take a minute.' He held out his hand, trying not to wince as pain shot through his shoulders and Cass nodded, producing her phone from her pocket.

'Thank you. Tell her that we're going back down to fetch the medical supplies. I think I know how we can get them across.'

It didn't come as any particular surprise that she had a plan. Jack imagined that Cass was the kind of person who always had a plan. She was tall and strong, and moved with the controlled grace of someone who knew how to focus

on the task in hand. Now that she'd pulled her hood back
her thick red hair, cut in a layered style that was both practical and feminine, made her seem even more gorgeously
formidable.

His text to Mimi was answered immediately and confirmed that it was Rafe that he'd seen. Jack texted again,
asking Mimi to pack whatever spare medical supplies they
had into a bag.

'Here.' He passed the phone back to Cass. 'She's waiting for your call.'

'Thanks.' She slipped the phone into her pocket. 'Now
you get warm.'

She led the way through to a large kitchen, bustling with
activity, which suddenly quieted as they tramped through in
their muddy boots and wet clothes. Beyond that, a corridor
led to a bathroom, with a sign saying 'Women Only' hung
on the door. Cass popped her head inside and then flipped
the sign over, to display the words 'Men Only'.

It looked as if he had the place to himself. There was a
long row of handbasins, neat and shining, with toilet cubicles lined up opposite and bath and shower cubicles at
the far end. The place smelled of bleach and air freshener.

'Put your clothes there.' She indicated a well-scrubbed
plastic chair next to the handbasins. 'I'll send someone to
collect them and leave some fresh towels and we'll find
some dry clothes. What size are you…?'

The question was accompanied by a quick up and down
glance that made Jack shiver, and a slight flush spread over
Cass's cheeks. 'Large will have to do, I think.' She made
the words sound like a compliment.

'Thanks. That would be great.'

'Do you need any help?' She looked at him steadily.
'I'm relying on you, as a medical professional, to tell me if
there's anything the matter with you.'

If he'd thought for one moment that Cass would stay and help him off with his clothes, instead of sending someone else in to do it, Jack might just have said yes. 'No. I'll be fine.'

'Good.' She turned quickly, but Jack caught sight of a half-smile on her lips. Maybe she would have stayed. Working in an environment that was still predominantly male, Jack doubted that she was much fazed by the sight of a man's body.

He waited for the door to close behind her before he painfully took off his jacket and sweater. Unbuttoning his shirt, he stood in front of the mirror to inspect some of the damage. It was impossible to tell what was what at the moment. A little blood, mixed with a great deal of mud from the dirty water. He'd shower first and then worry about any bumps and scratches.

A knock at the door and a woman's voice, asking if she could come in, disturbed the best shower Jack could remember taking in a long time. Hurried footsteps outside the cubicle and then he was alone again, luxuriating in the hot water.

After soaping his body twice, he felt almost clean again. Opening the cubicle door a crack, he peered out and found the bathroom empty; two fluffy towels hung over one of the handbasins. One was large enough to wind around his waist and he rubbed the other one over his head to dry his hair.

He looked a mess. He could feel a bump forming on the side of his head and, although his jacket had largely protected the rest of him, he had friction burns on his arms, which stung like crazy, and a graze on his chest from where the zip on his jacket had been driven against the skin.

'Coming in…' A rap on the door and a man's voice. A slim, sandy-haired man of about forty entered, carrying a pile of clothes and a pair of canvas shoes. 'Hi, Jack. I'm Martin.'

He was wearing a light windcheater, white letters on a dark blue background on the right hand side, in the same place that Jack's paramedic insignia appeared on his uniform. When he turned, the word was repeated in larger letters across his back.

'You're the vicar, then.' Jack grinned.

'Yeah. My wife seems to think this is a good idea, just in case anyone mistakes me for someone useful.'

'I'd always be glad to see you coming.' Hope and comfort were often just as important as medical treatment.

'Likewise. We're grateful for all you did to get here.' Martin propped the clothes on the ledge behind the washbasins. 'They look nasty.' His gaze was on the friction burns on Jack's arms.

'Superficial. They'll be okay.' Jack riffled through the clothes. A T-shirt, a grey hooded sweatshirt and a pair of jeans that looked about his size. He picked the T-shirt up and pulled it over his head so that he didn't have to think about the marks on his arms and chest any more. 'How's my patient?'

'Lynette's fine. She's over at the vicarage, drinking tea with my wife and complaining about all the fuss. She seems to have got it into her head that she's got some say about when the baby arrives.'

'You were right to call. At the very least she needs to be checked over.'

Martin nodded. 'Thanks. Cass has gone to get your medical supplies. Goodness only knows how she's going to manage it, but knowing Cass…'

Even the mention of her name made Jack's heart beat a little faster. 'She seems very resourceful.'

Martin nodded. 'Yeah. Bit too resourceful sometimes.

Now, important question. Tea or coffee? I don't think I can keep the Monday Club under control for much longer.'

Jack chuckled. 'Tea. Milk, no sugar, thanks.'

'Good. And I hope you like flapjacks or I'm going to have a riot on my hands.'

'You seem very organised here.'

Martin nodded. 'This church has been taking people in for the last eight hundred years. Wars, famine, fires… Now floods. I've never seen anything like this, though, and I've been here fifteen years. Half the village is flooded out.'

'How many people do you have here?'

'Just a couple of families staying overnight. We've found everyone else billets in people's homes. But everyone eats here, and we have an action committee…' Martin shrugged, grinning. 'That's Cass's baby. I confine myself to tea and sympathy.'

Jack reckoned that Martin was downplaying his own considerable role. 'And hospitality.'

'We've never turned anyone away before, and that's not going to start on my watch.' A trace of determination broke through Martin's affable smile and was quickly hidden. 'Anything else you need?'

'A phone? I'd like to call home.'

'Yes, of course. The landline at the vicarage is still working; you can use that.' Martin turned, making for the door. 'Come to the kitchen when you're ready and I'll take you over there.'

CHAPTER TWO

MARTIN OPENED A side door that led out of the kitchen and they walked along a paved path, sheltered by makeshift awnings that boasted a few scraps of soggy coloured bunting hanging from the corners. Then through a gate and into the vicarage kitchen, which oozed warmth and boasted a table large enough to seat a dozen people.

Lynette was red-haired like her sister, her features prettier and yet somehow far less attractive. She was heavily pregnant and Jack's first impressions were that she was in the best of health. Although she'd been having minor contractions, she seemed stubbornly positive that the baby wasn't coming yet. Jack begged to differ, but kept that thought to himself.

He left Lynette on the sofa by the kitchen range and sat down at the table, where a cup of tea was waiting for him. 'I'll be able to examine you a little more thoroughly when your sister gets back with my medical bag.'

'Thanks. But there's really no need to worry. First babies are always late, aren't they?'

Sue, the vicar's wife, frowned. 'Not necessarily. My Josh was early.' She pushed a large plate of flapjacks across the table towards Jack. 'If I eat another one of those I'll be sorry when I get on the scales. I wish the Monday Club would stop cooking...'

Lynette laughed. 'Not much chance of that. Mrs Hawes doesn't like to see anyone going hungry.'

Sue sighed, looking up as someone rapped on the glass pane of the back door. 'It's open...'

The door swung inwards and two bags were placed inside. Then Cass appeared, her hair wet and slicked back from her face, holding her muddy boots in one hand and her wet jacket and overtrousers in the other. Sue relieved her of them and disappeared to put them in the front porch.

'You got two across?' Jack bent to inspect the contents of the bags.

'Yeah, we got a line over about quarter of a mile down from the bridge. Mimi's okay and she's going back to the hospital with what's-his-name.' The corners of her mouth quirked into an expression that would have been unfathomable if Jack hadn't been able to guess the situation. 'She sends you her love.'

Jack nodded, drawing a stethoscope and blood pressure monitor from the bag. 'Right, ladies. If you're comfortable here, Lynette, I'll get on and do a more thorough examination.'

He'd given Lynette one last flash of those tender eyes and smiled at her, pronouncing that everything was fine. Lynette hadn't even noticed what he hadn't said, but Cass had.

'She's in the early stages of labour, isn't she?' Cass had shown him through to the small room behind the church hall, which had been earmarked as his sleeping quarters and already boasted a hastily erected camp bed in the corner, with sheets and blankets folded on top of it.

'Yes. Although this could be a false alarm...'

Another thing he wasn't saying. 'And it might not be.'

'Yes.' He scrubbed his hand back across his scalp, his

short dark hair spiking untidily. 'I have everything I need, and I've delivered babies plenty of times before.'

'Really?' Jack was saying everything she wanted to hear, and Cass wondered how much of it was just reassurance.

'It's not ideal, but we'll get her to the hospital as soon as the weather lifts. In the meantime, you've done your job and you can rely on me to do mine.'

A small curl of warmth quieted some of the fear. 'Thanks. This baby is…' Important. All babies were important, but this one was important to her.

'I know. And he's going to be fine.' His eyes made her believe it. 'Is the father on the scene?'

'Very much so. He's not here, though; Lynette's husband is in the Royal Navy and he's away at the moment. My father works abroad too; Mum was going to come home next week to help out.'

'So it's just you and me then.' He contrived to make that sound like a good thing. 'You're her birth partner?'

'Yep.' Cass pressed her lips together. Going to classes with Lynette had seemed like the most natural thing in the world. The most beautiful form of sharing between sisters. Now it was all terrifying.

'Good.' His gaze chipped away at yet another piece of the fear that had been laying heavy on her chest for days, and suddenly Cass wondered if she might not make a half decent job of it after all.

'I'd rather be…' Anything. 'I'd rather be doing something practical.'

He laughed. 'This is the most practical thing in the world, Cass. The one thing that never changes, and hopefully never will. You'll both be fine.'

She knew that he was trying to reassure her, and that his *You'll both be fine* wasn't a certainty, but somehow it seemed to be working. She walked over to the coil of ropes and pulleys that had been dumped here while she'd taken the bags through to the vicarage.

'I'll get these out of your way.'

'Let me help you.' Before she could stop him, he'd picked up the rope, leaving Cass to collect the remaining pulleys and carabiners up and put them into a rucksack. 'You used this to get the bags across?'

'Yeah.' Hopefully he was too busy thinking about childbirth to take much notice of what he was carrying. The cut end was clearly visible, hanging from the coil of rope. 'I borrowed the gear from one of the guys in the village who goes mountaineering.' She slung the rucksack over her shoulder and led the way through to the storeroom, indicating an empty patch of floor, but Jack shook his head.

'Not there; it's too close to the radiator and rope degrades if it dries out too fast. Help me move these boxes and we'll lay it flat over here.'

Cass dumped the rucksack and started to lift the boxes out of the way. 'You know something about rope?'

'Enough to know that this one's been cut recently, while it was under stress. Mountaineering ropes don't just break.' He bent to finger the cut end and then turned his gaze on to her.

The security services had missed a trick in not recruiting Jack and putting him to work as an interrogator. Those quiet eyes made it impossible not to admit to her greatest follies. 'I...cut the rope.'

Somehow that wasn't enough. He didn't even need to ask; Cass found herself needing to tell him the rest.

'Mimi shouted across, asking if we had a harness. They both seemed determined to try and get across, and medical bags are one thing...'

'But lives are another?' he prompted her gently.

'Yeah. I was worried that they'd just go ahead and do it,

and as soon as one of them put their weight on the ropes I wouldn't be able to stop them. So, when we got hold of the second bag, I cut the rope.'

He grinned. 'I couldn't see Mimi letting you haul a bag over and staying put herself on the other side. Nice job.'

Cass supposed she might as well tell him everything; he'd hear it soon enough. 'Not such a nice job. I miscalculated and the rope snapped back in their direction. Another few feet and it would have taken Mimi's head off.'

'It was…what, thirty feet across the river?'

'About that.'

'Weight of the bags…' He was obviously doing some kind of calculation in his head. 'Wouldn't have taken her head off. Maybe given her a bit of a sting.'

'Well, it frightened the life out of me. And what's-his-name…'

'Rafe…'

'Yeah, Rafe tackled her to the ground.'

Jack snorted with laughter. 'Oh, I'll bet she just loved that. Rafe always was a bit on the protective side where Mimi's concerned.'

'She didn't seem too pleased about it. What is it with those two? Light the blue touchpaper?'

'Yeah and stand a long way back.' Jack was still chuckling. 'Shame, really. They're both good people, but put them within fifty feet of each other and they're a disaster. Always will be.'

'I know the feeling…' All too well. Only Cass would be a disaster with any man. She'd never quite been able to move on from what Paul had said and done, never been able to shake the belief that he was right. She'd felt her heart close, retreating wounded from a world that had been too painful to bear.

He didn't reply. As Jack bent to finish arranging the

ropes so they'd dry out properly, Cass couldn't help noticing the strong lines of his body, the ripple of muscle. That didn't just happen; it must have taken some hard work and training.

'So you're a mountaineer?'

He shook his head, not looking at her. 'No. My father. It's not something I'd ever consider doing.'

That sounded far too definite not to be a thought-out decision. 'Too risky?' Somehow Cass doubted that; Jack had just braved a flood to get here.

'There's risk and risk. My father died when I was twelve, free climbing. Anyone with an ounce of sanity would have used ropes for that particular climb, but he went for the adrenaline high. He always did.' The sudden bitter anger in Jack's voice left Cass in no doubt about his feelings for his father.

'I'm really sorry...'

He straightened up. 'Long time ago. It was one of the things that made me want to go into frontline medicine. Going out on a limb to save a life has always seemed to me to be a much finer thing than doing it for kicks.'

'And of course we both calculate the risks we take pretty carefully.' Cass wondered whether Jack knew that the current calculation was all about him. She wanted to know more about the man who was responsible for Lynette's safety, to gauge his weaknesses.

He nodded. 'Yeah. Needs a cool head, not a hot one.'

Good answer. Cass turned to the door. 'Shall we go and see whether there's any more tea going?'

They collected their tea from an apparently unending supply in the kitchen, and Jack followed Cass as she dodged the few steps into the back of the church building. She led

him along a maze of silent corridors and through a doorway, so small that they both had to duck to get through it.

· They were in a closed porch. Arched wooden doors led
through to the church on one side and on the other a second
door was secured by heavy metal bolts. Tall, stone-framed
windows, glazed in a diamond pattern of small pieces of
glass, so old that they were almost opaque. A gargoyle,
perched up in a corner, grinned down at them.

'I reckoned you might like to drink your tea in peace.'
She reached up to switch on a battery-operated lantern,
which hung from one of the stone scrolls which flanked
the doorway. 'Martin's lent me this place for the duration.
I come here to think.'

It looked more like somewhere to hide than think. Jack
wondered why she should need such a place when she was
clearly surrounded by family and friends here. She seemed
so involved with her community, so trusted, and yet somehow she held herself apart from it.

All the same, for some reason she'd let him in and it felt
like too much of a privilege to question it. Jack took his
jacket off and sat down on one of the stone benches that
ran the length of the porch. She proffered a cushion, from
a pile hidden away in an alcove in the corner, and he took
it gratefully.

'You've made yourself at home here. It's warm as well.
And oddly peaceful.' Jack looked around. Listening to the
storm outside, rather than struggling against it, made the
old walls seem like a safe cocoon.

'I like it. These stones are so thick it's always the same
temperature, winter or summer.' She laid her coat out on
the bench and smoothed her half-dried hair behind her ears.

'Makes a good refuge.' He smiled, in an indication that
she could either take the observation seriously or pass it
off as a joke if she chose.

'Yeah. You should ask Martin about that; he's a bit of a history buff. Apparently there was an incident during the English Civil War when Cavaliers claimed refuge here. They camped out in this porch for weeks.'

Fair enough. So she didn't want to talk about it.

'I'd like you to stay with Lynette tonight, at the vicarage. Keep an eye on her.'

She nodded. 'I don't have much choice. My house is a little way downriver from the bridge. It was partially flooded even before this afternoon.'

'I'm sorry to hear that.'

Cass leaned back, stretching her legs out in front of her. 'I've been expecting it for days and at least I had a chance to get everything upstairs, which is a lot more than some people have had. It's my own stupid fault, anyway.'

'So you're the one, are you? That's been making it rain.'

She really was stunningly beautiful when she smiled. Warm and beautiful, actually, with a touch of vulnerability that belied her matter-of-fact attitude and her capable do-anything frame. But she seemed far too ready to blame herself when things went wrong.

'I wish. Then I could make it stop. The house has been in my family for generations and it's always been safe from flooding.'

'But not on your watch?' Jack realised he'd hit a nerve from the slight downward quirk of her lips.

'There used to be a drystone wall, banked up on the inside, which acted as a barrier between the house and the river. My grandparents levelled a stretch of it to give easy access to build an extension at the back. When they died they left the house to Lynette and me and, as she and Steven already had a place up in the village, I bought her out. I was pretty stretched for cash and thought I couldn't afford to reinstate the wall for a few years. Turns out I couldn't afford not to.'

'You're being a bit hard on yourself, aren't you? I'd be devastated if my place were flooded.'

Cass shrugged. 'I'm concentrating on Lynette and the baby. Bricks and mortar can wait.'

Jack nodded, sipping his tea.

'So how about you?' She seemed intent on changing the subject now. 'You have children?'

'A little girl. Ellie's four.'

She smiled. 'That's nice. I'm sorry we're keeping you away from her.'

If he was honest, he was sorry about that too. Jack knew exactly what it was like to have to come to terms with the idea that his father was never coming back, and he'd promised Ellie that he would always come back for her. Right now the storm and the floods made that impossible, and the feeling that he was letting Ellie down was eating at him.

Cass didn't need to know that. 'I'm concentrating on Lynette and the baby too.' He received a bright grin in acknowledgement of the sentiment. 'I'd really like to call my daughter to say goodnight, though. Would you mind if I borrowed your phone?'

'Yes, of course.' She stood up, handing her phone over. 'I'll leave you to it.'

'That's okay. Say hello to her.'

She hesitated and then sat back down with a bump. Awkwardly, she pointed to one of the icons on the small screen.

'You could try a video call. She might like to see you.'

'Yeah, she would. Thanks.'

Jack couldn't remember his sister's mobile number so he called the landline, repeating Cass's mobile number over to Sarah. 'My sister's going to get back to us.'

'Your wife works too?'

'I'm a single father. Sarah has a boy of Ellie's age and she looks after her when I'm working.'

'Sounds like a good arrangement.' She seemed to be getting more uncomfortable by the minute. If he hadn't already come to the conclusion that Cass could deal with almost anything, he would have said she was flustered.

He didn't have time to question why because the phone rang. Cass leaned over, jabbing an icon on the screen to switch on the camera and answer the call.

He was so in love with Ellie. Cass had reckoned that a wife and family would put Jack firmly out of bounds, which was the best place for him as far as she was concerned. But he was handsome, caring, funny...*and single*. She was going to have to work a little harder now, because allowing herself to be tempted by Jack was just an exercise in loss.

'Daddeee!' An excited squeal came from the phone and Cass averted her gaze. Jack held the phone out in front of him, his features softening into a grin that made her want to run away screaming.

'Ellie! What are you up to, darling?'

'We're having tea. Then Ethan and me are going to watch our film.'

'Again, sweetie? Doesn't Auntie Sarah want to watch something else on TV?' He chuckled as a woman's voice sounded, saying that if it kept the kids quiet, she was happy.

'Listen, Ellie...' He waited until the commotion on the other end of the line subsided. 'Ellie, Daddy's got to work, so you'll be staying with Auntie Sarah for tonight.'

Silence. Then a little voice sounded. 'I know. Miss you, Daddy.'

Cass almost choked with emotion. When she looked at

Jack, he seemed to have something in his eye. 'I miss you too, sweetie. You know you're always my number one girl. And I'll be back soon to give you big hugs.'

'How big?'

'As big as a bear. No, bigger than that. As big as our house.'

A little squeal of delight from Ellie. Cass imagined that Jack's hugs were something to look forward to.

'As big as our house…'

'Yeah.' Jack was grinning broadly now. 'Be good for Auntie Sarah, won't you.'

'I'm always good.' Ellie's voice carried a note of reproof.

'Sure you are. Would you like to meet my new friend?' He winked at Cass and her heart jolted so hard she almost fainted. 'She's a firefighter.'

'She has a fire engine?' Ellie was obviously quite taken with the idea.

'Why don't you ask her?' Jack chuckled and handed the phone over to Cass.

A little girl was staring at her. Light brown curls and luminous brown eyes. She was the image of Jack.

'Hi, Ellie. I'm Cassandra.' She wondered whether Ellie was a bit young to get her tongue around the name. Child development wasn't her forte. 'All my friends call me Cass.'

'You're a fire lady? With a fire engine?' Ellie was wriggling excitedly.

'Yes, that's right.'

'Do you have a ladder?'

'Yes, more than one. And we have a hose, for putting out all the fires.'

'Auntie Sarah…!' Ellie clearly wanted to share this exciting news.

'Yes, I heard. Tell Cassandra that you've seen a fire engine.' The woman's voice again, laughing.

'I've seen a fire engine.' Ellie turned the edges of her mouth down theatrically. 'It was a long, long, long way away...'

Suddenly Cass knew exactly what to say to Ellie. 'Tell you what. We're having an Open Day at our fire station soon. We're showing all the children around...' She was about to add that Ellie would have to ask her father if she might come, but that seemed to be a foregone conclusion.

'Yesss! Daddeee!'

Jack shot Cass a wry smile. 'Do I get to come along too, Ellie?'

Cass thought she could almost see the little girl roll her eyes.

'You have to take me, Daddy. I can't drive...'

'Ah, yes, of course. Looks like it's the two of us, then. Say thank you to Cassandra.'

Jack leaned in, speaking over her shoulder, and Cass swallowed a gasp, suddenly aware that his body was very close.

'Thank you, Cassandra.'

Ellie managed the name without even blinking, and Jack chuckled.

'Time to say bye-bye now, sweetheart.' Ellie responded by waving and blowing a kiss, then Jack took the phone from her to say his own goodnight to his daughter.

Cass stood up, her limbs suddenly trembling. It was impossible to fall in love in so short a time and over the phone. And, if she was honest with herself, she hadn't fallen in love with Ellie's brown eyes but with Jack's. But he was a grown man. It was much easier to admit that his child was all she could see.

'She's gorgeous.' Cass had let him finish the call, looking away when he blew kisses to Ellie.

'Yeah.' His fingers lingered lovingly over the blank

screen for a moment, as if he couldn't quite let go of the memory of his daughter's face, and then he handed the phone back. 'I didn't think she'd manage to pronounce *Cassandra*.'

The second time he said her name was just as disturbing as the first. Awakening thoughts of what it might feel like to have him whisper it.

'She must be growing up fast.'

'Seems too fast, sometimes.' He shrugged. 'She loves fire engines…'

'Yeah, me too. You didn't mind me asking her to the Open Day?'

'Mind…?' He laughed. 'Sounds like fun. Do I get to sit in the driver's seat?'

'No. Children only. Dads get to watch.'

CHAPTER THREE

THEY'D EATEN IN the church hall, the dreaded Monday Club turning out to be a group of perfectly nice women who cooked good food in large quantities and didn't mind a laugh. The evening was spent at the vicarage with Lynette and Cass, who persuaded Martin to make up a fourth for board games. Then Jack made his apologies and retired to his sleeping quarters, shutting the door and lying down fully dressed on the camp bed.

Suddenly he felt very alone. Ellie would be tucked up in bed by now and although he knew that Sarah would have given her bedtime kisses on his behalf, he hadn't been there to give them himself. Mimi was probably exhausted and looking forward to a good night's sleep. Cass was...

He wasn't going to think about where Cass was. He had a child, and he had to protect her. Jack had made up his mind a long time ago that the best thing for Ellie was that he remained single.

He must have drifted off to sleep because the next thing he knew was a tingle behind his ear, and his eyes shot open involuntarily as he realised that someone was rubbing their finger gently on his skin. He blinked in the light that was flooding in through the doorway and saw Cass.

For one moment all he could think was that this was a delicious way to wake up, coaxed out of unconsciousness by a red-haired goddess. Then the urgency on her face snapped him back to reality.

'Her waters have broken. Jack…'

'Okay. I hear you.' Jack swung his legs from the bed and shook his head to bring himself to. He'd been hoping that this wouldn't happen. He had the training and the experience for it, and this certainly wasn't the most outlandish place that he and Mimi had delivered a baby before now. But without the possibility of any backup, and only the medical supplies that Rafe had sent, it was a heavy responsibility, which he had to bear alone.

This was no time to panic. Contrary to all his expectations, Cass was panicking enough for both of them at the moment.

Keeping his pace brisk but unhurried in an effort to slow Cass down a bit, he picked up his medical bags and made for the vicarage. As they reached the back door they passed Martin, who was hurrying in the other direction, a sleeping child in his arms.

'Go through, Jack. Just getting the kids out of the way.'

Jack nodded. Following Cass through the kitchen and up the stairs, he found Sue and another woman on either side of Lynette, supporting her as she paced slowly up and down.

'We'll take her into my bedroom.' Sue looked up at him. 'There's an en suite bathroom, and the mattress in here is wet.'

'Thanks.' First things first. Jack smiled at Lynette, wiping a tear from her face. 'How are you doing?'

'Um… Okay. I think.'

'Good. You want to walk a bit more?'

Lynette nodded.

'All right. I'm going to get the other room ready for you, and then we'll take it from there. Tonight's your night, eh?'

'Yes… Thanks.'

Cass took Sue's place at Lynette's side, and Sue led him through to her own bedroom. Jack pulled the plastic under-sheet from his bag, silently thanking Rafe for thinking to pack it, and Sue set about stripping the bed.

When Cass supported Lynette through to the main bed-room, it seemed that everything was ready. She helped her sister sit down on the bed. 'Do you want your scented candles?'

'No!' Lynette's flailing hand found Jack's sweatshirt and held on tight. 'I want to keep a close eye on the guy with the pain relief...'

'I'm here.' Jack was calm and smiling. 'I'm going to wash my hands and I'll be right back, okay.'

'Yeah. Whatever.' Lynette frowned and closed her eyes.

Get the candles anyway... Jack mouthed the words to Cass and she hurried through to the other room to fetch Lynette's hospital bag.

When she got back, Sue waved her towards the bathroom door and Cass tapped on it tentatively. Jack was standing in front of the basin, his T-shirt and sweatshirt hung over the side of the bath, soaping his hands and arms. 'There's a clean T-shirt and some dressings in my medical bag. Will you get them, please?'

'Dressings? What's the matter?'

'Nothing. They're for me.' He grinned, turning round, and she saw the new bruises on his chest, the bright red gashes that ran across his sternum and upper arms.

Her sister was in labour. Now was a fine time to notice that his muscle definition was superb. Or to feel a tingle at the warmth of his smile. Cass swallowed hard.

'How did you do that...?' She pointed to the spot on her own arm to indicate the patch of red, broken skin on his. That had to hurt.

'It's just a friction burn. It's bleeding a little so best I cover it up.'

She nodded and went to fetch what he'd asked for. The dressings, along with a roll of tape and some scissors, were right at the top of the bag. Jack must have been thinking ahead.

'Okay, will you tape these on for me, please? Right around the edge so that there are no openings anywhere.'

Couldn't Sue do it? The temptation to run away and hide from his body almost made her ask. But her sister was out there having a baby, and Cass had already decided she'd do whatever it took.

He held the gauze in place and she taped around it for him. Trying not to notice the fresh smell of soap on skin. Trying not to think about how close he was, or how perfect.

'Thanks. That's great.' He nodded his approval and Cass stepped back, almost colliding with the linen basket. Then, thankfully, he pulled the T-shirt over his head.

'Ready?' His smile held all of the warmth that she could want for Lynette. Which happened to be a great deal more than Cass could deal with.

'Yes. I'm ready.' Cass had told herself that this was going to be the best night of her life. Being with Lynette all the way, seeing her nephew being born. Now, all she could feel was fear, for everything that could go wrong.

He was calm and quiet, soothing Lynette when the contractions eased and helping her concentrate and breathe when they came again. When Lynette became frightened and overwhelmed, he was there with reassurance and encouragement. When she wanted to change position, he let her lean on him. When she needed pain relief, he was there with the Entonox.

Lynette seemed almost serene when she wasn't crying

in pain, switching from one to the other with astonishing rapidity.

'Is this right?' Cass mouthed the words to Jack.

Jack's gaze flipped to the portable monitors at Lynette's side. 'Yeah, we're okay.'

'It's so fast…' Cass had been preparing for a long haul, but it had barely been an hour since she'd woken him up and already he was telling Lynette that they were nearly there.

'That's a good thing. Lynette's fine and so is the baby.'

Ten minutes later, her nephew was born. Jack cleared his mouth, rubbing his chest gently. Everyone held their breath and then the little man began to cry. Lynette squeezed Cass's hand so tight that she thought she was going to break her fingers.

'Say hello to your mum…' Jack laid the baby on Lynette's chest and covered him over with a towel. The two women lay on the bed together, cradling the baby, in a daze of happiness.

Suddenly, it was all perfect. Martin had welcomed the newest member of the village to the world, and Sue went to make tea and toast. Jack managed everything perfectly, melting into the background, clearing up and making the medical checks that were needed, without intruding into their bubble.

Then the call came from Lynette's husband, saying he'd received the photo that Cass had sent and was ready and waiting for a video call. Lynette was left alone for a few minutes to talk to him and show him their new son.

Cass waited outside the door, a sudden heaviness settling on her. However close she and Lynette were, however much her sister had needed her, it wasn't her baby. It was Lynette and Steven's. Their joy. One that she would only ever feel second-hand.

This wasn't the time. There were too many special moments ahead for her to spoil with her own selfishness. And they came soon enough. The moment when Jack helped Lynette to encourage her son to feed, and he finally got the hang of what he was supposed to do. The moment when his eyelids flickered open and Cass stared for the first time into his pale blue eyes.

'Do you have a name for him yet?' Jack was busy repacking his medical bag.

'We did have. But we've decided on something different.' Lynette smiled. 'We reckon Noah.'

'Very appropriate.' Jack chuckled.

'Is Jack a nickname for John?' She was beginning to tire now, and had lost the thread of what she was saying a couple of times already.

'Yep. Named after my grandfather. They used to call him Jack as well.'

'Noah John has a nice ring to it, don't you think?'

Jack turned. 'What does your husband think?'

'Steven suggested it. What you did tonight meant everything, to both of us, and we'd really like to have your name as his middle name. If you don't mind, that is.'

A broad grin spread over Jack's face. 'I'd be very honoured. Thank you.' He walked over to the bed, bending down to stroke the side of little Noah's face with his finger. The tiny baby opened his eyes, seeming to focus on Jack, although Cass knew that he couldn't really focus on anything just yet.

'Hey there, Noah.' Jack's voice was little more than a whisper. 'We guys have to stick together, you know. Especially since we share a name now. What do you say we let your mum get a bit of rest?'

'Will you and Cass look after him for me? I just want to close my eyes; I don't think I can sleep.'

'Of course.' Sue had prepared the Moses basket that she'd used for her children and Jack took Noah, setting him down in the cradle. But he immediately began to fret and Jack picked him up again, soothing him.

'Now what do we do?' Cass whispered the words at Jack. Sue and Martin had quietly left at the first suggestion of sleep, and Lynette's eyes had already drooped closed. It seemed that they were quite literally left holding the baby.

Jack chuckled quietly, nodding towards the easy chair in the corner of the room. 'Sit down. Over there.'

'Me?' She was suddenly gripped with panic. 'You want *me* to hold him?'

'I've got things to do. And it's about time he got acquainted with his aunt.'

It was almost a bitter thought. Holding her sister's baby and not her own. But in the peace and quiet of the room, candles guttering in their holders and a bedside lamp casting a soft glow, it was easy to forget that. Cass plumped herself down in the chair, wondering what Jack was going to do next.

'Suppose I drop him?'

'You won't.' Jack seemed to be able to manage the baby in one arm while he picked up a pillow from the bed in the other hand, dropping it on to her lap. 'Here you are. That's right.'

The sudden closeness felt so good she wanted to cry out. Jack's scent, mingling with that of a baby. Instinctively her arms curled around Noah and she rocked him gently, holding him against her chest. He fretted for a moment and then fell into a deep sleep.

'I just want to wake him up. See his eyes again…' She looked up at Jack and, when he smiled, Cass realised that all the wonder she felt must be written clearly on her face.

'Yeah, I know. Let him sleep for a while; being born is a tiring business.'

Jack fetched a straight-backed chair from the kitchen and sat in the pool of light from the lamp, writing notes and keeping an eye on everyone. When Cass could tear her gaze from Noah, she watched Jack. Relaxed, smiling and unbearably handsome. She envied the shadows, which seemed to caress his face in recognition of a job well done.

When Noah woke and began to fuss a little, Lynette was immediately alert, reaching for her child. Jack delivered him to her and this time there were fewer grimaces and less messing around to get him to feed. Cass watched from the other side of the bed and, when he'd had enough and fallen back into sleep, she curled up with her sister on the bed, holding her hand until they both followed Noah's example and slept.

The morning dawned bright and clear. Jack had managed to sleep a little, in the chair in the corner of the room, and now he had heard from the HEMS team. They were flying, and would take advantage of the break in the weather to take Lynette and Noah to hospital.

Despite the early hour, a few people had gathered around the village green. An excited chatter accompanied the landing of the helicopter and a ragged cheer went up when its crew followed Jack towards the vicarage.

He said his goodbyes to Lynette and Noah inside, keeping his distance as the HEMS team took them outside with Cass. Jack wondered if this would be the last he ever saw of her and, despite all his resolutions, he found himself staring at her, as if to burn her image into his mind. But she waited for Lynette and the baby to be safely installed in the helicopter and then jogged back to stand at his side.

'There goes your last chance of getting out of the village

today. The roads are still blocked.' Cass's eyes seemed to be fixed on the disappearing speck in the sky.

Jack nodded. 'Yours too.'

'What does that make us?' She turned her querying gaze on to his face.

Jack shrugged. 'It makes us people who know our families are safe, and that the village might still need us.'

'It's not easy…'

'I don't think it's meant to be.' Jack's decision to stay had been made in the small hours of last night and it had torn him in two. Doing his job and being a good dad was a complex and sometimes heartbreaking juggling act.

'Well, it's done now. The only thing I can do to justify it is to make today count.' She smiled suddenly. 'Hungry?'

'Famished.' He looked at his watch. 'What time's breakfast?'

'Not for a couple of hours. We'll raid the kitchen.'

The kitchen was empty and she made toast while Jack made the tea. She rummaged in the cupboard, finding a couple of jars, and picked up two bananas from a crate in the corner. Then she led the way through to her private hidey-hole in the church porch.

'What is that?' It appeared that instead of choosing what she wanted on her toast, Cass was going for everything.

'Chocolate spread, then peanut butter and mashed banana. Try it; it's really nice.'

'Maybe another time. When I'm planning on not eating for the next two days.'

'A good breakfast sets you up for the day. You should know that; you're a medic.'

'Yeah. Perhaps I'd better not mention the sugar in that.'

She shrugged. 'I'll work it off.'

They ate in silence. His first slice of toast with peanut butter and his second with chocolate spread. Jack supposed that since he was going to eat the banana afterwards, he couldn't really poke too much fun at Cass's choice of breakfast.

It was still early and the glow of a new day, diffusing gently through the thick ancient glass, seemed to impose a relaxed camaraderie. Grabbing meals at odd hours after working most of the night. Talking, saying whatever came to mind without the usual filter of good manners and expediency. It felt as if anything could be asked, and answered.

'Is there someone waiting for you when we get out of here?'

She shrugged. 'Lots of people, I imagine.'

'I meant a partner...' It was becoming important to Jack to find out about all the subjects that Cass seemed to skirt around.

'Oh, that.' Jack wondered whether she really hadn't known what he was talking about. 'Big red truck. Makes a noise...'

'You're married to your job, then?'

She nodded, taking a bite from her toast. 'You?'

'I never married. And I don't get much time for socialising any more; when Ellie came along I had to make quite a few changes.'

She turned her querying eyes on to him and Jack wondered whether she wanted to know about him as much as he wanted to know about her. It was strangely gratifying.

'Then you have a *past*? How exciting.' The curve of her lip promoted an answering throb in his chest which made it hard to deny how much he liked it when Cass teased him.

'It's not that exciting.' Looking back, it seemed more desperate than anything. Desperate to find the warmth that was missing from his broken home, and yet afraid to commit to anyone in case they let him down, the way his father had let his mother down.

She gave him that cool once-over with her gaze which always left his nerve endings tingling. 'Bet you were good at it, though.'

That was undeniably a compliment, and Jack chuckled. 'I kept my head above water.'

Her eyes were full of questions, and suddenly Jack wanted to answer them all. 'Ellie's mother was the daughter of one of my dad's climbing partners; we practically grew up together. I went off to university and when I got back Sal was away climbing. It wasn't until years later that we found ourselves in the same place at the same time, for the weekend…'

'Okay. I've got your drift.' Cass held up her hand, clearly happy to forgo those particular details. 'So what about Ellie?'

'Fifteen months later, Sal turned up on my doorstep with her.'

'And you didn't know…?'

'Sal never said a word. She only got in touch then because she needed someone to take Ellie while she went climbing in Nepal.'

Cass choked on her toast. 'That must… I can't imagine what that must have been like.'

'It was love at first sight. And a wake-up call.'

'I can imagine. Bachelor about town one minute, in charge of a baby the next. However did you cope?'

'Badly at first. Sarah took me in hand, though; she got me organised and offered to take Ellie while I was at work.' Despite all of the sleepless nights, the worry, it had felt so right, as if he'd been looking for something in all the wrong places and finally found it on his own doorstep. He'd had no choice but to change his lifestyle, but Jack had done so gladly.

'And Ellie's mother?'

'She never came back. Sal died.'

Cass's shoulders shook as she was seized with another choking fit. Maybe he should wait with the story until she'd finished eating.

She put the toast down on to her plate and left it there. 'Jack… I'm so sorry. She was killed climbing?'

'No, she was trying to get in with an expedition to Everest. Of course no one would take her; there's a waiting list to get on to most of the peaks around there and you can't just turn up and climb. She wouldn't give up, though, and ended up sleeping rough. She was killed in a mugging that went wrong.'

'Poor Ellie…'

Her immediate concern for his child touched Jack. 'She's too young for it to really register yet. I just have to hope that I can be there for her when it does.'

Cass took a sip of her tea. 'I have a feeling you'll do a great job of helping Ellie to understand about her mother, when the time comes.'

'What makes you say that?'

She flushed pink. 'Because you're very reassuring. You were great with Lynette last night. In between all the grimaces, that was her *I'm very reassured* face.'

'Well, that's good to know. And what was yours?' He pulled a face, parodying wide-eyed panic.

Cass giggled. 'That was my *I hope no one notices I'm completely terrified* face.'

'Thought so.' He leaned towards her. 'I don't think anyone did.'

'That's okay, then.' The sudden glimpse behind the barriers that Cass put up between her and the world was electrifying. Her smiles, her laughter were bewitching. If things had been different…

But things weren't different. Ellie had already lost her

mother. No one should feel that loss twice, and if it meant
that Jack remained steadfastly single it was a small price
to pay for knowing that no one would ever have the chance
to leave Ellie again.

He took a gulp of tea. Maybe it was better to just stop
thinking about any of this and focus on the here and now.
'So what are your plans for the day?'

Crisis bonding. That was what it was. Jack wouldn't seem
half as handsome or a quarter as desirable if it hadn't been
for the floods and a long night, filled with every kind of
emotion imaginable. A little sleep and a lot of coffee would
fix everything.

Somehow Cass doubted that. But she had to tell herself
something before she started to fall for Jack. Because, when
it came down to it, his expectations were most probably the
same as any other man's.

And she would never really know what his expectations
were until she was in too deep. When Paul had first pro-
posed to her he'd never mentioned children, but the pressure
had started to grow as soon as it became apparent to both
of them that there might be a problem. She couldn't risk
the pain of trying again and being rejected when she failed.
No man, not even Jack, could guarantee that he wouldn't
leave her if she couldn't give him children.

It was better to accept being alone. And to concentrate
on today.

'Martin and I were going to go and visit Miss Palmer.
She's eighty-two and won't leave her house. She's pretty
feisty.'

He chuckled. 'What is it about this village? It's like a
nineteen-fifties horror film—some poor hapless paramedic
washed up to find himself in a remote place where all the
women are terrifying...'

He wasn't terrified at all; he was man enough to enjoy it. Cass grinned. 'We *are* all terrifying. There's something in the water.'

Jack leaned back, his shoulders shaking with laughter. 'I'll stick to bottled, then. And I don't much like the sound of an eighty-two-year-old on her own in these conditions. Want me to come along?'

'Yes. Thanks. Maybe we can grab a couple of hours sleep first, though. And some coffee.'

CHAPTER FOUR

'I WONDER IF she's got any cake.' Sleep seemed to have made Cass hungry again.

'Almost certainly.' Martin opened the front gate of one of a small, neat row of houses. 'I gather that the Monday Club came round here yesterday, after your visit.'

'That's all right then. What we can't eat, we can use to shore up the flood defences.' Cass stopped at the end of the path and Jack decided to wait with her, leaving Martin to approach the cottage alone.

The door was opened by a small, neatly dressed woman who might or might not be Miss Palmer. She didn't look eighty-two.

'Vicar. Lovely to see you.' She craned around to look at Cass and Jack. 'You've brought reinforcements, I see.'

Martin's shoulders drooped. Clearly, reinforcements were exactly what he needed.

'That her?' Jack murmured the words to Cass and she nodded, turning her back on the front door.

'Yep. She's…'

'Cassandra!' Cass jumped and swivelled back to face Miss Palmer. 'Do turn around, dear; you know I can't hear you.'

'Sorry. I forgot…'

Miss Palmer pursed her lips in disbelief. 'Well, come

in and have a cup of tea. And you can tell me all about last night.'

'News travels fast.' Cass strode up the front path. 'They're calling him Noah. Eight pounds, give or take.'

'Good.' Miss Palmer beamed her approval, leaning round to examine Jack. 'Is this your captive paramedic, dear?'

Jack was beginning to feel as if he was. Captivated by Cass's smile, longing to hear her laugh. Wanting to touch her.

'Yes. We found him washed up by the side of the river and we've decided to keep him. We've had him locked in the church hall.'

Miss Palmer nodded, enigmatic humour in her face. 'Leave your boots in the porch.'

The sitting room was bright and frighteningly clean, with the kind of orderliness that Jack remembered from before he'd had a child. One wall was entirely given over to glass-fronted bookcases and another was filled with framed photographs.

'My travels.' Miss Palmer caught Jack looking at them and came to stand by his side. 'Papua New Guinea… South Africa…'

Jack studied the black and white photographs. Some were the kind a tourist might take, posed with landmarks and things of interest, and others told a different story. Groups of children, ramshackle schools, a young woman whose air of determination couldn't be disguised by time and who had to be Miss Palmer.

'You worked abroad?'

'Yes. I'm a teacher. I came home when my mother became ill and looked after her for some years. Then I taught in the school, here.'

'And this one?' A colour photograph of Miss Palmer,

done up in waterproofs and walking boots, standing on high ground. Next to her, Cass had her arms held aloft in an unmistakable salute to some victory or other.

'Ah, yes.' Miss Palmer shot Cass a smile. 'We climbed Snowdon.'

'Miss Palmer raised a whole chunk of money...' Cass added and Miss Palmer straightened a little with quiet pride.

'Surprising how much people will sponsor you for when you're in your seventies.' A slight inclination of the head, as if Miss Palmer was sharing a secret. 'They think you're not going to make it to the top.'

'We showed them, though.' Cass broke in again.

'Yes, dear. We did.' Jack found himself on the end of one of Miss Palmer's quizzical looks. She was probably checking that he understood the point that she'd just made. If she could do all this, then a flood wasn't driving her from her home.

'I'll go and make the tea. Make yourselves comfortable.' Martin sat down suddenly, as if responding to an order. Jack reckoned that any prolonged exposure to Miss Palmer would have that effect on someone.

'I'll come and give you a hand.' Jack ignored Cass's raised eyebrows, motioning for her to stay put. He wanted to speak with Miss Palmer on her own.

She bustled, tight lipped, around the small modern kitchen. Jack gave her some space, leaning in the doorway his arms folded.

'So. What are we going to do, then?'

Miss Palmer faced him with a look of controlled ferocity. Jack imagined that she was used to a whole class quailing into silence at that.

'I had assumed you might be off duty.' She glared at his T-shirt and sweater.

'I'm never off duty. I dare say you can understand that.'

Miss Palmer didn't stop being a teacher as soon as she was out of the classroom. And Jack didn't stop being a paramedic just because his ambulance had been wrecked and his uniform soaked through.

'Yes, I do.' She laid cups and saucers carefully on a tray.

'Your friends are concerned about you. My job is to find out whether that concern is justified. To check whether you're okay, and if you are to leave you alone.'

Miss Palmer's set expression seemed to soften a little. 'This house is well above the flood line, and I'm lucky enough to have electricity and my phone still. Is it so much to ask, that I stay in my own home?'

'No. And I'll do my best to make sure that happens, but you've got to help me. If we can address any potential problems now, then that's a good first step.'

'Is this the way you deal with all the old ladies?'

'Yes, of course. Is this the way you deal with all your pupils?'

Miss Palmer smiled suddenly, her blue eyes twinkling with amusement. 'A hundred lines, young man. *I will not answer back.*'

Jack chuckled. He could see why Cass liked her so much; they were birds of a feather. Both as feisty as hell, with a sense of humour. 'Are you on any medication?'

Miss Palmer walked to the refrigerator and drew out a cardboard packet, which Jack recognised. 'Warfarin. What's that for—you have a blood clot?'

'A very small one. The doctors picked it up on a routine screening six months ago. I had an appointment for an X-ray a couple of days ago, to see whether the clot had dissolved yet, but I couldn't make it.'

'Okay. When was your last INR test?'

'Two weeks. I can't get to the hospital.'

'I'll get a test sent over; I can do one here.'

Miss Palmer nodded. 'Thank you. My INR is usually quite steady but…'

'Best to check.' The Warfarin would be thinning her blood to dissolve the clot. The INR test made sure that the dose was correct. 'Do you have some way of calling someone? In an emergency?'

Miss Palmer opened a cupboard and reached inside, producing a panic alarm.

'Is that working?' First things first. Then he'd tell her that there wasn't much point in keeping it in the cupboard.

'Yes, I try it out once a week.'

'I want you to check it every evening. And I want you to wear it.'

He was expecting some kind of argument but Miss Palmer nodded, putting the red lanyard around her neck and tucking the alarm inside her cardigan.

'I want it within reach at all times. Particularly when you're in bed or in the bathroom.'

'You're very bossy, aren't you?' Miss Palmer seemed to respect that.

'Yeah, very. But I'll make you a deal. You wear the alarm and let me give you a basic medical check, and I'll get everyone off your back.'

Miss Palmer held out her hand and Jack smiled, stepping forward. Her handshake was unsurprisingly firm. 'All right. Deal.'

Jack had obviously been carrying out some negotiation in the kitchen. When he reappeared with Miss Palmer, carrying the full tray of tea things for her, it was apparent that they'd struck up some understanding. At least he'd got her to wear her alarm.

Tea was drunk and Martin excused himself, leaving to make a call on another family in the street. Cass concentratcd on her second slice of cake while Jack busied himself, taking Miss Palmer's blood pressure, asking questions about her general health and checking on her heart and breathing.

Finally he seemed satisfied. 'Congratulations. I can find absolutely nothing wrong with you.'

'Not for want of looking.' Miss Palmer gave a small nod as Jack slipped the blood pressure cuff from her arm and she rolled down her sleeve. She liked people who were thorough in what they did, and clearly she approved of Jack.

'I'll be back with the INR test, and I expect to see you wearing your alarm.' Jack grinned at her. 'I might try and catch you by surprise.'

Miss Palmer beamed at him. 'Off with you, then.' She hardly gave him time to pack his bag before she was shooing him towards the door. Cass followed, hugging Miss Palmer and giving her a kiss on the cheek.

'Go carefully, Cassandra.'

'I will. You too, Izzy.' She whispered the name. It was something of an honour to call Isobel Palmer by her first name, reserved for just a few dear friends, and Cass didn't take it lightly.

She followed Jack down the front path and walked silently beside him until she was sure that Miss Palmer could no longer see them from her front window. 'All right, then. Give.'

He turned to her, raising an eyebrow. 'I've done a deal with her. She gets to stay as long as I'm allowed to satisfy myself that she's well and taking sensible precautions.'

'I don't like it.' Cass would much rather have her friend looked after for the time being. Martin had offered a place at the vicarage and, now that Lynette was gone, there was more than enough room.

'I know you don't. Look at it this way. What's important to her?'

'Her independence. I know that. But this wouldn't be for long.'

'That doesn't make any difference. Her community has still told her, loud and clear, that she can't cope. How do you suppose that's going to affect her in the long term?'

He had a point. 'But... Look, I really care about her.'

'Yes, that's obvious. And if there were any medical reason for her to leave her home, I'd be the first to tell you. But I'm not going to provide you with an excuse to make her leave, because taking away an elderly person's independence isn't something that anyone should do lightly.'

Cass pressed her lips together. Izzy had helped her be independent when no one else could. Maybe it was fate that Jack was asking her to do the same for Izzy.

'Okay. You're right.' She pulled her phone out of her pocket and stuffed the earbuds into her ears. Before she got a chance to turn the music on, one of them flipped back out again as Jack nudged the cable with one finger.

'So what's the story with you and her? She was your teacher?'

'Yeah.'

'And you stayed in touch with her when she retired?'

He seemed to see almost everything. Which was obviously a good thing when it came to his patients, but Cass reckoned it could get annoying for everyone else.

'She was my teacher for twenty years. Still is, in some ways. I have dyslexia, and she took me on. I used to go to hers to do my homework after school every day and she used to help me.'

'And she let you struggle a bit with things?'

A grudging laugh of assent escaped her lips. 'She let me struggle all the time. She was always there to catch me, though.'

He nodded. 'Then perhaps that's your answer.' He picked up the earbud, which dangled on its lead against the front of her jacket, and gently put it back into her ear. Cass pretended not to notice the intimacy of it, but shivered just the same.

It appeared that even though the crisis was over, the bonding part wasn't. And wanting him, wanting Jack's strength and his warmth, would only end badly. She and Paul had tried for two years to have children, and by the end of it she'd been a wreck. Sex had become a chore instead of a pleasure and Cass had felt herself dying inside, unable to respond to a touch.

Worst of all, she'd become fearful. Afraid of a future that seemed to depend on her being able to have a child, and hardly daring to get out of bed on the mornings when her period was due. Fearful of the heartbreak that had come anyway, when Paul had left her.

That fear had paralysed her whenever she'd even thought about starting a new relationship, because any man would be sure to react in the same way as Paul had. So Cass had turned to the parts of her life where she'd already proved she could succeed. Her job. Taking care of her family and friends. Overcoming her dyslexia. If wanting Jack brought her loneliness into sharp focus then he would be gone soon, and the feeling would pass.

Cass had withdrawn into silence as they'd trudged back to the church hall. The weather was getting worse, rain drumming against the windows, and when Cass didn't show up for lunch Jack wondered if there was something wrong. It seemed almost as if the violence of the storm might be some response to the unspoken emotions of a goddess.

Nonsense. She might look like an ethereal being but she was all woman. Tough and proud on the outside but with a kernel of soft warmth that showed itself just briefly, from time to time. Each time he saw it, the urge to see it again became greater.

And that was nonsense too. His own childhood had been marred by loss and he wanted no more of it, not for himself or for Ellie. The uncertain reward didn't justify the risk, even if he did crave the sunshine of Cass's smile.

Cups and saucers were filled and the lines of diners started to break up into small groups, talking over their coffee. At the other end of the hall, Martin was on his feet, talking intently to a man who had hurried in, a small group forming around them. Someone walked out of the hall and Jack heard Cass's name being called.

Ripples of concern were spreading through the community, people looking up from their conversations and falling quiet. Jack stood up, walking across to Martin.

'What's going on?'

'Ah, Jack.' Martin's face was creased with anxiety. 'We've got a lost child…'

Activity from outside the hall caught Jack's attention. The shine of red hair through the obscure glass of the doors and then Cass was there, the man who had gone to fetch her still talking quickly to her, obviously apprising her of the situation.

'What do you want me to do?' Without noticing it, Jack seemed to have gravitated automatically to her side.

She looked up at him. The defeated droop of her shoulders that he'd seen earlier was gone; now Cass was back from whatever crisis she'd been facing. Full of energy and with a vengeance.

'We have a ten-year-old who's gone missing. We'll split up and search for him in teams. You're with me?'

Jack nodded. Of course he was with her.

CHAPTER FIVE

JACK FOUND HIS jacket amongst the others, hung up on the rack in the lobby, and pulled his boots on. People were spilling out of the church hall, finding coats and forming into groups. Everyone seemed to know what they were doing and Cass was at the centre of it all.

Suddenly, she broke away from the people around her, walking over to a young woman in a wet jacket.

'We're going to find Ben now, Laura.' Cass put an arm around the woman's shoulders. 'Can you think of anywhere he might have gone?'

'He might be looking for Scruffy. He ran off and we couldn't find him. Pete went out this morning, but there was no sign of him back at the house.'

Cass nodded. 'Okay. And where might Ben be looking?'

'I don't know…' Laura shook her head and Cass took her gently by the shoulders.

'It's okay. Take your time.' She was calm and quite unmistakably in charge of the situation. Just what Laura needed at the moment.

Laura took a deep breath. 'Maybe… Oh, Cass. Maybe he's gone down to the river. We take Scruffy for walks along there.'

'Whereabouts? Down by my place?'

'Yes… Yes, that's right.'

'Okay, I'll check that out.'

'I'm coming…' Laura grabbed hold of Cass's jacket.

'I need you to stay here so that we can bring him straight back to you when we find him. Join the group that's searching the church buildings and keep your phone with you so I can call you. All right?'

Laura nodded. Jack knew that Cass was keeping her away from the river, and the reason didn't bear thinking about.

'Let go of me, then…' Cass gently loosened Laura's fingers from her jacket and turned, leaving her with Martin. Her face set suddenly in a mask of determination as she faced Jack.

'I'll get my bag…' The heavy bag would slow him up but he might need it.

'Thanks. If you give it to Chris, he'll stay here with the car. He can get whatever we need down to us quickly.'

'Okay. Makes sense.'

Jack fetched his bag and handed it over to a man standing by an SUV which was parked outside the church hall. Then he joined Cass's group and they set off, moving quickly through the village and down the hill.

They passed the spot where the bridge had been washed away yesterday, and Cass stopped to scan the water. 'I can't see anything…' She stiffened suddenly and pointed to a flash of blue and red in the branches of a partially submerged tree. The wind caught it and it flapped. Just a torn piece of plastic.

'Where *is* he?'

The exclamation was all she allowed herself in the way of emotion. After surveying the river carefully, she started to walk again. They scaled a rocky outcrop which afforded a view across the land beyond it.

Nothing. Jack strained his eyes to see some sign of the

boy. The house ahead of them must be Cass's, stone-built and solid-looking, the extension at the back blending so well with the stonework at the front that it would be difficult to say for sure that it was modern if he didn't already know. He hoped that Ben hadn't got in there; the river had broken its banks and the place was surrounded by water.

'Ben…' Cass filled her lungs and shouted again. 'Ben!'

She stilled suddenly, holding her hand out for quiet. Nothing. Just the relentless sound of the rain. Then she suddenly grabbed Jack's arm. 'Can you see something? Down there?'

Jack squinted into the rain but all he could see was the swollen river, flanked on this side by twenty feet of muddy land. The river must have flooded up across it in the night and receded slightly this morning because he recognised part of the bridge sticking out of the quagmire.

She pulled a pair of binoculars from inside her coat and trained them down on to the mud. Then her breath caught. 'Got him. He's down by that bit of bridge. He's covered in mud and it looks as if he's up to his waist in it.' She lowered the binoculars, feeling in her pocket. Jack squinted at the place she'd indicated and thought he saw movement.

Cass handed a set of keys to one of the other men in the group. 'Joe, I've got a ladder in my garage and a couple of tarps. Can you guys go and find them, please?'

'Okay. Anything else?'

'Yeah, just pump out the water and clear up a bit while you're there.' A small twist of her lips and that wry joke was all she allowed herself in the way of regret.

She was off before Jack could say anything to her, scrambling down the other side of the ridge. The four men with them headed towards the house and Jack followed Cass, getting to the bottom before she did and catching her arm when she slipped in the mud.

'Careful…'

'Yeah, thanks.' One moment. There was no time to tell her that he was sorry to see her house flooded, and no time for Cass to respond. But her brief smile told him that she knew and she'd deal with it later. Jack resolved to be there when she got around to doing that.

They set off, jogging towards Ben. Jack could see him now, covered in mud, sunk up to his waist, right next to the remains of the bridge. And, huddled next to him, wet through and perched on one of the stones, was a small black and white dog.

'He must have seen the dog and tried to get out there to fetch him.' Jack supposed that Scruffy was light enough to scamper across the mud, but the boy had sunk when he'd tried to follow him.

'Yeah. Wonder how close we can get.'

Jack had been wondering that himself. It was likely that the ground all around Ben was completely waterlogged.

'Ben… Ben…' Cass called over to the boy and Jack saw his head turn. 'Ben, stay still for me. I'm coming to get you.'

'Cass…' The boy's voice was full of the excitement of seeing the cavalry ride over the hill. Full of the panic that he must have felt when he'd started to sink into the mud and found he couldn't get out.

'Ben—' Cass came to a halt at the edge of the mud. 'Ben, I want you to look at me. No…don't try to move. Stay still.'

The boy was crying but he did what she told him. 'I… can't…'

'I know. Just hang on in there and I'll be out to get you in a minute. Then your mum gets the job of cleaning you up.'

Her grin said it all. She was trying to replace Ben's terror with the more mundane fear of a ticking off at getting himself so dirty. Cass was edging forward slowly, testing

the ground in front of her before she put her weight on it.
Jack followed, ready to grab her if she started to sink.

'You'll be able to tell your friends at school that you got
rescued by the fire brigade.' She was grinning at Ben, talking to him as she tested the ground ahead of her and to either side, and the boy seemed to calm a bit.

Her foot sank into the mud in front of her, a good fifteen feet away from Ben, and he began to howl with terror.
'Okay. Okay, Ben. It's okay.'

She reached back and Jack clasped her arm. A brief smiling glance that seemed to sear through the urgency of the
situation. 'Don't let me sink…'

'I've got you.'

Another tentative step in the clinging mud. Another
and her boot sank as far as her ankle. Jack felt her fingers
tighten around his and he reached forward, gripping her
waist and pulling her back.

'I think that's as far as we'll get…' She looked around,
pulling her phone from her pocket and dialling.

'Joe, I need the ladder now. And there's a toolbox in the
garage—can you take a couple of doors off their hinges
and bring them over…?'

She turned back to Ben. 'All right, Ben. Just waiting for
my ladder. Then I'll be out to get you.' She was doing her
best to turn this into an exciting adventure and, although it
wasn't totally working, Ben was a lot calmer now.

Jack looked round and saw two men appear from Cass's
garage, one on each end of an aluminium ladder. Wading
through the water, they reached dry land and made for them
as fast as the muddy terrain would allow.

'Here we go, Ben.' Cass was keeping up a stream of reassurance. 'They're on their way.'

As soon as the men reached them, she stretched the double length of the ladder across the muddy ground towards

Ben. More than halfway. When it was extended fully, it would reach him easily.

'Thanks, Joe. Have you called the emergency services? She turned to one of the men who had brought the ladder.

'Yes. They'll do what they can. I called up to the church and they're sending the medical bag down. Pete and Laura are coming too.'

'Great, thanks.'

Jack and the other two men helped Cass drag a couple of heavy branches over, putting them under the end of the ladder to try and stabilise it. Then she took a deep breath, turning her face up to him.

'Cover my back, eh?'

'You've got it.'

He tested the ground at their end of the ladder and put all his weight on it to steady it. Cass began to crawl along it, pushing the extension towards Ben.

'We're going back to help with the doors.' He heard Joe's voice behind him. 'The screws are all painted in, so they're not coming off that easily.'

'She's going to need some help out there. Use a crowbar if you have to.' Jack knew that Cass wouldn't hesitate to say the same.

'Right you are.' Joe turned, jogging back towards the house.

Ben gave a little cry of relief when the end of the ladder reached him, grabbing it and wrapping his arms around it. There was a click as Cass locked the extension in place, and then she began crawling along the extension.

Jack applied all his weight to his end of the ladder. The other end seemed to be sinking a little, but not so much that it stopped Cass from reaching Ben. He wondered whether the boy saw the same as he had, when he'd been tangled in that tree yesterday and he'd opened his eyes and seen her there.

From the way that Ben grabbed at her, he did. He heard Cass laugh and saw her wrap one arm around the boy, trying to loosen the mud around his waist with the other hand.

'I don't think…' She called back without turning her head, 'I'm going to need a hand with this.'

It was as Jack had expected. 'They're coming with the doors now. I'll be out in a minute.'

'That'll be lovely. Thanks.' Her tone was much the same as if she was accepting a cup of tea, and Jack smiled. She was unstoppable. And quite magnificent.

As soon as the ladder had reached Ben, Scruffy had bolted from his perch, running across her back and over the mud to get to dry land. Cass kept her attention equally divided between not falling off the ladder and keeping Ben quiet and stopping him from trying to move. She could hear signs of activity behind her, along with general instructions from Jack about tarps and doors. Then his voice, calling over to her.

'I'm moving off the ladder now. Watch out.'

She braced herself as the ladder moved slightly, sinking another inch into the mud. Then, as someone else applied their weight to the end of it, it steadied again. Above her head, she heard the beat of a helicopter.

'Are they going to pull us out?' Ben was shivering in her arms, his head nestled against her shoulder.

'No, they can't do that.' Trying to drop a line and pull Ben out might tear him in half. 'They're probably just flying over to see what the situation is and how they can help us.'

'And then the fire engine…?'

'Yeah. Then the fire engine.' If Ben hadn't realised that

there wasn't a way for a fire engine to get to them, she wasn't going to disillusion him. 'But they won't have anything to do because we'll have you out before they get here.'

'Okay.' Ben sounded almost disappointed.

'Ben…?' Face down in the mud, Cass couldn't see what was happening behind her, but she recognised Laura's voice.

'Mum!' Ben's high-pitched shriek was directed straight into her ear.

'Ben, I want you to do exactly what Cass tells you. Do you hear me, darling?'

Good. Someone must be with Laura, calming her and telling her what to say. Jack, perhaps. Only she was rather hoping that Jack might be on his way towards her.

'Yes, Mum.'

'Tell your mum that you're all right. That you'll be out soon.' Cass grinned at Ben. It would do him good to say it, and do Laura good to hear it.

'Will I?'

''Course you will.'

Ben called out the words, this time managing to direct most of the volume away from Cass and towards his mother. Then someone tapped her ankle gently.

'Can I join you…?'

Jack's voice behind her.

'Feel free.' She squinted round as her kitchen door slid across the muddy ground towards her.

The door moved, and sank a little into the mud as it took his weight, and then he was there beside her. The relief was almost palpable.

'Hey, Ben.' He was lying on his stomach on the door, grinning broadly. 'How are you doing?'

'Okay, thanks.' Ben puffed out a breath. 'Are *you* going to pull me out?'

CHAPTER SIX

UNFORTUNATELY, PULLING BEN out wasn't an option. Mud rescue was difficult and physically demanding at the best of times, and this wasn't the best of times. The continuing rain meant that every time they moved some of the mud from around Ben's body, mud and water trickled back into the hole.

Working together, they found a solution. Jack reached down, scooping the mud up, while Cass shoved it as far from Ben as she could. As they worked, she became bolder, no longer shy of Jack's body. Using his strength to lever her own against, bracing her legs across his.

It was exhausting work. Ben was beginning to get really cold now and started to cry again, and Jack talked to him, encouraging him. Or was it Cass that he encouraged? She hardly knew, just that the sound of his voice kept her going, despite the growing ache in her arms.

'What do you reckon?' His eyes seemed almost brighter, warmer, now that the rest of him was almost entirely covered in mud.

'Yeah. Let's try it.'

'Okay. Be ready to take him.' Jack wrapped his arms around Ben. Gently, carefully, he began to lift him. Ben's feet came out of his wellingtons, leaving them stuck in the muddy pit, and Jack hoisted him clear.

A tremulous, excited babble of voices sounded behind them. Cass had almost forgotten that anyone else was here.

'Got him…?' Jack passed Ben over to her and the boy grabbed her, whimpering with cold and exhaustion.

'Yeah.'

'Okay, you shift over on to the door and I'll pull you both back.' Jack manoeuvred around her, working his way carefully back, and Cass felt him grip her ankles, pulling her back after him.

Her limbs were shaking with fatigue and Cass didn't know where Jack found the strength to drag her those few short feet. But he did, taking Ben out of her arms as soon as they were back on the grass and carrying him over to the SUV that was waiting to take them the short distance to the village. Laura and Pete followed, desperate to hold their son.

A hand gripped hers, hauling her to her feet. People clustered around her, patting her on the back and enquiring whether she was okay. Cass nodded shakily and, as she made for the car, a path opened up in front of her, everyone stumbling backwards to get out of the way.

Ben was in his mother's arms on the back seat of the car, Scruffy sitting close to him. The boy was wet, cold, very muddy, but seemingly otherwise unscathed. Jack gave Cass a nod in answer to her silent question. He was okay.

'We'll get him back now…' He signalled to the driver and got into the car next to Ben, Laura and the little dog. Pete pushed Cass into the front seat.

'Don't you want to go?'

'I'll see you up there…' Pete's eyes were glistening with tears. 'Go and get yourself dry.'

They drove to the vicarage and Martin ushered Jack upstairs, Ben in his arms. Laura followed and Sue propelled Cass into the kitchen.

'I'd hug you if you weren't so filthy…' Sue stripped off

her jacket and sweatshirt, nodding when she found that the T-shirt underneath was dry. 'Sit.'

Cass sat down, half in a dream. Sue's businesslike ministrations were just what she needed. She didn't need Jack to help her out of her overtrousers; he had other things to do. But a part of her wished that he didn't and that after the struggle that they'd shared so intimately they could have just a little time together.

'Feet wet…?' Sue loosened the laces of one of her boots, sliding two fingers inside as if she were a child. 'They feel all right. Drink this…'

Hot soup. Fabulous. 'Thanks, Sue.'

She sipped the soup, letting the warmth of the kitchen seep back into her bones. Then she laid her head on her hands. Just for a moment. She was so tired.

'Sorry about all the mess, Sue.' It seemed that Jack's voice alone, amongst all the other comings and goings in the kitchen, had the power to pull her back to consciousness. Cass looked up and saw him standing in the doorway. He'd taken off his muddy jacket and sweatshirt and his arms and face had been washed clean, presumably as a preliminary to examining Ben. His short hair glistened with a few stray drops of moisture.

'Nonsense.' Sue glared at him. 'How's Ben?'

'We've cleaned him up and I examined him. He's pretty tired now, and he had a nasty fright. But, physically, I can't find anything wrong with him.'

'Good. Anything I should do?'

'Plenty of liquids, something to eat. Keep him warm. Old-fashioned care.'

Sue smirked. 'I can do that. You two go and get cleaned up.'

Cass got to her feet and walked over to the sink. She'd

got mud on the table where she'd laid her head down. Sue whipped the wash cloth out of her hand.

'Leave that to me. Go.'

'No, it's okay…' Cass's protests were silenced by one slight incline of Jack's head. She was going with him.

He led her to the bathroom in the church hall, accepting towels from one of the Monday Club ladies who bustled in out of nowhere and left just as energetically. Putting them down on to the chair by the washbasins, he dumped a plastic bag he'd been carrying on top and then walked over to the door, flipping the lock.

'Boots.' His grin was warm, and far too tender to resist. Cass hung on to the washbasin while he unlaced her boots, pulling them off.

'What's this?' He'd tipped her face up to his, running his thumb across the sore spot in her hairline.

'Just a scrape. Is it bleeding?'

'Not all that much. I'll clean it up in a minute.' He searched in the plastic bag and produced a bottle of shampoo, which Cass recognised as her own, one of the toiletries that she must have left at Sue and Martin's. She reached for the bottle and he pulled it away.

'Let me do it.'

There was no desire in his face, no trace of wanting. Just the warmth of two comrades who finally had the opportunity to see to each other's needs instead of those of everyone else.

This would be okay. And she so wanted it. Someone to take care of her after a long night and an even longer day. There would be no complications, no threat of what might happen tomorrow, because Jack wouldn't be here tomorrow.

He pulled a chair over to the washbasin at the end of

the row, which was equipped with a sprinkler tap. Testing the temperature of the water, he told her to close her eyes.

Cass felt herself start to relax. He was good at this, guiding the water away from her face, rubbing gently to get all of the mud out of her hair. Massaging the shampoo through, his firm touch sending tingles radiating across her scalp. His leg pressed against her side as he leaned over her.

Maybe there was just a bit of sensuality about this. Along with all the nurturing and the warmth—the things that she reckoned it was okay to take from Jack. Cass dismissed the thought. It was what it was and she was too tired, too much in need to question it.

Then the warm water running over her head and finally a rub with a towel. Cass opened her eyes, sitting up straight.

'Better now?'

'Much. Thank you.' She rubbed at her hair and he handed her a comb. She winced as the teeth passed over the abraded skin at her temple.

'Let's have a look at that.' He didn't wait for her to either agree or disagree, just did it. Gentle fingers probed and then he reached for the plastic bag again. 'I think you'll live. I'll put some antiseptic on it, though.'

The antiseptic stung for a moment but even that was refreshing. Jack had a lightness of touch that set her nerve endings quivering, but that would have to remain her little secret.

'Do something for me?' He raised one eyebrow and she smiled.

'What do you want?'

A slight twitch at the corner of his mouth. Then he sat down opposite her and carefully removed a haphazardly applied piece of plaster from his arm. Underneath, the skin was red raw, a fragment of wood protruding. Cass caught her breath. He must have ignored the injury, the splinter driving deeper into his skin as he'd worked, and it was going to hurt to get it out now.

'Do you have a pair of tweezers?'

He leaned over, producing a pair from the bag, but when Cass reached for them he closed his hand over them, holding it against his chest. 'Gently does it, eh? I know you lot.'

'My lot?' Cass grinned. 'What's that supposed to mean? I'll have you know I'm medically trained.' All firefighters were.

'It's supposed to mean that you don't have to throw me over your shoulder and carry me out of here first. Then tip me in a heap on the ground and start pumping on my chest.'

'Think I couldn't? I have a technique, you know.' The truth was that she could just about manage it. He'd have much less trouble lifting her.

He was shaking his head, laughing. 'That's exactly what I'm worried about.'

He handed her the tweezers and pushed the bottle of antiseptic towards her. Cass positioned his arm on the vanity top and bent over it, looking carefully. He made no sound but the muscles in his arm twitched when she laid her finger close to the wound.

'You really should have a local anaesthetic for this.'

'Nah. Better to just get it over with. I've only got the strong stuff in the medical bag.'

And he was saving that in case someone else needed it. Cass gripped his wrist tight to steady his arm and drew out the first piece of the splinter. She was going to have to fish a little for the second piece, which had been driven deep into his arm.

She so hated hurting him but he was trusting her to have the nerve to do it. Trusting that her hand wouldn't shake and make things a whole lot worse. She steadied herself and pressed the tweezers into the raw skin, trying not to hear his sudden intake of breath.

'Sorry...' She had nothing to make the pain any better and Cass fought the urge to dip her head and kiss it away.

'That's okay. Got it all?'

Cass carefully examined the wound. 'Yes, I think so. Can't see anything else.'

'Antiseptic, then.'

She applied a generous measure, making sure that the wound was disinfected. 'Are your tetanus shots up to date?'

'Yes.'

'Then we're nearly done.' Cass leaned forward, stripping off his T-shirt, and Jack chuckled.

'What now? Is this all part of the technique too?'

'Just making sure there's nothing else you haven't told me about.'

She would have preferred to touch instead of just looking, but that would be a step too far. Cass found herself ignoring the scrapes and bruises and concentrating on the smooth contours of his shoulders and chest. Very nice. And, what was nicer still, he had the confidence to just sit there and meet her gaze without sucking in his stomach or trying to flex his shoulders. He was perfect, just as he was.

'Finished?' He raised an eyebrow.

'Yeah. I think you'll do. Do you want me to dress your arm?'

'We'll clean up first.' He gave her a bone-melting grin and stood up, picking his T-shirt up and throwing it over one shoulder. 'Stay there.'

He picked up the bag and disappeared around the corner, towards the showers. Then the sound of gushing water came from the only cubicle that contained a bath. He wouldn't. Would he? If he did, then she just might. Even thinking about it was sending shivers through her tired limbs.

'Come on.' He was back again, catching up two of the largest towels in one hand, and Cass followed him. When he opened the door of the cubicle a gorgeous smell hit her. Bath oil foamed in the steaming tub and there were candles propped on the window ledge and the vanity unit.

'You're not going to fall asleep in here, are you?'

She wondered what he'd say if she asked him to stick around and make sure. But he'd put one of the towels down on the rack and now he was halfway out of the door. It seemed he had no intention of staying.

'No. Just keep talking.'

'Right you are.' He closed the door behind him and Cass heard the sound of the shower in the next door enclosure.

She turned her back on the partition wall between her and Jack before pulling her sweater off and unbuttoning her shirt. As she slipped off her jeans, she caught herself instinctively glancing behind her as if his gaze, or perhaps her own fantasies, had the power to dissolve the partition while she wasn't looking.

When she stepped into the steaming water, sinking beneath the bubbles, she felt the warmth seep into her bones. Cass lay back, rubbing the ache out of her shoulders. Bliss. This was pure bliss.

Okay, so he'd been tempted. Jack would admit to that. But it was worth needing to apply a little self-control to have seen her face when she'd walked into the cubicle. When he'd found her slumped at the kitchen table, he'd known this was exactly what she needed.

'Still awake?' he called to her as the hot water drummed on to his shoulders, making the various scrapes he'd picked up over the last couple of days smart a little.

'Yes. You?' Cass's voice was clear, drifting through the gap between the top of the partition and the ceiling.

'Yeah, I'm awake.' Wide awake and trying not to think thoughts that he shouldn't. 'I'm sorry about your house.' He'd been meaning to say it for a while now, but Jack wasn't sure how to do it without hugging her. The partition between them rendered that now unlikely.

The sound of her moving in the water. 'It's okay. There are more important things.'

Yes, there were, and what had happened with Ben had underlined it. But that didn't mean that the loss of her house was nothing. Jack wondered when it was going to hit Cass, and renewed his promise to himself that he'd be there when it did.

'Thanks for the candles.' Her mind seemed to have drifted somewhere else. 'They're a nice touch.'

Jack couldn't stop himself from smiling. There was so little he could do for her. 'Wish I could have done more.'

'Cherubs? Or perhaps a few perfumed clouds hovering about…?' She laughed quietly.

'Both. Every cherub needs a cloud.'

'Ah. And a glass of champagne.'

'Why stop at a glass?' Jack smiled as he soaped himself, feeling the tension ebb from his shoulders. 'Want some caviar with it?'

'No. I'll take a burger. Home-made, with extra cheese. And chips. Plenty of salt and vinegar.'

'Of course you will. Anything else?' What would he do if she said the one thing he wanted to hear? It was a nice fantasy, but in reality he'd probably pretend he'd got soap in his ears and was temporarily deaf.

'Mmm. I'd normally say a mud mask, but actually I think I've had enough mud for one day. Someone to get the knots out of my shoulders.'

Jack didn't comment on that, for fear of sounding too interested in the position. 'And…?'

'A manicure. After I've had the burger, of course. What about you?'

Jack chuckled. 'Three or four handmaidens. One to hand me my towel and one to hold my champagne for me.'

'That's two spare. Send them in here, will you, I'll be needing some help with the after-bath beauty thing. And the swirling silken robes, of course.'

'Yeah. Naturally.' He stepped out of the shower and switched off the water, dabbing at the abrasions on his chest and arms. 'What about the musicians?'

'Nah. Tell them to wait outside; it's getting a bit crowded in here.'

Jack pulled on the clean clothes that Martin had found for him and unlocked the cubicle door. The image of Cleopatra, rising from her bath and being dressed in silks and jewels, was doing nothing for him. Cass, wrapped in a towel, tired from the effort of saving a young boy's life, was far more entrancing.

When he heard her get out of the bath and pad over to the row of lockers by the showers, Jack kept his eyes, if not his mind, on the task of clearing away the shampoo and wiping the basin. A pause and then she appeared. Pink-cheeked and dressed in sweatpants and a sleeveless T-shirt, a hooded sweat top slung over her shoulder.

'I…thanks. For the bath.' It seemed that fantasy was only permissible when they weren't actually looking each other in the eye.

'My pleasure.'

She shrugged awkwardly. 'I might go and lie down now. Close my eyes.'

Her hand was on the door handle before he remembered what it was he'd been meaning to say to her. 'Hey, Cass. Wait.'

'Yes?'

'Do you think we made today count? Enough to justify staying behind?'

She smiled suddenly. 'Yes. We did.'

CHAPTER SEVEN

CASS HAD BEEN opening out her camp bed when Sue intercepted her. Jack had apparently just happened to walk over to the vicarage and mention that Cass was going for a lie down and Sue had a comfortable, warm nest all prepared for her on the sofa in her kitchen. Far nicer than a rickety camp bed in one of the chilly communal rooms behind the church hall.

Warm and relaxed from her bath, she fell asleep until Sue woke her for an evening meal. It seemed that Jack wasn't joining them and after waiting in the vicarage kitchen for two hours, not daring to betray her interest in him by asking Sue where he was, she went back to sleep on the sofa.

She woke early the following morning. Everyone in the house was still asleep and she donned her jacket and boots and crept out of the back door and to the kitchen in the church hall.

'Sleep well?' A voice behind her interrupted her thoughts and Cass jumped guiltily, sending a teacup rolling across the worktop. It seemed that even thinking about Jack could summon him up out of nowhere.

'Yes, thanks. What are you doing up?'

'One of the guys on weather watch last night... Andy, I think...he woke me up early. Apparently the water levels have gone down overnight, and you've got a couple of escape routes already planned. He said the one down by the motorway…'

So that was the reason for his early start, and the fact he was wearing his ambulance uniform. He couldn't wait to get home. The only thing that was unexpected about that was the feeling of disappointment which tore at Cass.

'Yeah. We reckoned that was most likely going to be the easiest. We've got a boat down there, and my car's parked on the other side, so I'll give you a lift. I need to go and get some supplies.'

'Actually, I was wondering if you'd do me a favour.'

'Of course.' Anything.

'Martin and I made a few visits last night. There are a couple of people running low on repeat prescriptions, and there's a man who is overdue for a pacemaker check. And there's the INR test for Miss Palmer. I'll speak to the hospital; they should be able to make the testing equipment available to me for the day, so I can do it here.'

'You're…' The only piece of information that her mind seemed to comprehend was that Jack was coming back.

'It'll take me most of the day to get across to the hospital and collect what I need, do the tests and then take everything back again. I was wondering if you might help with that, so I get a chance to see Ellie.' His eyes were clouded. Jack obviously didn't much like asking for favours. But he needed this one.

'Of course I will. You go straight home and I'll go to the hospital, collect what you need and get the prescriptions. I can pick you up again when I'm done.' She held out her hand. 'You have a list?'

He hesitated, his hand wandering to his pocket. 'That's really good of you. Are you sure it's okay?'

'Stop arguing and give me the list. Go see your daughter.'

* * *

They'd been piloted across the stretch of water which blocked the A389 by one of the men from the village, drowsy and complaining in the early morning light. Then the dinghy turned around, leaving them standing alone.

'What now?' Jack looked around for any clues as to what he was supposed to do next.

'We walk.' Cass shouldered her backpack and set off, not waiting for his reply. 'It's only a little way. I have my SUV parked in the driveway of that house up ahead.'

Jack followed her pointing finger. 'That's yours? The one camouflaged by mud?'

'Hey! I'll have you know that my car has the engine of a…' she flung her hands up, searching for a suitable description '…a cheetah.'

'A cheetah? What's that—likely to eat you if you get too close?' Jack teased her.

'No! The bodywork's a bit splashed, from when I drove it out of the village when the motorway started to flood.' She grinned up at him. 'You want to walk?'

'I'll take my chances.' Jack upped the pace a little and she matched his stride. The day ahead of them seemed suddenly full of promise.

She'd delivered Jack to a large, neatly groomed house on the edge of one of the villages, close to town. He'd left her with one of his delicious smiles to think about before jogging up the front path and ringing the doorbell. Cass thought about waiting to see whether Ellie would come to the door, and decided not to. She had other things to do and her own list, along with Jack's, would take a good few hours.

It took less than that, but she'd promised Jack that she'd pick him up at twelve and being early would only deprive him of precious time with his daughter. Cass stopped outside a coffee shop and found a seat at one of the smaller tables to drink her coffee alone.

At five past twelve she drew up outside the house again. Grabbing the bag on the front seat, she wondered for the fiftieth time whether this wasn't going to make her look an idiot.

'Sarah…?' A dark-haired young woman answered the front door. 'I'm Cass.'

'Come in.' Sarah shot her a broad smile that reminded her of Jack's. 'They're through here.'

She followed Sarah through to a large lounge. One end of it was strewn with toys and Jack was sitting at the other end in an armchair, a little girl on his lap, a child's picture book laid aside on the arm of the chair.

Two pairs of brown eyes. One shy and assessing, the other smiling.

'You got everything?'

'Yeah.'

Ellie's small fist was wound tight into her father's shirt and she was hiding her face now. Cass stood her ground, wondering what to do.

'Say hello to Cassandra, Ellie…' Jack nudged his daughter's arm, speaking quietly, and the little girl shot her a brief glance. 'She's a bit shy.'

'That's okay. I…er… I went for a coffee and happened to see this as I was walking back to the car. For Ellie…'

She proffered the package awkwardly. It was a mass of brown paper and sticky tape, probably not particularly attractive to a child. And Cass wasn't sure now whether the contents would be all that appealing either. Ellie looked like a very girly girl, in her little pink and blue dress and pink cardigan.

Jack rose from the chair, taking Ellie with him. The little girl clung to her father, hiding her face in his shoulder. 'Hey, Ellie. Cass has brought you something.'

Ellie turned, looking at her solemnly. Then suddenly she smiled.

'Hi, Ellie.' Cass smiled back.

'Hi, Cassandra.' Jack chuckled as Ellie once again managed to pronounce Cass's full name.

'Maybe Cassandra likes to be called Cass?' He raised one eyebrow and his daughter looked up at him.

'I like Cassandra,' the little girl corrected him firmly.

'Well, it's not a matter of what we like. We should call Cass whatever she likes to be called, shouldn't we?'

Ellie turned questioning eyes on to Cass.

'I like Cassandra too. It's just that most people call me Cass because it's shorter. But I'd like *you* to call me Cassandra.'

'See…' Ellie gave Jack an *I-told-you-so* look.

'Yeah, okay. Far be it from me to interfere…' He shot her a delicious grin. That hard, strong body, the tender eyes. The tough, unbending resolve that was all too easy for the little girl in his arms to conquer. It was like an arrow, straight to Cass's heart.

Ellie was reaching now for the parcel in her hand, and Cass handed it over. Jack peered at it. 'What d'you have there, Ellie?'

'I don't know…'

'Well, say thank you to Cassandra and then you can unwrap it.' Jack looked at the sticky tape. 'Maybe you can ask her to help you.'

He let Ellie down and she ran to the chair, putting the parcel on to the seat and pulling at the wrappings. Jack shrugged. 'Or she'll just try it herself…' He smiled at Cass. 'Thank you.'

'You're welcome. I just happened to see it and…'

'Cassandra!' Ellie had torn most of the brown paper off and scattered it on the floor, but the sticky tape was too much for her. Cass grinned, walking over to her and kneeling down next to her, tearing at some of the tape.

'Wow! Look at that, Ellie.' Jack's voice behind her. Ellie gifted her with a bright smile and suddenly everything was right with the world. 'Say thank you, and go and show Ethan and Auntie Sarah what you've got.'

'Thank you, Cassandra...' Ellie threw the words over her shoulder as she ran to the kitchen, where Sarah was making the tea.

'Every girl needs a fire engine?' When Jack turned, the curve of his lips was all for her. Not the indulgent smile that he had for Ellie, but something raw, male. The trace of a challenge, mixed with the promise of something heady and exciting, should she wish to take him up on it.

'I think so.' She was caught in his gaze, unable to back off.

'You're probably right.' He reached forward, brushing a strand of hair from her brow. 'Take your coat off. Sarah's making lunch and she won't let you go without something to eat.'

Sarah and Cass were a perfect foil for each other. Sarah loved to cook, and generally did so as if she were feeding an army, and Cass was perfectly capable of eating like one.

Ellie was allowed down from the table and disappeared off into a corner, clutching her fire engine and a red colouring crayon. Cass leaned back in her chair, her plate empty.

'Thank you. Your spaghetti sauce is really tasty.'

Sarah smiled brightly. 'Would you like the recipe?'

'If you don't mind. I'd like to have a go at this myself.'

Somehow Jack hadn't imagined Cass doing anything as mundane as exchanging recipes. Charging to the rescue seemed more her style. Or maybe testing her strength against his at midnight, under a starry sky. But, when he thought about it, the idea of coming home to find her cooking was equally intoxicating.

'You cook?' He smiled, as if the question were a mere pleasantry.

'I like to eat.' She grinned back. 'That generally involves cooking first.'

'I'll email it through to you. Text me your email address.' Sarah collected the plates and turned to the refrigerator. 'Anyone for cheesecake?'

Cass's grin indicated that she was more than a match for cheesecake.

Ellie had presented her with a picture. A large figure, which seemed to be her, from the amount of red crayon that had been applied around the head, towering over a red box on wheels. Cass hugged the little girl, genuinely delighted, and felt Ellie plant a kiss on her cheek.

Jack had pencilled in her name under the figure and Ellie had returned to her corner to laboriously trace out the letters, her tongue stuck out in concentration. Then it was time to leave. Cass bade Sarah and Ellie goodbye and waited in the car while Jack hugged his daughter.

He dodged out, rain spattering his jacket, and Cass whipped Ellie's picture off the front passenger seat before he sat on it.

'Not a bad likeness.' He smiled at her.

'She's even put a ladder in.' Cass indicated the miniature ladder that the giant figure was brandishing.

'Yep. She's got an eye for detail, even if she's a bit wobbly on scale still.' He regarded the picture thoughtfully. 'And your hair…'

'Yeah. Rub it in.' Sometimes Cass wondered whether

hcr hair was all people saw about her. The phrase *'flame-haired firefighter'* had worn thin a while ago.

He gave her a reproachful look. 'I was going to say that Ellie did her best with the colours she had. It would be a bit much to ask for her to do it justice.'

The look in his eye told Cass that this was a compliment. The thought that Jack liked her hair suddenly made all the jokes about it worthwhile.

'Would you mind if we stopped off at my place? I want to get a change of clothes…'

Cass caught her breath. Maybe the change of clothes was just for today. Maybe he wasn't thinking about staying. She didn't dare ask.

'Yes, if you want.'

'That's if I still have a bed for tonight, in the church hall.'

'Of course you do. Thanks.'

'And if we could stop at the phone shop as well—it's on our way, and hopefully I'll have a replacement phone waiting for me.' He grinned. 'I called them this morning and asked, told them it was an emergency and that I'm a paramedic. The woman on the other end was really helpful.'

The grey, clouded sky suddenly seemed warmer, less forbidding. Cass started the engine, craning around to see over the boxes stacked in the back of the SUV, and reversed out of Sarah's drive.

Jack's house was only ten minutes away. He motioned for her to follow him inside and left her in the sitting room while he disappeared upstairs.

The room had a nice feel to it. A little battered in places, which was clearly the result of a four-year-old's exuberance, and the toys in the corner were stacked anyhow, as if they'd been hurriedly cleared away before Jack left for a day's work. But it was comfortable. The way a home should be.

A sudden vision of her own ruined home floated in front of her eyes and Cass blinked it away.

The open fireplace was obviously used, coal heaped in a scuttle beside it. The dark leather sofa was squashy and comfortable, piled with cushions, a couple of throws across the back rest. Bookshelves, on either side of the chimney piece, were stacked full, the bottom shelf clearly reserved for Ellie, as it contained children's picture books. The very top shelf boasted a set of leather-bound books and Cass squinted up at the gold leaf titles on their spines. She couldn't read all of them, the words that were faded and cracked were a bit too much for her, but it was obviously a set of Victorian classics.

Some framed photographs obscured the backs of the books on the lower shelves. Pictures of Ellie, growing up. Jack, with Ellie on his shoulders. A woman, sitting on an elephant, her bright blonde hair obviously owing more to a bottle of peroxide than nature. It was impossible to tell whether Ellie's mother was like her at all; her face was twisted into an open-mouthed expression of exhilaration.

Another shot, obviously taken at a beach bar, and next to that one taken on the top of a snow-covered peak.

'The Matterhorn.' Jack came into the room.

'Looks fantastic.'

'Yeah. It's a popular peak.' When she turned, Jack's eyes were fixed on the photograph and she felt a stab of jealousy for Sal. Not because of all the places she'd been, the things she'd done, but because she was the woman who'd made love with Jack and borne his child. And that was wrong, on so many levels, not least because Cass had decided that she was not going to feel anything for Jack.

'You must miss her.'

Jack shrugged. 'These photos are here for Ellie, not me.

I carcd about Sal as a friend, but there's a part of me that can't forgive her.'

Cass could think of a number of unforgivable things that Sal had done, but tact got the better of her. 'What for?'

'I'd hoped that when Sal got back from Nepal, we might be able to come to some arrangement so that Ellie would have a proper family. I was prepared to do anything to make that happen.'

'But...surely that wasn't her fault. She died...'

'Yeah. She never told me that she was going to Everest without the proper permits or a place on an expedition. It was just plain crazy and I would have stopped her if I'd known.'

Jack took a last look at the photograph. 'I didn't have the time with my father that I wanted, but at least I knew him. Ellie doesn't even have that; she doesn't remember Sal at all.'

'Ellie seems...' Cass tried to concentrate on something else '...very happy. Very secure.' She remembered seeing Jack hug Ellie when he'd left, and then, in a moment of still-ness between the two, he'd put his hand on his heart. Ellie had mimicked him and then let him go without any tears.

'She knows I'll always come back for her.' He shrugged. 'But sometimes I wish...' He shook his head, as if wishes couldn't possibly come true.

Cass hardly dared ask. But she did, anyway. 'What do you wish?'

A sudden heat in his eyes, which turned from fierce in-tensity to something warmer. 'I miss being able to ask a woman out to dinner.' The tips of his fingers were almost touching her arm. Almost reaching for her, but not quite.

'And you can't do that?' There were plenty of single fa-thers that did.

'I reckon that the one thing that's worse for Ellie than

not having a mother is having a succession of temporary ones. I can't let her lose any more than she already has. I wish it were different, but...'

'Yeah. I miss...' The warmth of having someone. The tingling sense of excitement every time Jack walked into a room had made her realise just how much she missed that.

'But aren't you married to your work?' He raised an eyebrow. 'You're not thinking of getting a divorce, are you?'

'No. That relationship's doing just fine, thank you.'

'Shame.'

The thought that maybe, just maybe, there was another option left her breathless. If they both knew that nothing could come of it, if no one ever knew, then there couldn't be any hurt. If neither of them expected anything, then surely neither of them could be disappointed.

Maybe it wasn't quite that simple. Jack had just the kind of body, just the kind of touch, which made sex for the sake of it seem like the best idea she'd had in years. But there was more to him than that, and his tenderness could make things very complicated.

She turned away from him, breaking the spell. 'We should get going if we want to get back to the village and then make another round trip this afternoon.'

Maybe her disappointment sounded in her voice. He smiled then caught up the bag that lay in the doorway, ushering her outside and then slinging his coat across his shoulders to run to the car.

CHAPTER EIGHT

As SOON AS they got back to the village they started on the round of visits that Jack had promised to make, Cass acting as his guide. The first on the list was Mr Hughes. He had refused to allow his wife to stay and watch while Jack checked on his pacemaker, and Mrs Hughes had refused to stay in the kitchen, so Cass waited outside the sitting room door with her.

'I really don't know why he didn't go to the hospital sooner. He missed his last appointment, and they said that he had to go in three months. He hasn't got much left on the battery...'

Cass nodded sympathetically, wondering when Mrs Hughes was going to stop with the barrage of complaints about her husband.

'Then, all of a sudden, it gets to be urgent and we can't go because of the floods.' Mrs Hughes gave a derisive sniff. 'Silly man. I wish he'd look after himself a bit better. I do my best.'

'I'm sure it'll all be okay.' Cass ventured some reassurance, based rather more on Jack's expertise than what she knew about Mr Hughes' lifestyle.

'He doesn't listen to me. I've told him more times...' Mrs Hughes broke off as Jack emerged from the sitting room. Behind him, Mr Hughes looked suitably chastened.

'I'm taking your husband's results to the hospital this afternoon.' He gave Mrs Hughes a smile and she brightened immediately.

'And…?'

'His consultant will review them and give you a call. There's nothing to worry about; his pacemaker is doing its job and there are no problems there, but I think that Mr Hughes may well benefit from taking a few measures to improve his general health.'

'Thank you, Doctor.' Mrs Hughes shot a look of triumph at her husband.

'I'm a paramedic.'

Mrs Hughes leaned towards Jack confidingly. 'I don't care who you are. Just as long as you told him…'

Jack nodded, clearly unwilling to commit himself about what he had or hadn't told Mr Hughes, and Mrs Hughes saw them to the front door. Cass followed him down the front path and fell in step with him.

'More exercise. Give up smoking and change his diet…'

Jack grinned. 'Very good. You want to take the next visit?'

Cass shook her head. 'Everyone in the village knows. I imagine the only person who *doesn't* know is the consultant at the hospital. When I asked Mrs Hughes if she'd spoken to him, she said she didn't like to.'

'Why not?'

Cass shrugged. 'Because he's far too important. And clearly far too busy to be worrying about his patients' health.'

Jack gave a resigned groan. 'Okay. He's actually a good man, and very approachable. I'll be making the situation clear in my notes and he'll follow up.'

'Thanks.' Cass swerved off the road and climbed over a stile, jumping down on the other side. 'Short cut.'

Jack had almost completely lost his bearings. Here, on the other side of the village from the river, the land sloped more gently and houses were scattered between fields and copses of trees. The ring of water that surrounded the area spread out into the distance, encroaching wherever it could through gullies and streams and into homes. But Cass seemed to know every inch of the place, and so far they hadn't even got their feet wet.

'Any other bits of interesting gossip I should know about?' It sounded as if the villagers knew who needed medical help long before anyone else did.

'Don't think so. Joe Gardener pulled a muscle yesterday, carrying my kitchen door.'

'He mentioned that last night when I saw him. The tube of vapour rub from the chemist is for him. What about you?'

'Me? Nothing wrong with me.'

Jack had expected her to say that. But he'd heard a little village gossip too, last night. 'It's just that if there was someone who'd been up all night on more than one occasion in the past few weeks, who'd been holding down a physically demanding job, digging ditches and looking after a pregnant sister…'

She shot him a warning glare, compressing her lips into a hard line. Jack ignored it.

'…rescuing kids, and then going through the trauma of having her own house flooded, I'd be a bit concerned.'

'Would you, now?'

'Do you want to talk about it?'

She stopped short, almost tripping over a tree root when she turned to face him. 'What's all this about, Jack? I'm fine. I told you.'

'Okay. Just asking.' If she wasn't going to talk about it, then he couldn't make her. 'But if you do need anything.'

'So I'm needy now, am I?' She frowned at him.

'No. You might be human, though. And if it turns out that you are, and you need a friend…' He shrugged. Why should she turn to him? She was surrounded by friends here and she never seemed to want to take any help from anyone.

Suddenly she seemed to soften. 'Jack, I…' She shook her head and the moment was lost. 'Will you do something for me? As a friend.'

'Of course.'

'Will you just shut up?'

He'd obviously gone too far and Cass was withdrawn and quiet as they circled the low-lying areas of the village, dropping off prescriptions and visiting anyone who might need medical support. But, whatever sadness she concealed, and Jack was sure by now that she was hiding something, she never hung on to it for long. Cass was nothing if not resilient, and by the time they'd walked back up the hill to Miss Palmer's cottage, she was smiling again.

'I can't wait to see what Bathsheba's going to get up to next.' Cass grinned at Miss Palmer. While Jack had been checking her over and doing the INR test, Cass had produced an MP3 player from her pocket and plugged it into a laptop which lay on a side table.

'Oh, I think you'll be surprised.' Miss Palmer smiled enigmatically.

'Miss Palmer's reading Thomas Hardy. I can read it myself, but it's easier when she does it for me.'

'You can concentrate on what's happening, you mean?' Jack liked the idea, and it obviously gave both Cass and Miss Palmer a lot of pleasure.

'Yes. I get to enjoy the story.'

'It's our little secret.' Miss Palmer was looking at him speculatively, and Jack was learning never to ignore any of Miss Palmer's looks. 'Just between the two of us. Or the three of us, I suppose.'

Cass's cheeks flushed a little, but she didn't seem to mind. And Jack had the sudden feeling that the brick wall that Cass had built around herself had just crumbled a little. Not so much as to allow him to see over the top, but if he put his shoulder to it a few more times who knew what might happen?

They'd retraced their route back along the flooded motorway and to Cass's car. She'd waited in the hospital car park for him, plugging the MP3 player into the car's sound system while Jack returned the borrowed equipment and made sure that the results of the tests he'd taken would reach the right people.

'What time does Ellie go to bed?' When he climbed back into the SUV, she looked at her watch.

'In about half an hour. But if we go now, we'll get back across the water while it's still light.' Jack knew what she was thinking. He'd been thinking the same himself, but it was too late now.

She started the engine. 'Won't take long to kiss her goodnight, will it? And I've got a flashlight in the back of the car.'

'Anything you *don't* have in the back of your car?'

She chuckled. 'I like to come prepared.'

They were in time for Jack to put Ellie to bed. He walked back downstairs to find Cass alone in the sitting room, still listening to her MP3 player.

'Ready?'

'Yeah. Thanks.' He said a quick goodbye to Sarah, resisting the temptation to go and wake Ellie up, just to say goodnight to her again, and followed Cass to her car.

When they arrived at the motorway, she pulled a large

flashlight from the car boot, switching it on. It illuminated the water in front of them as she swung it slowly.

'They must not be here yet.' There was no answering flash of light from the gloom on the other side. 'They won't be long.'

Suddenly, the men coming to fetch them could be as long as they liked. It could rain as much as it liked. Jack reached for her, wondering whether she would back away.

She didn't. Cass took a step towards him, the beam of the flashlight swaying suddenly upwards. They were touching now. Sweaters and coats between them, but still nothing to protect him from the intoxicating magic that she exuded.

'Switch it off.' His own voice sounded hoarse, almost abrupt.

An answering snap, and they were standing in semi-darkness. She pulled down her hood, rain splashing on to her face as she tipped it up towards him.

'Cassandra…' Jack had already lost sight of all the reasons why he shouldn't do this. All the things that stood between them seemed to have melted away.

'Jack…?' There were so many questions in the dark shadows of her eyes and he couldn't answer any of them.

'Yes?'

'… Nothing.' She whispered the word, her lips curving into a tantalising smile.

He was confused, torn apart by two equal forces pulling in opposite directions. Cass was the only thing that seemed real, the only thing he could take hold of and hang on to. He pulled her close, hearing the soft thud as the flashlight hit the grass at their feet.

CHAPTER NINE

His body was as strong, as delicious as she'd imagined it. When he held her there was no possibility of escape, unless he decided to free her. But Cass didn't want to be free of him.

Still he seemed to hesitate. Going slow, waiting for her to stop him. That wasn't going to happen. She pulled his hood back, laying her hands on either side of his face.

She could feel him breathe. Then he said her name again.

'Cassandra.'

'I'm right here, Jack.'

He touched his lips against hers, soft and gentle. That wasn't what she wanted and he knew it. When he came back for more, the sudden intensity made her legs wobble. Pinpricks of cool water on her face and the raging heat of his kiss. It was almost too much, but at the same time she didn't want it to end.

Layers of heavy-duty, high-performance waterproofing scraped together as he lifted her off her feet. Cass wrapped her legs around his waist and her arms around his shoulders, looking down into his eyes now. His hand on the back of her head brought her lips to his, their kiss annihilating her.

He could lay her on the grass... Suddenly the rain and layers of clothing meant nothing. The possibility that they might be discovered meant nothing. Nothing meant anything as long as he could find a way to touch her, in all the places that she wanted him to.

'Jack…' She moved against him so desperately that he almost lost his footing.

'Careful.' He nuzzled against her neck, the warmth of his lips against the cold rivulets of water that trickled from her wet hair. One hand cupped her bottom, supporting her, and the other seemed to be burrowing inside her jacket. Then she felt his fingers, cool on her spine, just above the waistband of her jeans.

His touch made her breath catch in her throat. Caressing, tantalising. If he could do that with one square inch of naked skin to work with, then goodness only knew what he might do with more.

Then, suddenly, he stopped. 'Cass… Cass, we have company…'

'Uh?' *No!*

'Feet on the ground, honey.' His voice was gentle, holding all the promise of what might have been if fantasy had any power to hold off reality. She slowly planted her boots back down on to the grass, feeling his body against hers, supporting her until she felt able to stand. When she turned, she saw lights tracing a path down towards where the dinghy was kept.

'Too bad…' She picked up the flashlight and switched it on, signalling to the group on the other side of the water.

His fingers found hers, curling around them. 'Yeah. I can't imagine…'

'Can't you?' She smiled up at him.

'Actually, I can. I'm imagining it right now.' He bent towards her slightly. 'What I'd do…'

'Don't. Jack…' Her skin suddenly seemed to have developed a mind of its own and was tingling, as if responding to his touch.

'What you'd do.'

'Jack, I'm warning you…'

'Yeah. I'll consider myself well and truly warned.' He squeezed her hand and then let it go, one last brush of his finger against her palm making her shiver. Lights shone across the dark water and the sound of the dinghy's motor reached her ears. And Jack's smile beside her, indicating that in his mind he was still touching her.

It was easy to tell himself that it had been a delicious one-off moment in time that wasn't going to happen again, when there was so little chance of he and Cass being left alone for long. They'd missed supper and ate in a corner of the kitchen, the bustle of clearing up after the evening meal going on around them. And afterwards there were people waiting to see Cass, to discuss plans for shoring up the makeshift dams which were keeping the water away from a number of houses in the village.

She didn't once mention her own house. A few times, Jack saw her press her lips together in an expression of regret over something she didn't want to talk about and he wondered whether he might get her alone, later. But by the time the meeting broke up, everyone was yawning, Cass included, and clearly they were all off to their own beds.

He hadn't kissed a woman since Ellie had come into his life. Maybe that was why he couldn't stop thinking about last night. Jack felt a quiver of guilt as he made his way to the church hall the following morning and deliberately slowed his pace. He shouldn't be so eager just to get a glimpse of Cass.

'Watch out!' A burly man in a red waterproof jacket cannoned straight into him as he walked through the lobby, and then shouted the warning in his face.

'Sorry, mate.' Jack stepped back as the man staggered a little. 'You all right?'

'Yeah. Sorry. Splitting headache this morning.' The man stopped and seemed to collect himself. 'Must be a stomach bug. The wife and kids have got it too; when I left, my youngest boy was throwing up.'

'Yeah? You need anything?'

'No, it's okay. The walk here seems to be clearing it.'

A slight prickling at the back of Jack's neck. It was probably nothing but he asked anyway, keeping his tone conversational. 'Any other families got it?'

'Not that I know of.' The man straightened. 'The power's off at my place and it gets cold at night, even though we keep the heater on in the hall. Probably just a stuffy head from too many blankets.' He took off his coat, hanging it with the others, and opened the hall door to let Jack through.

Cass was easy to pick out immediately, her red hair shining like a beacon that seemed to draw him in. Jack reminded himself that he had more important concerns at the moment, and that wanting to touch her could wait.

'Can I have a word?' He motioned her to one side. 'The guy in the brown sweater who's just arrived.'

Cass looked round. 'The one with the beard? That's Frank.'

'Where does he live?'

'Over on the other side of the village.' She shot him a questioning look. 'What's the matter?'

'Have you heard about anyone else with a stomach bug? Headaches, sickness?'

'No. We all know about the dangers of flood water, if that's what you're getting at. Everyone's drinking bottled.' She paused. 'The whole family usually comes up here for breakfast; the power's out down there.'

'He was on his own this morning. And he says that all of the family have had headaches and sickness, which clears in the open air.'

'You don't think…?' As a firefighter, Cass probably knew the symptoms of carbon monoxide poisoning better than he did.

'I don't know.'

'Best make sure.'

They found their coats, and Jack quickly packed a few things that he hoped he wouldn't need into a small rucksack. Cass led the way, turning away from the river, taking the path they'd taken yesterday. He wondered whether he should mention last night to her, perhaps even apologise, but Cass had already pulled her phone from her pocket and was scrolling through the contact list.

'No answer. Maybe they're on their way up to the church.' Even so, she quickened her pace, striding along the perimeter of a field of corn, the crop rotting where it stood. On the far side they slid down a steep incline and then back on to the road.

Cass had called again and there was still no answer. She and Jack almost ran the few feet along the road and then up the path of a large modern house. She banged on the door, bending down to look through the letter box.

'Someone's coming.'

The door was answered by a heavy-eyed lad of about eighteen. 'Cass?' He shielded his eyes against the light. 'What is it?'

'This is Jack; he's a paramedic. Can we come in, please, Harry?'

'Yeah. If you're looking for Mum, she's not very well. She and Alex have gone back to bed.'

'Are you okay?'

'Not too bad. I went out for a walk this morning and

it cleared my head. But it's so stuffy in here…' The lad shrugged, standing back from the doorway and eyeing Jack. 'I heard all about you…'

It seemed that most of the village had heard all about him, and at the moment that was a good thing because he could dispense with the usual formalities. Jack walked straight into the house and up the stairs.

Behind him, he could hear Cass telling Harry to wait in the hallway. There was a portable gas heater on the landing, which looked as if it had been hauled out of the garden shed and pressed into service when the power failed. Jack reached out, turning it off as he passed.

The first of the back bedrooms was in darkness, and from the mess of posters on the wall its occupant must be fifteen or sixteen. Jack opened the curtains and a drowsy protest came from the bed.

'Geroff. My head…'

'Alex, my name's Jack. I'm a paramedic. Get up.' Jack didn't bother with any niceties. He stripped the duvet off the bed and the dark-haired youth protested.

His speech was so slurred that Jack wasn't entirely sure what he was saying, but it sounded like a none-too-polite request to go away and leave him alone. He hauled the youth up on to his feet, pulling his arm around his neck. 'Walk. Come on.'

Jack supported the boy over to the bedroom door. He was showing all the signs of having flu—flushed cheeks, drowsiness and, from the way he was clutching one hand to his head, a headache. But flu didn't get better when you went out for a walk in the fresh air, and carbon monoxide poisoning did.

'Coming through…' Cass's voice on the landing. She was carrying a woman in the classic fireman's lift, her body coiled around her shoulders. She looked to be unresponsive.

'Harry, get out of the way!' Cass called to the lad, who was now halfway up the stairs, and he turned and ran back down again.

'Mum...? What's the matter?' He flattened himself against the wall of the hallway, letting Cass past to the front door, and Jack followed.

'Harry... What's going on?' The boy at Jack's side grabbed at his brother.

'You'll be okay, but you need to get into the fresh air. Now.' Jack tried to reassure the panicking boys. He seized a couple of coats from the pegs in the hall and thrust them at Harry.

Harry transitioned suddenly from a boy to a man. 'Go on and help Mum. I'll see to Alex.'

Jack followed Cass out of the front door and she led the way round to the car port at the side of the house, where there was at least some protection from the rain. He tore off his coat, wrapping it around the woman as Cass lay her carefully down.

'Her name's Sylvie.'

'Thanks. Will you fetch my bag, please?' Sylvie's breathing was a little too shallow for Jack's liking, but at least she was breathing. Her eyelids were fluttering and she seemed lost somewhere between consciousness and unconsciousness. Cass nodded and a moment later the rucksack was laid down on the concrete next to him.

'Oxygen?' She anticipated his next instruction, opening the bag and taking out the small oxygen cylinder.

'Thanks. Can you see to the boys? And try and knock for a neighbour; this isn't ideal.'

'Right you are.' Cass disappeared and Jack held the oxygen mask to Sylvie's mouth. 'Sylvie... Sylvie, open your eyes.'

A figure knelt down on the concrete on the other side of the prone body. Harry picked up his mother's hand, his face set and calm. 'Mum…'

'That's right. Talk to her.' Jack knew that Sylvie would respond to her son's voice better than his. He cradled her, holding the mask over her face.

'Mum… Come on now, wake up.' Jack allowed himself a grim smile. Harry's voice was firm and steady. 'Open your eyes, Mum. Come on.'

Sylvie's eyes opened and Jack felt her begin to retch. Quickly he bent her forward and she was sick all over the leg of her son's jeans. 'Nice one, Mum.' Harry didn't flinch. 'Better out than in…'

Jack grinned, clearing Sylvie's mouth and letting her lie back in his arms. She opened her eyes and her gaze found her son's face.

'Harry… I feel so ill…'

'I know, Mum. But Cass and the paramedic are here, and you're going to be okay.'

'Alex…'

'He's okay. He's gone with Cass.' Harry stroked his mother's brow.

'I'm going to put a mask over your face, Sylvie. Deep breaths.' Jack replaced the mask, and Sylvie's chest rose and fell as she breathed in the oxygen.

'That's right, Mum.' Harry's gaze flickered towards Jack and he nodded him on. 'Deep breaths, eh. Do as the man says.'

'Well done.' Jack didn't take his gaze from Sylvie but the words were for Harry. 'You just passed the first responder's initiation. Don't back off when someone's sick all over you.'

The young man gave a nervous laugh. 'What the hell's the matter with her…? With us?'

'I think it may be carbon monoxide poisoning. She

seems to be coming out of it now.' Sylvie was quiet but her eyes were open and focused.

'What…like car exhaust fumes?'

'Something like that. One of those heaters may be faulty. Where did you get them?'

'Dad's mate lent them to us. He uses them in his greenhouse.'

Sylvie stirred in his arms and Jack smiled down at her. 'All right. You're doing just fine, Sylvie.'

Cass knelt down beside him. 'Next door. They're waiting for us.'

'Thanks. Help me lift her?' Jack gave the oxygen tank to Harry to carry, more as a badge of honour than anything else, and Cass helped settle Sylvie in his arms. A middle-aged woman was standing at the door of the next house, and Jack carried Sylvie carefully up her own front path and back down her neighbour's.

The house was neat and warm. He was waved through to a sitting room, two large sofas placed on opposite sides of the room. On one sat a man, his arm clamped tightly around Alex's shoulders.

'She's all right, Alex. She just needs fresh air and she'll be okay. We all will.' Harry seemed to have taken over Jack's role and he relinquished it gladly to him. When this was all over the young man could feel proud of the way he'd acted.

He laid Sylvie gently down on the sofa. A roll of kitchen towel was produced, to wipe Harry's jeans, and Jack asked him to sit with his mother. Cass appeared from the hallway, pocketing her phone.

'You'll be wanting her seen at the hospital?'

'Yeah. All of them need to have blood tests for carbon monoxide.'

'Okay, there are a couple of cars coming now, and we'll

take them down to the motorway and get them across there. A lot quicker than calling an ambulance...' She stopped suddenly, reddening. 'What do you think?'

'I think we'd better get a couple of cars down here and take them across at the motorway. It'll be a lot quicker than calling an ambulance.' His eyes sparkled with amusement.

'Yeah. Right.' Cass wrinkled her nose at him and Jack tried not to laugh. She was irresistible when she second-guessed him, and that thing with the nose was the icing on the cake.

'How long?' He had to make a conscious effort to get his mind back on to the task in hand.

'Ten minutes. I'll go and get some clothes for them.'

'Just coats, from the hallway.' The front door must be still open and the air in the hallway would have cleared by now. 'I don't want to have to carry *you* out.' Though he'd carry her pretty much anywhere she liked if given half a chance.

'I'd like to see you try.' She turned her back on him and marched out of the room, leaving him to his patient.

CHAPTER TEN

SYLVIE'S HUSBAND WAS in one of the cars that arrived and the family was ferried down to the motorway together. Cass had disappeared, and Jack saw her waiting on the other side of the water with her SUV. She dropped the keys into Jack's hand and told him she'd meet him at the hospital and Jack helped Sylvie into the front seat, the rest of the family squeezing into the back.

He drove away, leaving her standing alone on the road. There wasn't any point in wondering exactly how she was going to get to the hospital. She'd said she'd be there, and Jack had little doubt that she would.

She arrived, pink-cheeked, nearly an hour later and sat down next to him on one of the waiting room chairs.

'Hey.'

'Hey yourself.' He wasn't going to ask.

'Everything all right?'

'Fine. They're being seen now.' Jack reached into his pocket and took out her car keys. 'Blue.'

'Blue?'

'When Sylvie was called in I nipped out and put your car through the car wash around the corner. Just in case you happened to be looking for it, it's blue.'

She gave him a sweet smile, refusing to rise to the bait. 'I'll bear that in mind. Thanks.'

They sat in silence for a few minutes. Cass took off her coat and dropped it on the chair next to her.

'You could at least ask.'

Jack smirked. He'd been determined that she would be the first to break. 'All right. How did you get here?'

'I walked for about a mile and then I hitched a lift. On the mobility bus.'

Jack snorted with laughter. 'The mobility bus? Didn't they want to see your pensioner's card before they let you on?'

'No, they did not. I showed the firefighter's ID card I have for home safety checks and cadged a lift.'

'And said you were on your way to a fire?' This was the first opportunity he'd had to sit and talk alone with Cass since they'd kissed. It felt almost as if he'd been holding his breath, waiting for this moment.

'Very funny. Next time *you* have a fire, don't expect me to put it out.' She turned her head away from him and Jack saw that she was blushing furiously at her own gaffe.

'I can put out my own fires, thank you.' Something about the delicate pink of her pale skin just wouldn't allow him to let this go. That, and the thought of letting her put out the delicious fire that her kiss had ignited.

She turned, grinning at him, and Jack suddenly wondered what he'd just got himself into. 'You're no fun, are you?'

That smile. Those dark eyes, full of all the things that might have been last night. She hadn't stopped thinking about it. It had been running at the back of her mind, like a piece of music playing over and over on the radio. Unnoticed for most of the time, but still there.

Maybe she should just get a grip. Put Jack away in a box, lined with tissue paper, ready to take back out again when she was old and grey and wanted to remind herself of what it was like to be young.

'That was a nice lift. Good technique.' He spoke quietly, almost daring her to rise to the challenge.

'Thanks. One of those things that firefighters do.' She shot him a smile, daring him back.

'Better than paramedics, you mean?'

'Much better.'

He was unashamedly sizing her up. Cass returned the compliment. Jack was a good deal heavier than her, but she'd lifted men before. It was all a matter of technique. And the stubborness to give it a go. Right now she'd do practically anything to avoid thinking about the responsibilities waiting for her back at the village.

He heaved a sigh, as if his next question had already been asked and answered. 'Car park?'

Cass nodded. 'Car park.'

Jack popped his head into the treatment area, checking that the family weren't ready to go yet, and they walked silently out of A and E.

'You're sure about this, now?' He was strolling next to her, his hands in his pockets.

No, she wasn't sure at all. Not about any of it. Cass stopped between two cars and stood in close, putting her right leg in between his, trying to imagine that he was a practice dummy. It wasn't working.

'Mind your back.' He chose this moment to grin at her and offer advice. Cass ignored it.

Grabbing his right arm, she positioned it over her left shoulder. Then, in one fluid movement, she bent her knees, wound her left arm around the back of his leg and lifted him off his feet.

'There. Easy.' She felt him put his free hand on the small of her back, balancing his weight and steadying her.

It wasn't quite as easy as she was making out, but she could walk a dozen steps before she swung him back down on to his feet.

'Impressive.' He looked impressed as well. Some men would object to a woman being able to carry them, others might suffer it in silence, but she'd never imagined that it might be a cause for congratulation. But then Jack was different to most men.

Or perhaps he wasn't. His lips curled, and suddenly she was pressed hard up against him, his leg between hers. 'Hey…!'

'Sorry. That's not right, is it?' He eased back a bit, turning what felt a lot like an embrace into the exact position for a lift. Then she found herself swung up on to his shoulders with about as much effort as it would have taken to swat a fly.

His right arm was wound around the back of her knee, his hand holding her arm. Perfect form. Perfect balance.

'Not bad.'

He chuckled. 'What's wrong with it?'

What was wrong with it was that the primitive beat of her heart actually wanted him to carry her off to his lair and claim her as his. He'd lifted her with no apparent effort last night, and she'd always assumed that he was perfectly capable of slinging her over his shoulder, but having him do it was something different.

'You're not running.'

He settled her weight on his shoulders and started to stroll slowly back to A and E. 'Paramedics never run when they can walk. We don't go in for all that macho firefighter stuff.'

'Cheek!' She smacked at his back with her free hand. 'Are you calling me macho?'

'Never. Takes a real woman to do what you do.'

She tapped his shoulder. 'Thinking of letting me down any time soon?' She was getting to like this far too much. His scent, the feel of his body. The sudden dizzy feeling that accompanied his compliments.

'Oh. Yeah, of course.' He didn't bend to set her back down on her feet, just shifted her around so that she slithered to the ground against his body.

'You lost marks there.' She stared up into his eyes.

'I know. Worth it, though.'

It was the most exquisite kind of letting go. Forgetting about the effort and the stress of the morning and taking something for themselves, even if it was just messing around in a car park, testing each other's strength. And if it meant any more than that, Cass was going to choose to ignore it.

'Suppose we should get back.' He nodded and they started back towards the hospital building. Back towards the cares of the day, the problems that still needed to be solved. And still neither of them had said anything about the one thing that she couldn't stop thinking about. That kiss.

The smell of a Sunday roast pervaded the church hall and people were busy smoothing tablecloths and positioning cutlery. Everything neat and tidy, as if the families of Holme were determined to show themselves, and each other, that despite everything which had been thrown at them in the last few weeks, life went on.

Jack popped his head around the kitchen door to ask what time lunch would be, fully expecting to be shooed away, but instead he was drawn in and questioned rigorously about Sylvie and her family. He imparted the news that they were all recovering well, that Sylvie was spending tonight under observation in the hospital and that the family would stay with her sister in town. In return, he was told that no one knew where Cass was, but that she'd gone out about half an hour ago, saying she wouldn't be long.

Armed with half a packet of biscuits, and the knowledge that it would be another hour before lunch was served, he walked through the winding passageways at the back of the church, losing his way a couple of times, but finally managing to find the corridor that led to the porch. When he opened the door, no one was there.

He wondered whether he should sit down and wait for Cass. This was her private place and it seemed like an intrusion, but he needed to talk to her alone.

He had to make a choice. He could leave, and thank his lucky stars that the constant demands of other people had meant that one brief but sensational kiss was all they'd been able to share. Or he could live with that mistake and not let it stop him from doing the right thing.

He heard footsteps approaching the door. When she opened the door into the porch she was rubbing her face, as if supremely weary. In that moment, Jack knew that he cared about her far too much to leave her here, with such a heavy weight of responsibility on her shoulders.

'Jack!' As soon as she caught sight of him she seemed to rally herself. 'What's the matter?'

'Nothing.'

She shot him a puzzled look, then dropped the pair of waders she was holding and took off her coat.

'Where have you been?' She pressed her lips together in reply and Jack gave up trying to pretend that he didn't know. 'Your house?'

'Yeah.'

Jack swallowed the temptation to say that if she'd told him he would have gone with her. 'What's it like down there?'

She sat down, clearly trying not to look at him. 'Wet. Pretty dismal.'

'And how are you feeling?'

Cass gave a grim smile. 'Pretty dismal too.'

He leaned across, handing her the packet of biscuits. 'Chocolate digestive?' It was little enough, but at least she took them.

She unwrapped the packet, her fingers clumsy, as if she were numb. 'What are these for?'

'I want to talk to you. I reckoned that offering you food might keep you in one place for a minute.'

She pulled a biscuit out of the packet, the ghost of a smile playing around her lips. 'You have my undivided attention.' She waved the biscuit. 'Almost.'

Jack smiled at her. It wasn't much of a joke, but then she must be feeling pretty horrible right now. 'You're going back to work tomorrow? Your fire station's the one in town, isn't it?'

She nodded. 'Yeah. Early start. I'm trying not to think about it.'

She was going to *have* to think about it tomorrow. Trying to use the showers without waking everyone else up. Getting across the water, alone and in the chill darkness of an early morning. Arriving at work already exhausted. Jack tried one last gambit before he suggested the only other solution he could think of. 'You don't have anywhere you can stay in town? A friend?'

'Normally I would. But there are so many people flooded out that no one's got any room at the moment.'

'I live pretty close to town. You could stay with me and Ellie.' Including Ellie in the invitation might make it sound a little less as if he was trying to make a pass at her. 'I have a spare room so you'd have your own space.'

She stared at him blankly. 'My own space?'

'Yeah.' Saying that the kiss had meant nothing was far too big a lie to even contemplate. 'Last night is…then. And today is…'

'Now…?' Tension hovered in the air between them and clearly Cass knew exactly what he was talking about. Perhaps she'd been thinking about it too.

'Yeah. Then and now. Concentrate on now.'

She shook her head slowly. 'I appreciate the offer. But I should stay here.'

'Cass, you know that's not going to work. Goodness only knows how long it'll take you to get to work from here. You'll do a demanding job, then come back here and find there are a load of other problems to deal with. It's too much and you know it.'

'I can manage.' Her voice was flat, measured. Jack knew that she was close to breaking point and if pushing her a little further was what it took to make her see sense…

'No, actually, you can't manage. This village owes you a great deal. But no one wants you here now. You need a break, and if you don't take it then you'll make a mistake. You and I can't afford to make mistakes, not in our jobs.'

Shock registered in her eyes and then she twisted her mouth in a parody of a grin. 'Kick a girl when she's down, why don't you.'

'If that's what it takes.' He'd resolved that he wouldn't touch her, that he'd demonstrate that he could keep his distance. But even a friend would offer comfort. Jack shifted over to sit next to her and wrapped one arm tightly around her shoulder. He might not have managed to persuade Cass, but he'd persuaded himself. Leaving her behind was totally out of the question.

He always seemed so warm. So solid. And she still felt as if the ground had been whipped out from under her feet, after the shock of wading through the dirty water that was almost a foot deep in the ground floor of her house.

'I suppose…' She shifted a little, wondering if he'd let her go, and gratifyingly he didn't take the hint. 'I suppose you're going to say that I don't have any other choice.'

'Nah.' He rested his chin lightly on the top of her head. 'I'm not going to waste my breath by telling you what you already know.'

Even now, he made her smile. If close proximity to Jack was hard, then continuing on here without him would be harder still. And since he seemed so intent on disregarding the kiss, then she could too. She could turn a blind eye to the clutter of Ellie's things around her and resist the temptation to pick the little girl up and hold her to her heart.

'Maybe just a couple of days. You won't know I'm there…'

'You can make as much noise and as much mess as you like. That's one of the rules of the house.'

Cass thought for a moment. 'I cook…'

'Great. Knock yourself out. We can take it in turns; I wouldn't mind a few evenings off.'

He had an answer for everything. And right now Cass couldn't see any further than a hot meal and a night's sleep, uninterrupted by worry. She straightened, disentangling herself from his arms, and Jack moved back quickly.

'Okay. Thanks.'

As soon as Jack made up his mind to do something, he just did it. No messing around, no fuss. Martin would keep an eye on her house while she was gone, and she was assured time and time again that she was doing the right thing. Jack had quietly overseen everything, and if the feeling that the whole village was handing her over to him was a little strange it wasn't a bad one.

Lunch had been eaten and Martin had stood up to make a brief speech, sending them on their way with the thanks and good wishes of the community. Hugs had been exchanged and they'd walked out into the sunshine.

'Not giving me a chance to change my mind?' Jack had propelled Cass firmly into the car that was waiting outside.

'May as well go now, while the rain holds off.' He shot her a sizzling grin. 'And I'm not giving you the chance to change your mind.'

By the time they reached his house, it was raining again. Jack showed her up to the spare room, told her to make herself at home and disappeared to collect Ellie, leaving Cass to sit on the bed and draw breath for the first time in what seemed like for ever.

She looked around. The room was clearly hardly used, meticulously tidy and a little chilly from having the door closed and the heating turned off. But it was bright and comfortable and, for the next few days, it was her space.

It was quiet too. After the bustle of the vicarage and the church hall, this seemed like heaven. She listened at the silence for a while. Maybe this hadn't been such a bad idea after all.

CHAPTER ELEVEN

THE EVENING HAD passed in a welter of good manners and keeping their distance. The next morning was rather less formal, on account of the rush to get Ellie up and both of them out of the house in time for work, but Jack reckoned that they were doing okay. Then he got the phone call.

He'd picked Ellie up from Sarah's in a daze of misery. Done his best to pretend that there was nothing wrong, until after he'd tucked Ellie in and kissed her goodnight. When he went back downstairs, the house was quiet.

'What's the matter?' Cass was sitting on the edge of one of the armchairs, looking at him thoughtfully.

'Nothing. Long day.' She'd come here for a break. He didn't want to burden her with his problems.

'Don't do that to me. I told you mine, and now you can tell me yours. That's the deal, Jack, and if you don't like it then I'm out.'

In that moment, Jack knew that this was all that he'd wanted. Someone to come home to. Someone he could share this with.

'It's Mimi. She's been hurt.'

'When?'

Jack slumped down onto the sofa. 'Yesterday afternoon. I heard about it this morning; Rafe called me when I was on my way to work. I went straight in to see how she was...'

He closed his eyes, the lump in his throat preventing him from saying any more.

The sofa cushions moved as Cass sat down beside him. 'And how is she?'

'She's in the ICU. None of her injuries are life-threatening, but she's in a bad way. I went up at lunchtime and they let me sit with her for half an hour.'

'Is she awake?'

He shook his head. 'It's better they keep her under sedation for a while.'

'Would you like to go back now? I'll stay here and look after Ellie.'

'There's no point. They won't let me in, and there's nothing I can do. Rafe's promised to phone if there's any change.'

He felt her fingers touch the back of his hand and he pulled away from her. That wasn't going to help. Nothing was going to help.

'What is it, Jack?'

'You think that this isn't enough?' He heard anger flare in his voice and it shocked him. When he glared at Cass, she flushed, pressing her lips together. Now wasn't the time for her to clam up on him.

'Just say it, Cass. You really can't make anything any worse.'

'Things could be a lot worse and you know it. Since when did you give up on anyone, Jack?'

'I am *not*...' The denial sprang to Jack's lips before he realised that Cass had seen a lot more than he had. Giving up on Mimi was exactly what he was doing.

All he wanted her to do was hold him. Maybe she saw that too because she reached across, taking his shaking hands between hers. Jack could never imagine that Cass's touch could be anything other than exciting, but now it was soothing.

'I'm afraid of losing her, Cass. She went into a building and it flooded...' He shook his head. 'Why did she have to go and do that?'

'Same reason you would, I imagine. This isn't really about Mimi, is it?'

Cass always seemed to see right through him, and right now it was the only thing that could bring him any comfort. 'I was so angry with my father when he died. I felt he cared more about getting off on the risk than he did about us. Sal too...'

Cass let go of his hands, curling her arms around his shoulders. Jack hung on to her as tightly as if he were drowning.

'I'd be angry too. But you have to forget that now because Mimi's your friend and she deserves your trust. You have to believe in her.'

She'd cut right to the heart of it. To his heart. The thought that once again he might lose someone who was important in his life had torn at him all day. He hadn't been able to see past his anger, hadn't even allowed himself to feel any hope for Mimi.

'I let her down, didn't I?'

'No. And you're not going to either, because you're going back to the ICU tomorrow and you're going to tell her how much you care about her, and that you know she's going to get better. Even if she can't hear you.'

'Perhaps she can. You always have to assume that even heavily sedated patients can hear what's going on.'

'Well, in that case you'd better make it convincing.' The flicker of a smile caressed her lips. 'Go on. Let's see your convincing face.'

She could make him laugh even when things were bad.

She might not be able to make all the worry disappear, nor could she drive away all the simmering fear and anger, but she knew how to give him hope. Jack gave an approximation of his most earnest expression and she shook her head, laughing.

'I'd stick with the one you gave Lynette. I wouldn't buy a used car off you if you looked at me like that.'

She made him a drink, and got a smile in return, but she could still feel the pain leaking out of him. He wasn't just dealing with Mimi being hurt; he was dealing with all of the remembered pain of his father's death. All of the fears he had for Ellie.

The best she could do tonight was help him to switch off for a while. She knew his gaze was on her back as she ran her finger along the books on the shelf, spelling the titles out quietly to herself.

Reaching for the book that she and Izzy had shared, she turned to Jack. 'I don't suppose you'd like to read…'

He grinned. 'I'd be honoured. Will Miss Palmer mind?'

'She'll understand.' What he needed was to let it all go, just for a few hours. And Cass didn't know a better way than this. She handed him the book, settling down next to him on the sofa, and Jack opened it and started to read.

Slowly, they slipped into another world together. The space between them seemed to diminish as they travelled the same paths, thought the same thoughts. And Jack's voice lost the sharp edge of stress that she'd heard in it all evening.

He finished the chapter and they embarked greedily on the next. But it was too much. When they stopped for a while, to talk sleepily, the book slipped from Jack's fingers and Cass caught it before it fell to the floor.

He looked so peaceful. Waking him up would only

bring him back to a present that he needed to forget for now if he was going to face it tomorrow. Carefully, Cass manoeuvred Jack round on the sofa, taking off his shoes, disentangling herself from his arms when he reached for her, and fetching the duvet and a pillow from his bed to keep him warm.

Maybe she should make some attempt to slip his jeans off; he'd be more comfortable. She reached under the duvet, finding the button on the waistband and undoing it. Jack stirred, and she snatched her hand away.

Enough. Go to bed. Cass left Jack sleeping soundly on the sofa and crept upstairs.

When Jack woke, the feeling of well-being tempered the knowledge that he wasn't where he was supposed to be. He was still in his clothes, but when he moved he realised that the waistband of his jeans had been loosened. He fastened the button again, a little tingle of excitement accompanying the thought that Cass must have undone it, and kicked the duvet off.

Exactly what clinical level of unconsciousness did a man need to attain before he didn't notice the touch of Cass's fingers? Jack dismissed the notion that she must have slipped something into his cocoa and sat up. A loud crash sounded from the kitchen, propelling him to his feet.

'Daddee...' Ellie was sitting at the kitchen table, holding her arms out for her morning kiss. Cass was on her knees, carefully scooping up the remains of a jar of peanut butter, and shot him an embarrassed look.

'Did we wake you?'

'No, he was awake.' Ellie settled the matter authoritatively. 'So we can make some noise if we like.'

Jack chuckled, lifting Ellie from her chair and kissing

her. 'Yes, but you still can't make a mess. What do you say to Cass?'

'Sorry. My hand slipped.' Ellie repeated her current excuse for pretty much anything, and Cass got to her feet.

'That's okay, sweetie. There wasn't much left in there.'

'There's another jar in the cupboard.' It didn't look as if Cass had started her own breakfast yet. 'Thanks for getting Ellie up.'

Cass grinned. 'Call it a joint effort. Ellie picked out what she wanted to wear and I helped with some of the buttons.'

He noticed that Ellie had odd socks on and decided not to mention it. He could rectify that easily enough when he got her into the car.

'I really appreciate it, Cass.' He tried to put everything that he felt into the words. 'Last night, as well...' Last night had helped him face everything a little better this morning.

For a moment her gaze rested on his face, asking all the questions that she couldn't voice with Ellie around. A sudden rush of warmth tugged at his heart, leaving Jack smiling, and she nodded.

'You're going in to see her today?'

'Yes. Shall I give you a call and let you know how she is?' That seemed important somehow. That Cass would be expecting his call.

'I'd really like that.'

Tuesday had brought no change in Mimi's condition, but Wednesday morning brought hopes that she might be woken later on in the day. Cass ate her lunch with her phone in front of her, on the table. When it buzzed, she snatched it up.

'Could I ask an enormous favour?' Jack asked a little awkwardly.

'Sure. Name it.'

'They're waking Mimi up today. Rafe and Charlie, her brother, are with her at the moment, but I'd really like to go in and see her after work.' A short pause. 'There are some things I'd like to tell her.'

'That's really good news. I'll get some shopping on the way home if you like.'

'No… We've got plenty of everything. I was wondering if you could look after Ellie for a while. It's just that Sarah's going to her evening class tonight…'

Cass swallowed hard. Shopping would have been the easier option, but Jack needed time with Mimi. She could do this. 'Yes, of course. Take your time with Mimi; we'll be fine.' Her voice rang with a confidence she didn't feel.

'Thanks.' He sounded relieved. 'I really appreciate it. Sarah will drop her home on her way to her class…'

She took Sarah's mobile number just in case. Then Cass placed her phone back on the table, wondering what she'd just done.

'Guys…' The ready room was buzzing with activity, and most of her colleagues had children of their own. 'I need some help here. I'm looking after a four-year-old this evening. What am I going to do with her?'

Eamon turned, chuckling. 'Easy. First thing to do is feed her. No sweets or sugary stuff, or she'll be running around all night…'

Pete broke in. 'Find her something she likes on TV for an hour, and then ask her to show you her favourite story book. She'll tell you what it says; they know their favourites by heart.'

Cass laughed, spinning a screwed-up ball of paper at Pete's head. 'I can manage a kid's storybook. Big writing, spaced-out words.'

'There you go then. If in doubt, go for princesses; they're all the rage at the moment,' Eamon added with a laugh. 'Sorted.'

Cass wasn't so sure. A menu and a schedule of activities for the evening was the least of her worries. Looking after Jack's child, in Jack's house, was a mocking counterfeit of all the things she wanted so much but couldn't have. She was just going to have to rise above that and maintain some kind of mental distance.

Tea was accomplished, albeit with the maximum amount of mess. Jack had called, saying that after having slept for the whole afternoon, Mimi was now awake and relatively alert, and Cass told him to stay with her.

Ellie selected her favourite cartoon and Cass sat down on the sofa with her to watch it, while Ellie kept up a running commentary of what was going to happen next.

'The monster's coming…'

'Where?'

'They're going into the forest. He's hiding…' Ellie covered her eyes.

'Hcy. It's okay.' Cass assumed that Ellie knew that too, but that didn't seem to erode the tension of the moment for her.

'Cassandra…' Ellie flung her arms around Cass's neck, seeming genuinely terrified, and every instinct demanded that Cass hug her back.

This moment should hurt, but Ellie was just a little girl and it was Cass's name she'd called. Cass felt herself relax, holding Ellie tight. It was just the two of them, and she and Ellie could protect each other from the monsters that lurked in both their heads.

When Jack got home the kitchen was empty, apart from the remains of a meal which looked big enough to feed a whole army of four-year-olds. Upstairs, Ellie was in bed and her room was uncharacteristically tidy. Cass was sitting by her bed, the closed book on her lap indicating that she'd resorted to improvisation for Ellie's bedtime story.

'Daddy...? I had a nice time...' Ellie's voice was sleepy and Jack leaned over, kissing his daughter's forehead.

Cass's face tipped towards him, tenderness shining from her eyes. He nodded in response to her mouthed question about Mimi, and she smiled.

'Do you want to take over?' She was halfway out of the chair next to Ellie's bed and Jack shook his head. He'd worried about Ellie becoming too reliant on Cass, but in truth it was he who was beginning to feel he couldn't do without her. Ellie was clearly a lot more relaxed about things.

'What's the story about?'

Cass thought. 'Well, there's this princess. Beautiful, of course, and she's got her own castle.'

'Naturally.' Jack sat down on the end of Ellie's bed.

'And she wants her own fire engine...' Ellie woke up enough to show that she'd been following the plot.

'Right. And does she get it?' Jack found himself smiling. Not the tight, forced smile he'd been practising for the last couple of days, but one which came right from the heart.

'Only after she passes her exams and the fitness test.' Cass was clearly intent on making the thing believable.

'And she's going to rescue the prince.' Ellie chimed in.

Jack chuckled. 'Don't let me stop you, then. This I have to hear.'

The soft light from the bedside lamp had transformed Jack's features into that very prince. Handsome and brave. Someone who could fight dragons and somehow turn an impossible situation into a storybook ending. When the princess had finished rescuing him, he rescued her back and everyone lived happily ever after.

When Ellie finally drifted off into sleep neither she nor Jack moved. Holding on to the magic for just a little while longer, despite there being no excuse to do so.

But this was no fairy tale. Jack wasn't hers, any more than Noah or Ellie were. Cass rose quietly from her chair, putting the book back in its place, and walked out of the room, leaving Jack to draw the covers over his sleeping child.

The air in the kitchen was cool on her face. She stacked the dishwasher and tidied up, then heard a noise at the doorway.

'Oh! You surprised me.' Despite all of her efforts to bring herself back to reality, Jack still looked like a handsome prince. 'How's Mimi?'

He nodded. 'Very drowsy, and a bit incoherent at times, but that's just to be expected. She's doing well. Thanks for looking after Ellie.'

'It's no trouble. How about you—are you okay?'

'I'm fine.' Cass sent him a querying look and he flashed her a smile. 'Really.'

Cass nodded, picking up a cloth and giving the worktop a second wipe. Jack didn't move and the silence weighed down on her, full of all the things they'd left unsaid.

'Would you like a pizza princess? There are some left over in the fridge. They don't actually look too much like princesses...' She was babbling and closed her mouth before anything too crazy escaped.

'I'd like to thank you—for what you said the other night.'

When she turned, the warmth in Jack's eyes seemed more like heat now. Delicious heat.

'I've been re-evaluating. Giving the believing thing a try.'

Something caught in her throat. 'H... How's that going?'

'It's...different.' His gaze dropped to the floor. 'Can I believe in you, Cass?'

She didn't know how to answer that. But it definitely needed an answer. She touched his hand and he gripped hers tight, pulling her towards him.

'I want you to know...' He shook his head as if trying to clear it. 'I didn't ask you here for this.'

'Anything can be re-evaluated.'

For a moment they were both still. As if the next move would be the deciding one, and neither quite trusted themselves to make it.

'I can't promise you anything, Cass. I'm not the man you want...'

He was exactly the man she wanted. No lies, no strings and none of the attendant heartbreak. He was saying all the right things, and making her feel all the right things too.

'Then we're even. I won't promise anything either.'

It was all either of them needed to know. There was no need to hide any more, and the air was electric with whispered kisses.

Then more. Much more, until the kitchen was no longer the place to be and the bedroom was the only place in the world.

They tiptoed up the stairs in an exaggerated game of having to be quiet. Jack looked in on Ellie, closing her bedroom door, and then turned to Cass.

'Asleep?' She allowed her lips to graze his ear.

'Fast asleep.' He led her to his own bedroom and as soon as he'd shut the door behind them, he pulled her close. 'Be quiet, now...'

That wasn't going to be easy. His kiss was just the start of it, and when his hand found her breast Cass swallowed a moan.

'Keep that up and I'll be screaming…' The thought of being in his arms, all the things that he might do, made her want to scream right now.

'No, you won't.' His body moved against hers, his arm around her waist crushing her tight so that she could feel every last bit of the friction. 'You're not going to have breath enough to scream.'

She could believe that. Cass fought to get her arms free of his embrace and pushed him backwards towards the bed. He resisted the momentum, imprisoning her against his strong body. 'Oh, no, you don't…'

Cass relaxed in his arms, letting herself float in his kisses. Balancing her weight against him, curling her leg slowly around his.

'Oof…' He fell back on to the bed, caught off balance, and she landed on top of him, breaking her own fall with her arms. 'Nice move, princess…'

'I have more.' She pinned him down, running her hand across his chest, luxuriating in the feel of his body. He gasped as her hand found the button on his jeans, and she felt his body jolt as she slipped her fingers past the waist-band.

'I just bet you do.' Suddenly she was on her back and Jack had the upper hand again. Holding her down, stretching her arms up over her head, dipping to whisper in her ear.

'I'm going to strip you naked… Then I'm going to find out just how many moves you've got…'

A shard of light from the hallway. Jack froze.

CHAPTER TWELVE

'DADDY! WHAT ARE you doing?'

The one question he'd never had to even consider an answer for. Jack closed his eyes in disbelief, feeling Cass wriggle out from under him.

'Don't hurt her, Daddy.' He heard Ellie pound into the room and he rolled over on to his back, feeling something soft smack against his legs. Ellie had obviously come armed with her teddy bear.

'It's okay, Ellie. It's all right…' How the hell was he going to explain this one?

'Ellie…' Cass's laughing voice. 'Ellie, it's okay. We were just playing. Daddy was tickling me.' Jack opened his eyes and saw Cass, on her feet and swinging Ellie up in her arms.

'Like this…' Ellie's fingers scrunched against Cass's shoulder in a tickling motion.

'Just like that.' She plumped down on to the bed, rolling Ellie on to her back and tickling her. Cass seemed to have a better handle on the situation than he did. Maybe because she didn't have to worry about surreptitiously refastening any buttons.

'What's the matter, Ellie?' He waited for their laughter to subside, wishing his wits would unscramble themselves.

'I had a bad dream.' Ellie remembered what she was here for and flung herself into his arms. 'Make it go away.'

'Okay.' He held her tight, flashing Cass an apologetic look, but she just grinned. 'Tell me all about it and we'll make it go away.'

It hadn't taken long to comfort Ellie and Jack had suggested that she might like to go back to bed, but she wouldn't budge. So Cass had put an end to the dilemma by getting Ellie to lie down on the bed next to her, with Jack on the other side.

'I'm sorry.' He mouthed the words quietly over the top of Ellie's head, a mix of uncertainty and regret on his face.

'That's okay.' This seemed so right, so natural. Lying on the bed with Jack, his child curled up against her.

'Really?' He stretched out his hand, brushing the side of her face.

'Not quite what I expected.' She whispered the words quietly so as not to disturb Ellie, and Jack dropped a kiss on to his finger and planted it on to her cheek. 'But it's really nice.'

'Could I hold your hand?' His eyes were so tender. When he folded his hand around hers, in the space above Ellie's head, it felt as if a circle of warmth had closed. One which included her. Cass had often wondered what this would feel like, and given up hope of ever knowing.

She had been so afraid of this, terrified of the hurt when she and Jack were torn apart again. But now that didn't seem to matter. It was complete, a thing of itself that couldn't be touched by anything. Tomorrow it would be gone—Jack wasn't hers to keep and neither was Ellie— but even that couldn't spoil tonight.

She stayed awake for as long as she could, knowing that when she slept it would be the beginning of the end. Ellie was sleeping soundly, and when Jack's eyes finally fluttered closed she watched him sleep. If tonight was going to have to last her for the rest of her life, and right now it felt that it could, she didn't want to miss any of it.

It had been almost forty-eight hours since he and Cass had lain down on his bed with Ellie. Thirty-six since he'd woken, stretching over to plant a parting kiss on Cass's fingers while she slept, before picking Ellie up and taking her into her own bedroom to get dressed. Jack had managed to spend one waking hour without thinking about it, largely due to a difficult call at work, although at night he wasn't doing so well. But he couldn't be expected to control his dreams.

He didn't speak about the shock of having Ellie walk in on them, or what had followed, which had somehow been so much more intimate than the night he'd been expecting. Cass said nothing either and their conspiracy of silence seemed to protect those few short hours from the indignity of careless words or doubts. Jack knew two things for sure. It had been perfect, and it mustn't happen again.

Then a girls' night out put all his resolve to the test. Cass had mentioned that she was going out on Friday night and so Jack and Ellie were on their own for supper. But when she came downstairs, fresh from the shower, her handbag slung over her shoulder and her car keys in her hand, what had seemed just difficult was suddenly practically impossible.

'Where are you off to?' He tried to keep the question casual but he heard a note of possessiveness in his voice. He was going to have to practise that and do better when Ellie was old enough to pick up *her* car keys and go out for the night.

'One of the wine bars in town. The one in Abbey Street.'

He knew the one. Quiet and comfortable, a good place to talk and a nice bar menu.

'Great. Well…' He suppressed the temptation to ask her what time she'd be home.

She glanced into the mirror in the hall, running her fingers through the burnished copper of her hair. The arrangement seemed somehow softer, brushed to lie heavy on her brow, and Jack could see sparkles of twisted silver hanging from her ears. Her lips were… Jack wasn't sure what shade of red that was. Delicious Red, maybe. Kissable Red.

'You look pretty.' Ellie supplied the words that he couldn't. She looked gorgeous. Boots, a black suede skirt and a sheer top with a sleeveless slip underneath, which allowed a tantalising glimpse of the curve of her shoulders and the shape of her arms.

'Thank you, sweetie.'

'I want a handbag like yours.'

'You like it?' Cass flushed a little at the compliment and Jack almost fainted. Was she actually trying to make him dizzy or did she really not know just how amazing she looked?

'I like the dangles…' Ellie ran up to her, tugging at the long fringe that hung from the sides of her bag. Jack imagined that when she walked it mimicked some of the graceful sway of her hips.

'Let Cass go, sweetie.' Ellie was about to throw her arms around Cass and the thought of rumpling such perfection was unbearable. 'She'll be late.'

'Bye, Ellie.' She bent down and gave the little girl a hug, somehow managing to keep her make-up intact and her hair just so. 'See you in the morning.'

'Yeah. Have a good evening.' Jack wondered whether he was going to wait up for her, and decided that if he did so it would be from the safety of his bedroom. Probably with most of the furniture piled up against the door, to at least provide some pause for thought before he marched out to ask her what kind of time she called this and then dragged her into his arms.

'Thanks.' She grabbed her coat, giving a little wave and a bright grin, and Ellie followed her to the front door, which gave Jack the chance to watch Cass walk down the front path and appreciate the fluid movement of her body.

Then she got into her car, a bright pearl shining in a sea of blue paint, mud and rust spots. Jack watched her draw away and turned, taking Ellie back inside. The house seemed suddenly very quiet.

He'd listened to the silence in the living room and then gone to bed early, just to see whether the silence in his bedroom might feel less grating. Finally, at eight minutes past one, Jack had heard the front door close quietly and then the pad of stockinged feet on the stairs.

The soft sound of her bedroom door closing allowed him to track her progress. Jack tried not to imagine her throwing her bag on the bed. Taking off her jewellery and slipping the sheer top from her shoulders. He turned over in bed and resolutely shut his eyes.

The silence seemed less a sign that something was missing and more an indication that all was well. Jack drifted off to sleep, but even then his unconscious mind was unable to filter Cass out of his dreams.

It seemed that Jack's unerring radar for detecting any signs of movement on Ellie's part had failed him once again. Cass, on the other hand, seemed to be picking up that instinct. Despite a late night, she woke early, to the sound of Ellie singing to herself in her bedroom.

She turned over in bed, trying to pretend she hadn't heard. Jack would be up soon and it was his job to look after his daughter. The singing continued, and she found herself out of bed, struggling into her dressing gown, before she had a chance to think about it any further.

'Go back to bed, sweetie…'

Ellie's answering smile indicated that she would do no such thing. She reached her arms up for a good-morning hug, and Cass gave in to the inevitable.

Toast and some juice were followed by coffee for herself and a glass of frothed milk for Ellie. The little girl sat at the kitchen table, carefully mimicking Cass's actions, sipping her milk slowly as if she too felt the caffeine bringing her round after a late night.

'Morning.' Jack was still bleary-eyed, his hair wet from the shower. Suddenly Cass was wide awake.

He looked good enough to eat. His washed-out jeans low on his hips, a dark shirt which seemed to have one of the buttons at the top missing, the extra inch or so of open neckline seeming to draw her gaze. Beautiful. From the top of his head to the tips of his sneakers.

Stop, it's not like that. I don't even fancy him. The lies she'd managed to half believe last night were coming back to slap her in the face this morning. And the questions from her friends about who she was staying with and what he was like had suggested possibilities that she'd been doing her best to ignore.

He bent to kiss Ellie and then turned his gaze on to her. 'Did you have a good evening?'

'Yes, thanks. Seems like an age since I've been out.'

He walked over to the kitchen sink, pouring himself a glass of water and downing it in one go. Cass got to her feet.

'I'd better get going. There's bunting to be hung.' She was trying not to notice what she fancied might be the re-mains of the look she'd seen in his eyes when she'd left the house last night.

'What time does it start, again?'

'Two o'clock.' Cass gave Jack a wide berth, making sure she didn't accidentally brush against him as she walked out of the kitchen, heading for the shower.

The fire station was decorated with flags and bunting, standing to attention in the stiff breeze, and the two fire engines on the forecourt shone in the sun. Cass looked up at the sky.

'Think it'll rain?'

Mike, another of the firefighters, glanced at the clouds.

'If it does, then it'll add some authenticity to the demonstration.' He chuckled. 'After the last month, I'm not sure I'll be able to get a ladder up unless it's raining.'

'Me too.' Cass tipped her helmet on to the back of her head. 'Shame we don't have bigger puddles out back. We could have done rope and water rescue as part of the demonstration.'

'Don't push it, Cass. Have you seen the roof of the office?'

'No?' She looked across at the prefabricated office, on the far side of the yard.

'Enough water on that flat roof to bath a donkey. I'm surprised it hasn't leaked yet.'

'Suppose we could always take a shot at waterfall rescue.' Cass grinned.

'Is that in the manual? Come on, I bet you know what page.'

'Everything's in the manual. And I wouldn't tell you what page it was on even if I knew; you'd just call me a swot.'

'You're a swot. Everybody knows that.' Mike watched the stream of cars turning into the car park. 'Here they come. Prepare for terror like you've never known before.'

* * *

Cass looked for Jack in the sea of heads and saw him with Ellie, who was dressed in red wellingtons and a matching waterproof coat. They were being guided across the yard with the first of the visitors and into the garage, where Mike was overseeing the most important part of the afternoon. The demonstration and being able to see a fire engine up close was the fun bit, but there was a serious message to get across as well.

Everything was distilled down into easy steps that a child might remember if faced with a fire or flood. Cass leaned against the front of the tender, listening to the kids' voices chanting along with Mike's. *Don't hide.* A child's first instinct, to hide away in the face of danger, was every firefighter's worst nightmare.

No nightmares today, though. Cass watched as the station commander's wife made a blood-curdling job of yelling for help from the roof of the garage, and four firefighters raced across the yard with a ladder. She was rescued with the minimum of indignity, as befitted her status, and to general applause. Then some of the smaller kids were lifted up on to a lower platform, where they were held safely by one of the crew until a shorter ladder was run across the yard to perform similar, if less hair-raising, rescues.

In between talking to the first of the groups which clustered around her and showing them around the fire engine, Cass saw Ellie on the platform.

'Help! Fire!' she called across the yard at the top of her voice. The firefighter squatting down next to her said a few words and then grinned as she waved her arms energetically above her head. 'Help! Fire!'

Ellie was duly rescued, received a round of applause and ran back to Jack. He hoisted her up on his shoulders and started to walk towards Cass, coming to a halt behind the family who had just approached her.

She bent towards the two little boys, seeing only Jack. Tall and relaxed, smiling at her.

'What…' She cleared her throat, trying to dislodge the lump that seemed to have formed. She'd already done this half a dozen times but she was suddenly acutely aware of being watched. And acutely mindful of the gentle dark eyes that were doing the watching.

'What have you learned today?' She waited for the boys' answers and then began to show them the fire engine, making a conscious effort not to rush them through. Finally they accepted the colouring sheets and badges that she handed them, along with the fire safety information for their parents, and walked away talking excitedly.

'Nice badges.' His lips were curved in a quiet smile. That smile of his should be X-rated.

'Sorry. Only for the under tens.' She dragged her gaze away from his and felt in her pocket. 'Which one would you like, Ellie? I've got a pink one here.'

Ellie nodded vigorously and Cass reached up, slipping the badge into her coat pocket. Her arm brushed against Jack's and she pulled it away.

'Would you like to come and see the fire engine, Ellie?'

'You missed a bit.' He lifted Ellie off his shoulders, setting her down on the ground, and leaned towards Cass, mouthing the words to her. *What about the message?*

'Ah. Yes.' This would be a great deal easier if he wasn't so distracting. Was it really legal to be so downright sexy, in public and in the presence of children?

'Ellie, what do you do if there's a fire?' She repeated the words numbly, wondering exactly why it was that suddenly all she could think about was Jack's touch. If she knew the answer, then that would at least be a first step to doing something about it.

'Don't hide.'

'Good. Well done.'

Jack nodded. 'And what else?' Cass frowned at him. He was pinching *her* lines now.

'You shout *Fire!* or *Help!*' Ellie decided to enlarge on the instructions. 'As loud as you can. And you could wave if you liked.'

'Yes. Waving's good too. You have to make sure that someone sees you and knows you're there.'

'Would you like to see the fire engine, Ellie?' Jack smiled down at his daughter.

'Do you mind? This is all very carefully worked out; I can't have parents stealing my lines.' Cass glared at him and he shot back a mouthwatering look, half-humour, half-remorse, and wholly delicious.

'Sorry. Carry on, I'll just watch.'

'Thank you.' Cass caught Ellie's hand, walking her over to the vehicle.

Jack watched as Cass showed Ellie the fire engine. Then stepped forward when Cass climbed up into the driver's seat, to hand Ellie up to sit with her.

She seemed to light up around children. She was a little awkward with them, in the way that he'd been before he'd had his own child, but she obviously loved their company. Why she'd made the decision to concentrate solely on her career, a marriage to her job which couldn't give her what she so clearly wanted, was just another of the imponderables about Cass.

Jack waited, handing up his phone for a few pictures of Ellie at the driver's wheel and then taking it back for a couple of Ellie waving out of the window at him. Then one of Cass and Ellie, hugged up tight together.

Then Ellie got down, accepting the colouring sheets and running back to him, waving the fire safety instructions that Cass had given her. There was nothing in there he didn't know and practise already; Jack had seen too many burns victims to be anything other than rigorous about fire safety in his own home. But it would be a good exercise to read them through with Ellie, and for them to go round and double-check together.

The next group of children was heading towards them and it was time for him to move on now. He'd hoped that the feeling of tearing himself away from Cass each time they parted might lose its sting, but it never seemed to.

'We're…um…we're all going for a drink afterwards. Friends and families—we're going to a place just out of town with a kids' playroom. If you and Ellie…' She left the sentence unfinished.

'Thanks, but Ellie's been invited to tea with one of her friends. I'm going to take the opportunity to pop in and see Mimi.'

'Yes, of course.'

'Next time, maybe…' This was crazy. Even here, now, he couldn't quite let go. Not while there was still some glimmer in her eyes which told him that Cass had been thinking about how close they'd come to being lovers.

'Yeah. See you later, then.' One short moment of connection, in which Jack fancied that they both shared an understanding of how hard this was. Then he took Ellie's hand, listening to her excited chatter as he walked away.

CHAPTER THIRTEEN

CASS SAW JACK'S car ahead of hers on the main road and flashed her headlights as he turned into the road that led to his house. His hazard lights winked on and then off again, and his car came to a halt outside the driveway. Cass drew level with him, winding down the window as he leaned across.

'You're early...'

'Yeah.' Cass had nursed a glass of orange juice for half an hour, then decided to go home. And then she'd driven back here. She wasn't quite sure when she'd started thinking of Jack's house as home, but she supposed it must have something to do with looking forward to being there every evening.

She leaned round and saw that the child's seat in the back of Jack's car was empty. 'Where's Ellie?'

'Her friend's mum asked if she'd like to stay for a sleepover. And when I went in to see Mimi she just about managed a hello and then fell asleep.'

'Ah. So you've been deserted.'

He chuckled. 'Yeah. No one seems to want me tonight.'

Not true. And from the look on his face he knew it. She should go. Pretend she'd forgotten her purse and had just popped back from the pub to collect it. Then come back later, when Jack was asleep and the coast was clear.

'Ladies first…' He gestured towards the driveway.

'No, you go.' Probably best to leave a getaway option, just in case. Cass watched as he turned into the hardstanding in front of the house. When she followed suit, she took the turn a little too wide and a bit too fast and jammed her foot on the brake, feeling her front bumper touch something as she came to a halt.

She was shaking as she climbed out of the car, leaving the headlights on so that she could see whether there was any damage to the back of Jack's. A piece of mud had fallen from the front of hers and on to his back bumper and she brushed it away.

'It's okay… I hardly touched you.'

'Yeah? Too bad.' He was facing her, not even glancing at the back of his car. 'Do you want to give it another try?'

'I wouldn't want to dent your bodywork.' Suddenly this wasn't about cars. Cass turned away from him with an effort, reaching for the switch on the dashboard to kill her headlights. When she looked up again he was gone, the front door open and the light in the hall beckoning her.

He was standing in the hallway, leaning against the sturdy newel post at the bottom of the stairs. Waiting for her. Cass stepped inside, letting the door drift to behind her, and Jack smiled.

'So… You think you can put a dent in my bodywork, do you?'

The house was quiet. No need to keep their voices down either, because Ellie wasn't asleep upstairs. Jack seemed to fill the space completely.

'I can't say. Not without a more thorough examination.' She wanted to touch him so badly. Blind to anything else but Jack, because there *was* nothing else.

'You can be as thorough as you like. Since we have a

little unexpected time on our hands…' His eyes held all the promise of everything they might just dare to do.

Jack walked towards her. Cass dropped her handbag, hearing her car keys spill out on to the floor as she pulled him close.

The kiss left them both breathless. No amount of air would be enough right now. No amount of that delicious feeling when his fingers brushed her face.

'Jack…' There was nothing left to say. They'd tried to keep their hands off each other and they'd failed. But at least they'd both failed together, and they both knew the terms of their failure.

'I can't do it, Cass… Can't pretend I don't want you.'

'Tonight you don't have to.'

He pulled the zip of her jacket open. No hesitation, but no rush either. She could feel his hunger as he kissed her.

His gaze never left hers as he reached behind her, pushing the front door fully closed. Cass heard the lock engage with a satisfying click and a little thrill of excitement ran through her veins. Locked in with Jack, and a whole house as their playground for the night.

He wrapped his arms around her shoulders, backing her into the sitting room and then settling her against him. 'Alone…'

Cass sighed. 'At last.'

Nothing short of an earthquake could stop them now. Cass could rescue him if the fire of their lovemaking got out of control, and he'd resuscitate her if she happened to pass out. They'd save each other from an impossibly long night spent alone.

Jack smothered the impulse to lead her straight upstairs and get them both out of their clothes as quickly as possible. The ultimate luxury had just dropped unexpectedly into their laps and they had time. Enough time to show her that it wasn't just sex he wanted, but a seduction.

'Light the fire.' Her lips curved. She knew just what he wanted. The thought of their limbs entwined in the firelight made him tremble but somehow the match sparked first time and he dropped it on to the kindling, which flared suddenly, licking around the coals stacked above it.

Each time he kissed her it felt new, different, like a first kiss. Jack helped her out of her coat and took his off, slinging them both on to an armchair.

'You are the most stunning woman I've ever seen. When I first opened my eyes and saw you, I thought that the heavens had opened up and you'd flown down to save me.'

She tapped her finger on his chest in laughing reproof. 'You should see someone about that. Want me to call an ambulance?'

'I think I'm beyond help.' He caressed the side of her face. 'My very own personal goddess…'

Cass giggled. '*Your* personal goddess? How possessive is that?'

He leaned in, whispering against her neck. 'Got a problem with it?'

'No, I don't think so. But if I'm a goddess, then perhaps you should kneel.'

The way she bought into his fantasies was the ultimate thrill. 'I can do that.'

'Naked…'

'I can do that too.' He nipped at her ear and she shivered, her thrill of pleasure echoing in his own chest. 'Keep that thought for later, eh?'

'Why? Going anywhere?'

'No. But we need to talk about…to agree on…some means of contraception.' The words sounded unexpectedly hard and unromantic, but that couldn't be helped. The wild, reckless days when *It's all dealt with* was enough to reassure him were gone. He'd changed. Even though neither of them wanted a permanent relationship, he could still care about her and while she was with him he'd keep her safe.

She flushed. Something seemed to stop her in her tracks. 'We do?'

'We can't just leave things to chance, Cass. That's a stupid risk.'

'I wasn't suggesting that… But… Can't you just…do something?'

He wasn't exactly sure what she meant. But a prickle of alarm was working its way round the back of Jack's neck.

'It's a choice we need to make together, isn't it?'

'Yes, of course… It's just… But…' She seemed suddenly desperate. As if he'd just suggested something impossible. 'Whatever, Jack.'

He wasn't prepared for the sudden confusion which ate away at his desire and for the wounded look in Cass's eyes. She seemed determined not to talk about it and the thought occurred to Jack that she was hiding something. If she wanted him to trust her, that wasn't the way to do it.

'I don't understand, Cass. Help me out…' One last plea, in the hope that maybe she would open up. But she seemed to be shrinking away from him with every passing moment.

'Fine. Have it your way.' He turned suddenly, choked by the sour dregs of desire. Walking from the room, he heard the door slam behind him.

CHAPTER FOURTEEN

CASS DROPPED TO her knees, staring into the fire, hugging her arms across her stomach. She hadn't meant to react like that. Why hadn't she just smiled and forced herself to have that conversation. It wasn't as if Jack had suggested anything outrageous. Of course they needed protection.

But to her ears, speaking about it so bluntly had sounded like a contract, some kind of business proposal. And all of the agony of the past, all her feelings of failure, had come flooding back. Even talking about protection, or the lack of it, brought back memories of the bitterness that had pervaded her old relationship. Memories of the months that she hadn't fallen pregnant ever since they had decided to do away with contraception and try for a baby. Thinking about the possibilities and consequences of sex each and every time. Making it a transaction instead of something sweet.

There had been no interruptions, nothing else to blame, and still they'd fallen at the first hurdle. A kiss, a touch, and then they'd torn themselves apart. They couldn't even manage a one-night stand.

There was no way she could stay here now. She was going to have to suffer the humiliation of turning up on a friend's doorstep and begging a bed for the night. She'd heard Jack go upstairs and the house was silent now. Cass opened the door, tiptoeing up the stairs. If she could leave without having to face him again and see that coldness in his eyes, all the better.

She quickly stuffed her clothes into her bag. Her toiletries were in the bathroom but getting them seemed like too much of a risk, and she could replace them. Zipping her jacket up, she picked up her bag and opened the bedroom door.

All clear. Wherever Jack was, he wasn't going to stop her. It was almost a disappointment, but then what would she do if he did try? Neither of them had said anything too hurtful yet, and it was best she got out of here before they had that opportunity.

She walked quietly downstairs. The hall light had been switched off and she put her bag down, scanning the floor for her car keys.

'Looking for something?' She looked up and saw Jack in the sitting room doorway.

'Car keys.' Keep it short and relatively sweet. Maybe he wouldn't see that she had been crying.

He held something up and Cass saw her key fob dangling from his fingers. She stretched her hand towards it and he snatched his arm away, tucking the keys into his pocket.

Cass swallowed hard. The urge to charge at him, knock him off his feet and grab her keys wasn't productive. Anyway, it probably wouldn't work. 'Can I have my car keys? Please.'

'Yeah. In a minute.' He turned and walked into the sitting room. It seemed she had a choice. Either thumb a lift or break into her own car and hotwire it.

Or she could follow Jack. She'd have to be insane to do that now. It was no particular comfort to know that she could remind herself afterwards that she'd known this was a bad idea and she'd done it anyway.

He was sitting in one of the armchairs, his dark eyes following her every move. Jack waved her towards the sofa and like an automaton, programmed to respond to his every command, she sat down.

'I overreacted, Cass. I'm sorry.'

'That's okay. My car keys…'

'In a minute. Hear me out first.'

'It doesn't really matter, Jack.'

'It does to me. Look, it never much occurred to me to ask what went wrong with any of my relationships. It didn't matter—they were never going to last and it was better just to paper over the cracks and part friends. I made that mistake with Sal too, and now I'll never really know what was going on in her head when she left Ellie with me.'

'This has got nothing to do with you and Sal. You can't use me to put the past right.'

'No. But I can learn from my mistakes.'

Cass sighed. 'Look, the best thing we can do now is to forget about tonight and decide to go our separate ways. As friends…'

'And friends don't talk to each other?' He let the thought sink in for a moment. 'I know I was blunt, and I apologise for that. But I was just terrified of leaving anything to chance, giving history a chance to repeat itself. Surely you can understand that?'

'Yes, of course.'

'You want to say anything?'

'I… No.'

He got suddenly to his feet, frustration leaking from every gesture. Cass thought he was going to throw her keys at her and storm out again, but he grabbed her arms, pulling her to her feet.

'Damn, Cass.' He was clearly in the grip of some powerful emotion that he was struggling to control. 'We were going to sleep together. Is it so difficult to trust me?'

'That's just what I wanted to do, Jack. Trust you and sleep with you. Not have to go through some kind of soulless agreement. I've got enough memories of that to last a lifetime.'

'What do you mean?' Jack was clearly not about to give up.

'I tried for a baby with my ex. Didn't happen.' The coldness she heard in her voice was her only defence. 'He left me, and I don't much blame him. All the charts and the dates, working out when we were supposed to have sex… It turned into a chore and I just used to close my eyes and get it over with. And then, afterwards, when I didn't…' She paused. 'Well, when you stopped things and starting talking about…what we needed to do, it brought back bad memories. I couldn't do it. I didn't want it to be like that with you.'

For a moment Jack seemed paralysed, shock registering on his face. Then he pulled her into a tight hug. 'I'm so sorry, Cass.'

'Don't be.' She held herself stiff and unyielding in his arms.

'You want to argue about *that* as well?'

Suddenly all the fight went out of her. He must have felt it because he sat her back down on the sofa, his arms still around her.

'Can I ask you something?'

'Whatever you like.' It didn't much matter now.

'Did you go to the doctor?'

'Yes. He couldn't find anything wrong with either of us. But there was something—we tried for nearly two years, and it must have been my fault because Paul… He left me because he'd made another woman pregnant.'

He wiped his hand across his face, uttering a soft curse. 'Cass, I'm so sorry that happened to you. But there's no blame attached to this. And sometimes the cause is to do with both partners...'

'Don't try to make me feel better, Jack. Paul has a child. It must be me.'

'Not necessarily. It could have been a combination of factors, some to do with you and some with him. Didn't the doctor explain all this?'

'He gave me some leaflets but I was so stressed out about it all...' The words had seemed to mock her, performing a *danse macabre* on the paper.

'And you didn't ask for help, either?'

'No. I didn't want to admit it to anyone.' The secret had driven a wedge between Cass and the people she was closest to. 'You know what some people in the village say about Miss Palmer? They say *"Poor Miss Palmer"* because she never had children.'

'Really? I'm not sure that's something it would ever occur to me to say. Miss Palmer's a force to be reckoned with.'

'I think so too. I want to be like her...'

'The best at your job? Terrifying? I think you've got that taped...' Jack chuckled as she elbowed him in the ribs, and somehow Cass found herself smiling. The secret was out but it hadn't turned on her like some wild beast. Jack had kept her safe.

He *had* trusted her. He *had* believed in her. It had given him the strength to be sure that there must be a reason for Cass's attitude, and when she'd shared her fears with him he'd understood that reason. The suffocating weight of his own childhood and his concerns for Ellie had seemed to lift, as if naming their fears could somehow allow them to put them aside for a while.

'Do you think… That I could go back and start again?'

'Right to the beginning?' Jack had often wondered the same himself. What it would be like if he could rewind and do it all again, knowing what he knew now. 'I don't think that's possible.'

'Just a week or so.'

That was a bit more attainable. 'Can we leave the part where I'm almost drowned out?'

'Yeah. No getting wet.'

'And I doubt that Ben's all that ready for a repeat of the mud incident either.'

Cass laughed. 'No. I don't imagine he is.'

Jack pulled her close, and when she tipped her face up towards him he dropped a kiss on to her cheek. 'Here?'

'That would be a really good place to start.' He felt her lips move against his skin and suddenly he was right back in the place he'd been an hour ago. With a second chance.

'You keep your eyes open when you're with me, though. I promise you that I'll take care of you and keep us both safe, but you have to let me know that it's me you see. Nothing else.'

'I see you, Jack. Not enough of you at the moment…' She tugged at his sweater and he chuckled.

'Hold that thought. I'll be back in a minute. Less, if at all possible.'

'I'll be waiting.'

Jack fetched a quilt from the cupboard upstairs to spread out in front of the fire, concealing the condoms in its folds.

She sat, watching his every move, the flickering light playing across her smile. When she stood, reaching for him, Jack shook his head and pulled his sweater off.

'Not yet. There's something I want to do for you…'

Her gaze didn't leave his face as he pulled off his clothes. Then he fell to one knee in front of her.

He wasn't prepared for this. Jack had worked hard enough to be confident about his body, but the effect of kneeling before her, naked as the day he was born and offering himself to Cass, was extraordinary. When her smile told him that she liked what she saw, he felt his limbs begin to tremble. She ran one finger over his deltoid muscle and Jack felt his shoulders flex in response.

'Look carefully.' Her gaze was running across his skin like electricity and he didn't want this to end any time soon.

She shot him a smile, targeting his chest next, and then his abs. Then she moved behind him and Jack caught his breath as he felt her warm hands on his back. Cass leaned over, bending to brush her lips against his ear and he groaned.

'Very nice. Exceptional, in fact.'

His heart thumped in his chest as she circled him again, stopping to face him. He caught her hand, kissing her fingers. 'All at your service.'

'That I like. Very much.'

'I'll take good care of you, Cass.' He wanted her to know that. Wanted beyond anything for her to believe it.

'I know.' She pulled her sweater over her head and Jack instinctively dropped his gaze to the ground. He'd never much thought about the seductive quality of listening to a woman undress, but this was beyond anything he could have dreamed. The soft scrape of material against skin. When he heard her unzip her jeans, his head began to swim and he gasped for breath.

'Jack…' Her fingers stroked his jaw and he raised his head. The picture of Cass, standing in front of him, naked, proud and strong, her red hair gleaming in the firelight, burned itself into his consciousness like a brand. Jack knew he would never forget this moment.

He was beautiful. Shadows contoured the honed muscles of his shoulders, slipping downwards towards slim hips and strong thighs. Like a fine sculpture of a man, every inch of which had been fashioned by a master craftsman, in perfect form and proportion.

A man less confident about his body might have objected to this. But Jack's strength allowed them to go places she'd never been before. Allowed them to act out the fantasy without the possibility of bruising his ego.

He wasn't just some abstract being, though. This gorgeous body would be nothing without Jack's warm eyes. The tenderness of his touch as he reached out, sliding his fingers along her curves.

'You are exquisite.' His hands moved to her waist and he drew her in, kissing her hip. Cass's legs began to shake and then gave way altogether, and his grip tightened, holding her as she fell to her knees. Then he pulled her against him in a movement of unashamed power.

Her gaze met his and he kissed her. The ache of wanting him so much was almost unbearable now and she clung to his neck as he picked her up, a tangle of trembling limbs, and laid her down in front of the fire.

Settling himself over her, one arm curled around her back, the other hand moving towards her breast. A bright shiver of anticipation and suddenly Jack stilled, his fingers just a moment away from her skin. Before he'd even touched her nipple it was tight and hard.

Just a breath, a brush of his lips, and then he turned his face up to her. 'Crazy for me?'

'You know I am, Jack.'

'Yeah. I'm crazy for you too, princess.' His hand trailed

down, caressing, learning her body. Each time she caught
her breath his fingers responded, lingering a little until he
tore a cry from her lips. Caught in his gaze, she could hide
nothing from him.

Jack didn't know how much more of this he could stand.
He felt as if he was melting. So very hard, and so very soft,
both at the same time.

She tightened the muscles which cradled him inside her
and he gasped.

'You like that…?'

'Yes would be an understatement. Do it again.'

'Your wish…' She did it again, grinning as he cried out.
'Is my command.'

'And yours…' He cupped her breast, stroking the nipple with his thumb, and felt her jolt against him. 'Is mine.'

They'd tested each other and broken every limit that Jack
thought he had. Balanced together on the edge of a precipice, one false move would send them over the edge. Jack
staved off the inevitable for as long as he could.

His sweet Cassandra. The words echoed in his head for
a moment as he saw her break, coming apart at the seams
so completely that she took him with her. And, when he
came, the sudden violence of each sensation robbed Jack
of everything. He belonged to her now.

They rested a little, grinning breathlessly at the racing beat
of each other's hearts. Jack folded her in his arms and they
lay staring into each other's eyes.

It was still early, though, and they both knew that this
wasn't even close to being over. A murmured conversation, stretching like cats in front of the fire. A bottle of
chilled Prosecco from the kitchen, which popped satisfy-
ingly, the cork hitting the ceiling. A book, chosen at ran-

dom from the shelf, which turned out to be a collection of short mystery stories.

He propped the book on her hip, their limbs tangled together. He loved this simple pleasure. Reading to her in front of the fire, feeling her intent gaze.

'Had enough?' Jack got to the denouement of the first story and she moved, sending the book slithering to the floor.

'Not nearly enough.' She picked up his glass, holding it to his lips, and he took a sip. Then she ran the cool rim across the heated skin of his chest.

'Hey… Two can play at that game…' He grabbed the glass from her, touching it to her lips and then her nipple and she yelped, laughing. And then everything else was forgotten as he rolled on to his back, pulling her astride him.

'How many times…' She leaned down to kiss him and he cupped her breasts in his hands. 'How many times can you do it in one night?'

An hour ago, Jack would have said that he wasn't going to be able to move for at least another two days. But Cass had a way of confounding every expectation. 'I have no idea.'

She shook her head in smiling reproof. 'Everyone should know that.'

'Yeah. I guess everyone should.'

No one should have that kind of stamina. The man should come with a warning, stamped across his forehead. *Danger. You will be putty in my hands.* By the time Jack tipped them both out of bed and into the shower, late the following morning, he'd pushed her to her breaking point. Then past it, into a rose-tinted world that seemed to revolve entirely around his smile.

Cass started on Sunday lunch while Jack went to pick

Ellie up. That afternoon he set about hanging wind chimes in the little girl's room, positioned so that they sounded every time the door opened. Ellie loved them, and Jack's grin made it quite clear that the loud jangling sound wasn't intended solely to amuse his daughter.

He didn't need to ask whether she would come to him that night, and Cass didn't need to answer. He was waiting, his eyes following her every move as she walked towards the bed. Jack's hand trembled as he pushed the silk wrap slowly from her shoulders.

During the day they never spoke of it, even when they were alone, and hardly even touched. Jack was a friend who had offered her a place to stay while her house was flooded. When darkness fell and the house was quiet, he was her lover. It was simple, intoxicating and they both knew that this relationship, with its split personality, couldn't last.

But for two weeks it did. A secret from everyone. Untouched by the past, because they both knew that there was to be no future to it.

CHAPTER FIFTEEN

'WAKE UP. WAKE UP…' Jack whispered into her ear, jerking the coffee out of Cass's way as she suddenly sat bolt upright in bed. That hadn't been quite the reaction he was looking for, but he'd watched her eyes flutter slowly open once already this morning.

'Uh… What's the time?'

'Eight-thirty.' She looked gorgeous when she woke. Particularly like this, the bedclothes slipping down to her waist, her hair in disarray.

'What?' Jack reared backwards as she shot out of the bed, affording him an even better view. Then she stilled. 'It's Saturday, isn't it.'

'Yeah.' He smiled. 'Coffee?'

She took the mug from his hand and took a sip. Then another thought occurred to her. 'Where's Ellie?'

'Downstairs. I heard her get up about an hour ago. I told her you were probably sleeping and not to come up here and disturb you.' Cass was up before Ellie during the week, and at weekends the wind chimes gave Jack a chance to head her off before she came into his bedroom. It had worked so far.

She took another gulp of coffee. 'I should be getting going.'

'Not without us, you're not.' Martin had called last night

to say that the flood water had receded from around Cass's house. He wasn't letting her go back there alone a second time.

'But I said—'

'Yeah. I said too.'

'Thought you might have forgotten that.' She pushed his legs a little further apart with her foot so she could perch on his knee. Jack took the cup from her hand, taking a sip.

'Post-coital memory loss isn't permanent. I'm coming to help. Whether you like it or not.'

'Too bad.' She took the cup back, raising it to her lips. 'It'll be cold and wet…'

'Are you even listening to me?'

She leaned forward, brushing a kiss on his brow. 'Yes, I'm listening. I'm just not sure how I'll feel about it all.'

'Then let me feel it with you. Whatever it is.' Jack stood up, tipping her off his knee and kissing her cheek. 'Get dressed.'

They were on the road by nine o'clock. The water had begun to drain away from the motorway and it was possible to take Cass's SUV across, Jack walking ahead to check the surface of the road for potholes while Ellie stared out of the window at the water swirling around the wheels. They drove up to the vicarage first to see Sue and Martin, and found Miss Palmer, drinking tea in the kitchen.

'I happened to pop in.' She addressed Cass, giving Jack a smile. 'Is this Ellie?'

Ellie clung to the bottom of Jack's jacket, trying to slide behind his legs. Miss Palmer smiled at her then bent to draw what looked like a large bundle of green felt out of a carrier bag at her feet. 'I can't get this quite right, you know. Oops.'

Something fell to the ground at her feet. Ellie peered at it then stepped forward to pick it up. 'Ah, thank you, dear.'

Miss Palmer took the plastic toy away from her and put it on the table.

'It's a dinosaur…'

'Yes, dear. I've got some more here somewhere.' Miss Palmer fiddled with the bundle of felt and another plastic dinosaur fell out. 'Ah, there it is.'

Ellie's shyness was no match for Miss Palmer and the little girl was hooked. She climbed up on to a chair next to Miss Palmer, craning across to see what she was doing. Sue went out into the hallway, calling up the stairs, 'Hey, you two. Dinosaur Park…'

Jack raised a questioning eyebrow in Cass's direction. 'Bit of a tradition around here. I used to love Dinosaur Park.'

By the time they'd drunk their tea, the felt had been rolled out on the table to display an impressive landscape— grass, rivers and desert—all sewn in a patchwork of colours. Ellie was wide-eyed, clutching a surprisingly lifelike volcano made out of fabric, and Sue's children were carefully arranging a waterfall made out of sparkly thread, which came complete with a pool at the bottom. Miss Palmer was talking to them quietly, lining up plastic trees and a variety of prehistoric creatures on the table, ready to complete the scene.

'She can stay here if she wants.' Sue nodded towards Ellie. 'I doubt they'll be finished before lunchtime, and then there's the battle to do.'

'Battle?'

'Yeah.' Cass grinned. 'Don't you know anything about dinosaurs?'

Ellie had to be prompted to give him a hug and a kiss goodbye and turned back immediately to the task in hand. Jack followed Cass down the steep path that led to her house.

She was quiet, seeming to be preparing herself for what

was ahead of them. Walking with her head down, across the mud which led to her house. Jack followed, wondering when she was going to stop and take a look around at the damage.

Clearly not until she got inside. The front door didn't move when she tried to push it open and Jack put his shoulder to it. It slowly opened, scraping across the carpet and making an arc in the sticky mud which covered the floor. A foul smell of damp and decay hit them.

This was worse than she'd thought. She'd expected the mud everywhere, the damp and the disgusting smell. Known that the plaster would be bulging and waterlogged, and that there would be brown watermarks on the walls.

And she'd known that it would be upsetting, but Cass hadn't prepared herself for feeling physically sick. She routinely saw a lot worse—homes that had been burned out or flooded. She hadn't lost her home and neither had she lost most of her possessions, as so many had. It was just a bit wet.

She produced a notepad from her pocket. 'Front door.' She wrote the words carefully, the first on a list that was undoubtedly going to get very long. But she was doing okay. She was getting a grip.

Jack followed her in silence as she walked through the hall, stopping to write things down as she went. In the kitchen it was the same story—mud, watermarks on all the floor cupboards and the same horrible smell. Cass had disconnected the cooker unit and propped it up on the worktop, but the unit which housed it was ruined, the particle board swollen and blown.

'Not so bad.' She tapped the floor tiles with the toe of her boot. 'I wonder if I can salvage these and re-lay them.'

'Cass…'

Not now. Not here. If he was too supportive, then she'd

just want to cry. Then he'd hug her, and that wouldn't do because they'd agreed that the pleasures of the night shouldn't leak into the day.

She turned abruptly, marching back into the hall and through to the sitting room. Forming most of the large extension at the back of the house, it was usually a great place to sit and relax—large patio windows which looked out on to the river and the trees beyond it. Now it was ruined. The empty bookshelves and TV cabinet were practically falling apart and the same oozing mud disfigured the carpets and walls.

She tasted bile at the back of her throat. Retching and crying, Cass made a run for the kitchen, wrenching open the back door.

'Don't touch me!' She was bent over, the fresh air stinging her wet cheeks, and Cass felt Jack's hand on her shoulder. She heaved in a couple of breaths, beginning to feel a little better.

When she straightened up again, she saw him standing by the back door. 'Sorry about that. Must be the smell. Turned my stomach.'

'Yeah. Must be.' He was watching her intently.

'I'll…get some water from the car.' She walked past him into the kitchen, wondering what Jack was thinking of her.

'Cass.' His voice behind her. 'What we have. It's only nights, right?'

She froze. Cass had known it was a mistake to let him come here. Talking about it was sure to mess everything up. 'Yes…'

'I want one day too. Now… Today…' When she turned, his eyes were dark, with the same intensity she saw in them every night. Jack walked slowly towards her and wrapped her in a hug.

Without any warning at all, she started to cry. Big choking sobs, while she clung to his jacket. Jack soothed her, kissing the top of her head, holding her tight.

She'd cried for a long time. Blown her nose and cried a bit more. Jack had fetched water for her from the car, along with the flask of hot tea, and they'd sat on the kitchen doorstep together, sharing a cup of tea. Despite the devastation around them, Jack was beginning to feel that he could get used to this daytime thing.

Someone banged on the door. 'Stay here. I'll get it.' Jack hurried through to the front door, heaving it open.

Martin stood on the doorstep. On the road a small group, mainly men but some women as well, all shod in wellington boots. Jack recognised Ben's parents, his father carrying a couple of shovels to help clear the mud from the floors.

'I know Cass doesn't want any help.' It seemed that Martin had been appointed to take the first crack at persuading her otherwise.

'She's taking any help she can get. Come in.' Jack stood back from the door and Martin beckoned to the group behind him.

What's going on? She mouthed the words at him as he entered the sitting room.

'Your friends have come to help you out.'

'They don't need...'

'Yes, actually, they do.' Jack put his arm around her, bundling her through to the hallway, which was filling up quickly.

'Martin...' Tears welled in her eyes again and she clutched hold of Jack's sweater.

'Thanks for coming.' Jack voiced the words for her and Martin gave a small nod.

'Where are we going to start, then?'

* * *

The amount that could be achieved by a dozen people in less than four hours was amazing. The house had been aired through, and mud shovelled into buckets to be carted out. Carpets had been taken up and some of the mud had been scraped from the floorboards. In the kitchen, the cupboards and floor were washed clean and the smell of disinfectant started to permeate the air.

The furniture left in the sitting room was beyond repair, and was dismantled and removed. At two o'clock Martin received a text, and called for everyone to down tools.

'Lunch in the church hall, ladies and gents. Half an hour.'

Cass had slipped from tearful and embarrassed, through red-cheeked and into beaming. Then back to tearful again as she stood at her front door, hugging everyone and thanking them as they filed out of the house.

'I don't know what to say…' She stood in the doorway waving as everyone made their way back along the track to the village.

'I think you said it, didn't you? Anyway, I think this morning was all about what the village wanted to say to you.'

'It was so good of them…'

'What goes around comes around, Cass.'

'Thank you. For today.'

He nodded. 'Do it again tomorrow?'

'No. You spend tomorrow with Ellie, and I'll come here. I feel better about things, seeing how much difference we've made today.'

'All right.' Jack would have a quiet word with Martin and make sure that Cass wasn't alone tomorrow. And maybe she was right. He'd asked for one day and she'd given it, and maybe that was enough for now.

CHAPTER SIXTEEN

THE WEEK HAD seen them slip back into their easy routine.
Jack had been looking forward to the weekend, wondering if perhaps Cass might be persuaded to take some time
off from her work at the house, for an outing with him and
Ellie. And then, suddenly, nothing else existed. The phone
call on Friday afternoon, from a parent of one of the kids
from Ellie's class, drove everything else from his head. Just
the need to drive, to be there.

He could hear sirens in the distance, and he willed them
on. Jack knew they were probably going in the same direction as he was, and if he couldn't reach Ellie then someone
had to. Anyone.

He took the turn into the small side road that led to the
school and slammed on the brakes, narrowly avoiding a
fire engine that was parked up ahead. Getting out of the
car, he ran, not stopping to even close the driver's door, let
alone lock it.

'Jack… Jack!' He heard a woman's voice and scanned
the crowd. 'Jack!' The mother of a little boy in Ellie's reception class ran towards him.

'Hannah.' He caught her hand, then put his arm around
her. 'What's happening?'

'All the other kids are out. But the annexe…' Hannah's
chest started to heave and Jack willed her to stay calm.

'Sarah told me that part of the building had collapsed.' Ethan had stayed home today with a bad cold, but Jack had dropped Ellie off at school this morning.

'Yes. The ground's so wet… The kids' classroom looks okay from the outside, but they're still in there.'

'Okay. Hannah, they'll get to them. The firefighters are trained for this; they know exactly what to do…' Jack wasn't sure whether he was trying to reassure Hannah or himself.

Stop. Look around. Assess the situation, then act. His own training came to the fore and Jack swallowed down his panic, the overwhelming need to have Ellie safe in his arms.

A pattern emerged from the chaos. A line of older children were leaving the main entrance of the school, shepherded by their teachers towards the sports field, which was some way from the building. There, children were being counted and checked, while a small group of parents waited anxiously.

He took Hannah's hand, walking swiftly around the back of the building, trying to control the feeling that he just needed to sweep everything in front of him away and find Ellie. What had once been the school hall was now a pile of rubble and the two-storey annexe beyond it, which housed the reception classroom, was completely cut off.

'They got the class on the ground floor out through the windows.' Hannah was hiccupping the words out through her tears. 'But Jamie and Ellie were upstairs. I saw her in the window, Jack.'

Jack looked up at the window, his heart leaping as he saw a small figure, climbing up on to the low, wide sill. *Ellie.* She was waving her hands above her head and seemed to be shouting.

'Ellie…' He roared her name, but in the general activity she didn't hear. 'Ellie!'

Someone held him back and he struggled free. The fire-fighters already had ladders up at the windows, and one of them climbed up. Jack saw Ellie walk along the windowsill towards him, reaching through the safety bars to press her hands against the glass.

They seemed to be talking. The firefighter called for quiet and a hush fell on the people below.

'Good girl. We saw you. Get down from the window now, sweetie, and stand over there.' The firefighter pointed into the classroom and Ellie obeyed him.

'Good girl. That's my good girl.' Jack sent the whispered words up into the air, wondering if Ellie knew he was here for her. Praying that she did.

'Why don't they just break the windows?' Hannah had her eyes fixed on the huge picture windows, which looked out on to the rolling countryside beyond.

'Windows that size…if they break them they might hurt the kids.' Jack shivered as he thought of shards of glass raining down on Ellie's head.

'Where's the teacher…?'

Good question. The thought of fifteen four- and five-year-olds alone up there made his blood run cold.

He wrapped his arm around Hannah, hurrying to the cordon of police and teachers which surrounded the scene. 'Let me through. Paramedic.' At the sight of his uniform he was waved through and, taking Hannah with him, he made for the two ambulances, parked next to a fire engine.

'Josie—' he recognised the paramedic who was waiting by one of the ambulances '—what's happening?'

'There's a class of fifteen kids and a teacher, trapped in there. No sign of the teacher, but there's a little girl who keeps coming to the window. There's a fire crew gone in.' Josie pointed towards a pile of rubble which almost filled a gaping hole in the wall. Above it, clean plasterwork with a line of pictures still pinned to it in a parody of normality amongst the destruction.

As he watched, one of the pictures fluttered from the wall on to the ground. A groaning sound, and a chunk of plasterwork flattened it as it detached itself from the wall and crashed down. Hannah let out a little scream of terror.

'Okay, Hannah. It's just a piece of paper...' He tightened his arm around Hannah's shaking shoulders. The image of frailty, crushed and broken, had torn at his heart too.

Josie was shaking her head, her eyes fixed on the classroom windows. 'She didn't hesitate. That woman deserves a medal...'

'What?'

'The firefighter. She saw the little girl and she was the first in, even though there have been great chunks of stuff coming down. Three of the men followed her.'

'Red hair?' A trickle of hope found its way into Jack's heart.

'Dunno, she had a helmet on. I didn't know it was a woman but I heard her call out to someone.'

Cass. It must be Cass. 'I'm going in...' Jack let go of Hannah and started to walk, and Josie pulled him back.

'Don't be an idiot.'

'Ellie's in there.'

Josie paled suddenly. 'All the same, Jack. If you get hit on the head by a lump of concrete then that's just another thing they'll have to deal with.'

He didn't care. 'Stay here, Hannah. I'll find them.'

'Jack...' Both Hannah and Josie were pulling at him now, and Jack shook them off. Then he looked up. Two figures had appeared in the window, with dark jackets and yellow helmets. Firefighters.

Cass. She and the other firefighter were making short work of the safety bars across one of the windows, and they opened it wide. Jack wondered where the other two men who had gone in were, and hoped that their absence didn't mean that there were casualties to attend to.

'Jamie…' The children were being lifted out one by one, into the arms of the men on the two ladders which had been raised to the window, and passed down to the ground. Hannah sprinted forward, pushing a policeman who tried to block her path out of the way in a surprising show of strength. She reached her son and fell to her knees, hugging him close.

Ellie. Where was she? Why wasn't she the first? Jack looked up at the window and saw Cass, with Ellie in her arms. She was talking to her, waiting for the firefighter on the ladder to be ready to take her, and Ellie was nodding.

Then a kiss. Jack almost choked with emotion as he saw Ellie handed safely from the window and into the arms of the man on the ladder.

Cass's attention was now on the next child, lifting him up and talking to him. But all Jack could see was Ellie. He ran forward and heard her voice as she was carried down the ladder.

'I shouted for help…'

'That's right, sweetie. Well done.' The firefighter was smiling as he climbed down.

'Daddeee! Cassandra rescued me.' Ellie held out her arms to Jack and then he felt her small body against him. He stammered his thanks to the firefighter, who nodded, climbing back up the ladder to fetch the next child.

'Are you all right, honey?' His first instinct was just to hold her, but he forced himself to check Ellie's small body for any signs of blood or injury.

'Cassandra came to find me. I got rescued…' There was clearly nothing wrong with Ellie's lungs.

'That's right, darling.' He looked up and saw Cass pass the next child out of the window. When she'd done so, her gaze scanned the people below her and found Ellie, who waved at her excitedly. Cass's grin told Jack that she'd seen what she had been looking for, and that she knew Ellie was safe.

The children were being marshalled into a group around the ambulances by parents and teachers so that each could be checked over. Jack walked across, holding Ellie tightly against his heart.

He saw Sarah running towards them and Ellie waved to her.

'I was rescued!' Clearly Ellie wanted everyone to know. Sarah flung her arms around them both and Ellie struggled to get out from between their bodies so that she could see what was going on.

The last child was being brought down the ladder and Jack did a swift headcount. Fourteen. He made only fourteen. And where was their teacher? He heard Cass's shout behind him.

'Paramedic…'

Josie looked up and grabbed her bag, making for one of the ladders. Jack reluctantly passed Ellie into Sarah's arms.

'Will you take her?' The words tore at his heart but he knew what he had to do.

'Of course. As soon as she's been checked over, I'll take her back home. I left Ethan with my neighbour so I don't want to be any longer than I can help.' Sarah turned to Ellie. 'Daddy's got to go and help Cassandra. We'll wait for him at home, eh?'

Ellie nodded. 'Are you going to rescue Miss Elliott?'

'Yes, sweetie. I'll be back as soon as I can.' Jack turned and made for the ladders.

* * *

It was no surprise that after the first paramedic was helped through the window, Jack appeared right behind her. Both of them had been provided with helmets and jackets.

'Just couldn't stay away, could you?' Cass grimaced at him.

'Nope.' Jack looked around the empty classroom.

Cass nodded. 'Good. Keep the helmet on.'

She led the way across the empty classroom, holding her arm out in front of him to keep him back from the door as she opened it. She heard Jack let out a quiet curse as he looked along the corridor, at the gaping hole in the floor that separated the classroom door from the far end of the corridor. 'How did you get through here?'

'We made it.' It hadn't been easy, and they'd been showered with lumps of loose plaster falling from the ceiling. But when she'd seen Ellie up at the window, Cass had remembered the promise she'd made to the little girl. *'If you go to the window and call for help, the firefighters will rescue you.'* That wasn't the kind of promise you made lightly.

'What's the situation?'

'The teacher's at the bottom of the hole, with the boy. He's lying underneath her and we don't know how badly either of them are hurt yet. There's a team trying to get to her from the back, on ground floor level, but the doorways are blocked with rubble and at the moment the only way is through here. So a second team has been working to get a ladder down to her.'

'Can you get me down there?'

'It's not safe.' The roof was still intact but cables and lumps of ceiling plaster dangled precariously over the hole. The other paramedic had already backed away into the safety of the classroom, and if he was going to stick to protocol then Jack should as well.

'Tell me something I don't know. Get me down there, Cass.'

She nodded. 'Okay. It'll be a minute before we're ready to go down.'

'Is she conscious?'

'We think so. When we came along the corridor we heard her groaning, and when we called down she replied. There was stuff coming down from the ceiling and she was covering the child with her body.'

'What happened?' Jack's face had formed into a mask of determination.

'I think the boy must have run out of the classroom and the teacher followed him. We found the door locked, and she must have thought to lock it behind her to keep the rest of the kids inside. Somehow, she and the boy both fell.'

He nodded. 'Can we get her up to this level?'

'We could, but it would be better to wait for the team coming in via the ground floor. We'll have to make a decision on that when you've assessed her injuries.' Cass looked up as someone called her name. 'They're ready.'

Jack followed her over to the mouth of the hole and Cass climbed carefully down, flattening herself against the ladder as a shower of dust and debris fell from the ceiling. Picking her way across the rubble, and what looked like the remains of a photocopier, she headed towards the woman.

'Annabel... Annabel, I'm Cass.'

Annabel's eyelids flickered and she moaned. 'Cass...'

'Lie still. Not too long now before we get you out of here.'

'Take him...' Annabel cried out in pain as she shifted slightly and a boy's dirty, frightened face peered out at Cass.

'Okay. Okay, we're going to take you both. Just hang in there.'

The boy started to crawl out from the crevice below Annabel's body. Somehow, even though she was clearly badly injured, she'd managed to get him into the safest place she could, protecting him in the only way that was available to her. Dust and plaster was floating down from above them and Cass crouched over Annabel, sheltering her and the child as best she could.

Jack was making his way towards her with the medical bag, which had been lowered down after them. As soon as he reached them, Cass let go of the boy, who wriggled free of his hidey-hole and straight into Jack's arms.

The boy was handed back to the firefighter who had followed Jack down, ready to be carried back up to the classroom where the other paramedic was waiting. Cass held her position, sheltering Annabel, while Jack started to check her over, talking quietly to reassure her.

A piece of something hit the back of her helmet and Jack glanced upwards. 'Okay?'

'Yep. Keep going.' Annabel was injured and defenceless. And she'd already shown such bravery. Cass would keep shielding her with her own body for as long as it took.

Jack gave her the briefest of smiles and then turned his attention back to his patient.

'Sweetheart. Annabel… I'm giving you pain relief. It'll kick in pretty quickly.' He murmured the words and Cass saw Annabel nod.

'The children…' She opened her eyes, trying to focus on Jack. 'You're Ellie's dad…'

'Yes, that's right. The children are all safe, thanks to you. And Shaun is okay as well—the firefighters are taking him out of the building.'

'I picked him up and the ground just… My leg…'

'You did just great, Annabel. You protected them all.'

Jack's sideways glance at Cass told her that he'd come to the same conclusion she had. Annabel and Shaun must have fallen together and she must have landed awkwardly, trying to protect him.

'So cold. Don't want to…die.' A tear dribbled from the corner of Annabel's eye and Cass shifted her position so that she could take her hand.

'You're not going to die.' Jack brushed the side of her face with his fingers to keep her attention. 'Hey… Annabel.'

'Yeah… Too much paperwork…' Annabel grimaced.

'Far too much. I know you're hurting, but you're going to mend. Just hold on to Cass and we'll be getting you out of here as soon as we can. Got it?' Cass knew exactly what the warmth in Jack's eyes could do. He could make her believe anything, and she hoped that Annabel would believe him now.

'Yes…'

News was passed through that the firefighters, working to get through at ground floor level, were almost there. Jack worked on Annabel quickly and carefully, preparing her to be moved. A neck brace and temporary splints for her legs. A thermal blanket, to try and warm her a little, and an oxygen mask.

Annabel's eyes followed him. Somehow, Jack had managed to become not just someone who could give her medical help but her lifeline. It was almost as if he was keeping her going, just by the sheer force of his personality, that warmth in his eyes. Staving off the shock which made Annabel's hand ice-cold in hers.

The noise of boots clambering over the rubble heralded the arrival of the stretcher. Jack slid a lifting board under her body and Cass helped him transfer her to the stretcher, quickly securing the straps and tucking the thermal blanket around her.

'Okay, sweetheart.' Jack smiled down at Annabel. 'We're on our way.'

CHAPTER SEVENTEEN

JACK WAITED UNTIL the ambulance had drawn away, carrying Annabel to the hospital. Cass came to stand beside him, watching the vehicle negotiate its way past the fire engines and down the lane.

'Brave woman,' she murmured.

'Yeah. Josie's going to find out how she is when she goes off shift, and call me.'

'Do you think…?' She shrugged. 'How did she seem, to you?'

'Shock. One leg broken, and the other is probably fractured. Cuts, bruises, and she's got a cracked rib and what looks like a broken wrist. I couldn't find anything else, but they'll be checking her over further at the hospital to make sure.'

Cass nodded. 'I hope she's all right. Are you going off shift now?'

'Yes, I want to take Ellie straight home.'

'Okay.' Cass turned towards the fire engine. 'See you later.'

He caught her arm. 'Cass. Thank you.' There was nothing more he could say. When he'd seen Ellie in Cass's arms his heart had almost burst with relief.

'Yeah. Any time.' She grinned up at him and he knew that she understood.

By the time Jack got Ellie home she was starting to ask questions, and to realise that her experience hadn't been just another game. Was her teacher hurt? Why did her school fall down—was their house going to fall down too? He tried to answer everything as honestly as he could without feeding his daughter's fears.

She wanted to hold on to him, and he settled down in front of the TV to watch her favourite film with her. Even that didn't seem to get her singing and dancing around the room, as it usually did.

Cass was a little later than usual and, when he heard the front door close, Ellie didn't get up and run to greet her. When she walked into the sitting room, she was smiling.

'Hey, Ellie.' She squatted down in front of her. 'How are you doing?'

'All right.' Ellie turned her solemn eyes on to Cass without letting go of Jack's shirt.

'I've got something for you.' Cass was holding one hand behind her back.

Ellie craned around, trying to see what it was. 'Sometimes we meet kids who are really, really brave. And we give them a special certificate.'

'Really?' Ellie's eyes widened, and Jack grinned. So that was what she'd been up to.

'Yes.' Cass produced a roll of paper from behind her back, tied with a red ribbon. 'So this is for you.'

Ellie took the paper and Jack pulled open the bow with his free hand and unrolled it on Ellie's lap. Her name was on it in large letters framed with curlicues. He ran his finger under the words.

'Junior Firefighter...' he read out loud. 'That's you, Ellie. And, look, everyone from the fire station has signed it.' He pointed to the group of signatures, strewn with kisses and hearts. Cass's name was there too, the writing careful and rounded.

He stopped to wonder for a moment how handwriting could possibly be sexy, and then turned his mind to the image at the bottom.

'And there's the fire engine.' The artwork was clearly downloaded from the Internet, but that wasn't the point. Cass had taken the time to print it off on thick paper, and to get it signed by everyone. And Ellie was proud of herself now, not fretful and worrying.

'Say thank you to Cass.' He turned his face up to her, mouthing the words for himself, wondering if she knew just how heartfelt they were. She smiled at him.

'What's for supper?'

Everything was clearly okay in Cass's world if she was hungry. Jack had come to recognise the signs. 'Pasta. Fifteen minutes. Why don't you take Ellie upstairs and you can find a place on her bedroom wall for the certificate. I'll get a frame for it, eh, Ellie?'

The bumps and bangs from upstairs, along with the sound of Ellie's chatter, indicated that there was rather more going on than just the choosing of a place on the wall. Jack laid the table in the kitchen and took the pasta bake from the oven, leaving it to cool. Curious to see what they were doing, he walked upstairs to fetch them instead of calling them down.

The curtains were drawn in Ellie's bedroom, and Jack's hand hovered over the light switch as he popped his head around the door. Then he saw the makeshift arrangement of sheets, held up with a couple of chairs and some twine, forming a tent at the end of Ellie's bed. The glow of torchlight and the mutter of voices came from inside.

For a moment he was transfixed. So this was what it was like. A family. He remembered playing in a tent in the garden with his dad before everything had been shattered and their home had become just a house where grief had pushed the laughter away.

Suddenly it hurt. That swell of pain, all the regret for things he'd never done with his father. For the first time, Jack wondered whether his father had really wanted to leave them like that. Whether, in those last moments, when death must have seemed inevitable, he had thought of his wife and children.

For a moment the feelings choked him. It had been so much easier to blame his father, to be angry at the choices he'd made. But perhaps he'd just been a dad, after all.

Quietly, he walked into the room. The sudden clatter of wind chimes startled him and Ellie came cannoning out of the makeshift tent, almost knocking it down. Jack hadn't noticed the trip wire at his feet.

'We got you, Daddy...' Ellie wrapped her arms around his leg, clinging on tight.

'Yeah, you got me.' He bent down to tickle her and she wriggled with laughter. Then he put one finger over his lips, assuming a stage whisper. 'Where's Cass?'

'In the tent,' Ellie whispered back, her hand shielding her mouth.

Jack dropped to his knees and followed Ellie. Inside the tent, a line of dolls greeted him, their faces impassive. And Cass, sitting cross-legged and a little nervous, as if she'd just been caught doing something she wasn't strictly meant to.

'Can I come in?' Jack grinned at her.

'Yes. Of course.' She shifted a bit to give him room to get inside the tent and Ellie clambered past him to her own spot, next to the dolls. 'Is dinner getting cold...? Ellie, we should go downstairs...'

'We could eat up here.'

'Yes!' Ellie gave him an imploring look and Cass reddened.

'Won't we make a mess?'

'Probably. That's what they make kitchen towel for.' He met her gaze. Today had changed things. When he'd seen Cass and Ellie together in the classroom window, he'd realised that trying to protect Ellie from Cass's love was not only useless; it was counterproductive. When they'd worked together with Annabel, Jack had wondered just how much else they could achieve together, given the chance.

And Cass had changed too. She'd created a comforting world for Ellie, and it was one that all three of them could share. They hadn't been together like this since he and Cass had slept with Ellie, on his bed, weeks ago.

'I used to have a tent, when I was little.' He smiled at Ellie. 'Grandma used to make burgers and chips, and she'd bring them out to the tent for Grandad and Auntie Sarah and me.'

Two pairs of round eyes gazed at him, Ellie's filled with interest and Cass's with astonishment.

'Auntie Sarah says that my grandad is the same as Ethan's grandad.' Jack realised that Sarah must have talked to Ellie about their father but that he never had, and she was struggling with the concept. It was an omission that he should have rectified by now.

'Yes, that's right. Do you want to see a picture of him? With me and Auntie Sarah when we were little.'

Ellie nodded vigorously.

'Okay. We'll have supper first, though.'

'I'll come and give you a hand.' Cass moved in the cramped space, trying not to knock any of the dolls over.

'It's okay. Stay here.' They didn't need to talk about this.

Tonight might be as terrifying in its own way as today had been, but it was long overdue.

They were having fun. The tent that Cass had intended as something to cheer Ellie up with, and would fit only two people and a line of dolls, had turned into a tent for three. Just like a proper family.

Jack had gone to fetch the photograph, disappearing for some time, and Cass supposed it was hidden away somewhere and he'd had to look for it. Ellie had drawn her own version, and Jack had watched thoughtfully.

'He looks like you, Daddy.'

'Yeah. He does, doesn't he?' There was no trace of the anger that surfaced whenever Jack talked about his father. He ran his fingers lightly over the photograph, as if he too were re-drawing it.

'Okay?' Ellie was busy with another picture and Cass ventured the question.

'Yeah. I think so.' Jack still seemed unsure about this, but he'd hidden the tremor in his hands from Ellie. 'You?'

It was nothing to do with her. It was Jack's father, his child, and his conflict...

But when she'd passed Ellie out of the window and seen Jack waiting at the bottom of the ladder, it had felt for a moment as if Ellie was her own child. As if all the pressure and fear were gone, swamped by their shared instincts to keep the little girl safe. Maybe...just maybe...there was some way forward for her and Jack.

'You?' He repeated the question, more pointedly this time.

'Yes. Fine.' Cass turned to the picture that Ellie was drawing, trying to avoid his gaze. 'That's beautiful...'

She'd spoken before she had even looked at the picture.

And when she did look, it *was* beautiful. A house. A red crayoned figure who she'd come to recognise as herself, along with a tall figure who could only be Jack. Between them stood four small figures.

'That's me.' Ellie planted her finger on one of the smaller images. 'And Daddy and Cassandra, and my brothers. And that's my sister.'

'Sweetheart…' Jack's voice was strained and Cass couldn't look at him. Didn't dare let him see the tears as her own picture of her perfect family suddenly imploded, smashing itself into pieces.

'That's very nice, Ellie.' She cleared her throat. 'I'm…'

What? Living next door? Coming to rescue Jack and his family? For a moment she couldn't think of any other reason for her to be in the picture than the one that Ellie so obviously intended.

'Okay…' When Jack pulled the picture out from in front of her, she almost cried out with loss. His other arm curled around Ellie and he took her on to his lap for a hug. 'I think it's nearly bedtime, don't you, Ellie?'

'No.' Ellie's voice was indignant.

'I think it is…'

Suddenly Cass couldn't take it. The nightly debate, which Jack always managed to win one way or another. The kiss, before Ellie ran to her father to go up to bed. She squeezed past Jack, almost knocking the tent down in her haste to get out.

'Cass…?'

'I'm going to stack the dishwasher.' She didn't wait for Jack's reply but ran downstairs, turning on the kitchen tap to splash cool water on her face. She'd done the one thing that she'd promised herself she'd never do again. She'd fallen for Jack, and dared to dream about a happy ending. One that could never come true.

Jack tried to get Ellie into bed as fast as he could, but hurrying always seemed to have the same effect. The more he tried to rush, the slower Ellie went. He read Ellie's favourite story, hoping she wouldn't mind that he'd missed a few bits out, listening for any sign of movement downstairs. When he finally kissed Ellie goodnight, the house had been silent for a while.

She was sitting at the kitchen table, nursing a cup of tea. Cass didn't need to look at him for Jack to know she'd been crying.

'I'm so sorry. She didn't mean it…' The words tumbled out. It was all his fault. If he hadn't talked about his own father, then Ellie would probably never have drawn the picture. Jack had broken his own rule, dared to include Cass in his and Ellie's tiny family unit. And he'd hurt her.

She shrugged. 'I know.'

'She draws whatever happens to be going on in her head at the time. It doesn't mean anything.' He was protesting far too much. Trying to deny the truth. It hadn't just been going on in Ellie's head; it had been going on in his. And, from the look in her eyes, it had been going on in Cass's too.

She shook her head. 'It's what she wants.'

Jack almost choked. 'Ellie has what she needs; this isn't about her.' On that level it wasn't. On another, deeper level, the thought of hurting her the way he'd been hurt, deliberately putting her at risk of losing a parent again, still terrified him.

'No? Then make it about you and me then. How would you feel, knowing that there was no possibility of having any more children?' The intensity in her quiet words made it very clear that they would have been shouted if there wasn't a sleeping child in the house.

'Honestly…?'

She looked up at him suddenly. Such pain in her eyes. 'That would be good. Honesty always is.'

'Honestly, I think it's you that needs to face that, not me.'

'My problem, you mean?' she flared angrily.

'No, I didn't mean that at all. I meant that you're the one who thinks it's a problem in our relationship, not me.'

'We weren't going to have this conversation, Jack. You said you'd keep me safe.'

The words stung because they were true. And wanting to change didn't mean that it was easy.

'It's been a hell of a day. Perhaps we should sleep on it.'

She nodded, her face impassive. 'Yes. I need to be up early tomorrow. I'm seeing the electrician at my house in the morning.'

Jack nodded. 'Are you coming to bed, then?'

He'd never had to ask before. Always known that Cass would go to her own room, to get ready for bed, and then come to his. The moments of waiting, which had seemed like hours in his impatience to hold her, were almost the best part of his day. Second only to when he actually did hold her.

'I don't want to disturb you in the morning. And I could do with some sleep tonight.'

Jack nodded. Saying it out loud had broken the spell. 'I'll see you for supper then. Tomorrow.'

'Yes.' She stood up, bending to kiss his cheek. That, somehow, seemed the most damning thing of all. That she still wanted him, maybe even loved him a little, but there was a gap between them which neither of them could bridge.

He didn't see her again until the following evening. She arrived home late, her face expressionless, and sat down with him in the lounge. Separate chairs, the way they always did, even if there would be no one to see if they curled up together on the sofa. It seemed almost normal, and strangely comforting after having brooded over the possibility that Cass might do what they'd agreed to do all along and take it into her head to call time on their relationship.

'How are things?'

'Fine. Good, actually. The electrician reckons it's safe to restore part of the power supply now, and that means I can get heaters in there to help dry the ground floor out a bit. The motorway's open again.'

One by one, the things that kept her here were disappearing. It was only a matter of time...

'I'm going to move back in.'

Jack swallowed. 'Already?'

'It's easier for me to be there. As long as I have somewhere to sleep, they're still doing lunches and an evening meal up at the church hall.' She pressed her lips together. Clearly she didn't want to talk about it.

'You have somewhere to sleep here.' His bed. In his arms.

'I know.' She sighed. 'But...'

Jack could feel it all slipping away. Protected by secrecy and the four walls of his bedroom, their love affair had blossomed, but as soon as they took it outside that, into the real world, it seemed unbearably fragile.

But maybe, with a little care, it could survive. 'Will you come out with me? One evening. A meal, perhaps.'

She blinked at him. 'You're asking me out on a date?'

'Yeah. I am. Sarah will look after Ellie...'

'I don't think that's a very good idea.'

'Why not?' Okay, so he knew the reasons. Had struggled with the reasons, and Jack still wasn't sure that they weren't valid ones. But surely Cass could give it a try?

'Because…' She stared at him for a moment, her gaze searching his face. 'Because there's no future in it, Jack. I know what it's like to want a child so badly that your whole life seems shattered every time your body tells you that you're not pregnant. I can't go through that again.'

'I'm not asking you to. All I'm asking is that we give it a little time. Find a way to work things out.'

She shook her head, her face suddenly impassive. 'No. That would be too cruel.'

She got to her feet, leaving the room without even looking at him and closing the door behind her in a clear sign that he wasn't to follow her. He heard her soft footsteps on the stairs and the sound of her bedroom door close. Then silence.

Jack stared into the gathering gloom, which had once been a thrilling first hint of the darkness ahead. Now all he could feel was anger. He'd risked everything for Cass, his own heart, and Ellie's. He'd trusted her enough to try to let her into his life but she was still too fearful to even make the effort, and now she was going to leave him.

Maybe she was right and it would never have worked out. And, if that was the case, then he needed to think of Ellie. He needed to protect her.

He sat for a long time, brooding into the darkness, then slumped round on the sofa, fatigue taking over from the what-ifs that were filling his mind. No point in going up to bed. He knew that Cass wouldn't be coming.

Cass was up and packed before there was any sound from Ellie's bedroom. By the time she heard the tinkle of wind chimes heralding the fact that the little girl was awake, she was sitting on the bed in the spare room, staring at the wall.

It was all for the best. This had never been anything other than something temporary, something that couldn't touch their real lives. It had been three weeks since their first night together. Just about the duration of a holiday romance.

The sounds of Jack and Ellie in the bathroom. The smell of breakfast. Everyday things, now tainted with sadness. She waited until she heard Ellie running around in the sitting room, ready to jump on the new day with her customary glee, and went downstairs.

Jack was drowsy and tight-lipped. He closed the kitchen door and turned to her, his face unreadable.

'You're going today?'

'Yeah.'

He nodded. 'Okay. I'm taking Ellie out to the petting zoo this morning. They've just opened up again after the floods.' His eyes softened suddenly and a thrill of hope ran through her veins. 'Take your time packing.'

Even Jack couldn't fix this. Neither could she. All they could do was to act as if nothing had happened, and that was easy enough. They'd been acting as if nothing was happening practically since they'd first laid eyes on each other.

'I'm ready to go now.'

He nodded abruptly. 'We'll be going soon. Then you can go.'

He couldn't help it. However much he was trying to come to terms with the past, he couldn't do it yet. Jack was cutting her out of his life, another casualty of loss, just like his father and Sal.

'May I...' Cass almost choked on the words. Surely he couldn't be that cruel. 'May I say goodbye to her?'

'Of course.' A glimmer of warmth again in his eyes and then he turned, opening the kitchen door. 'Take whatever time you need.'

It was cold comfort. Cass explained to Ellie that she was

going back home today and the little girl nodded, taking it in her stride.

'You're not going far.'

'No, sweetie, not far. You know where I live.'

'That's all right, then.'

Cass hugged her tight, squeezing her eyes closed to stop the tears. Jack called to her from the hallway, persuading her into her coat and wellingtons, and Ellie shouted a goodbye. When Cass went to the front door to wave them off, he didn't even look at her. If Ellie required a hug and a kiss goodbye, Jack obviously required neither.

CHAPTER EIGHTEEN

THE CLOCK RADIO blared into life and Cass cursed it, reaching out to shut it off. The sudden movement prompted a twinge in her shoulder.

Well it might. She'd been up until midnight last night, putting flat-pack kitchen units together, and they'd been heavier than she'd expected. Today, she might take some time to reflect on the considerable amount of work she'd done on the house in the last two months. Take a few 'work in progress' photographs to compare with the devastation of the 'before' photos and spur her on to the distant date when 'after' photos would be in order.

She took a long shower, still revelling in the fact that she had hot water again. Then padded back to her bedroom, sorting through her wardrobe and on a whim pulling out a skirt. Being able to wear something pretty in the house instead of muddying up her jeans yet again was novelty enough to smack of yet another new achievement.

She made coffee and then went back upstairs to her bedroom, sitting cross-legged on the bed and switching on the television. This was the one room in the house which didn't bear some signs of the devastation the flood had brought with it; downstairs was still a work in progress and the spare room was full of furniture. But here she could relax.

A film maybe. Watching TV on a Sunday morning

seemed like the ultimate luxury. Cass picked up the remote from the bedside cabinet and switched to streaming, flipping through the films on offer. No, not that one. Or that one. Definitely not that; she'd heard it was a weepie. Or that—it was a love story.

The only thing that seemed to drive Jack from her mind was hard work. And the only thing which drove him from her dreams was physical and mental exhaustion. Cass hesitated, looking at her jeans, folded neatly on a chair. Maybe she should put them on and get on with the kitchen cabinets.

The doorbell rang and she climbed off the bed and walked over to the window. Perhaps someone from the village wanted her for something. She almost hoped that it might be a problem which required her immediate attention.

Peering out, she jumped back in horror. Jack's car was parked outside in the lane. Maybe he'd brought Ellie back to renew some acquaintance he'd made here and decided to pop in. Didn't he *know* he couldn't just do that?

Cass watched the front path and saw him stand away from the door, scanning the front of the house. He was alone, and suddenly fear clutched at her heart. Why would he come here without Ellie on a Sunday morning?

She raced downstairs, sliding her feet into her wellingtons when she realised they were the only footwear she had in the hallway. Then she flung open the door.

'Jack…?'

He was making his way back up the path and he turned. Cass's stomach almost did a somersault as suddenly she realised that she hadn't remembered the warmth of his eyes at all. They'd always been so much better in reality.

'What's the matter? Where's Ellie?' Surely the only thing that could bring him here alone was if there was some kind of trouble.

'At Sarah's.' He paused for a moment and then strode back along the path towards her. 'May I come in?'

The temptation to slam the door in his face fought with the need to look at him just a little longer, and lost by a whisker. And she'd opened the door now. Not letting him in would betray the fact that she cared one way or the other.

She stood back from the door in silence and he nodded, wiping his feet and walking into the hall.

'Wow. Quite a difference from last time I saw this.'

Presumably he was referring to the new plaster and skirting boards, and the scrubbed floorboards. All Cass could think about was that the last time he'd been here they'd had something, and now there was nothing.

'It's been hard work.'

'I imagine so.' He seemed a little jumpy. As if there was a point to all of this and he was working himself up to it.

'What do you want, Jack?'

He turned his gaze on her, warm enough to melt chocolate. 'I've come for you, princess.'

No. *No!* What had made him think that he could do this? Leave Ellie with Sarah and pop back for a day spent in bed. Who did he think she was?

'Out.' She glared at him, hoping he'd go before she changed her mind. Her body had just caught on to the idea and was beginning to like it.

'Cass, wait. Can we talk about this?'

'There's nothing to talk about. You can't just drop in whenever you've got a free moment and you think you might like to warm your feet in my bed.'

Reproach flashed in his eyes. 'It's not like that.'

'Okay then, friends with benefits, whatever you want to call it. I'm not interested.'

'Neither am I. Cass, can we sit down...?'

'There's nowhere to sit. The kitchen's full of cupboards, and there's no furniture in the sitting room.' And she wasn't going to take him upstairs to her bedroom.

He rolled his eyes. 'Then we'll do it here.'

'No, we won't. Whatever it is.'

Suddenly he was too close. His lips just an inch away. Cass felt tears begin to roll down her cheeks. 'Jack, stop it. Please…'

'I don't want sex…'

'Stop it!' Didn't he know that friendship was just as much out of the question? She couldn't bear it.

'I want to marry you.'

Suddenly the air began to swim in front of her, distorting everything else. She felt her knees begin to buckle…

Jack managed to catch her before she hit the ground. *Stupid. Stupid.* He shouldn't have just come out with it like that but he was so afraid that Cass was going to throw him out before he got a chance to say it. He settled her in his arms and carried her upstairs, kicking open the nearest door and finding a room stacked with furniture. The other door revealed a large sunny bedroom with light oak furniture and white lace bedlinen.

She was already stirring in his arms and her fingers clutched at his shoulders when he walked over to the bed with her. 'Boots… Jack…'

'Okay. Just relax; I'll take them off.' The room was meticulously clean and tidy, and Jack knew that Cass would probably kill him if he let her wellingtons soil the bed. Sitting her down, he pulled her boots off and then guided her back on to the pillows.

His finger found the pulse in her neck. Strong, even if it was a little fast. His was probably faster.

'I'm all right.'

'I dare say you are. Stay down for a minute.'

She opened her eyes and their pale blue earnestness made his heart lurch. 'I must have just...'

'Have you been eating?' She'd felt light in his arms, and now that she was lying on her back he could see the line of her hips through the thin fabric of her skirt.

'I...' Her face took on a look of grudging contrition. 'I was putting the kitchen cabinets together last night and didn't stop for supper. I haven't got around to breakfast yet...'

'And so you fainted.' Jack decided not to touch on the immediate reason in case she did it again. He got to his feet. 'Stay there.'

'I'm okay. Really. Just a bit embarrassed.'

Not half as embarrassed as he was, for being such an idiot as to just drop a marriage proposal on her, right out of the blue. But now wasn't the time to mention that, not until she'd had something to eat.

'Stay there.'

'But...'

'No buts, Cass. If you move, I'll... Just don't move.' He tried to put as much authority as he could into his words before he hurried downstairs to the kitchen.

Cass could hear the banging of cupboard doors downstairs. Jack had asked her to marry him?

Maybe she'd got it wrong. Maybe he'd done it on impulse and was regretting it now. Or maybe he'd meant it, and she'd had to go and spoil the moment by fainting. It was her own stupid fault, but the constant hunger for Jack seemed to have overwhelmed everything lately, even hunger for food.

He appeared in the doorway, a glass of milk in one hand and a plate with a couple of croissants in the other. Sitting down on the edge of the bed, he waited for her to sit up before he put the plate on to her lap.

'Feeling better?'

'Yes, much. What were you going to say to me?'

'Eat first.'

How was she going to eat with the words she thought Jack had said bursting in her head like fireworks? She picked up one of the croissants and put it down again.

'I can't.'

He narrowed his eyes. 'Try. C'mon, Cass, I know you can do it.'

'I can't. Really. Jack…' *Please let this be what she thought it was. Please…*

He flashed her a grin. 'I'm glad you can't wait. Don't think I can either.'

'Then get on with it! I'm feeling a little nervous.'

He chuckled. 'Good. I'm feeling a bit nervous too.' Jack picked her hand up from her lap, kissing her fingers, and she nodded him on.

'Cass, you taught me how to believe. And I believe in you. There's only one choice and I've made it. I love you and I want to be with you for the rest of my life. We'll take everything else as it comes, face it together.'

It was everything she wanted to hear. There was only one more question and she had to ask it now, before happiness chipped away at her resolve. 'Are you sure you could be happy? If I couldn't give you children?'

'Wrong question.' He shook his head, smiling. 'If we can't have children *together*, then I can still be very happy. This is how sure I am…'

He reached into his pocket, pulling out a small box. When he opened it Cass clapped her hand to her mouth. The ring inside was beautiful, two diamonds twisted together in a gold setting.

'You're the only woman I'm ever going to want, Cass. You and Ellie are the only family I'm ever going to need. The only question is whether that's enough for you.'

'Me? Are you joking?' He was offering her the whole world and he wanted to know if it was enough?

His mouth curved into a smile. 'I'll let you know when I'm joking.' He snapped the box shut again and put it back in his pocket.

'Hey! Don't I get to look at it a bit more?'

'I thought you might like to think about it for a while.'

'Jack, ask me again. Please, I know my answer.'

He nodded. He knew her answer too. It had always been this way with Jack. Friends, lovers—they were like two pieces of a jigsaw that fitted perfectly.

He sat on the bed, holding her hands between his. 'Will you marry me, Cass?'

'Yes, Jack. I'll marry you.'

He took the ring out of the box, slipping it on to her finger.

They'd talked for hours, lying together on the bed, side by side. He'd told her his dreams and she'd told him hers. And all of those dreams began slowly to morph into plans.

He was so happy. It felt as if a great weight had been lifted off him, not just the weight of the last months, when he'd struggled to cope without Cass, but the weight of years.

'You want something more to eat?' Jack doubted it. In his remorse at seeing her so thin, he'd raided the kitchen again and she'd worked her way through two sandwiches, a banana and a pot of yoghurt.

'No. I... Were you serious when you said you didn't want sex?' The tone of Cass's voice intimated that she was pretty sure he hadn't been.

'I only want sex under certain conditions.' Her eyebrows shot up and Jack couldn't help smiling.

'Really? Well, you can't just leave me guessing. What conditions?'

'To show how much I love you. To celebrate with you, comfort you, be your companion.' He leaned in to kiss her lightly on the lips, his body burning with need. 'I'm not going to rule out cheap thrills...'

'I like the sound of *cheap thrills*. Would it be quicker to tell me what you *don't* want?'

'Yeah, much.' He eased his leg between her knees. 'I don't want you to be worrying about what time of the month it is, or whether your temperature's just spiked. I want you to see me, Cass. Only me.'

Neither of them had been able to deny that they wanted a child together, but they'd agreed that what they already had was enough. Now was the time to test that out, whether Cass could really leave her own past behind and risk all her broken dreams against what they had now.

'I'd really like that...' She gave him a dazzling smile. 'No expectations, then?'

He wouldn't go quite that far. 'Yeah, I've got expectations. That thing you do... The one that drives me crazy...'

'Which thing is that?'

'Every single one of them. All I see is you, sweetheart.'

'And all I see is you.'

She wound her arms around his neck, pulling him down for a kiss. Then she whispered in his ear, 'Take your clothes off...'

EPILOGUE

JACK FELT AS if he'd been sitting here for hours, although in truth it was probably only ten minutes. He looked around, towards the entrance of the church, and Mimi elbowed him in the ribs. 'Do that again and I'll be having words with you, Jack.'

'You're supposed to be looking after me, not haranguing me.' Jack had asked Rafe to be his best man and he'd refused, telling him that Mimi was the one he'd crewed an ambulance with for seven years. So convention had been thrown to the wind and both Mimi and Rafe sat beside him.

'She won't be late.' Rafe leaned over. 'Cass is never late.'

'She's already late.'

'No, she isn't.' Mimi looked at her watch. 'She's got another two minutes to go. If you don't stop this, so help me, Jack, I'm going to sedate you.'

A sound at the other end of the aisle. There seemed to be some activity in the porch, and suddenly Ellie appeared. It was the second time in six months that she'd been a bridesmaid and, after the petal-throwing debacle at Rafe and Mimi's wedding, Cass had decided that a sparkly wand might go with the pretty pink dress that Ellie had helped pick for herself.

Ellie waved the wand at the assembled company. Their families, their friends and half the village had turned out and squashed themselves into the church at Holme. Every head turned and the organist struck up the wedding march. This time Ellie didn't take fright and started to walk up the aisle, a look of intense concentration on her face.

Then Jack saw her. She had flowers in her hair and her dress fell in soft folds from an embroidered bodice, emphasising the fluidity of her movements. As Cass walked slowly towards him, her hand resting lightly on her father's arm, he was transfixed.

'Stand up, will you?' Mimi hissed the words in his ear, kicking him. Jack wondered whether his legs would be able to support him. Cass was the most beautiful woman in the world and she'd come here to be his wife.

'You've got the rings?' He turned to Rafe in a sudden panic.

'Of course we have.' Rafe propelled him to his feet and Cass smiled at him. And suddenly everything was not only all right; it was touched with more joy than Jack could ever have imagined one man could stand.

She'd made her vows and he'd made his. As they stepped out of the church and into the spring sunshine, a firefighters' guard of honour stood to attention. Miss Palmer was on the station commander's arm and Ellie capered around, swishing her wand. Everyone trooped across to the village green, where two huge interconnecting marquees had been erected, one to accommodate the buffet and the other for dancing.

Jack was by her side all the way, through the speeches, the cutting of the cake, the excited congratulations. Her soulmate. The hero who had saved her and brought her to a place where she was completely happy.

'Do you have a date yet? For moving in?' Martin beamed at Jack.

'A couple of months, we hope. We're taking our time and doing it properly.'

Both Jack and Ellie loved the house down by the river, and Holme was a good place for Ellie to grow up. They'd chosen the new decorations together and when Jack sold his place there would be cash to build a second storey on to the existing extension if they wanted. Cass found Jack's hand and felt his fingers close around hers.

'And I saw the new wall,' Sue chipped in. 'So, no more repeats of last year.'

'It wasn't all bad. Look what I found washed up on my doorstep.' Cass squeezed Jack's hand and he chuckled.

There was one more thing to be done. Jack had made her feel so happy, so loved, that she'd almost forgotten about monthly cycles and calendars. Until last week. She'd been to the doctor and taken a pregnancy test, just to be sure before she went on her honeymoon.

She'd run all the way home to tell him, stopping just yards from the house. He'd told her that he wanted to marry her without knowing what the future held and she couldn't deprive him of the chance to make that ultimate commitment.

Jack led her on to the dance floor. The weather was warm enough for the walls of the marquee to be removed, leaving just a high domed canopy, strung with lights over their heads. When their first dance was over, other couples started to fill the dance floor.

She felt Jack's chest heave in a long contented sigh and she smiled up at him. 'Happy?'

'I don't think it's possible to be any happier.'

She laughed. 'Sure about that?'

'Positive.'

She stretched up, whispering in his ear.

* * *

Mimi was watching the couples on the dance floor as suddenly Jack lifted Cass up, swinging her round. Then he set her back on to her feet again, hugging her tight as tears streamed down his face.

'Look.' She nudged Rafe. 'I don't suppose there's a bit more synchronicity going on, is there…?' It had become a joke between the two couples that Jack had set eyes on Cass at pretty much the same moment that Mimi had seen Rafe again.

Rafe thought for a moment. 'No. I don't.'

'Why not? It makes perfect sense.'

'But what are the odds, Mimi? Seriously. It would be wonderful, but…' His gaze wandered over to where Jack was still hugging Cass.

'Trust me, Rafe. Jack's got that same dazed expression on his face as you had last week, when I told you I was pregnant.'

'Really? I didn't look *that* bad, did I?'

Mimi stood on her toes so she could whisper in his ear. 'You were worse. And much more handsome.'

Rafe chuckled. 'Thank you. Would you like to dance?'

'I'd love to dance.'

* * * * *

MILLS & BOON®

MEDICAL ROMANCE™

THE ULTIMATE IN ROMANTIC MEDICAL DRAMA

A sneak peek at next month's titles...

In stores from 6th October 2016:

- **Waking Up to Dr Gorgeous** – Emily Forbes *and*
  Swept Away by the Seductive Stranger –
  Amy Andrews

- **One Kiss in Tokyo...** – Scarlet Wilson *and*
  The Courage to Love Her Army Doc – Karin Baine

- **Reawakened by the Surgeon's Touch** – Jennifer Taylor
  and **Second Chance with Lord Branscombe** –
  Joanna Neil

Just can't wait?
Buy our books online a month before they hit the shops!
www.millsandboon.co.uk

Also available as eBooks.

MILLS & BOON®

EXCLUSIVE EXCERPT

Luci Dawson's house-swap to Sydney starts with a surprise when she discovers she's sleeping in a gorgeous stranger's bed! Dr Seb Hollingsworth could be exactly what she wants this Christmas…

Read on for a sneak preview of
WAKING UP TO DR GORGEOUS
the first book in the festive new Medical duet
THE CHRISTMAS SWAP

Luci was pretty sure by now that it wasn't a burglar, but there was still a stranger in the house.

She needed to get dressed.

She switched on the bedside light and was halfway out of bed when she heard the footsteps moving along the passage. While she was debating her options she saw the bedroom door handle moving.

OMG, they were coming in.

'You'd better get out of here. I've called the police,' she yelled, not knowing what else to do.

The door handle continued to turn and a voice said, 'You've done what?'

When it became obvious that the person who belonged to the voice was intent on entering her room she jumped back into bed and pulled the covers up to her chin, grabbing her phone just in case she did need to call the cops.

'I'll scream,' she added for good measure.

But the door continued to open and a vision appeared. Luci wondered briefly if she was dreaming. Her heart was racing at a million miles an hour but now she had no clue whether it was due to nerves, fear, panic or simple lust. This intruder might just be the most gorgeous man she'd ever laid eyes on. Surely someone this gorgeous couldn't be evil?

'Don't come any closer,' she said.

He stopped and held his hands out to his sides. 'I'm not going to hurt you, but who the hell are you and what are you doing in my room?' he said.

'*Your* room?'

THE CHRISTMAS SWAP includes WAKING UP TO DR GORGEOUS by Emily Forbes and SWEPT AWAY BY THE SEDUCTIVE STRANGER by Amy Andrews

Available October 2016

www.millsandboon.co.uk

P916_2

MILLS & BOON®

18 bundles of joy from your favourite authors!

Get 2 books free when you buy the complete collection only at
www.millsandboon.co.uk/greatoffers